BLOOD OF THE DOGS

Book I Annihilation

Richard Cosme

To Patricia, my partner in all things.

To my mother and to Barbara Croissant, role models all.

FROM SARAH'S DIARY

OCT 2052

*M*y memory is not a straight line. Nor is it complete. The first nine or ten years are snippets. Actually two brief episodes. One was a reading class. I remember Miss Croissant with mahogany skin, a big chest, and white teeth. I could see the valley of her cleavage, beneath a big necklace which she always wore. Never the same one twice. She smiled a lot.

She taught us. Me, Malik, Cortney, Two-Tone Tommy, and One-Arm Jojo. Some other kids came and went. Every morning we went into the basement of one of the big houses and learned until we had to do chores. I don't remember the chores or anything else about that time. That lasted from one summer to the next. Luckily, I got all I needed before it ended.

The next thing I remember is about three or four years later, maybe age nine or ten. Would've been '32 or '33. I remember running silently, in the July darkness, with great energy and strength. I had on Nike cross-trainers, sweats, a hoodie, a White Sox hat. No socks, no underwear, no time. Fear drove me. As I ran, the fear dissipated. Distance provided relief, like moving away from a bonfire. I ran until I hit the woods.

In the morning I began scavenging and found a library. Libraries were among the safest places to be after The Collapse. The only reason people went there was to get fire starting material. My reading improved, as did my health. Books taught me how to eat from the forest and plant and harvest vegetables. I learned about guns and knives and trapping and skinning game. And I read happy books and mysteries and romances along with the fact books. From that point on, from the running, I remember most everything. I didn't care about much except food, survival gear, protective clothing and weapons, and my books. I didn't give a shit about The Collapse or what happened to the people. My feet hit the ground every morning and I started a new day of life. I survived nicely for six years. I scouted clans and indies encampments. They weren't doing as well as I was.

Then a new chapter. In '39, I saw Mac. Then I started to care.

PROLOGUE

When I was a few days old, and my parents had little time left to live, they took a strip of duct tape and wrapped something around my wrist. Our neighbors did the same thing to their kids. This was a week before The Collapse. Nobody ever came up with an official day for The Collapse because it happened different times and different ways all over the world. It took a few years to get going. The starvation came first, then the riots, then the disease, and the rot from within. The nukes and radiation brought it all to rest. When it hit our neighborhood, it was the post-nuke riot stage. They came fast, and even though everyone knew they were coming, not many lived through it. My family didn't come out the other side. The neighbors grabbed me as the houses burned. That was the deal for whoever survived.

They fled northwest with me and their two kids—into the woods and away from the power plants—and became indies. That was in in early '23 I learned later. My new family never told me the details of that first night. I consider that a kindness. My dark imaginings are probably far gentler than my birth parents' reality. When I was old enough, my new parents gave me what the original ones had taped to my wrist. They told me its significance, but it was not much more than a trinket post-Collapse.

They were good people and never made me feel outside. Never had a doubt about raising the dead neighbors' newborn child. They didn't tell me about my brother and sister. They made me family. So did the kids. The survivors of the first bitter winter scavenged shovels and hoes, wheelbarrows and seeds in the spring. My family had a Smith and Wesson long-barrel .38 special with a belt holster, a Winchester 12 gage pump, and a Marlin 336 30-30 lever deer rifle with a scope. We had a dog named Daisy. Australian Cattle Dog. Early warning system. She got skunked a lot, but except for skunks, was smart like all working dogs. And she took a liking to me.

We lived over a decade of good years up there. Found some other indies, had a little group, set up kind of a school. We learned to share our resources and abilities.

People did what they did best—knitting, farming, hunting, building, making furniture, teaching kids to read—whatever they could. They taught us that Earth had scourged the rot and She would protect what was left. Haven't seen that yet.

At our peak, we had nearly 30 families. We lived off the land and took care of our own. I think maybe we got too big. A clan noticed.

Daisy warned us when they came, and they killed her. My heart skipped at her yelp. Everyone scattered. I grabbed the only thing I had from my birth family, put it in my pocket, and ran so fast I thought I was flying.

Clansmen hunted us down. Killed the ones they could find. Did bad things first like they always do. I was too well hidden for them and was spared.

That was '38. I was 15 that year. No one ever told me which day I was born. Didn't make much difference. There were no calendars. I moved in closer to the old population centers. Scavenging was better. I stayed alone. Didn't trust a living soul.

Sarah found me in '39. Saved me is a better way to say it. Her, I trusted. We never let the other out of sight for over 10 years.

Duke came in '48. His vigilance gave us the courage to move in close to the Fox River. We were out from the indies, but close enough to scavenge if necessary. The river is what lured us. It had so much to give.

Weasel joined us in '53. He changed our lives more than anything up 'til that time. Until Stevie showed up.

PART ONE

CHAPTER ONE

STEVIE B.
MARCH 2054
ROUTE 59

In 2054, a year after Weasel had become part of the family, winter arrived early and angry. In March it was still going full bore. We always put back fruit and vegetables from the garden and grape vines and apple tree, so winter's severity hadn't affected us. And we could still ice fish is the Fox River shallows. But the bitter cold impacted the game. Deer were moving south, seeking better forage. Many succumbed to starvation. Weaker members of herds were easy pickings for the wolves. There were signs of dog packs' recent incursions into our area, seeking carrion or easy prey. As the winter dragged on we also noticed clan movement closer to us than ever before.

Craving fresh meat, Sarah and I were on a hunting trip, moving south on Rt. 59 to a forested area we thought might harbor a herd. The temperature had not gotten above freezing since a week before Christmas, but snowshoes weren't necessary. Snow was sparse in early '54.

Sarah was carrying the Browning 12 gauge pump, in case we ran across some turkey or pheasant. I had the Heckler and Koch HK81 with a scope. One of Weasel's many additions to our arsenal, it was an assault rifle that I used for hunting purposes. It fired a 7.62mm round, equivalent to about a .32 caliber, held a thirty-round clip and could be fired one shot at a time when I set it on semi.

A reliable army weapon, the HK was sturdy and able to take more abuse from dust, dirt and moisture than any 20th cen hunting rifle. Able to expend thirty rounds at full auto in just a few seconds, the assault rifle also served as an enforcer in the unlikely event we ran into any clansmen.

I also carried a Glock 17L, another of Weasel's contributions, holstered under my jacket. Semi-auto, seventeen 9mm rounds, light weight, easily accessible. I wasn't anticipating any trouble this far out, but being prepared had become habit, thanks to Weasel's tutelage. I was hoping we'd bag some venison, but a turkey would do nicely.

Duke was back home, guarding the fort. When we began dressing and gathering the weapons and gear, he started chasing his tail in circles, pausing every few seconds to bark a hurry-up message. He was plenty pissed when we made him stay behind. He'll sulk for at least two days, Sarah had said. But we both feared for his safety with the wolf and dog packs so close to our territory. Weasel promised to take him hiking close to the compound a couple of hours after our leave-taking.

We picked up deer sign about three miles south, a small herd, about a dozen, heading southwest.

"Look at this," I said to Sarah. I squatted across the game trail, counting the herd size. Overlaid on the hoof impressions was a boot print, about my size. The tread prints in the snow were very indistinct, indicating the boots had just about seen their last days. The right boot had a little circular hole in the bottom. The boot's owner probably had a wet foot. Not a big problem as long as he was moving and the temperature didn't get below fifteen or so, but a potential danger for frostbite when he stopped for the night, unless he made a fire and dried out his gear.

Sarah knelt next to me, inspecting the sign. "Let's forget this herd and get out of here. We don't know what kind of maniac might be making these tracks."

"That's exactly why we need to find out who it is. We're only about three miles from home with a perfect trail leading right back to the compound. We may have to take this guy out."

"Shit," she replied, regret in her voice. "Just because the poor guy is in the wrong place."

"…At the wrong time," I said. "Maybe we won't have to. Hell, I don't know. Let's just go see what we've got." I took the safety off the HK. Sarah did the same with the 12 gauge.

The trail entered a vast wooded area about two miles down—the deer searching for saplings that had not been picked clean by other herds, the man following behind. Two miles into the woods we came across pack sign joining the trail and skirting it on either side.

We stopped to examine it. "Dogs," I said. No matter how big a dog got, its paws were always smaller than that of a wolf. There were about twenty distinct sets of prints in the snow, mixed sizes, another indicator of dogs. Wolf paw prints generally ran about the same size. The signs in the snow told us the pack was between the man and the deer.

"Unless this guy's got a machine gun, he's in deep shit."

"Then let's leave it be," Sarah replied. "Let nature take care of our problem."

I was tempted. But not enough to drop it. I was also curious and concerned that our unknown hunter might follow our tracks back home. We needed to play the scene out.

We separated, each ten meters off the trail, moving slowly, frequently checking our respective outside flanks. The sounds came to both of us simultaneously, the braying of the hounds, the screams of a man.

A hill fronted us and we ran to it, belly flopping in the snow on its crest.

Below us, in a clearing split by a small stream running fast enough to keep from freezing, a fawn lay in the shallow water. The pack brought it down and gutted it. Our mystery man, wielding a huge dead branch was charging the pack, screaming and attempting to drive the dogs away from their kill.

"Jesus Christ," Sarah hissed. "He's fucking crazy."

I took the binoculars from my pack and examined the frenzied scenario below us.

"No he's not," I said. "He's half starved to death. Take a look."

The man had temporarily beaten back the pack and was squatting in the water by the carcass, eating what looked to be the liver, screaming and waving his club at the pack between bites of the raw flesh.

After a thirty second look, Sarah dropped the binoculars and grabbed my shoulder, yanking me face to face with her. "My God, Mac, that's not a man. That's just a little boy down there."

The concept of a little boy wearing size twelve shoes was a bit alien to me. I picked up the binoculars. Our mysterious quarry was dressed in rags, gloveless and hatless with long matted, dirty blonde hair. Scraggly tufts of facial hair sprouted from his chin. Even with his frame covered with his rag-tag winter outfit, I could tell he was emaciated.

She was right. He was tall and skinny and wild eyed…and only about thirteen or fourteen years old. Not a little boy to my mind, but Sarah often saw the world differently than I. The boy was either too young or too hungry to realize that he could not win a fight over food with the pack. In a few minutes the hungry animals would recognize that he was no real threat to them and add his bony frame to their meal.

As I watched, the three boldest of the pack were already edging in on the boy, taking blows from the club on their shoulders and backing away, just out of his reach, then feinting back in again. They, too, were hungry. Snarling in defiance, they began to surround the boy, employing the most successful strategy of all pack animals, including humans. I watched his eyes and saw in them the awareness that he would soon share the same fate as the fawn.

Then he did an amazing thing. He threw down his bloody prize and waded into the pack, screaming and whirling the club.

In my peripheral vision I saw Sarah jump up. "Fuck that shit," she screamed at me. "I hate those goddamn dog packs. Come on, Mac!"

She was already halfway down the hill before I could respond. I heard the sound of her chambering a shell into the 12 gauge and took off running after her, leaving the assault rifle behind and pulling out the Glock. I couldn't chance spraying bullets into the pack with Sarah and the kid nearby.

Sarah angled in from the side, keeping the boy out of the line of her fire. She started blasting from the hip when she got to within five meters, taking out three dogs on the outer edge, the 12 gage's force hurling their bodies three meters back.

Her attack drew the attention of half of the others away from the kid, who was still on his feet and swinging the branch, screaming at the top of his lungs. Eight of the pack whirled to face Sarah, the clamor of their snarling and growling added to the whines and yelps of wounded animals, making a wall of piercing sound, an ungodly cacophony.

The eight were attempting to circle Sarah, presenting themselves high rumped and low shouldered, no animal bold enough yet to step forward to deliver the first charge, all barking and howling and snapping and yelping, adding to the volume of the unholy din. I recognized mixed breed shepherds and labs and some watered down pit bulls and a mastiff—nasty, tough, city dogs, moved out of their regular urban turf by the extended winter. Sarah swung left to right, firing at the edges, protecting her flanks.

I got down on one knee and took out three on her left who were not in Sarah's or the kid's line. The retorts of the Glock were almost lost in the discord of the dog sounds and screams from three human throats. The 12 gauge reverberated four more times, Sarah guarding her right flank. The dogs that hadn't been downed by our shots retreated.

The kid still had six around him when Sarah and I burst through their circle, firing only when we were side by side and the boy was behind us. When four more succumbed to the pistol, the remaining animals scampered up the hill on the other side of the stream, out of range.

And then...silence, sweet silence. A meter over our heads, a thin layer of smoke hovered, still and impervious to the winter breezes that were deflected by the hills that surrounded us. The air was thick with the smell of cordite. I looked to Sarah. Her legs collapsed and she sat unceremoniously in the snow, which was no longer white, but flecked with pink. She gave me an upthrust thumb and a sheepish grin. She was uninjured.

I turned to the kid. Wild eyed and bedraggled, he backed away, darting glances between Sarah and me. "If you think I'm gonna share this deer with you," he snarled, "You're fuckin' nuts."

CHAPTER TWO

JANUARY 2053
HOME

It was a crisp, clear winter morning, temperature right around zero, and I could tell it wouldn't be getting any higher. It had snowed about six inches last night and the compound, the house, barn, stables, outbuildings and surrounding countryside had a clean, pristine beauty about them. If you didn't know what lay beneath the white covering, you'd think it was a beautiful land.

High had waltzed in behind the storm, cleansing the sky and dropping the temperature precipitously, rendering the snow cover into a blanket of light-refracting crystals. Mine were the first footsteps across the snow cover as I walked over to check on the pigs, goats, chicken and cattle. Their only concern was nuzzling away the snow to get at their feed.

Duke bounded past me, his nose plowing up the snow as he ran. He stopped, did a 180, stood stiff legged and barked four times. I agreed with him that it was time to play and charged him, wrestling him to the ground and forcing his muzzle into the snow. He leapt away, spun and charged. Try it again, he said.

I did. He was a real pushover even though he weighed in at a hundred and twenty pounds of wheat-colored golden lab. I'm pretty sure he lets me win our little battles.

Our match was interrupted by three dull thuds. Sounded like one of King Arthur's knights pounding on the castle door. Duke and I both froze. My glove came off and I pulled a .357 magnum from inside my parka, looking around the compound. Duke's hackles rose and he stared at the compound doors. A deep, almost subsonic growl rattled in his chest.

I put Duke on heel as I approached the doors and quietly climbed the ladder over the rolls of barbed wire to ascend the wall encircling our small compound and have a peek at the source of the intrusive sounds.

A three-foot platform ran across the top of the wall, just like the old forts in the cavalry and Indian books. Through a peephole I could see one set of footsteps in the snow leading across the vacant land surrounding the compound and running in a true line straight to our door. Slightly to one side of the footsteps there were what appeared to be two sets of thin parallel tire tracks. The snow between the parallel tracks was somewhat compressed, as if something had been dragged along. I was unable to see what kind of person and contraption had made these marks in the snow without sticking my head above the protection of the wall. The interloper had to be about twelve feet below me and slightly to my left, standing in front of the door.

Three more deep thuds rattled the door. I could feel their reverberations from where I crouched. Duke went nuclear, barking and snarling ferociously, charging the barbed wire which blocked his access to the door and backing away.

"If I let that dog loose, he'll tear your guts out and have them for breakfast," I hollered.

A somewhat high pitched voice with a Southern accent floated up in reply, "I don't want to cause no trouble and I don't want to kill no dog. I like animals."

"That dog would be at your throat in a heartbeat. I suggest you get the hell out of here. I don't have any spare food or supplies," I replied.

"I ain't hungry and I got plenty of supplies. Killing the dog would be no problem. But it would surely make me feel real bad. I suggest you take a peek over this pitiful little wall you got here."

Insulting my workmanship was not a way to get on my better side. Hurt feelings notwithstanding, I decided to take a look at the man with the big mouth and squeaky voice. I took a quick glance over the wall and pulled back to the shelter. Having ascertained that he didn't have a bazooka aimed in my direction, I stood up and looked down at my tormentor, allowing myself the time for a better evaluation.

What I saw made me on one hand want to laugh and on the other hand, shrink back again behind the safety of the wall. Beneath me was a spritely little gnome of a man bulked up by army issue winter camouflage gear and adorned with at least seven very high powered weapons, only three of which I recognized. At least half of them looked as if they could pulverize our walls in short order, not to mention what they could do to the three of us inside.

The man at my gate gazed up at me with eyes so green most women would have killed to have them.

"Howdedoo Mr. McCall. Name's Wendell Worthington Washington and I been your neighbor for about six months now. Thought it was about time I paid a social visit."

The way I had it figured, Wendell whatever-his-name was a complete lunatic. Whether he was a danger to us or not, I had yet to decide. But his weaponry made him a force to be reckoned with so I pushed a little button in the wall twice. The button was one end of a Radio Shack battery-powered home security and intercom system. The batteries were rechargeable on a solar charger. That sent lights flashing and bells ringing inside the house and put Sarah on red alert. Three pushes would have brought her out with the M 16 or 12 gage pump.

"Well Mr. Washington," I said in my best dealing with completely insane people voice, "it's real nice of you to finally drop by. We've really been looking forward to meeting you. And just how in the hell do you know my name? I haven't gotten around to putting up the mailbox yet."

Wendell looked up at me, looked down and sighed the sigh of a very disappointed man. Then he looked up again, a hard intelligence shining in his green eyes.

"Cut the shit, McCall," he shot back at me. "I ain't crazy. I ain't stupid. And I surely ain't no child to be talked at like that. I come here with some serious business to talk about. I never figured you for an idiot, but I'm rapidly changing my mind."

He took two steps back, revealing the source of the parallel tracks in the snow. It was a little red wagon, a kid's plaything with a long, black handle to pull it along behind you. Painted on its side in black script were the words, RADIO FLYER.

I could picture a little boy 60 or 70 years ago pulling it down a suburban sidewalk heading for his best friend's house all stocked up with plastic guns and toy soldiers. The wagon looked brand new. Its paint was a deep red, shiny and glossy in the early morning sun. Its contents were hidden from my sight by a neatly folded army blanket.

"Where I come from, Mr. McCall, it's good manners to bring gifts when you're calling on your neighbors for the first time."

"Where I come from, Mr. Washington, it is considered bad form to call on people you have never met carrying so much firepower. If I tried to visit any of the clans with so many weapons showing, they would shoot me full of holes, strip my corpse and feed it to the dogs."

Washington began removing some of the rifles and automatics strapped to his body. He laid them carefully on the wagon, saying, "Well sir, I apologize for putting a scare into you and your loved ones, but I intended most of these here weapons as part of my gifts to you…"

That definitely got my attention.

"And," he continued, "I'd be very happy to show you some of the very special features of these weapons. But you are surely making this a mighty difficult task."

I began to reassess my initial trepidation concerning WWW, but in the back of my mind I worried that his wondrous array of gifts could be blinding me to the potential threat he posed to our semi-safe existence. It had taken Sarah and me five years to build what we had and paranoia was a way of life for us.

I had at my doorstep a charming little man, spouting good neighbor platitudes and generally behaving in a most non-threatening demeanor. He was bearing gifts the value of which was incalculable in the world in which we lived. His weaponry could greatly enhance our chances for survival.

But to ignore the damage he could unleash upon the compound with the arsenal he had draped across his shoulders and nestled in the little red wagon would be pure avarice on my part. One of the automatics had what I recognized as a grenade launcher on it, and I had no doubt that he could blow a hole through our wall with one shot if he so chose. And what in the hell was under the blanket in the wagon? Plastique and a timer? Grenades? I hadn't seen a real grenade since I was six.

Paranoia won out over greed. As I looked down upon him from my perch on the wall, I tried to choose my words carefully. Pissing him off didn't look like a good plan.

"Mr. Washington, Before I say what I've got to say, I warn you that I've got a .357 in my right hand and if you make any quick movements I'm gonna shoot you. No matter where I hit you, you're probably gonna die."

To his credit the little man didn't bat an eye.

"This is a nasty world we live in," I began. "It makes me very sad to see the suffering and depravity beyond these walls. But here, inside these walls, we've got kindness and love and even education. And we've got respect. Outside there's killing and rape and mayhem and sodomy and even cannibalism. But in here the only violence we know is in books. And we know that the real world is far worse than any book we can read. In here it's a new, clean world."

I paused for a moment, then asked if he was still with me.

"Speak your piece, Mr. McCall," he said.

"We can't trust anyone but the two of us. Make that three. The dog is part of our family. We've seen too much. There's only two people and one dog in this world I know I can rely on. And you're not one of them."

His attention stayed on me, the expression on his face one of neutrality. A man pondering an issue.

"It's a pitiful situation, Mr. Washington," I continued. "God knows both of us dream of the day we could talk to another human being without pointing a weapon at them. We talk about having kids. But we're scared shit to try. I can't even count the number of corpses and skeletons of children and little babies we've found out there. It's so fucking bad that we don't even cry any more when we come across them. If you're not family, you are a threat to our existence."

I paused again to assess the impact of my message on the little man. There seemed to be a sadness in his eyes as he nodded for me to continue.

"So...Mr. Washington, me and you have got a problem. I can respect you, but I cannot trust you. And I can't endanger my wife. She's all I've got. Plus, she'd kick my ass. Right now she's sitting in the house, looking out the window, watching, waiting for a sign. She's holding a 12 gauge pump with the safety off. We have our rules and values. She trusts me not to forget, not to slip up. The only thing that worries her is that whoever I'm talking to might do me harm."

WWW sensed that I had finished with my spiel. He shifted his feet and cleared his throat, then began to speak in his distinctive high register twang.

"Well, Mr. McCall," he began, "that was an impressive piece of speechifyin'. I sure wish I could talk as good as you. People that talk as good as you got a better chance of gettin' listened to. Now me...I got this squeaky voice and don't know a lot of different words and most of the time people think I'm stupid so they don't pay much attention to what I got to say."

"I don't think you're stupid, Mr. Washington," I said.

"I know you don't," he replied. "That's why I"m gonna say my piece. The way I see it, is we got a bunch of different ways to go from here. I could take my stuff and go on home. Or I could leave my stuff here and go home. Or...I could take my stuff back about a hundred meters and start blowing holes in your fucking wall."

He paused to let that little option sink in.

"Now what you can do," Wendell continued, "is shoot me and take my stuff or let me go without my stuff. Or...we could both talk some more."

He paused, looking up at me, offering me the next move.

"What I think, Mr. McCall, is that you and me got more to say to each other. What's it gonna be? It's your call."

As Wendell finished, a strange realization came over me...This was the longest conversation I had ever had—except for my talks with Sarah—with another person during my life as an adult. I had read hundreds of books where people talked to each other at length. Seemed

15

like they could go on for hours. But this was a first for me…Sharing ideas with a person who wasn't a family member. This little man was weaving a spell over me. I didn't want to quit. I didn't want to banish him without learning more.

So I thought about it. Mulled over the pros and cons. Played with the options. Not going to shoot him and take his equipment. Didn't think he would withdraw a hundred meters and start lobbing missiles at us. Not in his make-up. If I asked him to go, he would go peacefully, I believed. If he stayed, we would talk some more. Certainly no harm in that.

But the problem of his having more armament at his fingertips than Sarah and I had in our entire house persisted. I decided that if we could solve the dilemma that WWW posed by being a one man armory, we would be able to resume our exploration.

"Mr. Washington," I said, "if we're going to continue this conversation, I feel the need to lay some ground rules to ensure our safety. But first, I'm asking you to call me 'McCall.' This 'Mister' stuff just doesn't feel right to me. Just plain old 'McCall' or 'Mac' sounds a lot friendlier to me and that's what my old family used to call me and what Sarah calls me now."

Wendell broke eye contact with me and looked to the ground, shuffling his feet in the snow. When he looked back up, there was a softer cast to his expression. I had stumbled my way to a crossroad and taken the correct turn. We would talk awhile longer.

"That is a most neighborly gesture," he said. "I'm honored to call you 'Mac.' And if I do, you're gonna have to call me by the name that most people have given me. Most folks call me 'Weasel.' I've never had what you would call a friend, and I know that most of the time folks are makin' fun of the way I look and talk. But I've grown fond of the name, and since I've studied on it, I learned the weasel's a pretty smart animal—ornery, wise and sneaky. He's a real survivor. The name suits me just fine."

The next part was going to be real tricky, because I was going to have to put Weasel through a whole bunch of hoops. I couldn't guess his reaction, but I hoped he would comply. In my mind was the feeling that Sarah and I might possibly be encountering something that had eluded both of us since the time she saved me—someone besides each other we could call friend.

"If we're going to continue, Weasel, you're going to have to put up with some, uh, ... unpleasantness. I'll try to make is short and painless, but I've got to check you out. No one besides Sarah and me has ever been inside these walls. If you are to be the first, I'm going to inspect everything but your asshole...And I may just have to check that out too."

"McCall," the little man replied, "I been watchin' you two for a long time now. I know you ain't dumb." He lowered his voice and added, "You ain't as smart as me yet, but maybe that can be fixed. I wouldn't expect anything less than best from you. Do what you gotta do."

I pressed the signal to the house once. The barrel of the shotgun preceded Sarah's head out the door. I turned my attention back to Weasel. "How do you take your coffee?" I asked.

"Cream and Sugar. Lots of both."

I turned back to the house and hollered across, "Bring me two cups of coffee the way I like it and an army blanket."

Sarah held up one finger, not the middle one, and disappeared back into the house. Two minutes later she reappeared at the door, standing there, two cups of steaming coffee held by their handles in her left hand and the shotgun cradled in the crook of her right arm, her finger on the trigger housing.

She stood there for a full sixty seconds, looking, feeling, sensing, sniffing the air like a dog. Satisfied, she high stepped through the snow to the base of my ladder. I never tired of seeing her, and as she advanced, I felt better with each approaching step.

We had each been alone for several years before we met. She had saved my life and nursed me back. When I awoke, the first thing I saw was her face. My left hand was sandwiched between her two. The first words I heard from her lips were, "It's about fucking time."

Since that moment, the closer she gets, the better I feel.

She was wearing a light sweater, jeans and leather hikers. A 9mm Taurus semi was holstered beneath her left arm pit. The cold never seemed to bother her. She said it was a matter of thinking warm. Mind over matter. I think it's a body fat thing, but I've never said it out loud. Her auburn hair was winter length. At 5'9" she is what the 19th cen cowboys would have called a handsome woman. That means she's attractive, big boned, curvy and unafraid of anyone or anything. All of that had nothing to do with why I loved her, although the soft slopes and curves were an added bonus.

I loved her because she was there each time I awakened, back when we first met, gently holding my hand in hers. I passed out again before I could ask her who she was and what had happened. When I came to again she was still there holding my hand. She didn't say anything that second awakening. Just smiled. That's when I started to love her, when I saw that generous smile…Then I passed out again.

As she approached the ladder, I told Weasel to take three steps away from the door. I told her to put one cup right outside the door, which took a while, because she had to negotiate through the little access area we had hidden in the barbed wire barricade. I covered Weasel while she did so, even though I felt he had no subterfuge in mind. When she secured the door and returned to the safe side of the wire, I invited Weasel to get his coffee.

"It's all right to leave the 12 gage down there," I said, and she climbed up with my coffee.

She looked at me questioningly, shrugging her shoulders and cocking her head to one side, silently asking what was going on.

I smiled at her. "Take a peek."

She took a quick look. Weasel was warming his hands with the cup as he sipped contentedly at the steaming coffee.

"What in the fuck is that?" she asked.

"That," I replied "is Mr. Wendell Worthington Washington, commonly known as Weasel to his friends, of which he has none, with the possible exception of me. I kinda like the little guy."

"What's with the arsenal?"

"They're mostly gifts."

She was astounded. I could tell by the way her mouth hung open.

"Very attractive face you're making," I offered. "Makes me want to take you inside and take advantage of your dimwittedness."

"Oh, I'm sorry. It's just that..." She took another look over the wall. "Christ, I don't know what half of those fucking guns even are. Do you?"

"Actually, no. But there's a good chance we're going to find out. In a peaceful way."

She took my cup and took a sip. "I'm going back in. If you're making progress with our mysterious visitor, having a third party around might just muck things up. You just make sure you're damn careful, Mac," she added as she climbed down.

I returned my attention to Weasel. He was sitting in the snow, white on white, his hands still drawing warmth from the coffee cup.

"Let's get started, Weasel," I said. "Take off all your clothes. Boots and socks too. Throw each piece up here."

"Jesus Christ, McCall," he hollered, "It's twenty below zero out here."

"I don't think it's quite that cold," I replied.

"When I get naked, that's what it's gonna feel like."

"Listen to me, Weasel, if you're in a clan, you've got a tattoo somewhere on your body. If you've got one, access to our home will be denied." I tossed the army blanket down to him. "You can use this while I search your clothes. I'll send your boots and socks back first so you don't have to stand in the snow barefoot."

Weasel stripped as quickly as possible, slowed by the fact that he probably had on over a dozen items of clothing layered to protect him against the cold. He threw each item up as it came off until I had a huge pile of clothes beneath me, and he stood in the snow, not quite naked yet.

His torso, arms and legs were adorned with an array of scabbards and holsters, each securing a deadly weapon. I recognized a Bowie knife, a fillet knife, an ice pick (secured to his right forearm with surgical tape), a derringer on the other arm at the wrist, a short barreled 38 special, a short barreled Baretta, and a couple of small spray cans about the size of a cigarette lighter.

He grinned up at me sheepishly. "I never leave home unprepared."

"Toss 'em all up," I said.

He complied, with a warning. "Don't be sniffing those cans. They ain't perfume. One's mace and the other's nerve gas."

I asked him to raise his arms above his head and do a slow 360. Aside from some very nasty scars front and back torso, he was completely clean. To my relief there were no tattoos. Without the bulk of clothing, he was smaller than I initially thought, skinny, but not emaciated, muscles wiry and long, belly flat. Weasel was a poster child for pale. Except for his pubic region and under his arms, his body was almost hairless. His hair was military cut, receding in the front, light brown in color. My scrutiny did not appear to make him uncomfortable.

"You want I should bend and spread 'em? Lift up my nuts?" He was smiling, putting me on.

"That won't be necessary," I responded. I quickly searched his socks and boots and threw them back down. "Relax a few minutes and I'll get the rest of your clothes back to you."

I threw the items down as I finished. The army pants and parka took a while. They contained more weapons than he had on his body. When I had finished, there was more firepower at my feet than Sarah and I had in our entire house.

I looked down at him. "I got more at home," he said reading, my mind.

Shaking my head in disbelief, I said, "Now, remove the blanket from the wagon and shake it out."

Under the blanket were two or three dozen square plastic boxes which I recognized as 21st cen compact discs and DVD's. He removed them, stacking them on one end of the little red wagon. "These here are presents."

Beneath where the discs had been was an Uzi and about twenty clips. He grinned up at me sheepishly. "You didn't expect I'd leave all these valuables unprotected, did you? This is also a present. I'm gonna take it by the barrel and toss it up to you."

Weasel returned the discs to their original position and rearranged some of the bounty, revealing a small rectangular black plastic box. He held the discs up to me, beaming proudly. "These things are what they call CDs and DVD's. Some play music. Others show movies. And performances by music groups. The quality is state of the art for pre-collapse. And that there," he said pointing his head toward the black box, "is a DVD and CD player, Blue Ray Max III, advanced digital signal processing unit, Dolby 10C Pro Logic Sound Enhancement, eight channel surround sound, and best of all, 3-D option. Consumer mags say this one is the best. Also got 4K and 3-D monitors back home."

I was completely astounded. "Weasel, this is unbelievable. I'm flabbergasted by your generosity. And please don't be disappointed, but I gotta tell you … We don't have any electricity. No one does."

Weasel responded with a grin that covered his face all the way up to his receding hairline. It was a wonder to behold.

"You will soon."

• • • •

I buzzed Sarah in the house and told her to call Duke in and get ready for a visitor. Nobody but us had ever been in our house. This was momentous. Weasel and I had expended fifteen minutes on getting him re-attired and my guiding him and his wagon through the barrier of barbed wire, grape vines and raspberry patch. I decided to leave the weapons where they were until we decided if Weasel was a fit for Sarah, Duke, and me and our little homestead.

"Nice touch," he said when he had made his way through the barbed wire. "Makes good sense. Keeps the bad guys out and supplies food at the same time. I suggest you go shopping and get a whole bunch of loud bells and attach 'em to the barbed wire. And go to a jail or prison and get some razor wire."

When the two of us and the wagon finally made it into the house, I was greeted by an astonishing scene. Sarah was in her 19th century rocker, Duke on his haunches by her side. The shotgun was in easy reach, but placed so as not be a primary concern to an observer. Between her and us, on a Queen Anne serving table was an assortment of cookies, a coffee urn, a pitcher of hot apple cider and three Nippon cups and saucers from one of her first forages (resting on early American lace doilies) and three Heisey glasses. In the center of the table was the Erte' sculpture, *Woman in Black*. Around the serving table were three matching Louis XIV chairs. Sarah never allowed me or Duke to sit in them.

We had now been together 14 years. Since we were kids, really. Never once had we been apart for more than a day or two when one of us had gone scouting. We did almost everything together. Cooked, hunted, fished, gardened, built, read, slept, cleaned, refinished furniture. We had found and furnished a house; built a wall and barricade; dug an escape tunnel; put in a garden; collected antiques, art and books; gathered chickens, cows, and pigs; built a stable; and generally made a hell of a nice life for ourselves—far enough away from the clans to be somewhat free from danger.

Which is not to say that we talked nonstop for 14 years or liked exactly the same activities. We each read, a solitary activity, and we each have areas that one is more proficient at than the other. She is the baker. I am the cook. She gardens. I butcher our meat. She cleans the fish. She reads non-fiction for the most part; I generally stick to fiction.

The only thing missing was kids. We figured out the sex part about 10 minutes after I could lift myself up to my elbows. That was about two weeks after she saved me. We didn't know much about sex, but we both knew babies could be dangerous.

Our first time, before we started, Sarah put her hand on my chest. "Wait a minute," she said. "I've been reading about this. We're gonna like this, but can't be having babies."

I nodded in assent. My mind wasn't processing clearly. "I'll follow your lead," I croaked. Good decision.

We didn't dwell on the issue. Survival took up most of our time. Tenderness and quiet moments are rare when wild dogs and deranged humans share your territory.

So when Weasel and I walked in the door and were greeted by Betty Crocker with a shotgun, I was a bit taken aback by this new side to her character. I was about to make a crack about the 50's when she cut her eyes at me, so I shut up. In retrospect, I see Sarah had a far better grasp on the situation than I. For this was not only a significant passage in our life together; it was also an occasion of profound magnitude for Weasel.

I took a step forward, turned to Weasel, then back to Sarah.

"Sarah," I said in what I imagined was a formal voice, "I would like to introduce my new friend, Mr. Wendell Worthington Washington."

She stood up and walked across the room to Weasel, offering her hand when she reached him. As he took it, she said, "Welcome to our home, Mr. Washington. Please let me take your coat. Won't you have a seat and join us for some nice hot coffee or cider and cookies."

I almost laughed. I fought the impulse.

Wendell shuffled his feet, hung his head and pumped her hand enthusiastically. After a few seconds, he got up enough gumption to make eye contact with her and said, "Howdeedo, Ma'm. I'd be honored to sit. And please call me Weasel."

Thus began the most amazing twenty-four hours of our life together and the flowering of a relationship that would send tidal waves of change through clan society five years down the road.

CHAPTER THREE

JANUARY 2053

We stayed up talking with Weasel for over twenty hours. As if recalling the way it should be from the words of 20th and 21st cen books and stories told by elders, all three of us made brave attempts at small talk. Three suburbanites circling an antique table filled with cookies, coffee and cider.

It didn't work.

It wasn't our world. The best of the 20th—families, ideas, church, schools, homes, neighbors—had gone up in smoke over three decades ago. Shells remained, barren and forlorn. Rusted vehicles frozen on rivers of concrete. Skyscrapers that would last for centuries, giant, functionless *objet d'art.* Hollow men and hollow women. There was no room for small talk in a society that required you to be armed every waking and sleeping moment.

Everything was big.

It was Weasel who finally got us down to business. "Ma'am," he said, "Sarah, I mean, I got something I gotta talk about. It's very important to me. And I'm not sure how to go about doin' it."

She leaned forward and refilled his coffee, then leaned back again, sedate and composed, trying, I knew, to allay Weasel's fears, diminish his discomfort with the situation.

"You just relax, Weasel," Sarah told our guest. "Mac here seems to trust you...and I trust him. We want to know what brings you to us. Whenever you're ready to talk, we're ready to listen."

As if in preparation for a monumental task, he took a deep breath and began. "It's a God forsaken world out there, Sarah. I've been alone in it for a lotta years, traveling and watching and movin' on again. Every time I moved it was because the people were hard. Too hard.

And empty. Didn't make any difference if it was city or country or small town. The people just didn't seem right. Like there was some part of them missin'. You know what I mean?"

"Weasel," I said, "for the past eight years Sarah and I haven't had the chance to know anybody except each other and the people in these books." I swept my arm in a circle, indicating the bookshelves along each wall, stacked with our library and bookstore withdrawals. "But we've seen the horrors going on east of us and we know what you're talking about."

"I moved up here about a year ago," Weasel continued, "and been scoutin' and collectin' ever since. I seen whole bunch of bad things. No worse here than the rest of the world, just more of it. I'm about five miles west of you, place called Montgomery. Just me and a few dirt farmers who trade food for some of the stuff I scavenge. But they ain't very friendly. Kinda mad acting all the time, like someone took somethin' from 'em.

"Been all the way into the city and up north and down south, too. Fox River and a canoe make a pretty good highway. Ran across you two about nine months ago. Been watchin' you ever since."

He saw the glance between the two of us and lowered his eyes, as if shamed by his disclosure.

"I never meant any harm. Thing is," he continued, "I never seen anybody like the two of you."

"How do you mean?" Sarah asked.

Weasel raised his head and looked at us, swinging his glance from one to another, then settling on Sarah, directing his words to both of us, but focusing on her.

"First time I saw you was near the end of winter. You were walkin' in the woods—holdin' hands and talkin'. I could see you were both smiling and I heard Sarah laugh. I never heard a woman laugh like that—all happy and gay, not laughin' at someone who was dumb or made some dirty joke, but just laughin' 'cuz she was happy."

He leaned forward, getting closer, sharing a secret.

"You two ever seen a movie?"

"No," said Sarah. "But we've read all about them. They sound so wonderful. But we have no power. No one does."

"I've seen hundreds of 'em," he revealed, leaning back, the secret shared.

"My God," said Sarah, excitement in her voice. "What are they like? Where'd you get them? Can we see one? How do you turn them on?"

"No worries. You'll see plenty. But that ain't why I'm tellin' you. Thing is, in the movies people act different from the way they do now. Except for science fiction and horror movies, they look different, too. In lots of movies people are nice to each other. They got families and kids and pets and friends and they joke around and laugh and treat each other good."

He got up and began walking around the room as he talked. "Now in the movies, somethin's always gotta go wrong. Otherwise, you got no story to tell. Some problem's gotta come up that makes people worry a lot and makes you scared somethin' bad's gonna happen to the ones you like. But in the end, it all seems to turn out OK."

Weasel was wandering as he talked, taking in our furnishings, inspecting the antiques, the art. He stopped at one of the bookshelves.

"I know how to read, you know. Taught myself with educational dvd's. Know how to use a computer, too."

That got our attention. We knew the potential of computers. But never thought we could operate one.

He returned to the table, knelt down between our two chairs.

"Whenever I'm not scavenging or building something, I learn on the computer or watch movies. My favorite's about this kid that finds a space creature and tries to take care of it, but it gets sick, and the government tries to get the creature, and the family helps the kid against the bad guys in the government."

He looked at us, each on a flank, listening attentively, fascinated by his account.

"You see…I watch my movies and wish I could have what those people have. It's real. I know life must have really been like that before the collapse. At least with some of the people. They couldn't have made it all up. Could they?"

"No. I don't think someone made it up, Weasel," replied Sarah. "Mac and I remember people telling us about families and life before the collapse. People that write books and make movies use their imaginations, but they build their stories around things that are real."

"Interesting," Weasel said. "We didn't have none of that where I came from. People being nice and happy. None that I recall, anyway."

"We didn't either," Sarah said. "Just what we heard people say…about what it was like before…"

Sarah and I sat quietly. Waiting.

"Every time I watch," Weasel continued, "I wish I could be part of something like they got…Have someone that cares what happens to you. People you can laugh and tease without worryin' about getting shot or beat up. Somebody that'll say nice things to you without wanting something. Then I seen you two, and for months you ain't never said a cross word to each other. You laugh and play with your dog and hunt together. Build a snowman. Work together. And you're always nice to each other."

He stopped, lowering his head as he knelt between us. Neither of us broke the silence. After a few minutes I saw his shoulders shaking. I looked to Sarah. She shook her head ever so slightly. No, let him be, she was saying. This is his time.

We waited, not uncomfortable with the silence, but concerned about Weasel's pain.

Head still down, he spoke softly. "Had a brother and sister, once. They were younger. Got killed in a food raid down south near Cairo, by the rivers. I was eight. Lived alone ever since."

Silence again.

He had been alone for twenty years, according to his calculation. He had found no one to trust, no one to care for the entire time of his self-imposed exile.

"I couldn't of saved 'em. Lucky I wasn't killed myself. They caught the bullets and I didn't. Just blind luck. We were all runnin' away from the shooting together. I was leadin' the way. Bullets got 'em all. Went back to 'em to check. But there wasn't anything I could do. They were gone. Little brother, little sister. Our mother, too. I just slipped away into the night."

We both sat across from him, silent, saddened by his tale, but not shocked. Each of us had endured similar tragedies.

He looked up at us, bittersweet smile on his face.

"Funny thing is, I never knew what I was missin' until I got electricity and movies. Probably would've gone through my whole life figurin' life's shit and that's that."

Weasel read the concern on our faces and quickly continued.

"Now don't you two worry about me none. I got a plan. What I got in mind is that I drop off these here presents and visit awhile. Then I leave and come back and we can set things up and I'll bring more things. That way we can get to know each other. If we like it, maybe someday we can be like, you know…a little family."

Sarah and I were silent, looking at each other. I didn't know how to respond.

She left her chair and got down on her knees, butt back on her feet, nice and comfortable. She took Weasel's hands in hers and turned him so they were facing each other.

"I've got a better idea," she said, looking up at me then back to Weasel. "We've got about five empty bedrooms in this house. Why don't you get some things you need and move into one and stay with us for a few weeks and we'll all see how we get along. But we don't want any presents. We just want you. You don't have to buy your way in. Just do your share and we'll all work together and get to know each other."

Weasel was struck dumb.

"Oh, I'm so sorry," she said. "I'm moving too fast for you."

"Oh no, ma'm. It ain't that." He looked up at me and back at Sarah again. "It's just that I never expected such kindness from strangers. You've only known me for a couple of hours."

"Pretty intense couple of hours," Sarah replied. "Plenty of time for us to decide. The amount of time Mac and I just spent with you is more than we've spent with anyone besides each other in …forever."

"I'm hearing what she's saying," said Weasel. "But what about you, McCall. What do you think about this?"

I grinned.

"I'm with her all the way. Only one thing, though. You think there's any way we could figure out how to see some of those movies you've been talking about?"

Sarah leaned forward and put her arms around Weasel, hugging him close, her head on his shoulder, looking up at me. His hands hung at his side, confused by what they should do, then went across her back in response. I could see the muscles in their arms tighten as they squeezed each other. A single tear coursed its way down from her right eye to her smiling mouth.

"Hot damn," he said. "Just like in the movies. You two wanna see E.T.?"

• • • •

We never got around to seeing a vid that night, nor for several nights. We talked until dawn, the three of us sitting around the table, Duke slumbering at our feet. The conversation ranged from the frivolous to the deadly serious. Much of our time was taken up with movie and music talk. Weasel was a fanatic about vids; Sarah was pretty much the same way about music. With nicads or lithiums, a portable cd player and her solar battery recharger, Sarah could listen to music for hours. We knew about i-pods, but we didn't know how to get music onto one.

We also discussed what Weasel saw to be our woeful state of defensive readiness. He possessed an extremely active and wide ranging mind; and, although he had little knowledge on the reason for the collapse, his take on the current state of affairs with the clans was far superior to ours.

"Don't make a whole lot of difference how we got here," he told us. "Stayin' alive is what we should be thinkin' about."

We were still in the living room, sipping homemade wine, a couple of hours beyond the reciprocal hug that had sealed our new living arrangement. It was our first foray into serious subjects. Weasel was up now, wandering and browsing the books, touching the antiques, viewing the cornucopia of oils prints and photos that Sarah and I had adorned the walls with. The house was a big, fancy one, the country home of rich people in the 21st, no neighbors for an acre or so in all directions.

But it was ours now, the fifteenth one Sarah and I had looked at when we first went house hunting. We had seen others that suited us, but in them had found evidence of the horrors that accompanied the collapse, corpses—actually skeletons—of whole families, sometimes even their pets, bullet holes, ominous dark rusty stains, massive interior destruction, as if an uncontrollable rage had possessed the interlopers who had invaded the homes and butchered their occupants.

We left those charnel houses and moved on, unwilling to live in the sites of such tragedy.

The house we finally chose was what they called a "model," the first finished in a development of country homes on wooded sites, surrounded by trees and invisible to the inquiring eyes of neighbors. A sign informed us we were at Falconcrest Glen where we would experience "Luxurious country living on private, wooded lots. From $1,200,000. Model Open." Falconcrest was never finished. A dozen houses were planned. Some were foundation only. Others, roof and walls. But now, in 2053, our home was encircled by pine, maple, prairie grass, and scrub trees. And only during winter could we see the shells of the unfinished neighborhood.

Our house was spacious and elegant, finished and furnished, clean and virginal, untainted by death and suffering. Three car attached garage bigger than some houses we had seen. And it was totally isolated.

The perfect starter home.

Weasel stopped to admire some prints and oils in the living room. Most of the walls in the spacious house were hung with artwork from various centuries and countries, the bounty of our years of scavenging in malls, galleries and museums and private residences. Some were prints; many, originals.

"I really like these," said Weasel, stopping in front of a grouping of four. "Kind of a dream like quality to 'em."

"Two of them are Atkinson Fox and two Parrish," I replied. "Both guys are American. Worked in the early 20th. I agree with you. I think both Sarah and I like their innocent quality."

"You mind if we take a look around upstairs?" Weasel asked.

Access to the upstairs was by a winding staircase from the living room or by the second story of a deck that wrapped around the back of the house. There were five bedrooms and three bathrooms upstairs. The bathrooms were nice to look at, but there was no running water. Our outhouse was a primitive reminder of the collapse.

"I think we can improve our bathroom situation and get rid of that pitiful outhouse," Weasel said. "You ever seen them portapotties. Kinda looks like a closet, but it's a shitter. We can get some up here and put 'em in that big ol' garage. Outta sight."

"What about the smell?" Sarah asked.

"They got chemicals," Weasel said. "We can get it figured out."

We moved down the hall and Weasel chose a corner room with plenty of windows for his own. Not until later did he tell us he chose it for its defensive capabilities, rather than the view. There was plenty of art on his walls, oils and prints, pencil sketches of European cathedrals and watercolors of nature scenes. Even several framed photographs, some portraits, some nature studies.

"Would I be asking too much," he asked, "if I wanted one of them scenes I liked downstairs for my room?"

Sarah was delighted. "Oh, Weasel, you can have one of each or even all four if you want. Everything we have is yours. If you see anything else you want for your room, just take it. You can check if there's anything in our bedroom you'd like to have too."

Getting into the flow, I offered my original Stan Lee posters, framed and signed. Fortunately, he only took two. But I still have visiting privileges.

"Let's go down and check the basement and that little ol' tunnel you got," he suggested.

"You know about our tunnel?" we both asked simultaneously.

"Shit, I know what kind of music you both play, where the dog sleeps, who reads what, what kind of weapons you got and a whole bunch of other stuff."

We were astounded.

"You mean you've been in the house?"

"Hell," he said. "Just because I like you don't mean I ain't gonna check you out before I make such a big decision. If you two were a couple of idiots, I might not have wanted to join up. Actually, that ain't exactly true. If you were dim wits, you'd need me more than ever. But I had to see what kind of people you really were. From what I saw, it was too good to be true, all that happiness and stuff. Remind me to show you LEAVE IT TO BEAVER when I get the vid equipment set up."

He paused and judged our reaction. "Jesus, I hope you ain't mad at me. It's my nature to check things out. I never came into the house when you were in it."

"No, I don't think we're upset," Sarah responded. "Just a little dumbfounded. We kind of thought the grounds were secure. How did you ever get past Duke?"

"Dipped my clothes in pig shit," he replied. "He never knew I was here. Had to throw away some nice duds though."

"Gee, what a shame," I replied.

"No problem," he responded. "Found a nice little Lands' End Outlet warehouse down south in an industrial park. Hope you don't mind if I borrowed a couple of books while I was here."

"Damn. I thought I was missing a couple. THE MOTE IN GOD'S EYE, right?"

"And another one called MORE THAN HUMAN," he replied. "Never read any books that long before. But I really liked 'em. I'll bring 'em back when we go over to get some of my things."

"What do you think of the tunnel?" I asked.

"Well, to tell you the truth, it's pretty pitiful. How do you think I got in? You can't let anybody get in that easy!"

Weasel steered us back into the living room and sat us down, standing before us, a professor fronting his students.

"Before we do any more looking around, we gotta talk some more."

He paused, thinking, I supposed, about presenting some tough material to us.

"You know," he began, "how I said I been watchin' you for a few months now?"

We nodded in affirmation.

"Well, I've been watching the clans too. Been into the city. All over. Different territories. Just easin' in and out. Hardly anyone ever knows I'm there."

"What happens if someone sees you?" I asked.

"Depends on the situation," Weasel replied, smiling grimly. "You saw how I travel. I carry at least ten weapons. So will both of you from now on. I always run first if I'm seen. Or else I try to talk my way out. Every once in a while, I get cornered or surprised. You saw the scars."

"I've never had any major problems." I said. "Well, amend that. I ran into The Babe a couple of years ago. Ever heard of him?"

"You sure it was the Babe?" Weasel asked. "Only askin' cuz you're still alive."

"Huge. Vicious. Smells like a sewer. That the one?" I asked.

"There's gotta be a story there. Tell me about it."

"There's a story alright, but I'd rather hear yours right now."

"You can thank God and good luck you're still walkin' and talkin'. They say the Lord looks after the feeble minded," said Weasel. "Cuz when you find the Babe, it it usually ends bad if you ain't wearin' the colors. Most of the time, it would probably be just me and Sarah here talking. It's only a matter of time until trouble finds you again."

"What makes you say that?" asked Sarah. "We chose this place because it's so far out from the clans. They have plenty to keep them supplied where they are now. There's thousands of stores and shops and warehouses. And more deserted homes and apartments than any of us can count. It will be another twenty years until they need to spread out into our part of the country."

Weasel come over and sat next to Sarah and me on the couch and turned to face her.

"Now please listen to me good, Sarah. It's real important you and Mac hear what I'm saying: It don't make no difference where you live. Trouble is gonna find you. Some one's gonna try to hurt you. Take away what you have. When my family got killed, we were over a hunnerd miles away from anything that looked like a city. Only about thirty of us. Doin' nobody any harm. Bunch of dirt farmers in a dip-shit abandoned town in Bum Fuck Egypt. A few huntin' rifles and dogs. We didn't have nothin' of any value. But we was easy pickings for them who like to take things from others."

"When I was a kid," I told Weasel, "we didn't have anything. Just indie farmers. But they still wiped us out."

Weasel fiddled with the silverware on the kitchen table, hesitating before he spoke. "Listen, Mac," he said. "They found you because they could see you. What I'm tryin' to say is you don't need to be stronger. Or tougher. Or have a big wall."

"Well then what in the hell do we need?" I asked.

"Invisibility," he said. "This place needs to disappear and look like every other abandoned or burnt out hulk in this little," he waved his hands, indicating the outside of the house, "neighborhood or whatever they call these things."

"But Weasel," Sarah said, "we're so far away. We chose this very carefully. There's nothing attractive to clans out here."

Weasel took Sarah's hands in his. "Please listen to me. Both you and Mac," he implored. "Some day—next year, five years, whenever—someone is gonna find this place. Just like I did. And they will want what you've got here. They will take what you love. Both things and people. If they can't carry it, they will destroy it."

"Why? Tell me why," Sarah begged.

"Because you have it and they don't. Because there's beasts out there. Human hunters and destroyers...and there ain't no rules."

CHAPTER FOUR

JANUARY 2053
HOME

Several hours after sunset and several glasses of wine later, Weasel pleaded exhaustion and went to bed. His stories and pleas for vigilance had frightened us. His character and ideas gave us hope.

Sarah and I cleaned up a bit and followed half an hour later. Duke walked up with us, but instead of coming into our room, his usual habit, he positioned himself outside Weasel's door. Whether it was because he didn't trust having a stranger in the house or liked our new house mate, we couldn't figure. Turned out to be the latter. We found them both sharing Weasel's bed in the morning.

I shut the door to our room, closed the shutters, lit three of the lamps and then stoked the wood burning stove. It would warm the room quickly. We used it only at night, afraid the day smoke would attract visitors.

I undressed and then engaged in one of my favorite hobbies, watching Sarah do the same. She folded or hung each article of clothing as it came off, lingering over the tasks as I knew she would. Dirty clothes went into our shared laundry basket, which was, fortunately, a walk across the room from where she shed her clothes. Naked, she returned to her dressing table, early American oak with a large shell mirror, sat on the bench and brushed out her auburn hair, shoulder length now, the way she wore it in the winter.

"Well, sweetheart," she said, smiling at me in the mirror, "we just changed the course of our lives forever. How do you feel?"

I sat on the bed and spoke to her reflection. "I was just following your lead. And Duke's. Weasel seems fine to me. I was surprised that you welcomed him in so quickly, though, without running him through some tests."

"Me too," she said. "It just happened. He struck a chord in me, that sad little man. There is warmth in there, Mac. I know he's battered and mean-looking in his scrawny little way, and probably as tough as any clan soldier, but he has the eyes of a poet...or philosopher. He's just so..."

"...Vulnerable," I said, watching her hair expand under the strokes of her brush. "And interesting. Not that our life is boring or any way lacking. But I was still surprised when you moved so quickly."

She looked at me through the mirror. "It's not the first time," she said. "It happened once before, you know. Acting on instinct like that." She grinned, teasing. "Turned out OK, didn't it?"

She was right. There was no time for her to think about it when she saved me, blasted her way through, pulled them off. Nothing but instinct. Whatever extra sense she possessed had guided her snap decision. She could have been killed as easily as I. And after it was over, and she patched and sewed me up, she could have given up some food and ammo and left me on my own. Didn't have to spoon feed me that soup. Sure as hell wasn't anything I did to impress her, being mostly unconscious and completely incomprehensible when I was awake.

"It was my rugged good looks back then," I said. "Made your heart flutter. You had to save me."

"You looked like a bowl of minestrone," she said.

"Before they got me."

"I couldn't really tell. You were moving too fast." She was almost laughing now. It was a ritual. We'd been through it many times. I think it reinforced our interdependence. We liked it that way, after those years alone—having another person to rely upon, even to the point of risking life.

"So what was it then, that drew you to me? Made you risk your life?"

She laughed then. So did I. "I had been following you for a couple of days," she recited. It was almost the same words each telling. "There was something about you. You seemed so sad...alone. You avoided the clans, the indies, the dog packs. But not because you were afraid. I could tell you were brave. Because it was smart. When the pack caught you in the open, it was just bad luck. But I figured you'd get out. Didn't know you had no ammo. When they took you down..." I started mentally recited with her, "...I could feel your pain. In my head I could almost hear you saying, 'Don't let me die alone.' I had to save you, Mac. You were only the second good man I had seen in my life. And the only one still living."

She turned from the table, rotating at her waist, and looked at me. Her eyes were misty. Always the same when she told the story, once every year or two. So were mine.

"And Weasel might be the third," I said.

"Right."

She turned back to brushing her hair. I was torn between my two views of her. I gazed upon her back, watching her shoulder muscles flow smoothly, hard and defined as she brushed, then allowing my gaze to drift down, tracing the curve that flowed into her waist then swept back out again over her hips. I loved her back and silently willed her to stand, offering me a full view.

I pulled my eyes back up to hers, willing my thoughts back to the conversation. "He's going to change our lives radically," I said.

"If he's right about..."

"He is," I said. "We just don't want to see it right now. We've got it too good—me, you and Duke. Weasel is going to change that outlook. The way we see things through rose tinted glasses."

"But you know something, Mac?" she said. "He's going to surprise us often. Bring joy to our lives. You wait and see."

"And he's gonna make us work," I said. "Everything we've done is coming down. We have to make our home look like every other abandoned home. No walls. No fortifications."

"Let's start that in the morning, sweetheart." That was a good sign. She continued brushing. "Are you tired?" she asked.

Invitation.

I looked back into the mirror, which reflected her from the waist up and decided for the moment that her front was now my favorite view. Her breasts rose and fell with the brushing motion, her eyes focused on her hair, as if she were unaware of the impact her body in motion had upon me. Her eyes shifted slightly and met mine in the mirror and she blessed me with a smile.

When the brushing was finally finished, she opened her top right dresser drawer, pulled out a pipe and loaded it. Swiveling her butt and legs around her dressing bench, she turned to face me, slightly parting her legs. She brushed her left nipple with her fingertip and it responded. Then she put the pipe on her dresser and slowly stood, allowing me, finally, a look at the whole package. She turned slowly, a full circle, then, hands on hips, inquired, "Had enough?"

Full front, a cornucopia of curves and soft skin and hard muscles, hidden little crevices and wonderfully responsive tissues that would spring erect at the touch of my tongue or the caress of my fingers...Yes that was definitely the best of all the options...for the moment, anyway. "Just another hour or so," I said.

She laughed and retrieved the pipe. "Now your turn," she said, walking over to me and kissing me softly on the lips. This is goose/gander deal here." She demurely slid under the comforter and lay on her back, only her head showing.

I stood up a gave a turn around, an awkward and ungraceful 360, but apparently it did the job. "Enough foreplay," I said. "Let's get it on." I hopped onto the bed.

"Hush," she replied, placing a finger on my lips. "Just a tiny bit more conversation."

Waiting was not a problem for me. I knew whatever was on her mind was best exorcised. When our minds were free, we always communicated better sexually. I climbed back into bed and lit the pipe with a kitchen match, took a hit and passed it.

She took a toke, held it a bit, and asked, "You're comfortable with the new living arrangements? You're right about it being a bit sudden. Could I have made a mistake?"

I put my arm around her and pulled her closer. "There was no mistake," I answered. "I trust your instinct. I had the same feeling when I was talking to him out in the cold. He's good for us. We'll be good for him. Besides, Duke seems to like him. What more could you ask?"

Turning onto her side under the covers, she put her arm around my waist and looked up at me. "Better now," she said. "We can stop talking. Wanna fool around, big fella?"

She sat up, letting the covers slip to her waist and took another hit and passed the pipe. I inhaled deeply and put the pipe on my night stand, then leaned over and gently placed my lips around her left nipple. I heard her sudden intake of breath. I was forever amazed and how she could instantly surrender to the physical. I knew that above me, her eyes were unfocused and her mouth slightly open. A rush of visceral response centered in my chest and flowed outward North and South.

Sarah reached down. "Ahh. So nice," she said dreamily. "Diamond cutter."

CHAPTER FIVE

Two days later, the four of us—Weasel, Duke, Sarah and me—hiked five miles through the snow south and west of the compound to the site of Weasel's home. Sarah and I kept increasing the pace, knowing we would soon be co-conspirators in Weasel's secret world of technology.

There would be no shock had we found his home in a cave...or even a tree house. Whatever it turned out to be, we knew it would be isolated, unique and stamped with Weasel's peculiar charm.

He didn't disappoint.

A three-hour hike brought us to a small development of modest looking suburban homes, the kind that were grouped close together and two homes were joined by a shared wall. They were called townhouses, even though there wasn't a town nearby.

"Whaddya see?" Weasel asked.

We were in the middle of a grouping of sixteen townhouses, eight each on either side of the road. We saw the homes, the indentation in the snow that demarcated the road that ran between the structures, a deer trail worn down deep enough to show brown grass and dirt, various other animal tracks and the signs of our own passing, Duke's paw prints and our own boot impressions.

"Nothing out of the ordinary," Sarah said.

"That's good," said Weasel. "Because I live right over there." He pointed to the end house behind us and to our left. "To get there, we gotta start over here." He pointed to the opposite end house of the grouping we faced. "Follow me."

Weasel retrieved a pine bough half-buried in the snow and using it as an eraser for our footsteps in the snow, led us around the back of the townhouse. We entered a kitchen area through the unlocked back door. "Don't have to worry much about prowlers out here," Weasel said. "But I do have a few surprises in case anyone shows up. You two wait up here with Duke while I attend to a few matters. It's safe to roam around up here, but don't come downstairs until I get back." He disappeared through a door that led to the basement.

Half an hour later he reappeared and escorted us into the basement, closing the door behind. We descended into the darkness, feeling our way along until we reached a carpeted floor. "Now," said Weasel's disembodied voice, "here's something I bet you've never seen before." In an instant the darkness was replaced with glaring light, causing us to turn our heads and shield our eyes.

"Jesus Christ," I said. "How in the hell did you do that?"

"Mac, that there is a demonstration of the wonders of electricity." He reached for a light switch, an item I was quite familiar with, but which I had never known to serve any useful function. Weasel flicked it down and the room returned to darkness, then back again to its lighted state with another flick.

Sarah was quite enchanted with the process and played with the switch several times before she asked, "Where is the power coming from?"

"I'll show you in a few minutes," replied Weasel. "But first, observe."

Two ceiling lights, the bulbs behind milky glass fixtures, provided the illumination. The room was furnished and obviously was meant to be a place for entertainment and relaxation. Couches and chairs faced a large television and there were stereo speakers in the corners. One wall was lined with cabinets, the others paneled in gray weathered looking format. Family photos and prints of art work were displayed on the walls. Nothing we hadn't seen before. At least there were no skeletons.

Weasel walked over to one of the cabinets and opened its door. He went down on hands and knees and pulled on something I could not see and then moved away, revealing an opening small enough for us to crawl through, connecting us to the neighboring home's basement. This new room was lit by one bulb. He turned out the lights in the room we had come from and closed the cabinet door behind him and then the hidden door in the new room's wall.

"Now, remember how I been stressin' the importance of safety and bein' suspicious all the time?" He pointed to a hand grenade that was held to the wall by the door we had just come through by two metal bands. A length of fishing line was in his hand. One end was attached to the ring in the grenade. "This line leads to an eye hook inside the door. I removed it before I opened the door when I first came down. If I hadn't done that, I'd look like the inside of a raccoon. That's what took me so long. Had to disarm several booby traps. What you do, is always live in a place that you feel is gonna be safe. Then you set traps all over the place, figurin' you'll never be safe. Works out pretty well that way."

"How many times have they been set off?" asked Sarah.

"None up here. Four times in about 18 years down south. Makes a pretty big mess when it happens. Plus I gotta move when someone comes across my place. Got five fellas once. I can guarantee you they weren't makin' no social call."

Except for in books, it was the first grenade I seen. I had read somewhere that in the early 21st there were approximately three hundred million privately held guns in the United States. But grenades weren't available to the general population in the 20th and 21st. They were a limited resource after the collapse. Within two decades, the clans had used them all up.

"How many of these things you got?" I asked.

"I got hundreds. Pineapples, frags, flash, concussion, smoke—You name it, I got it. Ain't a better scavenger in the world than me, Mac. Got some claymores, too. They make an awful mess. Armories and police stations. Just gotta know where to look."

He directed us to another hidden door and another basement. I quickly figured out that we were moving down the line of townhouses which were across the street from where his was located. We were on the wrong side of the road. I didn't bother to ask. Each door had been booby trapped similarly to the first. When we got to the last basement, there was a door in the wall left of us instead of straight ahead.

This opened to yet another tunnel, a passageway which obviously snaked under the street to the other group of townhouses. Two single bulbs strung along the ceiling provided light for our claustrophobic hands-and-knees sixty-foot journey. Every ten feet a vertical 4x4's led to lengths of 2x8's above our heads, bracing the ceiling.

"How in the hell did you build this?" I asked.

"Ain't as hard as you think when you got the right equipment."

As we entered the long tunnel, I heard a muffled sound unlike anything I had ever heard. Sarah and Duke picked it up too. As we moved down the shaft, I began to feel the sound as well as hear it. There was a faint vibration in the ground beneath my hands and knees. The sound was a deep drone, like a giant mosquito. Discernible within the drone was a rhythmic pulsing, but very fast, almost too rapid to pick up, but definitely there. Weasel crawled in front of me. I asked his butt what the noise was. His head laughed and told me I'd know soon.

After a few more feet, an unfamiliar smell began to accompany the sound. It was the odor of something burning. Similar to a kerosene lamp or burning fat, but somehow dirtier. We finally reached the tunnel's end and entered Weasel's domain, the noise becoming very loud. A smoky haze filled the new room—another basement.

The source of the noise and smoke and stench was vibrating in the middle of the room. It was a black tubular frame about three feet long and two feet high. In its middle, above the ground, the frame supported a black box which was making a huge racket and spewing forth blue-gray smoke. A thin, flexible pipe led from the box to the wall and, I guessed, out of the basement.

Weasel had to yell to be heard. "That contraption is a gasoline powered electric generator," he yelled. "Ain't never known another person to have one."

"How in the hell does it run?" screamed Sarah. "There isn't any gasoline anymore."

Weasel motioned us to follow him, and we exited into another basement and then a third before we could get away from the smell and noise. "It ain't the noise that'll kill you, it's the fumes. Full of carbon monoxide. Could drop you in a few minutes if you didn't get any fresh air. Believe it or not, most of the fumes were going out of the building through that exhaust pipe. That's what cars and trucks used to put out in their exhausts."

"How did people stand the smell? And my eyes. They're really burning," Sarah said.

"I know. Some cities were so bad, that they used to have 'alerts' for people with breathing problems. Crazy stuff. Saw it on some vids. That's why I'm looking into new generators. Real state of the art for the 21st. Propane and natural gas. Quiet and less junk in the air. I found some, but gotta figure out how to get 'em here and set 'em up."

Ten more minutes of crawling brought us into a different building, two basements away from the generator, and the fumes and noise had been left behind. The room was strikingly similar to the one we had first entered—quiet, comfortable, and peaceful.

"This is my relaxation room," explained Weasel. "Most of my supplies are in the rest of the rooms you haven't seen yet. We're safe here. The upstairs doors are sealed. The booby traps are all reset. Plus I've got a few escape tunnels you ain't seen yet. Sit yourselves down. Relax."

Duke explored every corner of the new territory, found a soft throw rug, curled up, and slept. I flopped down on a leather couch, glad to be finally out of tunnels and off of my hands and knees. Sarah stood in the center of the room, hands on hips, looking down at Weasel, who had taken root in a rocking chair, smiling contentedly. Proud.

I could see why. Across one wall, like a blank canvas, was a gigantic TV screen. At least three or four feet across. Beneath it was a shelving unit with a smoky glass door. Each of the six shelves held an impressive piece of electronic equipment. Weasel noticed where I was looking and walked over to the system, opening the door to the electronics.

"C'mon over here you two," he invited. Pointing to the whole system, he said, "You've seen these in stores or magazine pictures. Home entertainment system, finest the 21st could provide. TV is a Sony 40 inch 6K res. 3-D adaptable. These little fellas," pointing now to the shelves in the cabinet, "are a Bose wireless digital surround amp with subwoofer over there in the corner. Got eight speakers all over the place. You watch a blue ray on this little puppy, and you'll think you been transported to another time and place."

"Weasel," Sarah said in mock exasperation, "you can't drag us through forty miles of tunnels and show us the most amazing thing we've ever seen in our lives and then give us the specs on some stupid television." She grasped him by the shoulders and shook him. "Tell me about the electricity. How did you get gasoline for that generator? How does it work? My God, does this mean we can have a refrigerator and freezer and read at night without those smoky candles?"

Weasel laughed and steered Sarah to an easy chair, gently pushing her down. "Now you just get comfortable, little Miss Curiousity. I got a few surprises in store for both of you. But good things take time and the tellin' of a story and givin' of gifts is half the fun. All this stuff I got here and in the other rooms is wondrous indeed, but finally having someone to share them with makes 'em a thousand times more valuable."

He crossed the room and opened one side of a double door refrigerator and—wonder of wonders—there was a shining light bulb inside it. He pulled out a big glass pitcher with a brown liquid in it and retrieved three crystal glasses and a crystal bowl from the cabinet, filling each glass with ice cubes that came from behind the other refrigerator door. Weasel presented Sarah and me with the crystal glasses and Duke was the recipient of the bowl, which he promptly began lapping up, making big splashing noises.

"This here," said Weasel, holding up his glass, "is what's called instant iced tea. It's already got the sugar and lemon flavoring in it. Comes in brick form in big jars or can. You just chip off a little chunk, put it in water and stir it up. Not bad, huh? Would either of you care for some more ice?" Sometimes he could be a real show-off.

"No thanks, Mr. Technology," I said.

Weasel produced a pipe and a small tin fllled with fat marijuana buds, each as big as my thumb and laced with little red and purple hairs. "Got this stuff from a guy in Peoria. Traded him a big can of some powdered Kool-Aid for an ounce. Called it Kansas City Dead Dog. Said he found a huge plant growin' out of the carcass of a dead dog. Watered it a lot and waited a couple of months till it started budding 'fore he harvested it. Best pot I ever had." He fired it up and passed it to Sarah.

"It's time now for some explanations," she said, passing the pipe to me. "How'd you get the generators running?"

"Well," he replied, "you two know as well as me that there just ain't any gasoline out there anymore. And if there was it wouldn't be worth a shit. It loses its octane with age. Oil ain't a major problem. It gums up and separates a bit, but if its sealed well, it's generally usable. I just make sure I change it a lot when I'm runnin' the generator. Kerosene's available too. But you can't run no engines with it. Good for lamps though."

"Get to the point, Weasel," Sarah said. "How did you get the generator to run?"

"Keep your britches on, Sarah. You know I like to tell a good story. What happened was I was livin' in southern and central Illinois for a few years, and I kept comin' across references to ethanol. Found some writin' on it and figured out it was fuel that farmers made out of corn and soybeans when they used to have real big crops. Mostly they mixed it with gasoline. But if you wanted, you could run a car or tractor on straight ethanol by makin' some changes in the spark plugs, carburetor and timing belt. All I had to do was figure out how to make the stuff and then mess around with some engines tryin' to find the right combinations."

"What about going with solar?" Sarah asked.

"Good thinking," Weasel said. "Looked into it. First problem is age. Solar panels don't last forever. Most of them we can see on buildings are wore out now. Also, they got inverters. Change the current. Inverters last shorter time than the panels. Third thing is you gotta put 'em up. People can see that. I don't want to be seen."

I was on my third toke and decided it might be fun to go check out the refrigerator light. "So how'd you make fuel?" I asked on my way over to the fridge. I opened and closed the door a few times, trying to figure out whether it stayed on all the time or just when someone opened the door.

"Mac," asked Weasel, "just what in the fuck are you doin'?"

"Never mind," I replied. "I already figured it out. This little white knobby thing here on the side is actually a switch that turns off the light when the door hits it. No problem."

"The man could do brain surgery," said Sarah. "Just ignore him, Weasel. One time he spent an hour and a half reading one page of a novel when he was stoned. Just go on with your story."

"Yeah," I said, "but when you really got into it, there was about ten different levels of meaning to each line. It was very complex. Fascinating stuff. Got any books, Weasel?"

"I ain't given' you any books, Mac. I got a story that needs tellin'." He gave me the evil eye, and I returned to my seat. "Now makin' ethanol is very similar to makin' moonshine. It's just pure grain alcohol. You can use corn, soybeans, hell any dead plant will do. Can't use wood, though. Then you'd end up with methyl alcohol and that's poison for humans and engines. So I made me a batch. Several batches. Took months and months. Got to set up a still and fire it slow, watching the temperature real close. While it was cookin', I searched out car manuals and found out how to convert engines. Didn't tell me about little engines, like the one on the generator. But I just fiddled with the spark plug and carburetor a bit until I got it right."

"You make it sound so easy, Weasel," Sarah said. "This is so important. It changes our lives. Nothing will be the same now. It's unbelievable. The things we can do with electricity are mind boggling."

"It's got its limits, Sarah," he replied. "Can't run it all the time. Can't brew enough ethanol to keep up."

"Fuck the ethanol," I said. "Let's watch one of those video discs. I've been reading about 3D. You got any of that on disc?"

"Mac, we're gonna set up this whole system back home. No sense in cranking it up now. Besides, I got some other stuff to show you. Let's go next door."

It was in the next basement over that he showed us the computers. "I got Mac, Gateway, Lenovo, HP, LG...you name it," he said when we entered the room. Tables had been set up along all four walls. Each table held several computers and laptops and various types of printers and monitors and numerous magazines and tech manuals. Many of the machines were in various stages of disassembly. Tools were scattered about, and the disarray of his work room was a stark contrast to his entertainment area.

"Some of these machines work perfect," he told us. "But to tell you the truth, I haven't made much progress in fixin' the broke ones." He grinned sheepishly. "Been watchin' too much on that video disc player. But I don't think it will be a major problem gettin' them all runnin'."

He was right. They ran real good. They opened up the opportunity for us to learn what really caused the collapse.

FROM SARAH'S COLLAPSE JOURNAL
JANUARY 2053

Mac sees me writing and wants to get in. I told him write about his own stuff. I think I hurt his feelings. I don't want that. We have only each other—and Duke, that damn Duke, like a quiet person. But good and kind and loyal. Not like the people we see in the world.

Jesus Christ. Weasel arrived. Talk about changes. Suddenly I care about two people. When I started what I now call "The Collapse Journal" last year, it was a diary. Now with Weasel here, and his stories and the obvious signs of trauma on his body (what about his psyche?), I'm pissed at the world and want to find out how it got so fucked.

No more diary. Collapse Journal. I'm going to figure it out. I owe it to us.

When Weasel brought us limited access to electricity, a commodity Mac and I only dreamed about as we longingly looked at pictures of reading lamps, heaters, fans, and refrigerators in wrinkled, sun faded, water damaged magazines, a door that was rusted shut creaked a bit and opened a crack. I could see refrigeration, and fresh food, and eggs that lasted for weeks. I relished reading at night without the smell of candle wicks or kerosene. I could feel heat in our January bedroom and a breeze in our July kitchen.

But more than anything I viewed a window to the past. A time machine. Those little computers Weasel shared went to sleep in 2023. But Weasel woke them. The boxes and flat, square plates could talk to us. The machines were people and I wanted their knowledge. Not just their daily lives and the wonders of pre-Collapse, but the truth about how humanity became an endangered species.

I burned with curiosity. I knew we were alone. After 30 years, someone should have come to help us—or conquer us. We could read. No stupid people in this compound. In '23 the United States was huge and powerful. In the top three of most powerful countries. Someone was alive and organized and could fix us.

But no one came. Wrong. Weasel showed up. A solitary wanderer seeking a higher state of poverty. He was an emigrant, not an emissary. No one was coming to save us.

How, I wondered, could so many people be dead? In the whole world, how many humans were there in '23? The answers were in computers and electricity.

But life intruded and ten months later we sometimes played games on computers and read documents. We worked to survive from dawn to dusk. Dig, lift, carry, move, plant, stack, dismantle, burn. Then talked. Then read until the books fell from our hands. Discovering the how and why of The Collapse got pushed lower and lower on the to-do list.

CHAPTER SIX

T he blow came out of nowhere, an unexpected backhand, casually delivered by the woman who was his mother, a dirty, pathetic clan woman pissed at being disturbed while she gnawed on a stringy piece of venison. Thirsty, he tugged at her dress, seeking a sip from her cup. The blow would have been laughed off by a teenager, maybe would have stung a little to a child of nine or ten; but to three-year-old Stevie B., it was the hand of a giant crashing down upon his head. He left his feet, and, propelled backward, landed on his butt, his momentum snapping his head back until it impacted on a dirty, worn carpet of what was once the recreation room of a luxury apartment complex.

Blood flowed from his lip at the spot where the meaty flesh had come between the bones of her hand and his teeth. But he was familiar with the taste of his own blood. He was also well acquainted with broken bones and concussions, which he had received at various times from the other clan adults.

His was a mean, slimy world, as different from Sarah's and mine as vultures are from kittens. In his first three years of life, Stevie B. saw up close what Sarah and I had observed from afar—starvation, abuse, cruelty, insanity, rape, murder and torture. In the 20th and early 21st Stevie B., his life, his culture, his social interactions would have been called deviant.

Not anymore. Stevie B.'s brief life story made him a normal guy in our world.

When his head snapped to the floor, everything went black, then white, then lights twirled as the pain kicked in. He was too stunned and dizzy to cry. He was spared further abuse. Somewhere in his mind he knew it was wrong. It didn't feel right that mothers would hurt children, despite daily evidence to the contrary. He knew he shouldn't fear his mother, view her as just another adult—someone with power, someone to be feared. But even by age three, some instinct told Stevie that the world was askew. He crawled to the corner where he kept his blanket and wrapped himself in it, sucking his thumb and fantasizing about a woman who would hold him to her soft bosom and gently rock him. Sleep erased his pain.

• • • •

A month later Stevie came down with the case of influenza that forever changed his life. The disease generally killed kids — wearing them down, starving and dehydrating them. Sometimes it was the secondary cause of death. Stevie had seen sick children who demanded too much attention or nursing thrown outside by adult clan members and left to die—frequently helped along by dogs and various other scavengers. Children were not revered by the clans. Life was dangerous and demanding. Children were a hassle. If they made it to adulthood, the men mostly became scouts and soldiers, protectors of turf. Women were cooks, porters and providers of sex.

The bug hit Stevie hard. The intense fever caused him to sleep most of the time. When he was awake, he was too weak to cry. Sometimes he moaned, but that wasn't enough to get him expelled. His feeble cries weren't loud enough to warrant a beating.

His sick bed was in a corner close to the dog's territory. All clans have dogs. They are an essential early warning system. When times are good and food is plentiful, dogs are no problem. When times are lean, the clan can eat the dog. It's easy to steal a replacement pup from one of the packs.

Stevie slept curled up on pile of rags, his dirty blanket clutched between his arms and legs. Once he was awakened by a compelling thirst. Dehydrated and weakened by the intense fever, he crawled over and drank from the dog's bowl. The dog snarled, lunged forward and nipped Stevie twice, drawing blood, but the pain was a mere annoyance compared to what he had endured in his three short years of clan life.

After forty-eight hours Stevie's fever broke. He felt hunger pangs in his shrunken belly. While the dog slept, he stole her bones and eventually broke his way through to the marrow. That gave him enough strength to later skulk to the adults' table to partake in their scraps while they slept. He didn't have to compete with the dog. The mutt knew the price for excursions to the human's table was death.

Little Stevie B. survived the ravages of the flu. And the day he felt well enough to sit up and look around, he noticed a wondrous thing— no one was paying any attention to him! His brain provided him with the earth shaking realization that not one person had hit, yelled at, kicked, slapped or spat upon him in three days. Sure he was weak, but the only pain messages his body sent were from a couple of minor dog bites.

Stevie kept his silence. Two days later he asked one of the adult women for some food. A little experiment. He wasn't quick enough to dodge the slap that whipped into the side of his head. He crawled away, stifling his tears.

No one came after him to inflict more pain.

That was his last request of any adult. And that was how he learned to survive. He was lucky the teachers let him live. A decade later, when Stevie B. stumbled upon Sarah and me in the woods, much of his humanity had been leached away.

• • • •

Stevie B. spent his first nine years as a clan kid. He hadn't the vaguest clue as to what a family was.

To the clans turf is life. Their territory is their food and materiel source. Instead of pissing on corners like their animal counterparts, they mark their boundaries with elaborate and often strangely beautiful painted signs, much like the urban gangs of the 20th and 21st. Paint is easy to come by. The dried out cans of latex base in hardware stores and building centers can be salvaged by adding water.

Clan sign is everywhere. Crowns, stars, Playboy bunnies, tridents, swastikas, crosses, jokers, flying hearts, top hats and more—all painted with loving care and admirable craftsmanship, all demarcating territory, welcoming friends, warning enemies.

From the city on out to the suburbs, spreading north, south and west, most of the area that thirty-five years ago was called Chicago is now divided into little fiefdoms by the clans. Their territories stretch as far as the big shopping complexes. Where the malls stop, so do they.

Beyond this invisible wall is where we live. They haven't found us yet.

Large population centers give the clans bountiful resources for scavenging and salvage and ample opportunity for shelter. They squabble constantly, killing and maiming each other on a daily basis, but paradoxically often trade drugs—some clans have better chems than others—weapons and other items of hard currency. Jewelry, the real stuff, is highly valued and sought after.

When several million people suddenly died, they left behind their coffee, and cigarettes, and paper towels. And all those guns and ammo, machetes and knives. The survivors were ill tempered and intolerant.

Coffee is now worth as much per ounce as gold. With a Rolex and a pound of coffee, I can acquire a half dozen quality pistols or three assault rifles—or, were I so inclined, a reasonably healthy human being. Not a quality whore, mind you. They are high ticket items. But certainly a decent laborer.

Occasionally large scale battles occur among the clans. Sometimes ambitious leaders form coalitions and expand into other territories. These bonds are usually short lived. The leaders always seem to forget that when they expand, they have more turf to defend.

There are no clothing stores. Shoes and apparel are free for the finding. If someone craves another's clothes, there is a price. Grocery stores and supermarkets don't exist anymore either—except as empty buildings advertising a product that no longer endures. But there is enough food for our meager population. Game is plentiful. Huge herds of deer abound. Geese strut around like they're invincible. Ducks and chickens are easy prey for hunters. Raccoons, squirrel, turkey, and rabbits are prolific beyond our needs.

Many of us indies are farmers of sorts, raising chickens, cattle, pigs and sheep, harvesting crops of fruit and vegetables. In the spring and fall, the skies fill with flocks of geese and ducks beyond our ability to count. The lakes and rivers teem with fish—bass, bluegill, crappie, walleye, catfish, coho. More than enough to feed everyone. Humanity's passing has left the earth a sanctuary for their propagation. We are the only endangered species.

There are even some trading posts and bars that serve home cooked meals and aged whisky and newly distilled beer, wine and shine. In these smoky holes you can sometimes obtain weapons and jewelry. Frequently they have fresh meat and vegetables and fruit. Occasionally they have human beings for sale—whores, slaves, children.

Cars and trucks are abundant, but they don't run because there is no gas or oil.

Except inside the fortresses of the blue bloods on the lakeshore, doctors don't heal.

Telephones are silent. They have been replaced with long talkers or raised voices.

Police don't patrol.

Judges don't rule.

Juries don't listen.

There is no crime—for no one has established the norms to define crime. There are no transgressions because there is no law.

Nor is there any pollution.

Or dirty water.

Or smog filled skies.

Or fish floating belly up.

Or game squashed by cars.

There is no money. All exchanges are done on the barter system. The value of what you have is completely dependent upon the desire of the other person to possess it. If their desire exceeds their ability to pay, you could die.

There are no congregations of church goers, even though most churches still stand, gutted of their valuables and antiquities. Some say there is no God. Arguing to the contrary is difficult.

The most abundant of the legacies left from The Collapse are the skeletons. They are as driftwood on the lakeshore, fallen branches in the forest. We step over them, walk around them, see them but barely notice. Once there were millions. But after three decades of serving as toys for children and sources of marrow for the dog packs and other scavengers, they're no longer so prominent.

Outside of our walls, no one speaks of The Collapse, wonders how it happened that we were left this way—like we're living inside this huge, once beautiful engine, but are denied the knowledge and resources to engage the gears. I'm not sure if the culling left us with people who mostly don't care or if the rigors of survival are too demanding for them to have time to consider the causes. I'm leaning toward the former. The clans seem content in their savagery; most indies accept living with subservience and fear.

Inside, we know what caused The Collapse. Sarah figured it out. Took her over a year of research. Amazing what you can do with a little electricity and the guts of aged computers. When she told us, took us through the process of the collapse, we were stunned. Angry at first, although Sarah and I each received clues in our childhoods— stories from the elders, admonitions against technology and demagoguery.

Our anger dissipated into shock. Like seeing a slammer freak kill an enemy clan soldier just to see him die. Or someone shoot a deer, then leave its carcass for the scavengers. Not bother dressing it out or using all of it to feed your family.

Pity was what we finally felt. Seasoned with disgust. Poor dumb bastards. They saw it coming and were too fucking greedy to intervene. Took them nearly two years to kill most everybody off, shut off the power, silence the machines.

Except for us, no one that I know of has electricity. We are probably the first to use it since the collapse, over three decades ago. If the clans were to learn of our discovery, we'd be dead.

Weasel brought us electricity.

If someone were to ever figure out how to get the printing presses running and a book were to be written cataloging the clans, Stevie's clan would be found under the "S" listing as "Satan's Messengers."

They are one of ten clans we've identified as working within the area five miles east of our compound. West of us there is nothing but woods and prairie and a few indies hoeing their subsistence out of the fertile soil.

The other clans that are close enough to us that we have to keep an eye on their movements have equally inventive and descriptive monikers: The Insane Cobra Nation, The Glory Brigade, the Butt Rangers, the Gaylords, the Cannibal Crusaders, and Abortion Chunky Style are among the most barbaric.

But when it comes down to cold, calculating cruelty, depravity and viciousness, Stevie's clan, Satan's Messengers, is king of the hill.

In a world of beasts, Satan's Messengers is the Harvard of survival schools.

REMEMBRANCES OF STEVIE B.
2046 AGE FIVE

The back of his head stung from the sharp slap that came from behind, interrupting his meal of coarse bread and raccoon stew. The carrots were his favorite part and Stevie was carefully separating them from the chewy, stringy raccoon meat when the blow landed. A group of the younger children were eating their noon meal in the center area of their new home, a U shaped grouping of twenty rooms that had once been called The County Farm Motel. It usually took Satan's Messengers about six months to trash a new set of living quarters. Then they moved on to another apartment complex or motel, sometimes even a hotel. There were hundreds to choose from in their territory. Their new quarters were not elegant, but all the rooms and furnishings were intact.

"Give me your grub, you little butt licker," the voice behind him said. Stevie didn't need to look to know it was Paulie the Porker, a fat eight-year-old bully who terrorized the younger kids into giving him their food. Stevie was rail thin; Paulie was big-belly fat. That was the way of things. The bigger kids strong-armed the younger and smaller kids. The adults bullied and intimidated all the kids.

Paulie saw Stevie try to hide the carrots. He slapped him again in the exact same spot, still tender from the first blow and much more receptive to pain. Paulie knew that. He was a most accomplished bully. It wasn't easy to get fat eating clan food. Paulie was the master of getting more than his share.

Stevie hung his head and moved aside, giving access to his plate to corpulent Paulie. Snatching up the plate, The Porker brought it up to his mouth and greedily shoveled its contents down the gaping hole with his fingers, leaving only the carrots behind, little orphaned orange fingers with globules of fat from the stew adhering to them.

"You like these carrots, fuck face?" he asked Stevie.

Stevie knew an answer wasn't required. Paulie swept the carrots into the dust at Stevie's feet. "Pick 'em out, vegetable boy," Paulie laughed. "A little dirt adds flavor."

Stevie ignored the bully. A confrontation could mean serious pain, possibly injury. Paulie was a vicious little boy, highly respected in the eight-year-old community and already catching the eye of the clan grown-ups as a potential asset. Stevie kept his head down, avoiding eye contact, anything that could interpreted as further communication. Hunger was a far better choice than a severe beating.

And Stevie would go hungry. He didn't have the heart to take from the children smaller than he. And no one would offer him their scraps—no adults, no children. In the clan you had to hang on to your property. Either be tough or be low profile.

Paulie casually tossed the empty plate down in the dust. "I think there's a little gravy left, Scrote," he said to Stevie and left laughing.

The plate was lying face down in the dust. Stevie didn't bother to check.

REMEMBRANCES OF STEVIE B.
2048 AGE SEVEN

It wasn't unusual for Stevie to be awakened in the middle of the night by a fight. Two or more men battling over a hit of Slammer ... or a bottle of shine...or the flesh of a woman. Screaming and snarling, the soldiers sometimes battled to the death when their tempers flashed beyond the borders of reason, and they put their lives on the line for the transitory pleasure of sex or drugs. The loser's carcass would be dragged to the edge of the compound and left for the dogs.

But it was no ordinary fight that awakened Stevie this night, not a battle he could listen to and return to sleep when it finished. This one was coming right at him. If he didn't move, Stevie suddenly realized, he would be engulfed, swept away in the melee. This was hell.

The sounds of gunshots bounced off the walls of the Messengers' current home, a several hundred unit apartment complex arranged in a semicircle of three story buildings. In the brief silence between shots, Stevie heard screams of agony, of pain. As he sat up and rubbed his eyes, his brain slipped into gear and interpreted for him what his eyes and ears were registering. Through the flashes of rifle and pistol shots and the flickering flames that were beginning to dance up the sides of the buildings, Stevie saw hundreds of bodies running, falling, dripping black fluid.

Children skittered through the battle. Hands to their ears, eyes wide as an owl's in terror, mouths open in unheard screams, they were the first to fall, trampled by the fighting or fleeing clan adults, dispatched by stray bullets. No one tried to help the children. They were not valuable. More could be produced…or purchased. Survival was more important.

On his hands and knees, his sleeping bag crumpled beneath him, Stevie snapped his head left and right, frantically searching for a place to hide. Ahead of him, just a few meters away, a microcosm of the huge struggle drifted toward him, threatening to sweep him up in its ferocity. Two fleeing Messenger women had been tackled by four of the attackers. Backlighted by the growing fires, the men began ripping the clothes from the women's bodies. The women struggled and screamed mightily. The soldiers were laughing. It was much more fun to rape them alive than fuck their corpses.

Stevie knew the women by sight. They were of his clan. But by deed they had done nothing to ingratiate themselves to the boy. To them he was just another kid, high maintenance, low pay out. But Stevie knew it was wrong, what was happening to them, and scrambled towards them, a momentary lapse of reason from a young mind that had not yet turned savage, a futile gesture to help the helpless that luckily did not cost him his life. One of the attacking men jumped up and kicked Stevie in the ribs, knocking him back toward the edge of the action.

Breathless, retching from the blow to his side, Stevie crawled backwards on his hands and knees, away from the carnage, across the grass, over sidewalks, finally encountering a curb that dropped him a few inches to the pavement of the parking lot where he banged his back into a the old rusted hulk of a pick-up truck. The flattened tires raised the vehicle enough for his small body to fit under the truck. He was safe.

As Stevie watched from ground level, the battle, now just five minutes old, was going badly for The Messengers. It was mostly women and children and drugged-out or drunk soldiers who were absorbing the brunt of the attack. Resistance was minimal.

The attackers were a Folks clan, he saw. Right sided jewelry. The tattoos he could make out in the intermittent light were six-point stars. Folks were the natural enemies of People. It was the code.

It was from the other side of the compound, through the flickering flames and pockets of smoke, that Stevie saw The Babe coming. Flanked by six of his lieutenants, armed with an M-16 in one meaty hand and a Colt army issue .45 in the other, The Babe marched across the open area between the buildings barking orders and snapping off shots from his weapons. His lieutenants peeled off left and right to organize defensive forces to repel the invaders. The Babe kept marching, Stevie saw, toward what might be one of the leaders of the attackers, a man who was also screaming orders at his warriors.

A behemoth, a walking receptacle of lard, a monument to the pleasures of the flesh, The Babe was large enough to fill any doorway. Every man woman and child in the Messengers lived in fear of The Babe. He was a primordial force, ruling the Messengers with a savagery that was distinctive in a savage land, more brutal and depraved than the foolish attackers could have imagined.

As Stevie watched in fascinated horror, The Babe cut a path through the battleground, sometimes firing his weapons, sometimes using them as clubs, an eerie smile gracing his fat face. Stevie was familiar with the concept of body armor, but when puffs of dust flew from The Babe's massive chest, and the enormous man did not falter in his stride, the young boy shivered involuntarily. To his seven-year-old mind he was viewing pure evil, an invincible force incapable of harm from the actions of mere human beings. Many adult Messengers silently shared Stevie's view.

As The Babe waded through the bloodshed, the Messenger defenses began to coalesce. From the flanks, Messenger soldiers, led by the lieutenants, poured out of buildings, filling their noses with Slammer as they rushed into the action, firing assault rifles and pistols at the invaders, some brandishing bayonets and butcher knives, others machetes and axes, all screaming like demons.

The battle quickly compressed into a circle of action, a tight knot of writhing bodies. Rifles and pistols were discarded in favor of knives, clubs and hands. In the center was The Babe. Stevie saw him pick up two men, bash them together repeatedly until they grew limp and then drop them to the ground. He turned to search for other victims. Seeing two of his own men who were losing their personal battles with the invaders, The Babe poked his pistol into each man's stomach fired off three rounds…then dispatched their opponents with rib crushing body blows from the baseball bat that had been harnessed to his back.

The Babe suddenly saw two of the leaders of the attackers on the edge of the fray and rushed them, moving his four-hundred-pound bulk with uncanny alacrity. He was upon them before they could react, his huge paws grasping the fronts of their battle jackets and pulling them from their feet, bringing their heads close to his own. As The Babe bit off the ear of one man, the nose of another, spitting out the appendages in a spray of blood and laughter, Stevie shrunk beneath the truck. He could watch no more.

Soon the sounds of battle diminished, the grunts and groans, the clanks of steel on steel, the screams of the mortally wounded, the high pitched pleas for mercy. The Messengers were too much for the attackers.

There were no prisoners. The wounded were dispatched, often slowly. Stevie heard their cries. Weapons were gathered; clothes and jewelry were stripped; shoes were saved. The Messengers were a People clan, sworn enemy of all Folk clans. Then the corpses, torsos and foreheads, were lovingly carved up with the signs of the People—five point stars, up-side down crosses, five point crowns, the initials S M in curly script—and dumped into the Dupage River, which ran behind their compound.

As the buildings burned and the corpses drifted down the river, bearing the carved symbols of the Messengers' victory to be read by those who might find the bloated bodies, the victorious clan packed up and began the process of moving to a new location. Stevie went with them. They were all he knew.

They did not bury their dead.

• • • •

In Stevie's seventh year, when he first witnessed the horrors of clan battle, Satan's Messengers were getting big. Big meant noticed. Big was bad. It disturbed the balance. Clans the size of a couple hundred or so maintained the balance. Territories were manageable. Battles were brief and not so costly. But a couple of hundred soldiers was not enough for The Babe. His ambition was as mammoth as his body.

They were trying to punish The Messengers, pare them down to a more acceptable size, those clans who disturbed seven-year-old Stevie's sleep and nearly killed him in the process. But they were just a few months too late and a few I.Q. points too dumb. They hadn't reckoned on the power of The Messengers, hadn't calculated for the ferocity and organizational skills of their leader—savage, merciless, mountainous. The Babe was probably the first post-collapse man who wanted to be king.

CHAPTER SEVEN

REMEMBRANCES OF STEVIE B.
2050 AGE NINE
THE MALL

"Eric, Eric," Stevie gasped, out of breath from his run across the parking lot fronting their current address, "I heard the older boys talking. They found a huge mall. Hundreds of stores. Think about all the boxes we can find. Unopened ones. Maybe we can find some swords or real guns. Let's go, Eric. It's only about three miles."

Eric was Stevie's first friend, his only friend. Two lanky kids who looked down a lot and had the knack of being part of the background. They shared a love of exploring, scouting burned out and abandoned office buildings, stores and homes, pretending they were a two-man warrior team, escaping the enemy clans. Neither liked hanging around the clan compound. There was too much pain and abuse. In their imaginary warrior world, they did not receive pain; they inflicted it upon their enemies, saved other children from demeaning lives among the clans.

Eric and Stevie could journey near and far from their clan head-quarters. No one noticed their comings and goings. No one became concerned when they were gone for long periods. They attracted attention only when they wanted something or got in the way. Being the object of attention was not desirable. Both boys avoided clan adults and teenagers.

They left after lunch, pilfering some jerky of unknown origin, dried fish and bread from the cooking area because they planned a long trip. Spending the night was no problem. They would not be missed. They worked their way to the fattest road they could find running north and took it. When the road north ended and became dense woods, they went straight through, finding two excellent walking sticks within a few minutes.

Stevie and Eric loved the woods and would play in their shadowy coolness for hours, exploring and pretending to hunt deer. But when they came across a herd, they would always watch in awe of the animals' beauty and agility, breathing very shallowly and making no noise so the magnificent creatures would not discover their presence and bolt. They both ate venison. It was a staple of their diet. They confessed to each other that they were glad they were not the ones to make the kill.

The woods ended and they swung east and then north again, always watchful for other travelers. Strangers were to be avoided, but were seldom seen. Eric spotted two men biking south, toward the boys, on ten speeds.

"Get back," he said, pushing Stevie off the road and into the woods for cover. They hid just off the road, behind a gnarled oak and watched as the men rode by, their bikes weaving erratically on the road, wild laughter blaring from their mouths. Each was dressed in black and gold. No other color could be seen.

"Slammer freaks," whispered Stevie. "Insane Deuces love Slammer."

"Yeah, either that or wicki sticks," replied Eric in a hushed voice.

Whenever they saw someone on their journeys, the boys always hid. Friendship was as rare as love. Whomever they encountered was the enemy. Stevie and Eric were experts in being secretive and silent. They had to be. Neither was cut out to be a tough guy.

They first spied the mall from about a mile out—a huge, mysterious multilevel complex of connected buildings called Stratford Square. It was surrounded by acres and acres of parking lots dotted with rusted cars and trucks. Neither boy had ever seen a car move, but they both knew the vehicles were born to speed along the abandoned roadways that lined their world.

They played in the cars for two hours before they even made it to the mall. Buttons and knobs and handles and switches and foot pedals—these must have been for launching weapons as the vehicles sped along the roadways, battling enemy raiders. Eric would steer and

Stevie would launch rockets and fire machine guns, both supplying sound effects. They were very familiar with the sound of guns.

"Let's hit the mall," said Eric. "I've had enough of battles."

They loped across the parking lot, approaching a set of eight doors with all the windows broken out. Located between C PEN EY and K LS, the doors served as one of the main entrances to the mall. To the boys it was like the open mouth of a cave...and they loved exploring.

Inside, broken glass and leaves littered the floor along with yellowing papers, warped cardboard and discarded plastic cups. Skylights, some of them without glass, allowed the afternoon sun to enter the mammoth enclosed world, and as the boys walked down a hallway, they suddenly came to an opening that widened out to the main part of the mall like a gigantic cavern in a cave. Facing the boys were hundreds of stores, opening up invitingly on two levels before them, spreading out right and left and to their front.

"Jesus, Jesus, Jesus!" hollered Eric. "This is unbelievable, Stevie. This has gotta be the biggest mall that ever existed. You ever seen anything like this?"

"There's gotta be treasure in here," said Stevie. "I know we're gonna find something real big. Maybe knives. Swords, Eric. Maybe swords." Stevie took twenty steps and stopped to inspect his surroundings, noticing several more wide corridors that led to an even greater array of stores. "Holy shit, Eric," he cried. "It's even bigger than we thought. There's more over here."

The boys stood in the center, back to back, and did a slow turn, taking in their prospects for exploration. They were without limit. Windowless shops as far they could see. Floors littered with boxes and toys and broken electronic gear and articles of clothing. Unmatched shoes were cast about, doomed to be forever without a mate. Mannequins, naked and asexual or partially clothed, lay half in half out of display windows. Unbelievably, no signs of fire scarred the mall. Birds' nests filled nooks and crannies and light fixtures, and their chirping filled the mall with the sounds of the woods and grasslands. Raccoon droppings littered the floor. The masked scavengers happily nested in cardboard and paper or shredded clothing.

"Jewelry stores first," said Eric, breaking into a run. They knew jewelry would be valuable in trade. But all the stores were completely bare. No gold on this trip.

"Sporting goods," cried Stevie, breaking into a run. "Guns, knives, fishing gear and football equipment."

Another dry hole. But they were undaunted. Too much to see for discouragement to enter their minds.

An hour later Stevie came upon the door that led to the secret maintenance passageways and the air ducts. Deep in the maintenance hallways they discovered an open grate above their heads large enough to allow access to their thin frames. It beckoned them into the darkness. Eric found a closet. Inside was a step ladder.

"Let's go," said Stevie. "This could to something big, Eric."

Neither boy hesitated. Eric followed Stevie up the ladder and into the passageways that snaked through the mall walls and ceilings. They traveled from store to store on their hands and knees, moving from darkness to dim light and peering into each store through air grates, assessing their prospects from above and moving on until they finally discovered treasure.

On their sixth try, they found an opening through an air duct that gave them access to a bookstore storage room whose door had been sealed off by a roof collapse in the main store. The boys kicked out the grate in the air duct and climbed down into a treasure trove of books and magazines untouched and unseen for over 20 years.

They were amazed.

Eric and Stevie could not read. No one they knew could read. So there was no one to teach them. Reading was not a survival skill in Stevie's world. But they could look at pictures— beautiful, shiny color pictures of fancy cars and fast motorcycles, powerful trains and fanciful beasts, elegant banquets and luxurious homes, powerful football heroes, graceful basketball stars and willowy, sensual actresses.

"Stevie, Stevie," yelled Eric. "Check this out. Machines that fly. Guns and bombs everywhere. Wow if we had one of these no one would ever bother us. We'd be kings."

They had never seen an airplane until Eric found the book entitled, AIR FORCE JET FIREPOWER: 1960-2020. Their imaginations had never conceived of such awesome power. How could such huge machines get up into the air, they wondered.

And books and magazines full of photos of guns and knives. They knew about weapons. Their world was full of them. But not beautiful shiny ones like these. The guns they were familiar with, the weapons carried by all clan adults with enough clout to own one, were dark and unpolished, nicked and dented and scratched, but nevertheless lethal and ominous.

Then Stevie found the books with naked women in them. Lots of women showing all their parts to the boys. Modesty was not a virtue in the clans and the boys had seen everyone naked, children and adults, and had often observed couples having sex. The unclothed female form was not unfamiliar to Stevie and Eric.

But these women, these beautiful magazine models, were not like the women the boys had seen. They weren't pale and dirty. There were no sores or red blotches on their skin. Their breasts didn't sag. Their bellies didn't protrude and they didn't have bruises and scars and scabs like the women of the clan. Even their teeth were beautiful, not stained and rotting like some of the clan women's. And they were all so clean. They were beautiful.

It was Eric who came up with the idea that cost him his life. Stevie has always been grateful that it wasn't he who first proposed the plan.

"Do you know what the older boys would pay to look at these women?" Eric asked, a curious smile on his innocent face. "We could take some of these magazines and sell 'em. They're always tryin' to see the girls naked. Why not sell some to 'em, Stevie?"

Why not indeed, thought Stevie. He had a secret stash of canned food and could envision in his little mind adding to his larder. Maybe he could even get a knife to carry to impress the other kids with.

"Eric," Stevie replied, now beginning to understand why his friend was grinning, "we may never go hungry again."

And so back at the Messenger compound, they became young entrepreneurs and for two or three days became rich in their own, little boy way. When the older boys heard that the pictures were available, they sought out Stevie and Eric, bringing clothing and foodstuffs and army toys to the boys to trade for the magazines.

Oblivious to the attention they were attracting from parties other than the horny teenage boys, Stevie and Eric basked in the sweetness of their new found popularity.

CHAPTER EIGHT

Stevie B. and Eric were familiar with The Babe's leadership style. They had both witnessed one of the despot's answers to a challenge of his authority a month or two before their great adventure at the mall. The Babe had been talking to a thirteen-year-old girl in the yard area of the clan's apartment complex, pulling her close, touching her hips, stroking her back while he whispered in her ear. The girl did not appear pleased by his overtures. The girl's father witnessed the scene and, familiar with The Babe's proclivities when it came to young girls, in a rare display of fatherly concern, pulled her away from his boss and sent her home.

Stevie and Eric watched from their vantage point in a second story apartment which they pretended was their command post. The Babe stalked away. The man walked back toward his daughter. "I think there's gonna be big trouble," said Eric.

Stevie agreed. They both watched from the window, waiting for The Babe's response.

Five minutes later he reappeared, walking slowly and deliberately across the compound toward the girl's apartment, the Louisville Slugger firmly gripped in his huge right hand. The Babe called out the girl's father and, without and preliminary conversation, dispatched the offender with one swing, splattering nearby spectators with bits of brain tissue and fragments of bone. He retrieved the stunned girl from inside the building and walked her back to his apartment, gently guiding her with his arm around her shoulders, smiling solicitously and murmuring in her ear, dragging the gore smeared bat behind him, its business end a muddy mess of dirt, blood, bone and brain tissue.

The young girl's screams, emanating from his third floor apartment, lasted fifteen minutes. Ten years later, in the safety of our compound, Stevie told the three of us that he can hear the sound of the bat impacting the father's head as clearly as the day it happened.

"Sounded like a cantaloupe dropped from a second story window," he told us.

• • • •

At the zenith of the boys' first success in life, The Babe learned of Eric and Stevie's magazine sales operation. They were too young and inexperienced in the ways of the clan world to plan for subterfuge in their venture. They didn't know free enterprise was not encouraged by The Babe. Control was one of the main ingredients of his successful leadership. Dominance was perpetuated by maintaining a tight stranglehold over all activities within his organization. When he learned of the boys' venture, The Babe moved immediately to terminate their burgeoning enterprise.

The two boys were blissfully ignorant of the forces that were about to shatter their lives. On the morning that two of The Babe's men came to escort them to their chief, Eric and Stevie were taking inventory of their treasure trove and planning another excursion to the bookstore. Huddled in a corner of their second story command post in the Messenger camp, a five building apartment complex in a town once called Naperville, they were shocked when two lieutenants burst in and dragged them across the compound to their leader's third floor residence. They were dumped into the living room of a corner apartment, the door closed behind them.

Not a word had been spoken to them on their short journey. Nor had they spoken to each other. As they surveyed their surroundings, they remained silent, struck dumb by the abrupt change in their situation and the alien nature of the room they occupied.

A kitchen filled with filthy dishes and silverware was to their left. To their right, a wall dominated by dirt smeared windows overlooked the complex. Straight ahead, across the large living room, was a hallway with three doors, one on each side, one at the end, all of which were shut tight. From the door at the end of the hallway came voices and laughter, men and women's voices.

The living room was furnished with couches, cushions and coffee tables. Glasses and mugs covered the tables, some empty, some half-filled, some lying on their side. Candles and kerosene lamps were scattered throughout, ready for nightfall. Pipes and bongs and syringes and pills were abundant. A few little plastic bags with white powder in them were evident among the debris on the table, probably Slammer or Fuck-U-Up, maybe some new concoction from the Messenger's chems. The boys knew what they were. The room reeked with the odor of spilled homemade beer and wine, and the stench of urine filtered into the area, emanating from the hallway bathroom. The sweet, stale stink of hundreds of exhalations of marijuana smoke mingled with the other noxious odors that assaulted their noses.

Glittered, long-haired rock stars, poised and strutting, swinging microphones and wielding guitars like battle axes, looked down upon the boys from framed pictures on the walls. Joining the musicians were strange and terrible monsters and aliens and fantasy warriors, who battled dragons and defended women whose breasts were bigger than watermelons.

The Babe had found a poster store.

Stevie and Eric knew they were in trouble. They waited in silence, listening to the sounds from the room at end of the hall, surrounded by monsters with blood soaked fangs and razor sharp claws, each realizing that behind the door at the end of the hall lurked the real monster. For thirty minutes they were terrorized by their own imaginations. They spoke not a word.

Finally, the door opened and three women and one man exited the room. When they saw the boys, they laughed. The man pushed Stevie and Eric down the hall to meet The Babe. The boys were nearly in a state of fear-induced paralysis.

The soldier pushed them into the room, slamming the door behind them, leaving them alone with the biggest, ugliest, smelliest, most repulsive individual they had ever encountered.

The Babe reposed in a recliner, the kind that kicks out a leg rest when its occupant leans back far enough. Decked out in a brand new red and black Chicago Bulls warm up suit that strained against his protuberant belly and black Reebok high tops, he glared at them for a full minute. Then he spoke. His voice, deep and menacing, flowed from a mouth ringed by a raggedy beard, and highlighted by large, red, greasy lips. He licked his fingers and tossed a chicken bone in the corner.

"I understand that you boys like art. Did you like the living room? Pretty good shit, huh?" He leaned forward, his arm extended in a sweeping gesture. "Recognize any of the stuff in here? I keep my best pictures in here. The real art."

The terror stricken boys, who fifty years earlier would have been scrutinizing lions and elephants on the wall of Mrs. Wilson's third grade classroom, gazed at the walls that closed them in. They were surrounded by nude women, walls and ceiling. Breasts were thrust forward, languidly presented to the camera. Labia were spread by long elegant fingers with painted nails and offered willingly to onlookers. Smiles and pouts and pursed lips spoke silent invitations. Erect nipples were displayed, squeezed between thumbs and forefingers. Buttocks were presented and spread, revealed to the camera's inquisitive eye. There were no secrets.

Eric and Stevie were familiar with a few of the photos, ones that they had sold to the older Messenger boys.

"I'm looking to add to my collection," said The Babe. His voice was kind, solicitous. "This section over here is new. You boys ever seen this kinda art?"

Behind him was a section devoted to another type of photography. Eric and Stevie saw a wall of men. All nude. All offering the same type of things the women did, just with different equipment. Some of the men in the photos wore holsters with pistols in them or carpenter's belts filled with tools. Always displaying. Always preening. The boys looked away, afraid and repulsed.

"Whatsa matter?" leered The Babe. "You don't like this stuff? I thought you boys would be interested in this kind of art. Whadda you say you boys pose for some pictures? I don't have no camera. But we could practice. It could be fun. And I'll make sure you got some special presents. How about it?"

The boys backed away. The Babe read the disgust and fear on their faces. He took a new approach, falling back on his most successful strategy for dealing with people who had something he wanted.

He heaved his massive bulk from the chair and approached Eric and Stevie. Towering over them, he began to talk, quietly and menacingly at first; then building to a scream and bellow, spittle flying from his mouth.

"You two are selling magazines to the men. They are my magazines. Everything here is mine. Your food is mine. Your clothes are mine. Your mothers are mine. Your mothers suck my cock whenever I want them to. I can fuck them anytime I want. Same with your sisters. Same with you. I own your little asses. I can do anything I want with you. Nobody's gonna stop me. Nobody's gonna help you. I want you to tell me where you got them. I'm on top. You're the bottom. Think about it, you little pieces of shit."

He stepped back and flopped back down in his recliner, spent by his tirade, his face flushed and shiny with sweat, his beard spattered with spittle.

The boys were silent, struck dumb by the astounding performance of the gross three-hundred-pound creature in front of them.

The Babe waited, glaring at the boys, intimidating them into further silence. Stevie wanted to speak, but the words were locked in his brain. He couldn't get his mouth to work.

After a minute of stillness in the room, The Babe again extracted himself from the recliner, approached Eric, put a meaty paw behind his neck and guided him to his chair, forcing the boy to kneel between his massive legs as he sat back down.

"Did you like the magazines, Eric?" he asked. "Did the pictures excite you? Are you old enough to get hard yet? Remember what I said about you being mine?"

Hot, sweaty, pale, Eric took one look at the monstrosity before him and immediately lost control of his insides. A jet stream of chunk-filled yellow liquid rocketed from his mouth, splashing The Babe's ankles and feet. The stench of vomit and stomach acid filled the room. Panicked, terrified, lost, Eric pulled away from the monster's grasp, screaming, "No! No! No!"

The Babe lurched up from his chair, hastily stepping back. He tripped on the foot rest and fell backward, sprawled like a walrus on his filthy floor. The Babe rolled to his hands and knees and stood. His face was red with rage, fury flashed in his eyes as he picked Eric up by the collar and threw him across the room, screaming, "You puked on my Reeboks, you little shit!"

Eric's impact against the wall shook the room. His body slid to the floor, still and silent, no sobs, no sounds. The body of Stevie's friend was motionless. A small stream of blood leaked from the interior of one ear. One eye stared at Stevie. No recognition there. No more fear. The other eye was shut.

The Babe whirled to face Stevie B., who stood stunned and shocked by the violation of his only friend. "Where are my fucking books, you little toad! Tell me now or I'm gonna hurt you real bad."

Stevie fell to his knees, sobbing uncontrollably. He felt the monstrosity's footsteps approaching, lifted his head and, between sobs, told the beast where to find the magazines.

The Babe lifted Stevie off the floor and brought him to the level of his face. His feet dangling in the air, Stevie found himself nose to nose with his worst nightmare. He pulled his head back as the fat man's repugnant breath assailed his nostrils.

The Babe bared his teeth and snarled at Stevie, "You stay here while I find out if you tell the truth. If you're lying, I'm gonna slice open your little friend and make you eat his guts. If you're not, I'll show you how to use your little butt for something besides shitting."

He dropped Stevie and left. The boy crumpled to the floor, curling into the fetal position, eyes closed, his brain replaying over and over the horror he had witnessed.

Time passed. (Stevie has never been able to tell us how long), and Stevie absorbed the nightmare of being imprisoned in the same room with his dead only friend. Stevie was alone again. The knowledge that he would he was about to become dead or worse seeped in. The dead part didn't feel so bad. But he knew he couldn't count on dead.

Children had value. Alive with Satan's Messengers was worse than dead.

His options were few and terrifying. Stay, die, become a slave, run, die, survive alone. No way that a kid who had survived the worst the clan world could throw at him was going to wait in an apartment for a deranged, soulless, leviathan.

Stevie slowly stood. Shook his head. Did a slow 360. Assessing. First thing Eric. He walked over and closed his friend's one open eye. He told him goodbye. Out loud.

Stevie turned and listened. No threat. The Babe had probably taken his crew to find the magazines. The rest of the clan had resumed normal camp life. No one would come to the apartment except one of the Babe's crew.

He gave himself two minutes. Three water bottles, a pound of jerky, a buck knife and a skinner, a pair of Jordan's, not The Babe's, two hockey jerseys, a backpack. No need for the drugs. No guns.

Stevie walked from the back bedroom through the hall and living room and tried the door. It was unlocked. Returning to the bedroom, he slipped the backpack into position. Then he walked out the door. Down three flights of stairs, out of the building, and through a group of clan women who had pulled lunch duty. No eye contact. Steady pace. His brain and heart wanted him to run. Wanted it so bad that Stevie thought others could hear his heart beating like rain on a tin roof. He waited for the shout that never came.

He walked out of the camp, into the street, and disappeared in a residential neighborhood. He had no destination. He had no plan. His brain was not directing his actions. Stevie continued his trek all day, through the night, and into the next day. He munched jerky, drank bottled water and walked until his body gave out. Before dark on the second day, Stevie found a sturdy house, crawled into the basement, and crashed into unconsciousness.

He rarely spoke to another human being for six years, until Sarah and I found him in the woods about four miles from the compound, just a few seconds away from learning the ultimate lesson.

CHAPTER NINE

REMEMBRANCES OF STEVIE B.
THE YEARS ALONE 2050 TO 2054

O n the edge. Stay on the fringes. Hunt at night. Sleep when the sun was up. Explore. Seek in the dark. Stay out of the light.

Nobody taught him. But when he got hungry enough the first time, two full days and nights after he had fled from the Messenger compound and The Babe's sadistic interrogation of him and Eric, his mind flashing the flight signal over and over to the exclusion of everything else, Stevie found food while the curtain of night covered his movements.

He located the camp of another clan. The secret soldier games he and Eric had played, their natural inclinations to be furtive and silent, got him in, past the sleeping dogs and snoring clansmen, into the cooking area where dinner scraps and venison bones were his reward. He left the same way he came—silently. His first victory.

During his years alone, the survival lessons were hard and cruel. The brown bear taught him never to leave bones and food scraps open to the wind which could catch their rotting fumes and carry the odor to carnivores and omnivores that shared the night with him. He was awakened at dawn by the sound of 900 pounds of raunchy smelling fur accentuated by razor claws and tenacious teeth ripping its way into his basement shelter, enticed by the rotting meat the boy had discarded. Stevie scrambled out a basement window, all of his food and clothing 80left for the bear.

Never eat where you sleep.

• • • •

The dog packs taught him about back doors. He was twelve then, a boy alone returning to his home in a suburban basement after a night's foraging: five cans of vegetables—corn, French cut green beans, peas and two others he didn't recognize—a freshly killed rabbit from a clan cooking area and two kitchen knives with the edges that had lots of curves and indentations. As the sun began to lighten the sky in the east, they caught Stevie in the open, having heard the alien night sound of cans clinking together when the boy adjusted his back pack.

When its eyes confirmed that the sound was a possible food source, the pack's leader swung in Stevie's direction, signaling with a bark for the pack to follow, and began to close the hundred meters that separated the dogs from the ten year old boy with dead rabbit on his belt. Stevie swung left, then right. He was in the middle of a road with five lanes. Twenty meters to his right was a five-story office complex. With the dogs closing behind him, he rushed to the building, dashing through the doorless entryway and into a hopelessly barren area devoid of cover. Elevators. No way to close the doors. Stairs to his right. He ran to them and decided up was better than down. He knew what was below him. A dead end.

The dogs hit the building's entrance as Stevie flew up the stairs, his footfalls alerting them to his location. First floor…second floor…third floor. He was panicked. The pack was going to rip him to pieces. That's what they did. He had seen it happen to animals. Deer, sheep, even their own kind. Their baying echoed in the stairwell as Stevie reached the fourth floor and ran through the doorless entrance to the offices. Scrambling down the hallway, seeking an office with a door still in place, he had the presence of mind to throw the rabbit carcass which had been banging against his hip down the hall where the dogs would appear any moment.

The pack hit the fourth floor doorway and clamored through, bouncing off one another, slashing and biting as all fifteen tried to squeeze through the narrow entrance at the same time. The leader burst through first and caught sight of Stevie's back and began a frenzied barking which the other animals immediately echoed. The hallway reverberated with their call to the kill as they rushed toward the boy, now only fifteen meters in front of them, frantically searching for a defensible position. Hiding was out of the question.

The dead rabbit, only enough to feed one of them, stopped them in their tracks. They set upon it with a fury, all fifteen wanting their share, clambering over themselves in the narrow confines of the hallway, drawing more blood and chunks of flesh from their brethren than they did from the single carcass. The head and legs went in five different directions and the torso disappeared in seconds, ripped apart and gulped down in one piece by four separate animals. Those that missed out on the prize, furiously set upon the dogs who still had parts of the rabbit to gnaw on.

Glancing back, it seemed to Stevie that the pack had become one huge rolling organism, dominated by teeth and claws.

The rabbit gave Stevie about sixty seconds. It took the pack that long to figure there was nothing left. Not even a tuft of fur. He found a bathroom with a stick figure of a woman in a dress on a white plaque on the door. A door. Half open. Enough to allow him entry. More than enough for fifteen dogs, too. Even the biggest ones, the labs and shepherds that got close to a hundred pounds.

He squeezed through and turned his shoulder into the door as the sounds of the pack changed in tempo and grew louder as they closed on their quarry. The rabbit was history. Stevie was to be the next victim of their hunt.

The door moved slightly against his weight, but seventy pounds of scrawny boy wasn't enough to break the twenty-five year old bonds of rust and corrosion on the hinges. He took ten steps back and ran and launched his body at the steel door. Mass and velocity broke the hinges free half a second before five of the pack hit the door from the other side.

The huge black head of the pack's leader, a ferocious shepherd and pit bull mix was trapped between the door and the frame. Stevie looked down at the disembodied head, its lips curled back, fangs slashing out seeking purchase on Stevie's body, eyes rolling madly like huge white marbles trapped in the sockets, and increased his weight on the door. The dog yelped as the two unyielding surfaces pinched his neck. It tried to extricate his head, which was much bigger than the opening, and caused itself even greater distress.

Stevie kept up the pressure. From the other side of the door, he heard the pack in a renewed paroxysm of frustrated rage. They wanted in. They wanted Stevie. The clamor on the other side of the door increased and the leader, still trapped by Stevie, writhed in anger and pain, howling and yelping in agony until only the whites of his eyes showed. The dog's strength slowly diminished minute by minute and suddenly Stevie understood what was happening. The leader was being eaten alive from the hindquarters forward by the remainder of the pack. He was paying the ultimate price for failure.

The leader's growls became whimpers and the light in its eyes slowly dimmed as the pack behind him reached his vitals, gnawing away at his life the same way the leader had done so many times to the weak and the slow of foot. The dog's head sunk to the floor as his front legs finally gave out. The pack tried to pull the carcass into the hall to finish off the head and shoulders, and Stevie lessened the pressure on the door ever so slightly, allowing them to pull the dead leader back into the hallway. When the head disappeared, Stevie pushed the door shut and sat with his back to it, listening to the pack, inches away, devouring one of their own.

When they finished the feast, they tried again to get at Stevie. But the door was secured and he searched for an exit while they yapped in the hall and threw themselves against the door. There was no way out except the now gore-smeared doorway he had entered. Had there been a window, it would have been of no help. He was too high up to escape.

It was impossible for the pack to breach the steel door. And equally impossible for Stevie to leave. The dogs remained for two full days and nights, knowing prey was close, waiting for it to break. In the wild they knew a rabbit or squirrel would eventually panic and run. Humans didn't always follow the rules.

After the first day, Stevie no longer feared the pack. He knew they would leave to find easier pickings eventually. He now feared starvation or worse yet, discovery by animals that could work a doorknob—clan soldiers. His knives were too flimsy to open the canned vegetables, his only source of nourishment. He could have burst the cans by repeatedly banging them against the porcelain sinks, but noise was his enemy. He went for two days without food or water, until the pack finally gave up and went to search for unintelligent prey. Stevie slipped out on the morning of the third day, afraid to escape in the darkness in case some of the pack lingered, thankful no clansmen had found him trapped in the fourth floor bathroom.

The dogs taught him well. Always stay close to cover. Carry food and water. Get a can opener. Or a big knife. And never, ever, be without a back door.

CHAPTER TEN

REMEMBRANCES OF STEVIE B.
THE YEARS ALONE 2052 TO 2054

T wo years later Stevie, now a lean fourteen-year-old, confident and more adept at survival, learned two new lessons, painful experiences about the value of weapons and the price of being noticed. He had been working in daylight for about a year, staying away from heavily traveled areas, always near cover. The scavenging for food and supplies was much better when he could see where he was going.

He found an army issue Colt .45, the most common of the thousands upon thousands of handguns that survived the collapse. Stevie did not know the weapon was probably over fifty years old. Or that millions just like it had been manufactured. He just knew he had seen similar weapons and they worked just fine. The Colt was under the mattress in the master bedroom of a two-story suburban home, one of hundreds in a neighborhood where all the houses looked very similar—short driveways, many with the cars still in front of the garage, small lawns, little patios in the back, every third one identical in style.

In addition to a cleaning kit which included some oil in a plastic container and a spray can that oozed a few drops of foul smelling greasy fluid and two thin wire brushes, he found two extra clips and a box of ammo. And a holster. With the holstered gun around his waist, the heavy, cold steel menacing and powerful, ready for his grip, Stevie discovered that the old fantasies he and Eric used to share, the two-man warrior team, returned to his consciousness. Only this time Stevie was a one-man avenging squad, protecting the weak against the evil clan warlords, working alone, his partner vanquished in a glorious battle in years gone by. It was the first time he had been able to think about Eric without crying.

He holstered the .45 and practiced drawing it and aiming at imaginary clan foes, remembering how the older boys handled weapons when he had lived with the Messengers. When he left the suburban house, the weight of the Colt resting on his hip, he was much tougher than when he had entered. The feeling didn't last long.

Stevie's current shelter was the small office area of a huge, one-story warehouse in an industrial mall a few miles beyond the normal routes of clan soldiers. The office was a 15x15 square with walls of smoky glass and one door in, two windows out. He changed residences every month or so. All of his belongings fit easily into his backpack.

He settled into a corner and began to disassemble the gun, playing with its action and analyzing the movements of the parts until they all lay on the floor before him. He knew from his clan days that the weapon had to be cleaned and oiled before it could be used. As each part came off he remembered how it was linked to the others and laid it down next to the piece that had preceded it.

The whole process of taking it apart and putting it back together came very easily to him. Before him lay springs, bullets, the barrel, trigger housing, the clip, safety switch—parts big and small that in his mind he could visualize coming back together to form a pistol. He could visualize and rotate the parts in three dimensions. A parts catalogue in his brain. The ritual of cleaning and oiling and polishing was relaxing, and when all the parts came back together so easily under his hands, he felt as if he had accomplished something.

The next day Stevie hiked five miles west and found a meadow where he could work with the weapon. He had practiced with it empty, no bullets in the clip, and knew to pull the barrel back to chamber a round and to make sure the safety was off for the trigger to work. And even though the barrel was clean, shiny and dust free, his first shot was taken with extreme caution. He found a tree large enough to reach around with both hands and bellied up to it. The gun was extended in his left hand on one side of the tree. His face was pressed against the other side. If the weapon blew up, everything was protected except his left hand and arm.

When he pulled the trigger, the jolt and noise were so powerful that he thought his hand would certainly be a bloody mess. The gun had recoiled with such force that it had propelled him arm back, jumped out of his hand, bounced off the tree and landed in the leaves two meters to his left. The smoking pistol was still in one piece. Stevie wasn't so sure about his hand, which still remained out of sight on the other side of the tree.

Reluctantly, he drew his hand back around the tree, making it reappear at his eye level, slowly, inch by inch, so he could inspect each section of his wrist and hand until he got to the fingers, which he figured would probably still be on the other side of the tree, little bloody sausages lying in the leaves. With great relief, he found all his fingers still attached and when he asked his brain to move them, they moved, even though he couldn't quite feel them the way he normally would.

Stevie massaged the fingers and when feeling returned retrieved and inspected the Colt and decided to expend a couple of clips on a tree across the clearing, thirty meters away. From shots nine to fourteen, delivered in the two-handed fashion he had seen the clan soldiers use, he hit the tree every time. Wise enough to stop while shells remained, he promised himself he would return when he found more ammo.

Holstering the pistol, he walked across the clearing to inspect his accuracy and the damage done by the powerful bullets. Satisfied with his marksmanship and awed by the devastation the bullets had inflicted upon the tree, Stevie turned toward home and saw three men standing by the tree where he had first tested the gun. Each had a shotgun in the crook of his arm, and Stevie could see that all three men had fingers on the triggers.

One of them waved an arm, beckoning him to their position. Stevie considered a dash into the woods behind him. He had seen what shotguns could do to a human body and knew the woods weren't thick enough to absorb three rounds before they reached his back. Besides, even if he managed an initial escape, he was in unfamiliar territory. They would find him easily. He walked slowly across the clearing, keeping his eyes on their weapons. As he got closer, he identified three

12 gages, two of them double-barreled, one side by side, the other over and under.

The men were obviously indies. Dirt farmers, no doubt. No colors, tattoos or jewelry. Beards, dirty denim and old work boots. Indies farmed out west, beyond the clan boundaries, Stevie knew. Other groups also lived among the clans, between or on the edges of territories. They were somewhat tolerated by most of the clans, but always on the edge of violence, easy targets for the unpredictable outbursts of the clan warriors. It was preferable, if he had to be cornered, to be at the mercy of an indie. Clan warriors would likely kill him or sell him. With indies he might survive. Like the difference between being spotted by a dog pack or wolves. With the wolves at least you had a chance. They would likely ignore you.

The one on Stevie's right, the oldest, spoke first. "Boy," he said, "you're scarin' away our game makin' all that ruckus. How we 'spected to feed ourselves if all the animals get scared off by some little clan boy don't have enough sense to stay outta the woods?"

The words filtered through a dirty, bushy gray beard, stained with some type of brown expectorant which he now spat at Stevie's boots. His brow line jutted out over tiny, menacing eyes. His two hunting companions shared similar features. Intelligence did not sparkle in their hooded eyes as it did in the old man's. Stevie could see trouble coming, but he kept walking toward the man. He was committed.

"I think this little piss-ant trespassin' on our land is one of them clan fellas, Pa. Look at them pants," said the one directly to the old man's right, confirming Stevie's theory. A father and two sons. Or maybe two brothers and one son. The man was looking at Stevie's army surplus pants, signature apparel for clan members.

Stevie didn't know anything about inbreeding or the need for populations to be constantly interjected with new genes. He just knew that three dumb-fuck indies had shotguns on him. And he was in deep shit.

"Whatcha doin' out here, boy?" asked the third. "Figure to do a little tree huntin'?" He cackled at his joke, joined by the man next to him in the high-pitched laughter.

"Shut up, you two," commanded the first man. They immediately complied. "You sound like a couple 'a old women."

He turned to Stevie, looking him up and down, assessing the value of his clothing. "Boy," he said, "we came out here to get away from the likes of you. Don't want your kind out here."

"Let's have a little fun with him," said the third man. "String him upside down and gut him. Watch him wiggle."

"I told you to shut up, Eugene," the old man replied. "I gotta think on this." He turned to the man in the middle, "Michael, you take this boy's gun and hand it to me."

Stevie handed the gun over and stood quietly. Except for his fantasy warrior games, he hadn't spoken for two years and saw no reason to begin now. The old man took the gun and examined it, feeling its heft, aiming it at imaginary targets. He took the two steps that separated him from Stevie and, without warning, smacked the side of the pistol into the left side of Stevie's head, the force of the blow knocking the boy into the air sideways and on to the floor of the forest clearing.

"Hot damn," hooted Eugene, "You sure knocked him good, Pa. Can I do him some?"

"Shut your hole, damn you," the old man snapped. "I ain't gonna kill this boy. It's just not my way. Just 'cuz the clans kill children ain't good enough reason for us to do it. You two boys keep that in mind."

Stevie's ears were ringing and the pain on the left side of his head was immense. But not a sound came from his lips. That lesson had been learned early. Blood dripped on to the leaves beneath his head. I'm still alive, he thought to himself, silently hoping the old man would allow him to return home.

"Listen to me boy," said the man who had struck him. He squatted down beside Stevie. "You leave here and don't never come back. We see you again and we're goin' huntin'. Ain't no call for your type out here. You got everything you need in the city. This here's our territory."

The old man looked to his two companions standing by the tree, enjoying the entertainment. "Take this boy's boots and belt and holster. Find the extra ammo. He's probably got some."

"What about them trousers, Pa," asked Eugene, pointing to Stevie's army surplus pants.

"We got plenty of pants, boy," replied the elder. "The boots we can use. Let the boy walk back home barefoot. No need to strip him naked."

The the two younger men searched him and let him go, getting in a couple of kicks to his ribs while the old man wasn't looking and sharing conspiratorial smiles. Stevie walked home shoeless, his prized weapon a memory. Five miles with no shoes, plus another two it took him to find another pair.

What have I learned? Stevie thought to himself.

Never stand out. Never draw attention to yourself.

Don't trust anyone. He already knew that one. But it didn't hurt to be reminded.

Always keep an extra pair of shoes back at the crib.

He was confused about the concept of the gun and pondered on it for several hours as he walked home. It felt wonderfully powerful and certainly could be useful for protection. But it wasn't any good unless he was willing to use it. His instincts hadn't been sharp enough to kill the three indies the minute he caught sight of them. So, he thought, the only purpose the gun had served was to focus the indie's interest; get the shit beat out of myself.

Had he encountered clan soldiers instead of indies, he considered, they probably would have killed him for the pistol. Certainly would have administered a more severe beating. And if he miraculously transformed himself into a fearless warrior willing to use the guns when threatened by others, what good would one pistol do against someone who carried an M-16 assault rifle—and a couple of pistols and knives—as most of the clan fighters did?

Guns, he finally figured, were more trouble than they were worth. He never carried one again in his years alone. Probably saved his life.

• • • •

The lessons continued. Month after month. Year after year. He learned to deal with the predators—human and animal—trap and scavenge and forage for food. He lived for nearly six years that way, growing bigger and stronger and more suspicious and increasingly wary of every man, woman and animal with each new sunset.

It wasn't until March 2054 that he met an opponent he couldn't handle by stealth—a dog pack that wanted the same thing he did. And it wasn't until that moment that he met human beings who were good, and decent, and true. Trouble was, Stevie didn't know how to recognize these traits.

And when he told me and Sarah, "If you think I'm gonna share this deer with you, you're fuckin' nuts," he truly believed we were the enemy.

CHAPTER ELEVEN

MARCH THROUGH SEPTEMBER 2054

After we saved Stevie from the dog pack, an action he seemed to genuinely resent, Sarah and I were essentially stuck with him. If we left him to fend for himself, the remaining dogs would have finished him off. Even if we had destroyed the rest of the pack, he still would have been helpless, staggering through the cold and snow with no winter gear, a hole in his boot, and a rotted tree limb as his weapon.

So we brought him home with us. More accurately, he followed the food because we told him he couldn't eat it raw and the only place it was going to get cooked was back in the safety of the compound. He followed us at a distance of twenty meters or so, close enough so we could hear the curses he threw our way. Sarah is a really good curser, but the kid put her to shame.

"Don't worry, Hon," Sarah said, her heart filled with the warm glow of good deeds. "Once he gets some food in him and figures out we mean him no harm, he'll come around."

She didn't make too many bad calls. But on this one she was as wrong as wrong can be. I didn't bring her error in judgment up into the light of day too many times during that first six months. His entrance into our growing family did not go nearly as well as Weasel's, who had been with us for over a year. The way I calculate it, Stevie's first night lasted six months. Hell, we didn't even learn his name for five weeks. Stevie B., he finally said. If it's any of your fucking business, he mumbled as an aside.

The second we were back safely in the house, Weasel looked at Stevie, looked at us, and pulled his Glock—pointing it at the boy's face.

Stevie looked at Weasel, spat on the oriental carpet Sarah had scavenged from a mansion in Wayne, and said, "Go ahead and shoot, you mangy little toad. I can't eat my deer, may as well die here and now."

"Damn!" Weasel said, "Reminds me of myself when I was a kid. Welcome to the block. What's your name, kid?"

"Fuck and you, midget."

Stevie was tough as squirrel meat and nastier than a badger with PMS. He was mean-spirited, filthy mouthed, untrustworthy, violent tempered, vile and obstreperous. And it wasn't until he began to finally have real conversations with us that we learned of his history with Satan's Messengers.

Stevie B. wouldn't talk about his life for months. He didn't trust any of us. Except Duke. Which seemed odd...because Duke nearly ripped Stevie's throat out the first time Stevie attacked me. But I got the "Duke No!" command out quickly enough to avert disaster.

I then formally introduced Duke and Stevie by sitting them both down and letting Duke get the Stevie scent and experience.

"You fuck this up," I told Stevie, "this fucking dog might rip you up. You treat him right and Duke accepts you into the pack and protects you—forever."

Stevie mumbled something about the dog being stupid, protecting an asshole like me. But the boy seemed genuinely smitten by the dog and intrigued by the concept of being protected. The fact that Stevie had nearly lost his life to dog packs twice seemed to have no bearing on his affection for Duke.

Looking back, I think that was the first tiny crack in Stevie's armor. The dog won the boy's heart the same way he had with Weasel. I think Stevie respected Duke for his loyalty. He had seen that attribute in only one person in his life with the clan. No longer living, he later told us.

After three days with Stevie, days filled with verbal abuse and temper tantrums, bad manners and general refusals to do anything any of us suggested, Sarah, Weasel and I had a sitdown.

Our physical environment was at an all-time peak with the advent of electricity, supplied by two of Weasel's generators. Electricity provided us with entertainment in the forms of vids and music. It also opened up educational horizons, for we now had several hundred educational dvd's, covering spelling, reading and writing for little kids as well as advanced video academic videos and documentaries. It was on this equipment that Weasel had taught himself to read and write.

But the most fascinating gifts of all that came with the electricity were the computers and hundreds of data discs. Textbooks, math, history, encyclopedias. We still had not completely solved the riddles of their set up and utilization but were making progress.

We picked each others' brains constantly and worked incredibly well in the three-mind format. Weasel analyzed and ruminated, interjecting his comments and stories with movie references. Sarah philosophized and brainstormed, throwing out ideas like hailstones in a thunderstorm. And I tried to keep them both on the subject at hand, which was at that moment, Stevie B.

"What we've got here," said Weasel, "is failure to communicate."

"Thanks, Warden," I replied. "But since we can't throw the boy in the hot box, what in the hell are we going to do with him?"

"Weasel is right about communication," responded Sarah.

"Yeah," said Weasel. "Sounds real simple. But he ain't gonna talk to us until he trusts us. We don't know anything about this kid except what we can see. And what I see is he don't trust no one, no how. Period."

"And all he's got now is the three of us," Sarah said.

"Plus Duke," Weasel said. "That damn Duke. He's like another person."

"And saving the kid's life wasn't enough to get him to trust us," said Sarah. "So what does that tell you about his life?"

"Maybe worse'n mine," Weasel responded. "And that's sayin' a piece. But you never know how a person is gonna react to a certain situation. Maybe little Stevie ain't as, well, you know, smart as some other people."

"I don't think so, Weasel," I said. "Stevie's no dummy. I can see intelligence in his eyes. He's very wary and always watching interactions among the three of us. This kid's got a good brain in there. And I'll tell you another thing. That little guy is not afraid of anyone or anything."

"So let's see what we've got so far," said Sarah, her pacing in temporary abeyance, hands on hips, ready to expound. "We've got a boy whose life has been so bad that he's wandering around in the snow fighting dog packs for food. He's brave. Probably intelligent. In addition he hates our guts—we being the ones that recently saved his life and are now feeding him and protecting him from the elements—and probably hates the guts of every adult he's ever seen."

She raised her hands over her head in frustration. "Christ what a mess. Now we've not only got to try to figure out a way to get this kid to trust us...Anything else, Mac? Like maybe providing him a college education while we're at it."

"Jesus Christ," I yelled. "What a great idea. There's no way this kid knows how to read and write. And we've got a teacher sitting right here." I pointed at Weasel. "If Stevie is going to contribute and be part of us, he definitely needs an education. We've got books; we've got computers; and we've got a man who knows how to teach reading and writing. It'll definitely give him something to do and Weasel can show me and Sarah some of the lessons and we can take turns."

I was greeted by silence. Weasel was thinking, mulling it over. Sarah remained rooted to her spot, hands still on her hips. Then she took a chair and pulled it back into the circle.

"You know, Mac," said Weasel, "that ain't a bad idea. This boy must thinking pretty poorly about himself. I mean he ain't got nothin' and he can't do nothin'. So what's there to be proud of about himself? And nobody seems to like him except old Duke and the kid don't do anything to try to change people's minds. What the hell is that all about?"

Sarah spoke up now, directing her comments to Weasel. "I don't want you to take this the wrong way, Weasel; but I think you and Stevie share many traits." She paused, letting it sink in, assessing his reaction. "Why did you spend 20 years avoiding contact with people?"

"Cuz I didn't like the way they treated me," he replied, then smacked his forehead with the heel of his hand. "Oh, shit, I see what you're getting at. People treated him real bad, too. He's just waiting for us to start acting the way he's used to people acting all the time."

"In his mind," said Sarah, "it's just a matter of time until we turn into monsters."

"But there's one huge difference between Weasel and Stevie," I responded.

"What's that?" asked Weasel.

"You like yourself."

"O.K. you two, my turn now," I said. "Stevie's asleep. We've got about eight hours or so to come up with a plan, because we sure as hell haven't accomplished anything in the last three days. The only one that has made any progress is the dog. First question: How do we get him to trust us?"

• • • •

We worked through the night, drowning ourselves in coffee, finishing about an hour before Stevie woke up. All three of us practiced on the technique to restrain Stevie when he got out of hand. We had plenty of rug burns before we finally got it down pat.

While I served as the record keeper, we formulated a philosophy on how we would deal with Stevie. The whole plan was built around several fundamental rules:

We would never strike Stevie.

We would praise him often.

We would always respect him verbally and be careful not to invade his physical space unless he let us in.

We would trust him, even though we figured we might get burned on it a few times.

We would always be truthful.

We would stay united.

We would remain ourselves, for after all, everybody, including the dog, loved everyone else, so why fix what ain't busted?

We would set up rules and for him about violence, and chores and other people's property and respect. When he broke them, and we knew he would early and often, we would talk about it—unless he was acting violently. Then we would stop him from hurting himself or us or breaking the place up.

We would provide schooling for him 6 hours daily, 5 days a week.

"Whadda we do if he nukes out?" asked Weasel.

"Shit, that could easily happen," I said. "And we have a bunch of stuff that we would like to keep together. Like computers and such."

Sarah came up with a plan, which was implemented on Stevie's first day of school.

Weasel came up with the final idea for the night. "The boy needs to learn about weapons. He needs to know how to protect himself if running ain't an option. We teach him to shoot, he gains confidence and sees we trust him."

• • • •

The three of us were incredibly proud of our plan. And presented our ideas to Stevie in the morning over a two-hour breakfast.

Stevie told us to stick it. We smiled wisely and patiently, two wise men and one wise woman, secure in our wisdom, pillars of common sense and erudition.

By 9:10 the next morning, just a few minutes after the start of Stevie's first school session, he had all three of us on the floor.

Sarah and I were in the kitchen, looking over Weasel's new plan for easier-to-operate hand pumps for our well, when the screaming started. Point of origin: the newly reconfigured living room which now was our school. We both walked to the archway separating the two rooms to observe. We arrived just in time to see Weasel duck two books which Stevie had hurled at his head.

"Take your books and shove them up your ass, you shriveled up little bald fuck," he screamed at Weasel.

"Doesn't seem like a positive student teacher relationship," I whispered to Sarah, receiving a poke in the ribs in response.

Weasel picked up the books and put them back on the table. "Let's give this another try," he said in with great restraint. The veins on his neck were popping.

Stevie threw the books at him again and Weasel nodded to the two of us, the signal to take control. I approached and when I was close enough Weasel and I both grabbed an arm, giving Stevie no warning, and pressed in close to him, pinning his arms to his side.

It was like someone shot a jolt of electricity through the boy's body. He was barely 100 pounds, less than half my weight, but his rage gave him uncommon strength.

We couldn't control him from a standing position and put him on the floor in a flash, sweeping his legs and guiding him down without harm. He was on his stomach, Weasel across his legs and me on his shoulders, controlling each arm with one of mine. He still managed to wrest an arm free, so Sarah joined the battle, securing the arm.

He was trapped and plenty pissed about it.

"C'mon you mother fuckers. Let me take you one at a time. Takes three of you chickenshits…Hey Squirrel, got any nuts?…Get off me you fat assed bitch…Hey, Sarah, I'll bet needle dick here is one lousy fuck, ain't he… C'mon you pieces of shit, hit me, take your best shot…You're all a bunch of butt fuckers…"

The cursing and insults went on for at least 15 minutes. All three of us remained completely silent during the tirade. During the whole time he was struggling with all his strength. Finally, the fight went out of him all at once, just drained away, and he went limp. Sarah later said it was chemical. His body couldn't produce any more adrenaline, and he crashed.

After a couple more minutes, I could feel his shoulders begin to shake and big uncontrollable sobs shook his entire body. I gently stroked his head and Sarah rubbed his back. We remained silent.

When the sobbing subsided, I said, "When you feel like you can control yourself and get back to learning stuff, we will let you up."

"Fuck you, asshole."

"You let us know when you're ready." I turned to Weasel. "I think we're O.K. now with just the two of us if you have some things you need to do."

He winked in response. "Well you know, I think I'll take a little break, get something to eat and take Duke for a walk. I'll check in on you every 15 minutes or so."

The three of us, in alternating shifts spent the next two hours on the floor with Stevie. He got up twice in that time, but each time we put him back down quickly, once for taking a swing at me and once for screaming epithets at Sarah concerning her breast size and fondness for farm animals. He was down again later that first day and then once daily for the next five, the rages always associated with school work.

The second week he began to pick up letters and recognize words, receiving buckets of praise from all of us, which he pretended to ignore. But the takedowns decreased in frequency and when Weasel came up with the idea of tying successful completion of homework to watching videos in the evenings, progress was even more rapid.

Stevie's violent outbursts slowly decreased, week by week, while at the same time his fertile mind rapidly picked up the reading and writing and we moved him into basic math and sciences. His mind was ready for more advanced concepts before his reading abilities were capable of handling the texts, so we spent much his school time having him view educational videos—particularly something called "The Khan Academy"—and documentaries from Weasel's massive vid library.

After the first month of school, we began taking him on hikes miles from our compound to practice with weapons. If anyone heard our shots, they wouldn't link them to where we lived. We went shooting every Saturday. When done, we dismantled, cleaned, and reassembled all the weapons and returned them to the basement armory.

When Stevie watched educational vids, either Sarah or I always watched along with Stevie, available to answer his questions, but usually learning with him. It was during these video sessions that we received our first glimmerings as to the cause of the collapse.

We began to include Stevie in on our planning and discussion sessions as to the household defenses, modifications in the building, additions to the compound, scouting trips to be taken and supplies or hardware that we sought among the detritus of the 20th cen. He never contributed or asked questions during these sessions. But he was soaking in every word.

During the third week he allowed us to cut his scraggly hair and began showing interest in new clothing. I showed him how to shave his wispy facial hair. It was a ritual he undertook daily, even though once a week would have been fine.

Whenever any of us spoke to him, it was in the same tone and respect that we used among ourselves. He was another person in the house, an equal. Our hope was that Stevie would return the respect. He failed in these expectations often, but never received derision or disrespect in return.

In the fourth week he began voluntarily speaking, usually commenting on videos. He seemed to identify with Dorothy in THE WIZARD OF OZ and loved to discuss the film.

We learned his name on the fifth week. "You can call me Stevie," he said to Weasel during a science lesson. "My full name is Stevie B."

During the seventh week he mustered up enough courage to ask if he could use the compact disc player. His musical tastes, much to Weasel's consternation, were similar to Sarah's and mine—heavy duty, pulsating, muscular rock— IGGY POP, THE SISTERS OF MERCY, CHEAP TRICK, and a Chicago group called ELEVENTH DREAM DAY. But for his favorites Stevie went back to the more visceral groups of the 60's and early 70's, BLACK SABBATH and DEEP PURPLE. Weasel preferred country music, John Prine, Hank Williams, and 50's and 60's ballads and listened to "that Mozart guy" when he was tinkering with electronics or working on the guns.

• • • •

Progressed continued, each week or so bringing some small new skill into Stevie's repertoire. But about himself and his past, Stevie remained silent. By mutual agreement, none of us pressed him on the issue. Stevie spent much of his time with Duke and all three of us had observed him conversing for long periods with—or rather at—the dog. Duke was the perfect listener, attentive and nonjudgmental, and never, ever broke a confidence or divulged a secret.

During the fifth month Stevie's violent outbursts, now a seldom seen phenomena, stopped completely. They never returned. He did, however, remain quiet, reticent, reluctant to talk to any of us at length—except for school related questions and music or vid comments and discussions. His past remained locked.

In the middle of Stevie's sixth month with us, Fall of 2054, all four of us were at the kitchen table hashing out a problem Weasel was having with one of his new ideas. He wanted to bring us portable toilets, like big boxes that had doors and a toilet inside. Portapotties, he called them. Stevie suggested shit stations.

Duke was asleep on the floor by Stevie's feet. I was brewing coffee. Weasel, Sarah and Stevie were pouring over a stack of books on the table, looking for references to increasing production and strength of marijuana plants.

I had grown them for years. Weasel also smoked. We wouldn't allow Stevie to partake until he got older, although he did sometimes drink home brewed wine with us at meals. We argued back and forth that we were being stupid, but Sarah put it to rest with, "His brain has been badly damaged. Let's allow it to heal."

Primo marijuana was a valued commodity to most of the population east of us and the clans controlled its sale and distribution. But much of the marijuana was planting your favorite seeds and smoking the crop or harvesting ditch weed. We were looking for the next level. Whenever we traded with the clans, they always asked for high grade marijuana and so we wanted to increase our production. All of us were looking for data on temperature and humidity control, proper soil preparation, fertilization, ph balance, and cross breeding.

Weasel closed the book he was reading with a resounding thud, frustration in his voice. "I remember a few years back seeing a magazine called HIGH TIMES. It was all about pot and mushroom growing. I've looked for it on discs, but can't find any references to it."

"It's ironic, isn't it," commented Sarah. "Pre-collapse they had all kinds of references to alcohol and beer and cigarettes and wine. But they seemed to be afraid of marijuana. Toward the end, several states legalized it, but most politicians were afraid of pot. But I can't find any hard data on discs that indicate that it's dangerous, like cocaine or heroin or meth." I could see her starting to warm up to the subject. "You know what I think," she said, not waiting for a response. "I think that men were afraid of pot. The legislatures were controlled by men and they were afraid of the reactions people had to pot."

"How so?" Weasel asked.

"Think about it," she said. "What does pot do to people? What reactions are common?"

"Well, they laugh a lot," said Weasel.

"And they sure talk a lot," I said. "It also makes some people spend their time thinking and ruminating. Although you can never remember what you're thinking about. And it's great when you're making love."

Sarah kicked me hard on the shin under the table, cutting her eyes over toward Stevie.

"Oops. Sorry."

Stevie gave me a wink and a smile, kind of a man thing, brother to brother, although he hadn't seen a grown woman besides Sarah probably in years—except in the vids.

"Now out of all those behaviors you mentioned, which ones are feminine in nature and which ones are generally associated with masculinity?" she asked us.

"All of those behaviors, except for laughing, are generally feminine attributes," I responded.

"So there's my point," she said. "Male dominated legislatures would not allow a drug to be legalized that would cause men to behave in a manner that was generally associated with the female gender. Liquor was fine. It made men behave like men. Beat each other up. Holler. Scream. Break things. Rape. Pillage. But pot would break down communication barriers between the sexes. Not good. I rest my case."

She crossed her arms and sat back.

"Do you think these guys who made the laws really knew they were thinking this at the time?" I asked her.

"Truthfully...No. But I think that's what was going on. And remember, many states legalized or decriminalized for a few years. But then the feds cracked back down in what they called "The New Prohibition" in the mid 20's.

"Enough of this philosophy crap, you two," interjected Weasel. "We got a problem to solve here so we can increase our value to the clans. Might save our lives when we're passing through their territory. Might help us acquire some supplies or information we need. I need more references. Wish I had that magazine."

"I know where there's 100's of magazines," said Stevie, shocking us all into silence.

Weasel was the first to recover. "That's great, boy. Unbelievable. Where. How'd you come across 'em?"

Stevie had a strange look on his face. Pensive. Fearful. He didn't respond to Weasel's questions for several minutes. He looked at the three of us, his teachers and friends, his adoptive parents, his long-time tormentors. Duke, roused from his sleep by something beyond our senses, yawned and took a wakeful position by Stevie's chair. The boy reached down and stroked the dog's neck.

Stevie kept watching us, challenging each with his eyes, not backing down, finally concluding he was unafraid of what he saw reflected there. With a sigh, he made his decision, cast his eyes downward and very quietly, haltingly began telling the story of The Babe and Satan's Messengers.

He faltered several times. But always gathered his strength and continued. We never spoke a word. None of us moved from our chairs, fearful a small noise would make us miss his softly spoken, compelling words or perhaps startle him into silence.

Two hours passed. When Stevie finally finished, his tear-filled eyes came up and met ours. He saw our tears and bowed his head and began to softly cry. In that instant when his eyes met mine, I saw relief and gratefulness and shame in his eyes.

It was the first time he had ever trusted us. Probably the biggest risk he had ever undertaken in his life. For if we had let him down, then all of his fears and hate would have been justified. And he would have returned to his world of silence and violence.

Sarah recovered first, rushing to him and whisking him into the living room, arm across his shoulder, gently comforting him.

Weasel and I sat facing each other across the table, fire and loathing in our eyes, jaws clenched, still fighting back tears. I gave up the battle and wept softly.

I heard Weasel say, "That man is gonna die real hard." I could only nod my head in affirmation.

After Sarah had worked her wonders soothing Stevie and we had regained our own composure, Weasel and I went to Stevie. We told him he did good. We were proud of him. Eloquence abandoned us.

Stevie, Sarah still by his side, her arm across his shoulder, said to us: "Thanks Mac. Thanks Weasel. I didn't think I could ever tell that story. Was even beginning to think maybe it wasn't real. But I know it is now."

He paused and looked to Sarah, then back to us. "Me and Sarah been talking. I've never felt like this in my whole life. I never imagined that anything like this could exist."

His hands spread apart and swept the house, then came together and pointed to Sarah, and then to Weasel and me. He looked us in the eyes. "Sarah said I should ask you guys. Can we stay like this? Can all of us keep on being together? Me, you guys, Duke?"

It was Weasel who responded. "Goddamn it, kid, we sure as hell can. Welcome to the family. I'm glad you're one of us."

With that he gave Stevie a hug and we became five.

CHAPTER TWELVE

SEPTEMBER 2054 TO AUGUST 2055

On the morning following Stevie's catharsis, Weasel woke us all before dawn and herded us into the kitchen. He was wearing his usual outfit, Merrill hikers, some kind of jeans or sweats, and a ratty old t-shirt. Usually with some country band's name. Today it was Steve Earle. When it got cold, he would add a hooded sweat shirt. This morning he was wearing an apron over his shirt and carrying a spatula. When Weasel cooked, it was a big deal. He waved us to the table. It was set. Even napkins. Cloth ones.

"I got bacon from the pig we shot when it got in our garden, eggs from our chickens, biscuits from the flour indies down near Monee gave for a bag of Starbucks beans. Butter from that damned goat. And, blueberry preserves from them hippies out in DeKalb. I'm cookin'. Then we're talkin'."

No arguments. Weasel was a breakfast genius.

"You know," I said, pointing a buttery knife, "back in the good times, they had restaurants that served only breakfast. See them all over the place."

"When the world gets sane," Sarah said, "we're opening one of those with Weasel as chef."

Weasel was still at the stove. Finishing up the bacon. Duke was a statue by his right foot. He knew Weasel would be dropping a scrap. Weasel turned and smiled wistfully, "That's a hell of a dream. I could do that. Or maybe fix stuff." He went back to the bacon. "I think there's gonna be a few years before we have restaurants."

He finished the bacon, threw a dozen scrambled eggs on a platter, and magically produced a doggie bowl bacon and egg breakfast for

Duke. He served us with a flourish. "Dig in everyone. After breakfast, we're going to work."

• • • •

We ate seriously, no talking. Silverware clinked and scraped, frequent "mmm's" escaped, salt and pepper journeyed back and forth. We didn't applaud when we were done, but Weasel was gratified with by our performance. Finished, Stevie and I cleared, Sarah started to wash, and Weasel and Duke searched for that special last scrap. As we took the breakfast plates to the sink, Weasel started.

"If a clan finds us, we run. So first plan is more escape tunnels and ground routes."

Stevie returned to the table and jumped right in. "Why can't we fight them? There's four of us and we know how to survive."

"Think about it. Think about our lives," Weasel said. "We all shared parts of our stories. Each of us has had to fight. But mostly we ran. They never come alone. Always seem to have numbers. We run. We survive. We ain't ready to fight yet."

Stevie hunched over his coffee. I wondered how long the anger would remain so close to the surface. Maybe forever. "I want to get those fuckers," he said. "I don't want to run. I want to see them lose like we do."

"Tell you what, kid," Weasel said. "I got that same fire burnin' in me. And so does Mac and Sarah. But we can't do nothing until we're safe. Ain't no revenge in dyin'. And this here," doing a 360 with his hands, "This ain't losin'."

"Weasel's right," Sarah said. "This is special. The five of us. We need to build and protect what we have. All of us should be safe."

"Let's start basic here," Weasel said. "Toilets, water, tunnels. Toilets get us comfortable and ... what's a word here Sarah?"

"Sanitary."

"Yeah, sanitary. We keep that part of our lives separate."

"Uh, Weasel," Sarah said. "Remind me again about the portable toilets. How's that work?"

"It looks like a closet and uses chemicals to keep the stink away. Findin' 'em is easy. Gettin' one here is hard, but not impossible."

"Uh, Weasel," Sarah repeated. "Ever thought about two? Toilets, I mean. I don't really desire to share a sanitary facility with the three of you." She eyed us like one of those school marms from the vids. "No disrespect intended. You three just seem to have different…philosophies…when it comes to that entire excretory area."

"Not sure what you just said," Weasel replied, "but takes a day or two to get one. No problem in getting another. We ain't keepin' them forever. This place has a well somewhere. All these houses had to have water and I don't see any signs of underground piping. We find a well, power it into the house with a big pump, and we got indoor plumbing. We already got a septic field. We get water to the top, gravity does the rest and no one can see it."

"You mean like showers and baths and such?" Sarah asked.

"You bethca. But…portables first and then tunnels before finding the well. I know you like your little tunnel, but we need more and better."

"Well, shit," I said. "That's the hardest, dirtiest, most boring job ever invented. Sarah and I looked like pig farmers at the end of every day. And we went through ibuprofen like M & M's."

"Weasel," Sarah asked, "how did you build all those tunnels by yourself?"

Weasel's eyes squinted and he tried to suppress his sly I've-got-a-plan smile. "Technology, Little Miss Missy Miss," he said. "I got me some technology on one of my missions. Sometimes I call 'em a "foray," he said with a hand flourish. "Got that one on my vocabulary dvd."

"How in the hell did you get a tunnel digger?" Stevie asked. "Don't imagine they're very easy to carry around."

"Got a little story here," he said. We all hunched forward. His stories always had potential.

"Told you I'd been up here for a few years. Lot a wandering about the territory in that time. In my head, I have to know the land. I see it like a picture. Lot a mind mapping and even some drawings about what's over here and what's over there. Who's got toilet paper? Where's the coffee? Winter gear. Building supplies. This here 20-30 square miles," he waved his arm around his head, "there's treasure out there no one knows about. 'Cept me, of course. And now you."

"Like what?" Stevie asked. "Me and Mac and Sarah live here too. We been around. Know where stuff is. How you think we stayed alive all this time?"

"Well, I'll give you that, boy," Weasel said. "But all of us are survivors. Let me ask you some questions. All of you. Just jump in when you know the answers."

"Fire away," Sarah said.

"OK. How about well pump repair?" No reply.

"Let's try this, then. Small engine parts."

"Got lawn mowers all over the place," Stevie answered.

"Ok. I'll give you that."

"I know where 25 boxes of powdered milk are," Stevie said.

"Good. Need water for that. How about water filtration?" Weasel asked. "We only got about three months of them Brita things left."

Silence.

"Ok, then. Name five armories that ain't been found."

"You know to get more guns and ammo?" I asked. "That's big."

"Yeah, too big for the clans to know. How about water purification pills. Antibiotics. Pain killers. Grenades. I even got me a missile launcher with five missiles. Lucky we don't need 'em."

Stevie was smiling. I could tell he was thinking about one of those James Bond movies.

"Check this out" Weasel continued. "I know where there are at least a thousand rolls of toilet paper. The good stuff. Not that stuff in rolls as big as tires that chap your ass."

That got everyone attention. Nothing worse than red ass.

"Here's the big one," he said. "Can you tell me where to find a compact horizontal drilling auger?"

"Shit, Weasel," I said. "We can't even say it. What are you talking about?"

"Few minutes ago," he said, "Sarah asked about how I built those tunnels and you were cryin' about how hard it is. On one of my forays in '53, I came across a huge construction site. Big rigs, cranes, trucks. Tires bigger than one of them old time basketball players. One company had some crazy looking machines. Like a praying mantis on steroids. Bigger 'n one of them semi-trucks."

"What was it?" Sarah asked.

"I got curious and started looking in the buildings to figure stuff out. Couldn't read, but most places had these papers with pictures and such. These machines were giant drills for making tunnels. Tunnels big enough to drive trains through and small enough to run water pipes or electric wire. So I figured some of these augers might have what you call 'labor saving potential,' and I stayed for a week looking at them papers and crawling over machines. Finally found myself what I now know was a 36 inch horizontal drilling auger. It was a machine that could dig tunnels. But…and here's the real big thing, it was about the size of one of them big Harley motorcycles. Little longer but near the same."

"Interruption here," Stevie said, waving his hand. "How far away from your secret castle were you?"

"Maybe eight, ten miles."

"How'd you carry a couple of thousand pound machine ten miles, let alone get it running?"

"I can get any small engine runnin' that ain't froze up," Weasel said. "Gettin' the fuel's a whole 'nother matter."

"The tunnel digger," Stevie said. "How'd you get it back to your basement?"

"After I checked to see if it ran, I took it apart and brung it back piece by piece. Took me a month to break it down, bring back the pieces, and put it back in working order."

"Amazing," Sarah said. "Do you have any idea how smart you are, Weasel?"

"Well, Sarah, I don't know about all that smart stuff. Seems to me you got all the brains. And the rest of us is just waitin' to see where you take us."

Sarah gave an aw shucks gesture, waving the compliment away.

Weasel continued. "Figure that tunnel digger that took me a month is gonna be in our basement in a week with all four of us hauling and Duke doing the guard duty. That's our first job."

He was right. It took a week. We set the drilling equipment up in the basement, started cooking fuel in an abandoned home a couple of miles away, and became miners.

• • • •

While two of us mined, the other pair began reshaping the house and "compound" to look like every suburban home—aged, abandoned, and decrepit.

We demolished the wall, scattered the remnants in other unfinished luxury homes. Instead of fortress, we went with subterfuge, surrounding the house with blackberry bushes and thistle woven through rolled razor wire, the kind you see at prisons. We added more bells in the barbed wire, heavy enough to not be bothered by wind, but animal or human movement would start them ringing.

We replanted buckthorn saplings from the woods all over the lot. They grew like dandelions but were a soft wood tree with nasty thorns. Like dandelions, the could not be killed and within two years they would be a formidable barrier in combination with the razor wire. For added support and food supply, we planted more green and red grapes under the razor wire. Added to the ones we had, the vines would soon resemble a thick rope barrier, making quick passage to the house nearly impossible. We now had two types of grapes and raspberries for Sarah's turkey salad.

Flower beds and vegetable gardens now appeared wild and un-attended and moved further away from the house and into the backyards of our dead neighbors. The chickens could remain, but had to be free range and we lost many to foxes, raccoons, and coyotes. The pigs and cows we gave to the indies way out west. They had pens and fences and their settlements were too far away for clan forays. The indies let us have bacon and such whenever we could hike or bike out there.

• • • •

One night, a month into the process, Sarah put down her book and said, "Mac, have you ever thought about what has happened?"

We each had our retro little reading lamps scavenged from Penny Mustard. The blackout curtains were tight. Weasel and Stevie were either reading or watching vids with headphones or earbuds. Duke was in the hallway, as close to the middle of the four of us as possible. It felt safe. All of us knew it was an illusion. But it was a warm, comfortable fantasy.

"I'm not sure if you're referring to the house, our group, or the collapse," I said.

Even in the limited light of the reading lamps, I could see her green eyes sparkle. "This," she said spreading her arms to welcome the world. "Us. A year ago it was you, me, Duke, an outhouse, rain barrels and water buckets, and a flimsy medieval wall."

I said, "I've thought about how one day, one decision, changed everything. Me and you meet this strange loner who has lugged an arsenal and half of an electronic store over to us in the snow..."

"And invite him to live with us in less that 24 hours. That's not normal behavior for us," Sarah said.

"It wasn't random," I said. "He had been scoping us out. Hell of good people reader. Weasel might have known more about us than we ourselves did. It was a huge risk for him, not physically, but psychologically. Saying hi to the neighbors. Bringing gifts. Telling us we were idiots."

Sarah laughed. "And he was right. We have learned so much from him. And I'll tell you what, Mac. We have just begun to scratch the surface of what's going on in that man's mind."

CHAPTER THIRTEEN

EARLY OCTOBER 2055

During the huge remodel, nearly a years' hard labor, when we ultimately became nearly invisible, no one forgot Stevie's horrific tale. Nor did we forget the Babe. But from the moment he described his journey from clan kid to feral child, Stevie grew with us, became part of our fabric. He wasn't a victim of a depraved tyrant any more. He was one of us. And we were all victim's of The Collapse. After the night he revealed the horrors of his life as a member of Satan's Messengers and victim of The Babe's legendary appetites and then his years alone, Stevie was no longer a crippled thing we were nurturing. Stevie became part of our family.

No longer was it, there's Stevie. The poor thing. What a horrible hand life dealt him. It slowly became, there's Stevie. He's getting better at some of our daily tasks than we are. Isn't it great to have him as part of the family. So we didn't forget Stevie's tale. It gradually ceased to be the defining characteristic in our view of him.

Weasel, however, had a more active memory bank than the rest of us. Allow tragedy to make you stronger, he believed. Also let it make you more vigilant. He never spoke of Stevie's past and never treated him differently. But he was also secretly scouting for information the beast who almost ended Stevie's life at the innocent age of nine.

In October of 2055, at the breakfast table where the five of us met at the dawn of each day, Weasel turned to me and said, "Pack up for a two day trip. I got something to show you."

"What about the rest of us?" Sarah asked.

"There's a certain amount of, ah, subterfuge involved," Weasel told her. "Two of us is all we need. And we don't want our place here unoccupied."

Sarah raised one eyebrow, soaked up some egg yolk with a piece of wheat toast. "'Subterfuge,'" she said. "I'm impressed."

"It was in one of them James Bond books," Weasel said. "Had to look it up. Pretty nice little word."

"Yeah," Stevie said. "Sounds like some kind of engineering part." He went into his pompous teacher voice. "Well, son, if you don't incorporate a subterfuge to your foundation, you're gonna get water in your basement every spring."

"What about Duke?" I asked Weasel.

He usually accompanied Sarah or me whenever we left the compound. At the mention of his name, he lifted his head. Maybe a piece of food, he was thinking. I scratched his ear, tore off a piece of my biscuit which disappeared down his gullet.

"Two's plenty," Weasel repeated. "There's only four of us hear. Two should always be max for scouting. One pair here, one, out there. Duke's our wild card. But today he stays home."

"Is this going to be dangerous?" Sarah asked.

"No more dangerous than any day someone leaves the compound," Weasel told her—the implication being that it was always perilous.

"Well," she said, "you two just better be careful out there. Stevie, Duke and I will keep working to make this place look like an abandoned dump. And don't forget, Mr. Secret Mission People," she added with a twinkle in her eyes, "it's your day to do the breakfast dishes. I assume this trip won't preclude your doing chores."

• • • •

Weasel and I headed north, the Fox River on our left, but not close enough to see it. There were decent north/south roads that were passable on foot or bike. Plus game trails and what appeared to be networks of walking or bicycle riding paths. It seemed like everyone pre-Collapse had a car and they all left them on the roads and walked away. It was still common to find skeletons in cars. Sometimes whole families. Sometimes bags of bones with guns and trucks or SUV's pocked with bullet holes.

"We ain't gonna break until we get there," Weasel said. A good sweat was popping and our pace was brisk, maybe three miles and hour. "Figure us for an hour and a half. Got a spot picked out."

"What's our plan?" I asked.

"You know them vids where the cops are sittin' in a van all day, watchin' someone, fartin' and belchin' and generally stinking up the place?"

"Yeah, stakeouts."

"Right. That's what we're gonna do. A stakeout operation. Like Bronson or Bruce Willis."

"But without the van," I said.

"Right. Fresh air and sunshine for us."

"Whose the target of our surveillance?"

"You know the fat fuck that's makin' everybody miserable and nearly killed Stevie?"

"The Babe? We're staking out The Babe? Jesus Weasel! We need some more bullets or armor or machine guns or something."

"Don't plan on gettin' close. Just watchin'. He's got something going on."

"I've seen him up close already," I said. "It was … unpleasant."

Weasel stopped walking. "You were in the same room with The Babe?"

"I was in an indie bar up near the old airport," I told Weasel. "The big one up north, O'Hare. Our winter larder was low. Sarah and I needed some shotgun shells for hunting. I had a three pound can of coffee for barter. I'd be able to get an excellent return. Ammo was abundant. Coffee rare. This was spring, 2050, two and a half years before we met you.

"Sarah and I had more luck than smarts. We were smart enough to live in isolation, but not smart enough to realize I needed schooling when I went into the occupied areas. Like how to always sit with a clear line to an exit. I hadn't figured that one out.

"Sitting along a back wall of the indie bar, sipping a rancid home-brewed beer, I scoped out the dozen or so patrons, looking for hunters or clan soldiers. I had a 12 gage Winchester leaning against the table and a long barrel 38 Special in my back pack on the floor beside me.

About five minutes into my search, the Babe and four of his clan came in."

We resumed walking, heading north. Weasel said, "This here is settin' up to be a real good story. And here you are with all your arms and legs."

"Like I told you, More luck than smarts. Before I could process what was happening, most of the customers scurried out the back door. Two of the Babe's soldiers immediately positioned themselves by the front and back exits. A feeling of overwhelming dread washed over me. It made a lousy combination with the adrenaline. I had to use two hands to set down my beer. For the first time since my years alone, when fear was as common as the sun and moon, I was afraid. I could die here, in that nameless, dusty hovel."

We continued the hike. Weasel tapped his head. "You got some smarts in there, somewhere, cuz you're telling me the story."

"Maybe a bit," I said. "I visualized Sarah. In about 24 hours, she would start to worry. Just a little. She'd talk to Duke, keep busy, maybe tend the vegetable garden, take Duke hunting for quail or turkey, maybe fish the Fox, anything to take her mind off my absence. Day two she'd get serious about worrying. Day three, she'd know. I was dead or hurt bad. She'd load up some ammo for the Mossberg, take the Glock too, and she and Duke would start to search. Hoping, but knowing they were probably never going to find me.

"So there we were—me, the bartender and one other customer— some poor bastard who was too drunk to move and was dressed in the wrong color scheme."

"You were wearin' your camo, right?" Weasel asked. I nodded. "You see," he said, "not so dumb."

"The Babe and two of his men walked to the bar. They were all dressed red and black. The men at the exits were white guys, as was the Babe. The two soldiers who flanked him at the bar were Hispanic and black. The Babe towered over them. If you put both soldiers side to side, they wouldn't have equaled his massive girth.

"I felt like a rabbit in tall grass. I put both hands on the table, wrapped around the glass of tepid beer like it was a portal to sanctuary. Didn't move a muscle, except for my eyes. Watch The Babe, then the drunk at a table across the room. Then back to the Babe. The guy at the table was dressed in black and gold."

"You knew that was a bad choice."

"Oh, yeah. Everyone knew The Babe and his colors. He walked over to the soldier in black and gold. He said something in Spanish. The guy replied and the Babe spat in his face, pulled his .45 and shot him in the face, blowing him off the chair.

"He turned and looked at me. I stayed frozen as he walked to my table, extraordinarily graceful for a man his size. His hands were at his side. The .45 in the right, smoke curling up its barrel. He held it casually, softly, like a tiny pet. I watched, squeezing my glass in both hands so he couldn't see my hands shake.

"The Babe looked down at me from what appeared from my perspective about twelve feet up. Beady eyes inspected my clothes. Camo pants, sweatshirt, hiking boots, back pack. John Deere cap. No colors.

"Indie," he growled.

I nodded.

He glanced at my Winchester. His meaning was clear. I reached out with my right hand, grasped the barrel and handed it over to him.

"What else you got for me, Indie?" he asked.

I reached down for my pack.

"Careful," he rumbled and took the pack. He put it on the table and began pulling everything out. There was a turkey sandwich and an apple in a brown paper bag, some ammo for the Winchester, the coffee can, two clips for my Glock, some underwear and spare shirts and a skinning knife.

The Babe took everything but the clothes. Then he took my Glock and clip knife. He ripped open the brown bag and devoured my sandwich. With a mouth full of turkey, lettuce, tomato and mustard, he said, "Get the fuck out of here, Indie."

I stood, stuffed the clothes into the backpack and walked briskly to the front door, eyes straight ahead. As I walked, I wondered if I would hear the retort of a pistol shot before the bullet hit my back.

"In 60 seconds it was over. And what I remember most was being pissed. Not at him, but myself. The anger probably masked my fear. In the winter we wear coats so we don't freeze to death. We don't get mad at the winter. It is what it is. So is the Babe. Evil, vile. Everybody knew it. And he wasn't the only thing. There were other clans, dog packs, infections, cholera, small pox, wild boar, wolves, tornadoes, blizzards. If you weren't careful, you were out of the gene pool.

"You know better now," Weasel said. "And today you get to pay another visit. But I don't think we'll be in the same room with him. This here's a stakeout, not an attack. James Bond would call this intelligence gathering.

• • • •

Weasel and I were on a bluff overlooking the DuPage River, a beautiful little crystal stream that meandered about ten miles east of its big sister, the Fox River. In most places you could walk across it, but it had some great fishing holes and served as a north/south canoe highway. Below us, across the river about a hundred meters from the bank, was a development of thirty or forty townhouses. There were no rusted vehicles on the streets and a few of the peripheral buildings were obviously unfinished. The development was another victim of the collapse. No one had moved in before the hammer came down.

Oak trees dominated the bluff, blanketing us in shade, protecting our backs from the August sun. Weasel and I had been on our stomachs for about an hour, passing the binoculars and canteen back and forth. The birds and small animals had long since decided we were no threat and scampered, whistled, and scolded and in the canopy above us, oblivious to the small arsenal that lay between the two of us.

In a concession to comfort, we had stripped ourselves of weapons. It was warm enough for t-shirts. Weasel wore a Merle Haggard concert shirt. I was wearing a Roxy Music shirt Sarah has scavenged. Beside me was a portion of Weasel's armory—replacements for our old M 16s, the most common American assault rifle, and the cheap semi-auto pistols we had carried pre-Weasel. I had chosen a Hechler and Koch HK 81 assault rifle as my primary weapon. Weasel went with a Galil SAR. Both had magazine capacities over 30 rounds and fired 7.62 mm shells, heavier than the 5.56 rounds used by the M 16s, the most commonly held clan rifle.

Beside the assault rifles were two machine pistols, an Uzi and a
TEC 9, both adapted for 36 round magazines firing 9mm rounds. We
each also carried two pistols, a couple of Glocks, a Beretta 93R and
Steyr GB Auto. You ain't never leavin' the compound, Weasel had told
us early on, without at least a hundred rounds at your finger tips and
another two hundred in extra clips. Between us, as we lay on the bluff
overlooking the activity below us, we had six hundred rounds available.
And I knew Weasel had more weapons hidden beneath his clothes—
pistols, knives, ice picks, even safety pins. Both of us were wearing
vests, Kevlar IV, crotch to neck, beneath our pants and shirts. They
were true 2023 state of the art. Found a military armory down in
Springfield he told us. Wasn't easy carryin' all that stuff he groused.

"Today," he told me when had settled into our position, "is
moving day. They got themselves new quarters. We're gonna keep an
eye on these boys' operation. Then we're gonna try'n figure out what
kind of deal they got goin' on."

"And this is where The Babe lives?" I asked.

"Satan's Messengers. Stevie's clan. "Here," he said, handing me
the binoculars, "watch for half an hour. Tell me what you see."

The binocs brought the activity below into sharp focus, allowing
me close enough to see what people were doing, recognize individuals
by clothing and body movement, even make out some facial features.

I counted about 200 in the clan, making them considerably larger
than most. Men were predominant—only one in ten were children,
who were either ignored or made to carry items from one location to
another. At first I saw no women at all, until I noticed that one of the
laborers with a shaved head had a pair of prominent breasts. Looking
closer, within five minutes I found nearly 20 women, each completely
bald.

"Son of a bitch," I said to Weasel, "the women have shaved
heads."

"Seen it down south a couple of times too," Weasel said. "Hair is
important to most women. Sarah's a perfect example. Gives 'em a
sense of individuality. Also makes 'em feel pretty when they work on it.
I can remember my mother always had a different feel about her after
she washed and fixed her hair."

"Half these women are clan sex slaves," I said. "How come they don't want them to feel pretty? You'd think they would do their job better if they felt pretty."

Lying next to me, a meter away, Weasel looked across and smiled.

"You haven't known many whores in your life, have you?" he commented.

Truth was, the only women I had known were my mother and sisters and Sarah. She was the only one left, Sarah was. I shrugged and Weasel continued.

"After a woman's been whorin' in a clan for a while, it don't make no difference any more to her. The men don't care, her life's total shit and she knows she's gonna be used up in a few years anyway. What the head shaving does is make them all look the same. They lose their sense of being individuals. It's part of making them easier to control, Mac."

"Subjugation," I commented.

"That's a good one," he said, pulling a short pencil and scrap of paper from the pocket of his safari shirt. We always wore clothing with multiple pockets. "Spell it."

I spelled it; then commented, "And while we're at it, it's 'doesn't make any difference', not 'don't make no difference'."

"Noted," he said. "Thanks. What else you see down there?"

I lifted the binocs and continued to observe. The bulk of the work was done by the women. The men mostly lounged around in the shade, barking orders, cleaning weapons, napping. Five obviously pregnant women watched over the younger children. The older children helped with the move. Any transgressions by the kids were handled with kicks or backhands. Occasionally one of the women would break off from her back breaking labor to breastfeed an infant. Near noon, five began to cook at a central campfire.

That was when The Babe showed up. At over four hundred pounds, he didn't pass up any meals. He came out of one of the houses near the center of the new camp. A young girl followed behind him, shoeless and shirtless, breasts flopping, her legs moving in double time to keep up with his long strides. I saw her mouth moving. The fat man stopped and turned. His beefy hand grasped her head as if it were no larger that an apple, and he shoved her back. She landed on her fanny and scrambled back toward the house.

I put the binocs down. "The fat man brings back bad memories," I said. "I've alway felt he bested me".

Weasel read the regret in my voice. "He did. Time and place, Mac. You're a much different man now. Let's see if we can get some information from this group. Get some future payback. The fat man owes Stevie a big debt. Keep looking. I been watching for months, Mac. I never seen anyone fuck with him. They don't even like to look him in the eye, lest he see it as a challenge."

"You're talking about some pretty nasty looking men," I said.

"Most of those soldiers are as mean as anyone I've ever come across't," he replied. "Ain't never seen a one of 'em even look cross ways at the fat man."

The Babe was dressed completely in red and black, Chicago Blackhawks' hockey gear. He had a big head, made to appear larger by a scraggy full beard. Small eyes were close together, sunken back into his skull as if being swallowed by folds of fat.

Across his belly he had an M 16 strapped. What appeared to be a .45 hung from a shoulder rig. Another pistol was holstered at his side. From behind his left shoulder, an object protruded.

"What's on his back," I asked Weasel, "sticking out on the left side of his head?"

"The handle of his famous baseball bat," Weasel said. "He's got it rigged so he can draw it like a sword."

At The Babe's appearance, the men who had been lounging, stood as if on command. Four of the fiercest looking men trotted up to him as he made his way to the cooking area. He grabbed a huge bone from one of the women and began gnawing on it while he spoke to the four soldiers. They dispersed immediately and put a dozen other soldiers to work carrying large crates into a house two doors down from his dwelling.

He walked over to a group of women, stopped before one of the nursing mothers and pulled her roughly to her feet. She hastily passed the infant as he guided her back to his quarters, speaking to no one else, slamming the door behind him and the hapless woman.

"Shit," I said, disappointed by my brief observation. "He's gone." I wanted more of the colossus.

"Doubt he'll be coming back out for awhile," Weasel said. "Man spends half his time indoors. After dark is when he's most active. Like a rodent."

I resumed scanning the Messenger camp. Off to my right, two clan soldiers, tools in hand, tended to a long line of bicycles, tightening bolts, adjusting chains, oiling derailleurs.

"Tell me about traffic patterns," Weasel said.

I put the binocs down and began pulling food from the back pack. Turkey sandwiches, biscuits, some of Sarah's cole slaw, horseradish and mustard from the garden for the sandwiches. Well water from the canteens.

"They're set up in a semi-circle," I said between bites. "About twenty, twenty-five buildings. Figure that will give them close to a hundred bedrooms for what looks like two hundred of them."

"The women and children," Weasel said, "will go out on the edges. They'll cram them into a couple of houses, take the rest for the warriors. Each man will have his own bedroom. They need a whore, they'll just come down and grab one. Fact that the women and children are out on the edges, hardest to defend, first to go down, pretty much shows you their value."

"I noticed," I said, "that most of the boxes and crates are going into two of the buildings in the center."

"What's your take on that?" Weasel asked.

"One of them is obviously an armory," I said. "I can read the labels on the boxes. Army issue M 16s. Crates of ammo. Looked like body armor, too. Football and hockey gear. Some police stuff. The works. What's interesting is that they have more weapons than they have men to carry them."

"If they were at war," Weasel said, "the other building would house prisoners or slaves. Might even be a sex pen, too. When they're fighting these clan fucks get awful randy. But that isn't what it's for. How do you read it?"

"I don't know," I answered. "You tell me."

"I got a pretty good idea," he said, wiping oatmeal cookie residue from his mouth. "Important thing to notice is that both of the buildings are smack dab in the center. Right next to The Babe's quarters. Easiest to defend. They're both important. We'll find out for sure tonight."

"What do you mean?" I asked.

"We're gonna take a look. Get some hard facts," he said with a smile.

My first emotion was fear. I was going to die in a few hours. Weasel was a survivor. A jungle fighter. An urban guerilla. I was a toy soldier. I would bring us both down.

Fear was replaced by my need for revenge against the beast who had almost turned Stevie into a nomadic feral shell of human being— and my need to protect our lives, which was threatened every day by the Babe's existence.

"Can we kill him?" I asked.

"You just spent a few hours watching this guy," Weasel said. "He ain't gonna die easy. We get lucky, yeah, he dies. Our lives get better immediately. If not, we get solid info on his operation and buy us time. Time to get stronger, smarter."

"I'm hoping you have a plan."

"Them two buildings we been watching, the ones in the center. The armory goes. We try for the other one, too. I think it's just as important to them."

"Then the plan is all worked out?"

Weasel shrugged. It meant we were playing part of it by ear.

"Great," I said.

"Are you sure you want to do this with me?" I said. "I don't want to fuck up and get you killed."

"The fact that you're still alive past the age of twenty," Weasel replied, "shows me you got a hell of lot more savvy than you give yourself credit for."

• • • •

An hour after sunset we slept. Six hours later, Weasel's internal clock awakened him, and we prepared to infiltrate the Messenger camp.

"They party half the night," Weasel said. "Shine and Slammer. Acid. Meth. Herb or xanax or paxil to come down. Whatever else they can pop or snort. They should be winding down soon. We'll go in couple of hours before dawn."

As we checked our gear—body armor, silenced pistols, pen lights, freshly charged ni-cads, knives, Uzi and TEC nine—I asked if he had any further instructions for me. He sensed my discomfort, didn't read it as fear, more like a healthy wariness of the unknown. This was a new activity for me.

"Listen to me, Mac," he said. "You're gonna be fine. If I expected trouble, we wouldn't be going in."

"On the other hand," I said, "you tell us to always expect trouble."

"Always be looking for someone to fuck with you. But sometimes you know it's going to happen. You'll run across that someday, a time when you know you just stepped into it. This ain't one of those times. We're going in real quiet. Look around. In and out."

"What if we run into someone?"

"Then we deal with them quietly. Hands or knives. Silenced pistol if they're too far away."

I thought about what he had been teaching Sarah, Stevie and me. When we all had become proficient with the weapons, he moved us on to hand to hand. Most crucial thing, he told us, was to always keep your legs. Center of gravity down low. Stay on your feet. Keep your balance. No fancy shit, he said. Take them out fast, before they can do some damage. Eyes, throat, nose, nuts, solar plexus and knees. That's what you go for. Go for the eyes, nuts, solar plexus or knees to temporarily disable them. Fist or club to the throat or nose will inflict enough pain to stop them for a couple of seconds. Most important thing, he kept emphasizing, is to just do it. Don't analyze it. Do it.

• • • •

Leaving the backpacks and the assault rifles behind, we crept down the bluff, crossed the river and slipped into the Messenger compound. The embers of three campfires glowed in the center of their new camp. From the weak light I saw that several of the clan had decided to sleep under the moonless sky.

"No guards?" I whispered.

"No one's at war now," he replied into my ear. "They'll rely on the dogs."

We crept behind the townhouses, entering at the end of the semicircle that was closest to the river. On our right side, our shoulders brushed the townhouses. On the left, the woods had encroached to within a few meters. Thirty meters down, we encountered the dogs. Not a pack, but the clan mutts. A wild pack would have tried to take us down. The clan dogs made noise. They wouldn't be serious about dealing with us directly.

From a small knapsack, Weasel pulled several items, tossing them in the direction of the dogs. He pulled my head close and whispered, "Bunch of bones, plus a touch of animal tranquilizer," he explained.

"Jesus," I whispered back, "It's been over two years and I never knew you had tranks."

"Never needed 'em 'til now," he replied. "Sit awhile. It'll take about five minutes."

As we sat in the dark, my ears took over for what my eyes were missing. Night sounds—the hoot of a barn owl, the high pitched trill of a male cicada, a mosquito's whine, a coon foraging, rustling from the woods as the little life/death game between predator and prey was played out. I heard a log drop as it shifted in one of the fires. Sparks danced upwards and faded into the night. Occasionally human sounds would intrude, a laugh, a shrill scream, the cry of a baby.

Weasel jostled me.

"Let's move out."

Ten buildings down we stopped. Weasel tried the door, which responded with a squeak of the hinges. From his knapsack he pulled a little can; squirted something on the hinges. WD 40 I found out later. Sealed cans lasted for decades.

Inside, the ground level floor was uninhabited. It served as a warehouse, where they stored their arms. We flicked our penlights on, began a quick inspection.

"Get a rough count," Weasel whispered. "That's all we need."

We moved silently from room to room, counting boxes, randomly opening a few to make sure what was inside was what was advertised.

We came up with nearly two hundred M 16s, five hundred clips and another 50,000 rounds of 5.56mm ammo. We also ran across other assault rifles—Enfield, Galil, AK 47, Baretta, Colt. But it was predominantly M 16s, the weapon of convenience of the clans.

They also stored body armor, most of it the old bulky SWAT stuff, only a few pieces of Kevlar IV—the early 21st model that we used. We saw bayonets, telescopic sites and several hundred semi-automatic pistols.

"Let's blow," Weasel said. "We got what we need. We're going next door."

Next building over, we entered the same way, stood quietly inside the door listening for human sounds. There were people above us on the second floor, moving around. But they seemed content to remain up top.

"Let's take a peek," Weasel said, snapping on his mini light.

We entered through the kitchen, which had been turned into a little laboratory. Beakers, candles, kerosene burners, fat burners, jars of chemicals—the counter space was covered with paraphernalia for cooking and mixing chemicals. None of it ready to go. They were still in the set up stage.

"Damn," I whispered. "It's a chem lab."

"What I figured," Weasel said. "These boys been real active on the market lately. That's where some of those guns came from. Traded for chems. Messengers got themselves a new cook. Bought him from the Two-Two Boys. Gold and whores."

"How in the hell you know all this stuff?" I whispered.

"You travel. Meet people. Give 'em stuff they want. Be a friend. They start talking to you. Something you need to start cultivating. Now let's see what else we find."

We split, moving from room to room on the main level, using the lights sparingly, avoiding obstacles. In the bay window of the front room I found over fifty pots of cacti—little buds and spineless vertical breeds. Peyote and mescaline.

Another room was filled with garbage bags of pot, needing to be cleaned. Pot grew wild everywhere, but the good stuff was bred, crossbred and cultivated. There were also cans and jars of chemicals, liquid and powder, none of which I could identify.

When I came across two fifty gallon drums of chemicals and a floor to ceiling stack of car and truck batteries in one of the bedrooms, I searched out Weasel and brought him into the room. He inspected the two huge drums and looked carefully at the batteries, some of which had been broken open.

"Can these things still work?" I asked.

"Oh yeah," he said. "If you replace the water and the acid's still active. Plus you need power to recharge 'em. Which they ain't got."

"'don't have'," I whispered.

"Thanks. I need to work on that. Let's get the hell out of here. We got what we…"

…which was exactly the time that three Messenger soldiers came calling for a refresher on their crystal meth supply. The front door slammed open and a voice screamed, "Yo, Lab Rat, get your scrawny ass down here. You keep fuckin' those bitches, you gonna get cock rot. That's some real nasty pussy, boy."

We heard two men stumble in behind him, laughing loudly. We were in a bedroom at the end of a hallway which was on their right. There was only one door. We had three Messengers in the house.

"Windows," Weasel whispered.

We crept silently to our exit, released the latch on the window frame and pulled up, exerting gentle pressure, increasing our effort as the window failed to cooperate. Cheap buildings, warped window frames.

"Lab Rat," came another voice, "get your ass down here. We need some more crank. This shit's wearing off."

We heard movement above us, a slammed door, steps coming down to our level. Light began to show through the open doorway. Kerosene lantern from the chemist coming down the stairs.

"You guys are fucked," said the voice of the man from upstairs. "I can't find anything in this mess. You gotta wait until tomorrow. Maybe day after."

"Fuck that, pencil pecker," came the voice of the original man. The light began bobbing up and down. Grunts of pain came from the chemist.

"If this starts to get out of hand," Weasel whispered, "we're busting out before they bring half of the clan over here."

From the alcove where the doorway met the stairs came the voices of the other two soldiers intervening.

"You fuck with this guy, The Babe will crucify you," said one. He didn't mean it figuratively.

They continued talking to him low, intense. In my mind I pictured two of the soldiers slowly pushing their companion back, separating him from the chemist, calming him down. It grew quiet in the other room. For a moment I thought we would be safe.

Then, knowing the volatility of clan warriors, particularly those on speed, not completely confident of his own safety, the chemist spoke.

"Fuck it. I'm already down here. Let's see if we can find it. We're looking for a green cooler."

They began searching then, room to room, grousing and complaining, inexorably working their way back to me and Weasel. In about ten minutes, a time span in which sunrise slowly leeched into the darkness, as they worked towards our room, the four men went into the room next to ours, temporarily dimming the lamp light.

"Hope they have good luck in there," Weasel whispered, pulling an ice pick from his sleeve. "By the door, Mac. One of us on each side. If one comes in, I'll take him. Two, you take the second." He grabbed my arm and squeezed it. "Don't worry. Don't think."

We were each on a side when the man with the kerosene lantern, the soldier who originally burst into the house, the one with the least patience, left the other room before his companions, entered the hall and turned into our room, several steps ahead of the three others.

The light entered the room, followed by the man, whom I could see clearly, only a foot away, and who looked directly in my eyes just as Weasel stepped across the doorway, wrapped his left arm around his throat and snaked around with his right, plunging the ice pick into the man's heart. Surprise registered on his face. His eyes dimmed. Then went blank. Not a sound had been made.

The light moved, and I realized a beat too late that the muscles in the hand that had been holding the light had lost their ability to contract, and the lamp was headed for the floor. The crash was loud, startling. The light grew much brighter as the fuel spread, taking the fire with it.

Making no conscious decision, I pulled the Beretta 93R and dived into the hall ahead of the flames. All three Messengers had already begun to react. The chemist was running back down the hall, screaming, "Fire. Fire."

One of the soldiers had a pistol barrel headed my way. The other was just beginning his pull. I put two 126shots in the center of the first man's chest with the Beretta. The other man took two steps and kicked out at my gun hand before I could swing on him. As the gun bounced off the wall and the soldier began stomping all over me, I rolled to my back, sweeping my right arm with all my strength across his heels as I did so.

The man's feet left the floor, and he landed flat on his back.

I jumped up and kicked him hard in the nuts. He grunted and began flopping like a fish. As he jackknifed forward in response to the groin kick, I punched him square in the nose. Then for good measure, I hit him in the throat.

Weasel grabbed me from behind, pushed me forward, and we both ran down the hall, the flames following, took a right into the dining room and headed for the kitchen, where we slipped out the back door.

"You missed the solar plexus," he said. "Cover me a minute."

He sprinted to the armory, unclipped two grenades, pulled the pins and tossed them through the window.

Weasel loped back. "Let's get some distance between us and that building." As we ran toward the river, I could feel him smiling at me in the dark. There were two explosions in the armory, followed by several others, each more powerful than the former.

By the time we had returned to the safety of the bluff, the chem lab was engulfed in flames. The adjacent houses, one side the armory, the other, The Babe's, were also ablaze. In the flickering light of the flames, we watched in fascination as The Babe stomped and bellowed, his chemist at his side, sending men into the fiery chem lab to save what they could. It wasn't much.

A similar operation was occurring in their armory. Scores of men rushed in to retrieve the weapons and ammo. One of them balked when two more explosions rattled their compound, and The Babe pulled the .45 from his shoulder rig and put two shots into the man's faced. The remaining soldiers' work ethic suddenly improved. They saved some of the weapons and ammo before the building crumbled in the flames.

Weasel and I watched as a gentle pre-dawn breeze from the west nudged the flames from one townhouse to the other, finally stopping at the end closest to the river where the fire ran out of fuel.

"Damn," he said, fascinated by the progress of the flames. "That sure worked out fine. It'll set them back at least six months. Wish their arms warehouse would have gone up faster."

"Set what back six months?" I asked.

"I'm not sure," he said. "But he's building something. And it's based on the guns. The drugs get him the guns. He's been working up to this for about five years now. Whatever it is, it ain't good for anyone who isn't a Messenger."

"What was with all those batteries?" I asked. "And those two drums of chemicals?"

"There's a new drug out. Being marketed by the Messengers as the next generation of Slammer. Hits quicker, peaks higher, lasts longer. That chem we saw is the guy who's making it. I would have iced him if I got the chance."

Slammer was a powerful drug, a narcotic for soldiers. It pumped them up, created a mental myth of superiority, enhanced their reflexes, they imagined…for a few hours. It was a combination of methamphetamine, PCP and LSD. A more powerful version in the noses of clan warriors was not pleasant to contemplate.

"They're calling the new drug Bad Boy. Been on the streets a couple of months. It's a white crystal with grey flecks in it. I wanted to see what was in it. Think I know now. I'm pretty sure those two drums were embalming fluid."

It was a common ingredient in wicki sticks—a joint enhanced with PCP and embalming fluid.

"I think the new Messenger chem is distilling battery acid to add to the Bad Boy. Pulverizing the residue and blending it into the final batch. That's what the grey stuff is. What we got is probably PCP, crystal meth, embalming fluid, some kind of hallucinogen and the distilled battery acid."

"Jesus," I said, "how in the hell they come up with these ideas?"

But I knew the answer. The clans had been experimenting with substances that could get them up for years. Paint thinners, old spray cans, chemical solvents, varnish—you name it; they tried it. If someone died or went into a coma, they tried something else. I once saw two guys sprinkling their weed with the chemicals people in the 20th used to keep algae out of their swimming pools. If someone went into convulsions, but managed to come back out, it was a sign to them that they were on to something good. Just needed another ingredient or two. Maybe an adjustment in the dosage. No surprise that someone came upon battery acid.

So now we had a newer, nastier drug...and the Messengers selling it for guns and ammo.

Upside—we bought some time.

Downside—the Babe lived.

CHAPTER FOURTEEN

All the pain I hadn't felt while I was getting stomped in the Babe's camp, seeped into my bones as the adrenaline leeched away. My back, near the kidneys, my ribs left side, left thigh, and the start of a good black eye.

"Getting a little hitch in yer get along," Weasel said on the hike back. "Need me to carry some of your gear?"

I shot him a weak smile, more of a grimace. No way he was carrying anything. It would take 10 years to work that one off.

As the sun peeked over the horizon, we entered our east neighbor's basement, neutralized the booby traps, opened Weasel's door that no one but us could see, (sometimes I thought he played too many video games), traversed the tunnel, and entered our basement.

The door protested loudly, just as we wanted, and on the other side in the middle of a brightly lit bare room with four concrete walls was Sarah with a Franchi SPAS-12 combat shotgun, Duke with a kevlar vest and ears at high mast, and Stevie pointing a HK G36 at us.

"When the alarm went off, but we didn't hear an explosion," Stevie said, "we figured it was you two."

"Good job," Weasel replied. "Just like we rehearsed."

"One thing," Sarah said. "A surprise. Duke alerted before the alarm. That's before you opened the tunnel door nearly 80 yards away."

"Nice," said Weasel.

"You gents look a little worse for wear," Sarah said. "Let's get you upstairs."

"I'll reset everything," Stevie said, disappearing down the tunnel.

In the kitchen, Sarah helped us get out of our gear and shed our weapons. "Seems like a lot of blood here for a simple scout," she commented.

"Most of it ain't ours," Weasel said.

"Before I start on Mac," Sarah said to Weasel, "anything you need looked at?"

"Nothin' a good night's sleep won't take care of." He could have had his arm bitten off and said the same thing.

"Me too," I said. "Little sleep and I'll be good as new."

"Get that shirt off," she told me. She began a close inspection of my face and torso. I felt like a prize cow. Sarah poked a finger between two ribs.

"OWWWW!!"

"Enough of your macho bullshit, Mac. Let me see what's going on. You need to get the pants off too. You have serious trauma here."

All of us knew how to set bones, sew someone up, clean wounds, inspect for injuries, apply tourniquets and compress bandages. If I could walk several hours back home, I was going to be ok. But Sarah was always thorough, and forever our paladin, veterinarian, and house physician. We knew about internal bleeds, and that was her concern.

She inspected and prodded while we broke down and cleaned the weapons, waiting for Stevie to return before detailing our journey.

The tunnel door squalled like a haunted house and Stevie stomped back up the stairs. He grabbed the Steyr 93R and started disassembling. Looking at my face, he said, "Gotta be a story here."

Weasel said, "We were scouting The Babe's new camp. Got into a bit of a scuffle."

Stevie stopped working on the Steyr. Sarah stopped futzing with my bruises. Weasel watched Stevie.

Stevie got tighter. LIke he was being compacted. His fingers curled in. Head came up. Shoulders hunched. Duke rose and moved to his side, ears up. He didn't say much, but it came out slowly and deliberately. A struggle to keep the words from breaking the dam and flooding the room.

"You know where The Babe is, when he's gonna be there, and you don't take me with you? What the fuck! That"s low, Weasel. I thought we were all open and honest here. Not like out there."

"Plenty of reasons for that. You want them all now?"

"Yeah, every single fucking one."

Weasel paused a couple of beats. Pushed the parts of the HK to the side. "Ain't givin' you all the reasons. In your mind you know all of them. But you need to remember this. We all want him dead, Stevie. I was watching him before Mac and Sarah and me teamed up. He makes a lot of noise. Always something. And it's getting more noisy. But here's the thing, Stevie. I never seen anyone come close to killing him. We'll do it, son. But only when getting it done means we get to survive and stay together. And all of us will be there when he takes that last breath."

Sarah walked over to Stevie's spot at the table and a pulled chair next to him. She leaned in a bit, but didn't touch him. "You forgot about trust, hon," she said quietly. "I can understand that. All of us can. Trust takes time to grow. The mission was two people home and two on the scout. Logical. We are not going to betray you, Stevie. All of us have a bond."

The tension in the spring eased. Stevie's shoulders loosened up. His hands opened. The muscles in his face relaxed. He looked like a teenager again. A little pissed and confused. But that was what normal looked like.

Weasel and I gave them the chronology of the scout. The weapons, the drugs, camp life. The dust up at the end and the camp's destruction.

Stevie said, "I don't like having to remember those years, and most of the camp operation sounds the same, but a couple of things are different. First it sounds like there's more soldiers and what maybe we'd call grunts or laborers. Also slaves and sex women. Plus I never saw an armory or drug house. Everybody had their weapons. Drugs were just always there. Huge quantities of booze and home brew too. Every camp had a still. Clans aren't big on storing and organizing."

"That helps," Weasel said. "I been thinking for a bit that the fat man's got something going. Only a few reasons to have an armory."

"First, you plan to acquire more soldiers," Sarah said.

"Or, you plan to trade for something else," I countered.

"Which presents two more problems," Stevie chimed in. "Where do your new soldiers come from?"

Sarah finished the thought. "What are you looking for in trade that's more valuable than weapons?"

"If you're going to war," I said. "Who's your enemy?"

Weasel looked around the table. Shook his head. "We got a big story here. Started when Stevie was a clan kid. Gonna end with The Babe dead. Got some people in the story. But we don't know nothin' else."

"And we don't know how long it takes to get to the end. And we do know The Babe isn't telling anyone his plans." Sarah said.

"You just described every day of our lives," I said. "We wake up, have a goal, survival plus making life better, but have no idea how we're getting there."

"Well, hell. When you put it that way," Sarah said, "It doesn't sound so big anymore. We have the whole day ahead of us, let's go to work."

CHAPTER FIFTEEN

FEBRUARY 16, 2056

O nce we understood computers, we figured out the that the little stick wrapped around my wrist in duct tape by my parents was a flash drive. But I wouldn't let anyone open it. It drove Sarah crazy and she kept on my until I finally relented.

"OK," I said. "But you look. Then tell me."

Sarah took two days with the flash drive. She came to me evening of the second day. She showed me a new side, a vulnerable one. Her vulnerable was easier to deal with than my wrapped up tight crap. Her eyes were red. She sat on the bed and hugged me, and began to quietly weep.

I couldn't understand my emotions, but I was good at supporting hers. I held her, stroked her head. Didn't say anything. Eventually, she reached into her nightstand and pulled her stash, selected Mississippi Mellow, a sleepy Indica, and we smoked a bowl. I put on *Yo-Yo Ma Plays Ennio Morricone* and we drifted off a bit, holding each other.

An hour later, I squeezed her shoulders and asked, "That bad, huh?"

She looked up at me. "No," she said, "that good. I'm crying for the beauty. There is so much of it on the drive. The truth of Armageddon is also there. The information on The Collapse isn't beautiful. That story makes me angry. In the morning we all learn the truth, the bad stuff. Tell the boys to get some sleep."

"But we don't talk about my stuff yet, right?" I said.

"You let me know when you're ready," she said.

• • • •

Dawn. Weasel was making coffee. Stevie setting the table. Sarah's was preparing pancake batter to accompany the eggs and sausage from the Dekalb hippies. I fed Duke and took him for a walk.

"Got big stuff going today," I told him. "Gonna learn more about The Collapse. Maybe the final pieces of the puzzle. Might learn why some of your doggie friends are so mean."

He gave my hand a snuffle and headed back to the house. We were behind the barrier, but I dragged a huge pine branch over our tracks just in case. A little wind, a dusting of snow, and we didn't exist.

• • • •

Duke took his spot underneath the table, we all sat with our coffee or hot chocolate and waited for Sarah to begin.

"Unintended consequences and Mother Earth," she began. "That's what brought on the environmental cataclysm. Earth was suffering from a plague of humans and she needed to eradicate the infestation. The coexistence of humans and the planet was not sustainable."

Before she could continue, Weasel jumped in. What followed was our first major conflict. Sarah said later that she was tired, on edge, on a roll, and not open to criticism. Weasel communicated as he always did. Directly with no obfuscation. (Gotta tell him that word.)

What follows is the blow by blow of the Weasel/Sarah War:

Weasel: What is "she"? Who ya talkin' about?

Sarah: The key word is "sustainable", not "she". Earth survived and healed. We survived and have yet to heal. Which would be a better bet to be prospering hundred years from now? Humanity or the planet? Dogs might have a better chance than humans.

Weasel: Who decides? We gotta say in this, don't we?

Sarah: Earth decides. She is sustainable, self-healing.

Weasel: Waddya, crazy? You sayin' Earth is alive?

Sarah: Well, she…

Weasel: She???

Sarah: She certainly has a circulatory system, and a respiratory system...

Stevie jumps in: And an excretory system. She gets rid of all kinds of crap.

Mac jumps in: Digestive? She's self-sustaining. Energy, photosynthesis, biodegradation. Renewal, four seasons.

Weasel: Blah, blah, blah. *Sheeee* (he bent the word) can't think. Got no nervous system. Boo ya!

Sarah: There's lots of electricity, Weasel. And all the solar energy you could want. She cleans up, creates new life, buries the dead. And has been alive almost forever in our terms. I say there is a nervous system. Therefore, the capacity for thinking.

Weasel: Well, shiiit. I ain't ever winnin' this one. Just keep movin' and we'll save this for later.

A pause here. A brief silence. Enough for me to study Sarah's face. There's something new, I said to myself.

Sarah: No! (Emphatic and bright eyed and finger pointing) There is no later! Look at us, Weasel! Hurricanes, typhoons, drought, flooding, heat waves, cold waves, virus, bacteria, fungi. Earth can bake us, boil us, freeze us, drown us, starve us, rot us from the inside, attack us with her beasts large and small, and allow us to think we are superior to her. We were here only with her permission. It got revoked.

She slammed her fist on the table, pushed back her chair with enough force to topple it and left the table.

Things got quiet.

• • • •

Sarah went to make more coffee. She cleared our cups and rinsed them in the sink. The cups made more noise than usual.

Stevie helped Sarah. Weasel and I sat. Quiet.

"I didn't mean no harm," Weasel whispered.

"You need to tell her that," I said.

Weasel pushed back from the table. The kitchen was big. He walked like the distance from the table to the sink was ten miles with a heavy load. Weasel stood behind Sarah, shuffling from foot to foot. She knew he was there.

Stevie did a quick trot back to the table.

"Who's gonna say something first?" he whispered.

"A week of dishes says Sarah," I said.

"Done."

A full minute of silence passed. Weasel stopped shuffling. Sarah messed with the coffee, doing the same thing over and over.

"I ain't never had to to this," Weasel told Sarah. Her back was still to him.

"Do what, Weasel?" she said. "Realize that someone other than you knows something?"

"No… I mean yes."

She turned. Her eyes glistened. Her mouth and chin quivered. I went on high alert. This was rare. And very important. The last time this happened was when I told her about meeting the Babe at the airport and experiencing the knowledge that maybe I would never return to her.

Stevie was still as a June sunset. I didn't know what the right words for Weasel were. For me they would have been I'm sorry. That was selfish and petty. You deserve more from me. The key would have been that it was true. The key was respect.

But Weasel wasn't me and he hadn't lived with Sarah for 15 years. He had been alone for more years than Stevie. Weasel had no subterfuge, or tricks, or ploys. Whatever came next would be a first time event for him.

Weasel's head was down. Two feet separated them. Sarah silently, patiently stood. "I do know more than you in some ways," he began. "And it gives me great comfort to pass my knowledge on. Nobody ever respected me for what I know."

Sarah remained still. Weasel's head came up a bit. Eye contact. Then he straightened. Shorter than Sarah. But with eyes locked. "You and Mac and Stevie," he said, giving a shoulder turn to indicate the two of us at the table, "you show me respect. And the dog, too. That damn Duke. He's like another person. And I guess maybe I don't quite know how to take it."

Sarah nodded.

"Back in Southern Illinois, when I was left to fend for myself, my future was one day. That's what my knowledge bought me. Every sunrise was a victory. Then I came up here. It started turning into week to week. I had a longer future."

Weasel paused. Looked down. A full thirty seconds. Then he gave a little shake, like a dog waking up. Head up, shoulders back, he found his words.

"You, Sarah, have taught me that I am no longer myself. I am you. I am us. You know more than I ever dreamed of knowing. And you teach me every day. I will never disrespect you again."

I got a little misty.

"Damn!" Stevie whispered, "who would've thunk?"

A tear slid from Sarah's eye. She pulled Weasel in and wrapped him up. Her chin rested on the top of his head. She made eye contact and gave me a crooked smile, then gently patted Weasel on the back. Weasel slid his arms up around her waist and they remained that way until Sarah dipped her head and whispered. Weasel squeezed harder and then they separated.

"How about a break while I finish making this coffee?" Sarah said.

Nobody pointed out she had already done it fifteen times.

We broke for bathroom and stretching. I followed Weasel on to the deck. We had a nice snow cover. 180 degrees of our sight lines were woods and prairie. No roads, houses, or abandoned vehicles.

"You bring binocs?" Weasel asked.

I handed him a pair of Niko camo binoculars and he swept the view. Our deck was in need of repair and we kept it that way. The hand rails remained covered with snow. We didn't approach the front edge. During snow season we left through tunnels and camouflaged our entrance/exits. The tunnels were seriously booby trapped. No tracks back. No safe entry.

"Sorry about my fuck up," he said, handing back the binocs. "I still gotta fight that loner in me. It's been planted pretty deep."

"We're all new to this, Weasel," I said. "Each one of us has spent years and years alone. Hard to practice on relationships when you don't even have a mirror."

He handed back the binocs. "We're clean. Got a turkey tryin' to hide about 150 yards out by the scrub pine. All hunkered down."

I looked. Couldn't see a thing. Sometimes I think he just messes with me with his insights and abilities.

"You know what Sarah said to me?" he asked.

"No."

"She told me she loved me. Whispered it right in my ear. Nobody ever told me that."

He reached over. "Give me those glasses," he said. "Think I see a doe."

I realized at that moment that if we were explorers, Sarah was our captain.

• • • •

Three minutes later, Sarah called us back in.

"We're quitting for today," she told us. "Let's return to who we are and remember what we mean to each other. But know one thing. All of this Earth talk is interesting and debatable. But what the planet did or how she responded to our assault on her sovereignty, was not enough to kill several billion people. Humans are too tough and ornery. Something else happened. Something human. That's what's next. That's what's on Mac's flash drive. And we learn it tomorrow morning."

• • • •

A new day, a new breakfast. I predicted a conflict free zone.

Sarah began. "Earth can tolerate 7 billion bees or 7 billion ants or 7 billion birds. She obviously had trouble with 7 billion human beings. Seven billion apex predators."

"Hell, said Weasel, "I don't particularly care to be in room with any more than two or three."

"Amen to that," Stevie replied.

134

Sarah grabbed a biscuit, slathered it with cherry jam. "We continue with a question: If you wanted to kill large numbers of a species, what's your best strategy?"

"Easy," Weasel replied. "Group 'em. Herd 'em."

"Yeah," Stevie said. "Ant colonies, buffalo herds, schools of fish, whale pods."

"Turns out," Sarah said, "humans in the 20th and 21st were very compliant in forming groups. Of the seven billion humans, a huge percentage grouped themselves in urban areas. Some of the mega cities stretched for hundreds of miles."

"Sweet Jesus," I said. "We hastened our own extinction."

"What I think," Sarah responded, "is that we encouraged it."

"How?" I asked.

"In North America in 2020, Canada and United States," Sarah said, "over 80% of the population lived near coast lines. That included oceans, gulfs, rivers and the Great Lakes. If you look at the old satellite pictures of North America at night, most of it is dark. 80% of humanity is living on about 5% of the land mass. This is how civilizations developed thousands of years ago and we never changed. If you consider the whole surface of the earth, 90% of humanity lives on approximately 1% of the planet's surface. This is important, because humans affect not only lands, but also oceans and rivers and fresh water lakes."

"Don't shit where you live," Stevie said.

"You gonna start with the Earth is alive stuff, right about now, right?" Weasel asked.

Sarah cut her eyes at him and moved the biscuits out of his reach. She continued:

"Humans grouped together because it was efficient and comforting. Their basic needs were shelter, jobs, division of labor, food, and water. If we're talking about 10 or million people living in a small area, they needed huge networks and systems to keep everything running smoothly. Once the support system shut down, humans were helpless. Many of the survivors of The Collapse lived on farms or in small towns or what they called 'off the grid'. They were the indies of pre-collapse industrialized nations. Others who made through were tough urban dwellers, who got lucky or had extremely good genes. Smart like rats and tough as cockroaches."

"The clans," Stevie said.

"Think about this," Sarah explained. "In the 21st even the small cities had a million people. In China, there were over 45 cities with more than a million people. The big cities, and I'm talking all over the world, not just here, had between 15 and 35 million people. They had their phones, their cars, their antibiotics, their electricity, food, water, work, public transportation. Everything dependent upon the power grid. And the power grid totally dependent on coal and oil.

"We're going to do the effects, not the causes. Easier that way. First thing to go was food. Drought, floods, and storms of biblical proportion for several years. Holes in the ozone. Crops failed. Europe, Asia, Africa, North and South America all had rich breadbaskets thousands of miles deep and wide that just gave out.

"In '21 climate change slammed the planet. Monumental hurricanes, blizzards, typhoons, tornado swarms. Eventually the grain silos are bare, the food warehouses are empty. All aspects of human feeding revolves around grains. Cattle eat it, bakers bake it, tacos and pita contain it. Chickens peck at grains and seeds. People begin to panic. Sad thing was they didn't know they were going to die of thirst and anarchy long before anyone starved to death.

"Let's take this in order. Remember, we're talking a three-year span for the endgame. But it took over a hundred years to get there.

"First, all the food goes because of droughts in some areas and floods in others. How many trucks you think a huge grocery store needs a week? Big stores, 10 or 20 every week. Huge trucks. Some of the stores open all day every day. Think about how much food and drink 10 million people consume in one day. Multiply that by every large city on the planet.

"If you are beginning to starve, job one is feeding your family and yourself. Everything else goes away. Cops go home, train engineers stay with their families, fire fighters don't report to work, planes have no pilots.

"It didn't take long for power to die. They got electricity from burning coal. Coal came from engineers driving trains and someone on

136

the other end mining and loading the trains. Electricity ran the water delivery and filtration systems. And directed waste from millions of toilets and hundreds of factories away from drinking water supplies. And don't forget cars. Gasoline came out of the ground with electric powered pumps.

"Trucks stop coming because the drivers are staying home to find food or can't get gas because of power outages. Then what?

Riots.

Train engineers stay home to protect family. So do cops and soldiers.

No coal for turbines to generate electricity. Nuclear power plants take up the slack. Until their technicians are killed or starved to death or just don't come in.

National Guard comes in. Citizens are better armed than they are. Guard retreats. Or joins citizens.

No power, no food. No heat or A/C. Millions of gallons of bottled water disappear real quick. Whaddya drink? Surface water. Contaminated because sewer and water treatment is gone. Imagine 100 million people from New York down to Miami without fresh water or sewer and garbage disposal. Where does urine and feces from 100 million humans go when there is no sanitary system? What's it like in a week? Or two? Or a month?

Cholera, dysentery, hepatitis. If you have access to well water, you are good until someone with bigger guns finds out.

The nuclear power plants start to meltdown. We had three. Braidwood, Dresden, and Zion. All were near water supplies. Those are our hot zones now.

Groups began to coalesce. Farmers, gangbangers, cops, rich people, hoarders, preppers. The old, the young, the disabled couldn't keep up. Within a year or two, the groups turned on each other. The ones with the most fire power won. The old, the young, the crippled, and the stupid—all dead. Thirty years later, the winners are the clans and everyone else is an indie.

Now add this into the equation. Antibiotics and vaccinations are gone. What happens. Bad tooth or hangnail can kill you. Polio, smallpox, diptheria, measles, cholera, mumps, AIDS—all of them unchecked. Millions of rotting bodies, millions or rats and mice, thousands of unchecked dogs and cats. And the Black Death. Who you gonna call?

So if you lived in a rice paddy, or a remote fishing village in Scotland, or a farm in Nebraska, you were ok. Unless of course you were near a nuclear silo or power plant. But if you were self-sufficient, independent, not near other humans, you survived. This is where we are now—19th century agrarian. Maybe 18th. I don't know how many people are alive.

"Sarah," I said, "even with humanity's grouping instinct and dependence on technology and fossil fuels, Earth's fury wasn't enough to erase most of humanity from the planet."

"You're right, Mac," she said. "And humans were smart enough to race from a few million people to seven billion in a few centuries and unfortunately smart enough to wipe most of us the surface in a few weeks. Thanks to your flash drive, I know how it all happened."

"Bathroom break," she said. "This next stuff is brutal."

• • • •

"My research had taken us to days before the final Chicago riots in '23, Sarah continued. "Earth was in the global collapse state. But not the Armageddon stage. Billions of humans could have survived starvation and hardship. We are, after all, a resourceful species.

"In the 21st, any person with a computer and link to the internet could talk to the entire world. And they did. Thankfully, many saved their conversations and threads on hard drives and flash drives. I even found audio and video files from the final days. Deciphering Armageddon was not difficult. Those conversation threads, and e-mails and news documents and pictures and videos were on Mac's flash drive. There is so much information on there that I can't begin to crack it. But there was a nice file that contained everything we needed. It was labelled, "I hope someone can read this." It gave me a two-month chronology of the events. It is chilling. This is what I learned:

So when humanity is stumbling toward extinction from a series of catastrophic environmental events, a small group of men gives the human race the final push. The last straw was human, not Mother Nature.

She pauses a beat, dredging the last of her cocoa before continuing. "There was a group of countries that had nuclear weapons. They had them since the mid-20th and didn't want anyone else to get them. They had — and still do have — thousands and thousands of nuclear bombs, rockets, warheads, missiles, suitcase bombs—you name it, they had it. United States, France, England, Russia, bunch of others."

"So right now," Stevie said, "there are thousands of nukes laying around the world."

"Bad news, yes. Good news, no one knows how to set them off. And why bother? There are no more nations."

Sarah continued. "In '23, all but three of the world's countries wish nukes didn't exist. And the three that love them are led by either a psychopath, sociopath, religious fanatic or combination of the three. The first was a country that developed nukes that didn't mind selling them. Pakistan. There was another country led by a clinically insane man that developed its own nukes. Korea. And finally, there was a relatively new state—a terrorist state carved out of parts of Iran, Iraq, Kuwait, Syria, and Turkey in 2019. It was a big country full of deserts, oil wells, a few big cities, and a terrified population.

The new nation, was controlled by its religious leader, Hassan Dadras. Dadras came to power through a coup, taking over power from Sayyed Ali Khamene, who was considered a danger to the free world and all Muslims who were not of his sect. Dadras, the new guy, had complete, total control over all aspects of the nation and was a far more dangerous version of the guy he ousted. The new country named themselves The New Islamic State. The rest of the world labelled it as a Rogue State.

Under Dadras, The New Islamic State espoused the belief that all people on the planet should follow their brand of Islam. Which happened to be Shiite, an extreme and relatively small Islamic religious minority. Only 15% of world wide Muslims are Shiite. Everyone who was not Shiite—Christians, Catholics, Jews, Hindus, women, homosexuals, Sunni Muslims—were despised and should be converted, enslaved, or killed. Most Shias lived in Iran, Iraq, Pakistan, and India.

Now most people who fought fanatics at the time felt that Dadras was a 21st century version of Hitler, or Stalin, or Pol Pot. He was a ruthless dictator who wanted to take over the world. He used religion as his cover. The others used nationalism, separatism, or just plain old let's kill everyone but us.

Each mass murderer had a published reason for their reign of terror. And all of them were successful writers and sometime intellectuals. In the end, each of them had the same idea. Total control of every aspect of civilian life. Food, work, sleep, entertainment, religion, sexual practices. Some used nationalism. Others politics. The Christians in the Middle Ages, used the same reason as Dadras. Religion. That was the rationale behind the Crusades. You die in the name of our superior religion.

So Dadras was just a crazy killer hiding behind religion, Weasel commented.

Pretty much, Sarah said. But he got it done. Better than anyone in the history of humanity.

Most successful mass murderers, serial killers, dictators are brilliant. Dadras was off the chart. Among his many skills, he was also a world class chess player. He started his "world game" in 2019 when he came into power. The first things he needed was nukes, which he didn't have.

Where did he get all of his nuke making materials? Stevie asked.

It takes billions of dollars and several years just to get military grade nuclear bomb material, Sarah said. Not to mention ICBMs. So Dadras just went out and bought what he needed. Dadras bought them from the military leader of Pakistan. With a little help from North Korea, whose leader thought Pakistan, The New Islamic State, and, his country, North Korea, were all *sympatico.*

Pakistan started its nuclear program in 1972, motivated by India, their neighbor and enemy, which had a headstart on Pakistan. Pakistan became an official Islamic state in 1956. What followed were decades of military coups, civil wars, poisonings, assassinations, and terrorist bombings.

So Pakistan has nukes, lots of nukes and a general named Muhammad ul Haq who takes power in a few years before the collapse. General al Haq is very willing to sell nuclear weapons to

Dadras and his New Islamic State. He needs money to fortify his personal army and build some upscale palaces and castles. It ain't easy being a dictator.

So Dadras buys nuclear weapons from Pakistan. Slowly. Since the New Islamic State didn't have a delivery system, Dadras buys and begins stockpiling suitcase nukes.

Explain suitcase nukes, Weasel said.

Small enough to carry, but large enough to destroy several city blocks and release deadly radiation that lasts for decades and spreads through the air.

Stevie asks, Why they didn't just buy some rockets from the other bad guys?

Sarah says, "Dadras couldn't buy and hide ICBM's because they are so huge. Can't hide them. But suitcase nukes were perfect for his plan. They are powerful and dirty, and easy to smuggle into enemy countries. Not as powerful as the ones in the movies that can destroy and entire city. Less than Hiroshima. But a nuke is a nuke and it gets everyone's attention and heads of state lose their objectivity when you say, 'It's just a small nuke.'"

• • • •

So from 2019 to 2021 in the Middle East, through a series of complicated and ingenious moves, Hassan Dadras acquires 11 suitcase nukes. During the year of 2022, he sends out agents and places eight of the suitcase bombs in lead-lined hidey holes in cities all over the world.

Dadras initiates his plan during the ecological catastrophe that is already crippling most urban areas. In early 2023, during the peak of one of the most extreme northern hemisphere winters in modern history, Hassan Dadras embarks upon his chess game. The prize—world domination.

The fact that he begins in winter is brilliant because several of the bombs are ignited in the northern hemisphere cities—where millions are totally dependent upon technology to keep them from freezing to death. Imagine 9,000,000 people in New York City, many isolated in their boroughs by closed bridges and tunnels, losing all their food, water, power, transportation, and forms of communication when it is ten degrees below zero. That's what happened. Before all electronic communication went dark, one of the last messages from NYC was that with the arrival of Spring, you could smell the rotting corpses from 10 miles out.

Back to Dadras and his plan. The first move of his chess game occurs on January 16, 2023.

Written memos from news organizations stated that January 16 in 2023 was Martin Luther King Day in America. Dadras despised all things American, particularly the concepts of diversity and equality. For Dadras, everything wrong with the world was caused by America's influence and the only cure was his brand of Islam. So America is his endgame. But like all good chess players he takes a while to get there.

Remember, in 2022 his agents planted lead-lined suitcase nukes in major cities all over the world. He bragged about how easy they were to hide. And they were set up to be triggered by a remote device. Some of the nukes were detonated by smart phones, but most by on site terrorists. Some with devices as simple as a child's walkie-talkie.

DAY ONE
JANUARY 16, 2023

First move—in the name of his god, Dadras nukes his ally, North Korea — twice. One in the capital of Pyongyang and another in the second largest city, Hamhung. Both bombs explode in the business districts of the cities near monuments of the Supreme Leader, Kim Jung-on. The problem with playing chess with human pieces is that they don't always do what you intend or stay where you put them.

North Korea's leader, Kim Jung-on, a kid in his early 30's with no conscience and no restraints, flips out. Gets really stupid and tries to nuke the United States. Small bomb, big missile. It doesn't even make it past Japan before a U.S. nuclear sub blasts it out of the sky. Problem is the Korean nuclear weapon explodes over Japan and irradiates population centers. Japan does not have nukes and can't figure out who to blame.

Kim Jung-on launches two more missiles, but one fizzles out and crashes in the Pacific Ocean and the other is shot down over the northern Pacific by one of the U.S bases in Alaska.

Every nuclear country on the planet goes to high alert. And that's at least 13 countries. The world waits for the Kim Jung-on to react.

That was day one.

DAY TWO
JANUARY 17, 2023

North Korea's leader can't get his nukes to the U.S. And he really, really hates America. He is sort of allied with China, his next door neighbor. So he's not messing with them. But—South Korea is right next door. And protected by the U.S. He hates South Korea and if he attacks them, he attacks the U.S. by proxy.

So he flies two big nukes over South Korea with his fancy Chinese built bombers and blasts the southern part of the peninsula into the dark ages. He drops half a dozen nuclear bombs in the 20 to 40 KT range. The weather is crazy and the radioactive fallout is blown by a southern wind back over North Korea and into parts of China. Most of China's population is south and west of the fallout, but China has so many citizens that over 100,000,000 Chinese are in the path of the nuclear radiation cloud. Those people are doomed. China is pissed.

That was day two. Nations with nuclear weapons are talking nonstop both internally and with the other nuclear powers. Everyone wants it to stop. Each country is already dealing with starving citizens and food and water riots.

DAY THREE
JANUARY 18, 2023

China has decades of history as a semi-ally of North Korea. China knows where all the secret shit is hidden. All the bases, all the bunkers, all the ships and subs. China's leadership sends over planes — giant bombers with tons of bunker busters and non-nukes — and wipes *all* of North Korea's military capacity off the map.

And the world takes another deep breath. And waits. Nobody really knows what's going on. All leaders are satisfied with a nuke-free day. Nuclear powers are all scrambling to find out who nuked North Korea on the first day and why. And most of them are looking to the wild cards, Pakistan and The New Islamic State. The nuclear nations presume Kim Jung-on is toast. So now all the attention and diplomacy and bribes and threats are headed in the direction of the sociopath, General ul Haq of Pakistan, and the religious fanatic, Dadras, leader of The New Islamic State. The nuclear countries do not realize that Dadras has nine more suitcase bombs.

Dadras is ready for stage two.

DAY FOUR
JANUARY 19, 2023

With the help of Mother Nature, Dadras has the world close to the edge. Now he needs to nudge it some more. As a true religious fanatic, Dadras feels his only allegiance is to his holy mission—make the world live under Shia rule. He does not worry about money or infrastructure or civilian deaths. Even if his war kills Shiite men and women, they will have a guaranteed sweet spot in the afterlife based upon his holy war.

His next target is Pakistan. His other ally. His supplier of nuclear material. What's brilliant about his is that over half of the human population on the planet is in Pakistan, China, and India. Dadras's second move has him putting billions of people to death. He knows India and Pakistan have deep religious and political hatred going back decades. He knows they both have nukes. And China is the northern neighbor of both. Big bonus, India is politically aligned to the United States. So what does he do?

He knows the President of Pakistan is bat shit crazy like the dead Korean guy, so he sets off two more nukes in Pakistan. One bomb in Lahore, in northern Pakistan and near the border with India. Lahore and its surrounding communities have a population of over 10,000,000. The other is Karachi, in the southern region, and it is huge, over 25,000,000 people. One of the top ten largest urban areas in the world at the time. Like all of the suitcase nukes, the bombs are relatively small compared to ICBM types of weapons. But the bombs make big, dirty explosions in two Pakistani cities, and the whole world knows about it. Most of the deaths and casualties are Muslim, but it works out for Dadras because over 70% are Sunni. Sunnis have no afterlife. And the Shiites who perish? No problem, they've got heaven, after all.

A quick weather update here for World War III. In India and Pakistan, the cyclone season ended in November 2022. It is summer in the Southern Hemisphere. They don't worry about freezing to death, but they are experiencing a three-year drought. There are no food surpluses. Citizens of India are already starving. Corpses are piled outside of villages and on roadsides in the rural areas. In the cities there is an endless march to the dumps to dispose of loved ones.

DAY FIVE
JANUARY 20, 2023

Pakistan has two major urban areas that have been nuked, a population in full panic mode, and a need for revenge.

Back in the New Islamic State, Dadras watches his chess game proceed as he had envisioned for the past several years. He did not know that our planet's weather and climate spasms would be beneficial to his pogrom. But he did plan for the president of Pakistan to nuke India. And he was correct.

New Delhi went first. The second largest city in the world with a population of over 30,000,000 people. A beautiful sunny day in the 70's. Most people were looking for food and fresh water or for a way to get out of India. Pakistan helped with the latter. At 8:15 in the morning, a Ghauri-I missile rose from the Sulaiman Mountain Range of central Pakistan and streaked across the clear skies of India and landed in the middle of New Delhi. The yield was 60 kilotons, five times larger than Hiroshima or Nagasaki. Many parts of the world still had power and we have video of the missiles approach and the impact zone. Pakistan claimed credit and said another was coming. Two for two he said. Only two—one for Lahore and the other for Karachi.

Two hours later another missile bursts from the Pakistani mountains and rushes toward Mumbai, a magnificent city of 25,000,000 whose citizens are already rationing food and water and slowly starving to death. Mumbai is a seaport that juts into the Arabian Sea. A blazing sun bakes the city in 90 degree temperatures when a 60 kiloton Pakistani missile destroys the center of the city and irradiates the sea water for several miles along India's coast. Within a few days all information from Mumbai and New Delhi ceases. But it is clear that the initial burst of both weapons killed millions. But nearly everyone else died in the following weeks from burns, injuries, radiation poisoning, rioting, starvation, or dehydration.

DAY SIX
JANUARY 21, 2023

Amazingly, Dadras and The New Islamic State have seven suitcase bombs remaining. Each bomb has been in place for years. He has caused the deaths of nearly 100 million people by detonating four relatively small bombs.

China's got the biggest problem. Both India and Pakistan are on its southern borders and both are starting to move nuclear clouds in China's direction. It had the same problem on its eastern borders because of the North Korea's aggression. China's nuclear arsenal is in the thousands, equivalent to that of Russia and the United States, with missiles and submarines to deliver them against any enemy. Nobody wants more missile launches. But China solved its North Korea problem by destroying North Korea's military capacity. Both India and Pakistan are aware of this. And when China calls them to the table, they show up.

China says if you don't stop now, we will enter the fray. China's delegates tell the counterparts from India and Pakistan to get in touch with their military people in Vishakapatnam in eastern India and Karachi in southern Pakistan and stay on the lines. Within five minutes, both bases have been carpet bombed. Most casualties are military personnel. Planes, supplies, ammunition, battleships, submarines, are reduced to smoldering scrap metal. The Pakistani/Indian War is over. China did not use nuclear weapons.

DAY SEVEN
JANUARY 22, 2016

Dadras has not predicted this. But in chess there are always two players. Dadras is very good at countering an opponent's move. And he has seven suitcase bombs left.

First item on this agenda is to nuke Washington D.C. and New York. Then Moscow and St. Petersburg. It is winter in all four cities and he detonates his devices as the cities are sleeping. All four cities perch upon the edge of catastrophe with food, water, and power shortages. With their resources stretched to the maximum, the cities in the United States and Russia collapse under the weight of this new man-made assault and begin to slip into extinction. It makes no difference if the people try to hunker down or escape. There is no other side. They are doomed. Most freeze to death before radiation kills them.

Dadras waits approximately three hours—until the sun has risen over The New Islamic State—and nukes two of his own cities. Esfahan and Kirkuk. Why? There are still some satellites remaining and internet and speculation ranges across the globe that The New Islamic State was attacked by Israel, or France, or another terrorist group. A couple of posts suggest he is doing to himself to deflect blame. Other experts and commentators say that Dadras is doing this to his own people to keep Israel out of the game. If Israel thinks the New Islamic State is under attack, Israel will stand down.

Experts who speculated that Israel was Dadras's greatest fear were correct. Israel had over 200 nukes and plenty of delivery systems and would back down from no one. Dadras knew that Israel's fire power was impossible to withstand. But in Dadras's mind, if he controlled the world, he could attack Israel from all directions.

Israel was not buying. On day seven, after the two nukes in Esfahan and Kirkuk, Israel's defense ministry met and unanimously decided to implement one of the plans that they had in place for decades. It was called "Operation Well-Oiled Machine."

All of oil fields of the New Islamic State were identified and targeted. All of the possible locations of Dadras and his leadership, as well as his navy and army bases, were also constantly updated in Israel's targeting computers.

Israel pushed the buttons and sent the planes and missiles on their paths. For the oil fields, they started with bunker busters, opening up the top surface of the oil fields and destroying the machinery. They followed with nukes. At least 15 oil fields were nuked to the level of the oil itself. Israel irradiated the future of oil for the middle east and much of the world for centuries to come.

Israel also hit every New Islamic State ship, army or navy base, garrison, and bunker they could see or had locations on. They used a combination of nukes and conventional weapons.

Within 24 hours, of Israel's response, everything went dark and there is no information except journals, diaries, and word of mouth.

• • • •

No one spoke. Our table was a statuary.

Sarah waited a few beats and said, "I'm not done yet."

Weasel said, "You know those anti-depressants we found in the hospital in Winfield? Shoulda brought some back."

• • • •

Sarah says, So back to Weasel's question about the missile silos and power plants. That's where we're going now. All of the nuclear weapons in the world had what they called "fail safes." No would could launch them without codes and more than one person agreeing. In other words, if missiles flew, it wasn't by accident.

As for nuclear power plants, in 2023 there were over 300 in operation. Most of them in America, Europe, and Russia. At least a hundred more were under construction. Any power plant that was not shut down with the proper procedure continued to run and eventually became a dirty bomb.

What happens next is mostly speculation. But accurate, I think.

Some ability to communicate electronically existed in pockets in the United States. We have reports from witnesses who were over a hundred or two hundred miles away from major cities that multiple locations were struck. Consistent descriptions of huge mushroom clouds and a roar like no other. Some people said they had drones up to see the devastation. We have accounts that people read text messages that went dark mid-word. But most information is second or third hand.

After Israel nullified the New Islamic State and radiated future middle east oil production for centuries, someone in the big three loosed the dogs of war. Probably all three—China, Russia, United States. We have some insight to the North American destruction. Nothing else. We don't know about Europe or Asia or Russia. Many of the 21st cen nukes were 1000 times more powerful than Hiroshima and Nagasaki. And we've all seen pictures of that destruction.

So here are our best guesses. There were at least three EMP's on American targets, probably more. One each in New York, Los Angeles, Chicago. There were multiple nuclear hits across the country. Probably hundreds. From diaries and photos and word of mouth, we have witnesses to many rockets blasting from United States' cornfields, suburbs, small towns, submarines, and ships in response to the attacks. The United States had thousands of nukes, based all over the world. How many did we launch? No one knows.

For America, there were several strikes in water. One in the Gulf of Mexico near the west coast of Florida. The intent probably was to make Florida disappear and flood coastal cities like New Orleans. Lake Eerie got one, not sure why. But there is an industrial corridor and a huge fresh water supply endangered. Or maybe someone just missed a target. There were two hits between Milwaukee and Chicago. I'm guessing those were supposed to hit Chicago.

On the east coast of the United States, the urban corridor with over a hundred million citizens, nuclear strikes in Chesapeake Bay and Long Island Sound severely damaged New York, Washington D.C., and Baltimore. The west coast was hit several times, as was Atlanta. Chicago got an EMP and two nuclear plant meltdowns. Nothing in St. Louis or smaller midwestern cities. Nothing nuclear, that is. No cities survived the aftermath.

Who launched first, how long did it last, how many world-wide hits? We don't know. More than a hundred nuclear bombs landed in the United States. Probably several hundred. But we do know that we probably could have survived a nuclear war or an environmental apocalypse with all of our support systems in place. But the human race couldn't survive both.

Do we know what happened to Dadras? I asked.

If not dead, he's probably in cave in Afghanistan with goat herd and a flock of sycophants.

So, Weasel said, his situation is similar to ours.

Question, Stevie asked. Did you say Dadras had eleven suitcase bombs?

You noticed, Sarah said. Yeah, only ten got detonated.

END OF PART ONE

PART TWO

CHAPTER SIXTEEN

EARLY MAY 2056

"You and Duke," Sarah said, "be careful."

We were in our basement, next to one of the tunnel doors. Duke and I were doing a night scout. Sometimes we would solo, usually two, never more. In this case me and a dog. Duke's read of any environment was far beyond our capacity. He was a good companion.

In a world where a broken ankle could be a death sentence and an ingrown toenail could lead to an amputation, we were always careful. We knew about the collapse now. Were aware that our group was alone and should remain so in order to be safe. After nearly a year of hard work, the compound was nearly invisible. Our escape routes were plentiful. None of us had encountered any clans within miles of our location. Nobody spoke the words, but a feeling of well being was creeping into our lives.

"I've got Duke," I told Sarah.

"Yeah," she said. "He's a great partner. Keep him safe too." She hugged me, knelt down and fluffed Duke's ears, and went upstairs to Stevie. "I love you," she tossed over her right shoulder.

"Thanks, Babe. Me too."

The door in the wall opened. Weasel stuck his head out. "You done with the lovey doveys? Ready to go?"

I smiled. "You're just jealous."

"Maybe some truth in that," he said.

"There's a song," I said.

"Yeah, yeah," he laughed. "The Runt. *Gotta Get You a Woman.* Have one of his shirts. Maybe someday."

Tonight he was wearing a Son Volt shirt. Nice alt-country band. Black shirts were mandatory for night work. We moved through the tunnel, Weasel accompanying us down the length of the shaft to secure the outlet behind me. This particular passageway exited in the basement of a burnt out Tudor about 100 meters West of our compound. When I come to the door to the Tudor's basement, I located the oil can and lubricated the hinges.

The door was Weasel's invention. From the inside of the Tudor's basement, the door appeared to be part of the paneled wall—complete with burn marks from the fire that had destroyed the suburban home. In the highly unlikely circumstance that someone found entry into the Tudor's basement, they would see only scorched and scarred redwood paneling. Behind the paneling we had inserted our new door.

Weasel had found an old solid steel warehouse door and enlisted Sarah, Stevie and me to haul the thing back to the compound, the three of us pulling its three hundred plus pounds on a contraption Weasel had made out of wheel barrow wheels and a pick-up truck bed. The trip was five miles but wasn't backbreaking, thanks to the way he had rigged the vehicle. Sarah commented that in a past life Weasel was an engineer in the Roman Empire.

The door was fastened to 4 X 4's and we brought the entire set-up with us plus some Weasel pickings that looked totally useless to me. But Weasel's particular genius was visualizing his environs in a way that no one else could. I have never seen him throw anything away. We had to remove the door from the frame to get it down the tunnel and then set up the 4 X 4's again to rehang the door.

After I oiled the door and four heavy duty locks, I slipped the bolts and cracked the door open about four inches and sat for five minutes and listened.

Three a.m. The predators, both human and animal, were winding down their night's work as their circadian rhythms began preparing for the next cycle. In the thirty plus years since the collapse, timber wolves and cougar have worked their way down from Canada and Minnesota, Wisconsin and upper Michigan to take advantage of the proliferation of deer, farm animals, horses, and house pets that have returned to the wild. Brown bear also flourish. Noisy and generally ill-tempered, they are solitary vegetarians and have no interest in meat from my bones.

But the biggest danger to me and Duke, excluding human predators, are the roaming wild dog packs.

Wolves never seem to come near a human, unless the animal senses an injury. But the dogs, which in the last thirty years have transformed from loving pets to fierce predators and bred themselves into a position of power, seem to have no fear or respect for humans. To them, we are meat.

I didn't hear or sense any threat, so I turned to Weasel and gave him a nod, slipped through the door with Duke, closed it and listened as it locked it behind us. I would return by the front door.

Working my way silently through the Tudor's basement, I found the stairs and entered the first floor. I paused to appreciate the star dance through the rafters of the roofless house, a million tiny beacons providing enough light for me to see obstacles in my path. I loved the night and when I scheduled night missions I adjusted my internal clock a few days before and after the trip so that I was always awake when it was dark, usually retiring to catch five or six hours of sleep in mid-morning.

It was a gentle summer night, about 60 degrees. A south breeze carried the gifts of lilacs. Our destination was a house in a neighboring suburb where Weasel had found a survivalist cache, watched over by four skeletons in the burned out shell of a two bedroom ranch. Probably the family, thinking they were safely ensconced in their basement shelter, safe from all human harm, had been deprived of oxygen when their house went up in flames. It was a slow, horrible ironic death to be killed by the very structure they had built to ensure their safety.

Weasel brought back a shotgun, a Baretta 70-223 assault rifle with twenty-five extra 30 round clips, a Ruger P-85 semi-auto 9mm pistol and an old .38 special along with several hundred rounds of .38 magnum ammo. He had left behind various knives and utensils as well as a prodigious supply of canned pop, magazines, how-to books and— most valuable of all—nearly a hundred cans of coffee and more than 30 bags of sugar. My empty backpack could carry 30 kilos. Duke could carry another 10K's on kevlar III side saddles. Weasel figured we'd need at least three trips.

I set out at a ten minute mile jog, giving myself a couple of hours to cover the five miles and an hour to stock up before the sun started to rise. On day trips I would usually take the ten-speed mountain bike, but it wasn't safe for night travel—too many obstacles to spill me from the bike. We would sleep there during the day, spend some time scoping the area and return the following night. It's nice to have plans—even when they don't pan out.

I was wearing a lightweight long sleeve night camo sweater over a KevlarIII vest. My pants were army issue with plenty of pockets. On my feet were a Reebok light all purpose trainer type shoe—all black, no reflector tape. They were light, comfortable, moisture wicking and silent.

In my holster nestled the Glock 17L. In each of four of my pants pockets I carried two extra clips, taped together so they would make no noise as I ran. The Glock rested horizontally on my left side in a reinforced nylon holster, which was much lighter than leather. The whole rig was about a kilogram, and I hardly noticed the gun until I needed it.

In my backpack was a Wesson double action Alaskan Guide .445 Super Mag. I carried six extra speed loaders for the Wesson. The gun was big and heavy and when it was fired it could be heard for miles around. But in the 20th it was used as a hunting pistol and if I needed to stop a man or animal with one shot, this was the pistol to do it. Weasel tutored Stevie and me in adjusting the single action pull to 2.5 pounds to enhance long range accuracy. The double action feature allowed me to fire the gun almost as rapidly as a clip gun, even though the pull, at eleven pounds was much heavier.

On my belt was a clip knife, a buck knife in a pants pocket, and an Australian combat knife sheathed to my right leg. Across my back was a SIG SG-541 assault rifle, which fired 5.56mm rounds from 30 round clips.

Jogging through the former suburbs at night was always and forever an unnerving ordeal. On a clear night, even if the moon wasn't in phase to provide light, the millions of stars provided enough illumination to amplify the unearthly presence of abandoned and sometimes burned out homes, duplexes, apartment buildings, businesses, and schools. I was running through miles and miles of cemetery, the tombstones flanking me right and left, many of them two or more stories in height, each a silent testament to the ultimate cost of America's greed and consumption.

Having Duke by my side eased the eeriness. The follies of my forefathers have no place in his dog world. We are his life. He is our protector.

The flora and fauna of the American midwest did not mourn the passing of millions of the planet's dominant mammal. They thrived in ever increasing numbers, culling themselves in their own cruel way when one species became too abundant. The maple trees seemed particularly pleased with our passing. Every spring for the last thirty years, millions of their ubiquitous little helicopter seeds took root and our maple syrup harvest was an annual spring ritual.

A common sight is a maple towering twenty or thirty feet over a house, having taken root in a living room or kitchen and burrowed its way year by year through floor and foundation until it was firmly planted right in the middle of the of a suburban ranch house.

As Duke and I ran, we often disturbed the night hunters and their prey—horned owls, field mice, rabbits, red foxes, coyote, raccoons, deer, possum, woodchucks. The wolves usually stayed away from the areas that weren't heavily wooded, but the dog packs preferred their existence to be closer in to the remnants of civilization. Duke never pulled away from my side, even when tempted by rabbits or other small prey.

It was he, on this night, who sounded the warning, a low rumble in his chest, a change in his pace. We slowed. I kept him on heel and looked to see what direction he was sighting on. It was straight ahead. We were coming up to a junior college. I was familiar with the area. We had pulled hundreds books, disks and hard drives from its library when Sarah started researching the collapse.

The campus buildings stretched ahead of us on the right for about a kilometer. On our left were apartments, burned out shells that once housed young students and families in a town called Glen Ellyn. Between the road which we traveled and the college were huge expanses of parking lot, several acres of weed infested blacktop, complete with thirty or forty rusting vehicles. It was on the parking area that Duke focused.

As we crept closer, crawling to within twenty meters of the spot Duke was focused upon, sounds filtered to us—clangs of metal on metal, grunts, screams. I began to pick out figures in the dim light of the stars. Men grappling and parting; charging and being repelled; standing over prostrate figures and kicking or clubbing their downed adversaries.

I immediately recognized the macabre dance for what it was—a clan battle. Like most of the clashes I had witnessed, this one was hand-to-hand. They loved to fight, but most of the time held back the use of pistols and rifles. More survivors that way. Wouldn't want to fuck up your favorite hobby by getting everyone killed.

The rule was: Once you started fighting hand-to-hand, you kept it that way. Knives, bats, spears, machetes, golf clubs, nunchuks—no problem. Get the football equipment on, paint your face, gobble some Slammer or Fuck-U-Up, a combination of dirty meth and acid, and lets have at it. But no guns for close in work. Takes the fun away.

One of the figures stood out from the others by reason of his height and girth. He was in the middle of the melee swinging what I knew to be a thirty-four ounce Louisville Slugger. My ears registered the sickening thuds as his club impacted upon ribs, arms or an opponent's head.

This was my third glimpse of The Babe. I had a rush of fury when I realized it was him. Stevie's story of what that fat beast had done to him and Eric, flashed through my mind. Unbidden, the mental picture of the corpulent, smelly psychopath terrorizing Eric and Stevie played like a vid behind my eyes. I could see poor Eric's body crumpled against the wall.

I momentarily fantasized having the Mauser sniper rifle with night scope in my hands, the cross-hairs centered on one of his knees. I wouldn't kill him; I'd cripple the bastard. Shatter his fucking knees with dum-dum rounds. Let him spend the rest of his sick life crawling in the filth he created.

The sounds of hand to hand combat were suddenly stilled by three pistol shots, the deep reverberation of an army issue Colt .45, a favorite clan weapon because of its abundance and reliability. The flashes of the weapon's discharge briefly shattered the dim starlight over the parking lot/battle ground. Five more shots followed, spaced out with three or four seconds between each one, emptying the clip.

Someone was breaking the unwritten rules of clan combat.

Then complete, total silence. No sounds of battle, no breeze rustling the leaves, no night birds, no animals scurrying to their warrens. Nothing.

By the light of the stars, I could see the vague outlines of about a dozen figures grouped around the huge bulk of The Babe. Then they separated, moving across the battle ground in disparate directions, occasionally squatting down, as if looking for something lost or inspecting their fallen comrades and foes for signs of life. I put a hand of reassurance on Duke's flank. He was quivering, spooked by the ominous silence.

Then the screams started—horrible, God awful, nauseating, gut wrenching, agony-filled shrieks of fear and despair. A chill crept up my spine. The hair on the back of my head tingled. I shivered involuntarily and was very much afraid, fighting the primitive part of my brain's command to cut and run. Duke's hackles rose. He whimpered and I pulled him close to me. We remained in hiding to wait out the two hours until sunrise.

Individual words were discernible within the wall of screams, their meaning an assault on my mind as the sounds hurtled across the parking lot and were processed by my brain. "NO!" "OH, MY GOD!" "PLEASE, NO MORE!" The abhorrent noise, the shrieks of eight or ten men, eventually tapered off. But as the vanquished soldiers succumbed one by one, the impact of the shrieks, and pleas, and moans became more intense as the wails of agony became the death knells of two individuals, each terror-filled voice distinguishable from the other. Two men, distinct individuals, being tortured, dying slowly, each second a year of pain. Two men whom I could not help.

Then, finally, silence again.

The remaining figures in the parking lot moved off to the East, following the big man. I could hear them laughing, celebrating a job well done, glorifying a game well played.

I curled up in a fetal ball, awaiting the dawn, my mind filled with hate, dreading what I would find when sun pushed back the night.

• • • •

Before the eastern sky lightened, the birds sang in the sunrise. An hour had passed since the slaughter's end. I uncurled and stretched, preparing myself for the ghastly task that awaited us. I pulled some rations for the two of us from the back pack—fruit and rice for me, biscuits and raccoon jerky for Duke.

As we broke our fast together, we both heard the barking and yipping to our north, becoming louder as they moved closer. There was a breeze from the south, carrying the smell of the battle blood northward, toward the dog pack which had picked up the blood scent and was rushing to investigate. I wasn't worried about danger to us. The pack would be completely focused on the parking lot and we were far enough away to be no distraction to them. But I was concerned that the pack would destroy information that I sought as they ravaged the corpses in the parking lot.

Our survival depended on accurate knowledge of what was occurring in our immediate environment. Who is up? Who is down? Who's migrating? And in what direction?

A pack is dangerous under three circumstances. If they catch you by surprise, you're dead. But this is unusual, because they are generally noisy lots when prey is in sight. If you are injured, you are dead. Even if you can defend, they won't give up or back down when they sense a kill. If the pack is starving, you are dead. Its members will behave with extraordinary ferocity. They will not try to conserve energy for another attempt. The attack will be all out...do or die.

None of these three criteria applied to the situation Duke and I were in. The last time I saw a starving pack was at least 10 years ago, during the two month drought. Predators and prey had, for the most part, either died of thirst or starvation or moved out to seek better food sources. When the bottom of the food chain left the area, those predators above followed.

Since I wasn't injured, and knew the pack was not starving and was fully aware of their exact location, my decision was to face them straight on, diminish their number and get on with my business. I had to check the battleground, and the pack wanted to feed. Mutually exclusive objectives.

I checked the loads for both pistols, choosing the .445 Magnum for my primary weapon, planning to pick off several of the attackers at long range before they could get organized. The assault rifle didn't pack the punch or provide the long range accuracy I needed.

The sun was a semicircle on the eastern horizon when Duke and I moved twenty meters east, found a position approximately ten meters in front of last night's victims and faced to the north to await the pack's arrival. As its members picked up Duke's scent, the pack increased its clamor, each bark and yip provoking more of the same as they whipped themselves into killing frenzy.

They broke through, nine of them, almost in unison, between two apartment buildings about sixty meters in front of us, halting abruptly about ten meters later when they saw us positioned directly in front of them. Having prey take a stand was not something they had experienced before. The pack did not know that Duke and I were not prey.

The leader was mixed shepherd and black lab, big crested and long haired, unafraid but cautious in this new situation. He approached slowly, fangs bared, hackles up, growling a threat. Duke growled in response, wanting a piece of this interloper, but he stayed on my right flank.

I brought the .445 up, sighted and took out the big male with a chest shot. Before the others could react, I got off five more rounds, snapped the revolver open, dropped in a speed loader.

Surveying the scene, I saw that with the six shots I had taken down five of the pack, three clean kills and two crippling shots. The wounded dogs were whining and trying to pull themselves to some spot away from the danger. The four remaining animals had taken flight. A pack's courage is always positively correlated to its number of healthy members.

I returned the .445 to the backpack and unholstered the Glock as I walked toward the wounded animals. I put each away with a head shot and returned to where Duke waited and sat next to him, talking him down and keeping my back to the parking lot and the grizzly business of investigating the horror we had witnessed in the night.

• • • •

Everybody has them. Can't operate without them. Neanderthal, wolves, deer, Australopithecus, lions, hyenas. We had them too. Rules, sanctions, norms, limits. Without them we would be expelled from the gene pool.

Before the collapse, the industrialized countries broke one of the rules. The one about shitting where you live. As a result, about 100,000 of us now live in an area that supported nearly seven million people just thirty-five years ago. There are now hundreds of clans, primitive tribes existing in the empty shell that once represented humanity's highest technological achievement. Each clan consists of from fifty or so to several hundred members.

About eight or nine years ago Sarah and I sat down and tried to figure out how many people live in the area and how many are members of clans. It was all guess work, based on our travels, observations and information from each of our families—before they were lost to us. Our best guess was that 4000 are clan members. Meaning that, at most, less than four per cent of our population lives the clan life. So most people are like us, Sarah, Weasel, Stevie, Duke and I, in that they are NOT clan members.

The clans control the rest of us by systematic campaigns of random terrorism. They don't have a rule book. Probably don't even know how it works. Sharks don't go to school. They just troll the depths, and all the fish stay the hell out of their way. Our predators had their origins in the urban street gangs, fraternities, and athletic teams and evolved into two-legged dog packs.

During the latter stages of the collapse, they grabbed the weapons and they organized, ruling with an iron fist, recruiting the best, subjugating the rest. If you had something they wanted—guns, jewelry, food, a pretty woman—they took it. That's why most indies live hand to mouth. It's not healthy to appear well off.

When Sarah and I first met in '39, we each had what we carried. Together it added up to our clothes, three pistols, an M-16, a shotgun, four knives, 432 rounds of ammo, two sleeping bags and some jerky and dried biscuits. By indie standards, we were rich. The weapons and ammo were invaluable. They could provide us with food and defense…and also draw the attention of the clans to us. Double-edged sword. The clans discouraged indies from having weapons.

Two 16 year old kids.

We headed out beyond the clan zones and hid. Low profile.

Sometimes the the clan soldiers will mess with you just for fun. This is why all of us live in fear. The random violence. The clans are havens for psychopaths, sociopaths and mental defectives. The former, with their high intelligence unencumbered by conscience or decency, found their way into leadership; the latter are perfect followers. By yesterday's standards, indies are probably what you'd call middle class grunts. The clan leaders are politicians or CEO's or career criminals.

Chems are a big part of clan life. Slammer, Bad Boy, Wicki, Fuck-U-Up, weed, shine—they snort, drink, smoke, swallow, inject whatever they can get. A good chemist or brew master finds himself way up in the clan hierarchy. They are rare. A good batch keeps the men happy and horny, provides a valued commodity for trade. Weapons for chems is a common transaction. The clans with the best chemists are the most powerful. Right now The Babe and Satan's Messengers had the best chem on our little part of the planet.

Not all the clans are ruled by lunatics. A few are commanded by predictable, fair-minded men. Survivors who are doing what is necessary to get by. I have traded goods and information with these groups. If they trust me and I know their rules and obey them and pay the appropriate tolls and tariffs, I can move freely in their territories.

In the city, I trade most often with the Black Gangster Disciples. Usually I get Lake Michigan fish for pot or information. The BGD's also let me scavenge the high rises that grace their turf. Closer to our compound, between us and the lake, is the Insane Cobra Nation. I work well with them too. In both cases, all they know is that occasionally a man and a dog will show up, negotiate a scavenging fee, offer to trade for some ammo, brings good weed, coffee, Jordans or Yeezes. Never shows fear; always manifest respect.

But the Disciples and Cobras are unique, solitary meadows of sanity in a forest of aberration. Most of the clans would just as soon shoot me as talk to me if I set foot on their turf.

That was why I needed to know what had transpired in the parking lot behind me and Duke. I had to know who had gone down under The Messenger's onslaught and what it might mean to our future movements. Were new alliances being formed? Were the The Babe and Satan's Messengers moving west toward our area as Weasel had been prophesying for years? We were very conscious of turf and borders. Cross the wrong border and it could get you killed. My concern was with what boundaries had been changed by the battle in the parking lot.

Clues to The Babe's plans, would be valuable information. To learn more, I would enter the slaughterhouse. I put Duke on guard at the parkings lot edge and began to walk among the corpses.

I felt no sorrow. An hour ago each of these men would have killed me as easily as a dog pack. I was looking for nation. After nation, I could figure out clan. Their clothing and tattoos would tell me what I sought.

There are between 50 and 100 clans. The clans fall under two "nations," Folks and People. Each nation has its own code of conduct, colors, signs, symbols, numerology, and back story.

Over the years we catalogued their identifiers—colors, hand signs, symbols, numerology, key words and "lit" (literature).

The clans' complex I.D. rituals helped them set borders. If an individual or small group has to journey through several different territories, their survival depends upon knowing the affiliation of those whom they confront. A zebra who could not identify a lion would soon find its genes in the great recycler.

All the clans fall under one of two "Nations." They are either "Folks" or "People." Folks didn't fight Folks, and People didn't fight People. But each nation passionately hate the opposition. The only excuse Folks need to kill People is a visual sighting. And vice versa. Why? I haven't figured that out yet. I'm not sure I ever will. It isn't racial or religious. Clans are often mixed race and formal religion is non-existent.

If you map out old Chicago on a grid, you will a Folks and People checkerboard. So if a small group is twenty territories away from their home ground, it is vital to their existence that they be able to identify everyone they encounter.

Clan members always travel in neutral colors unless they are at military strength. So if you are Folks ten miles from home and run into a group of People, you run like hell or fight. If you run into other Folks, you sign—an elaborate ritual of hand signals—and talk and go through the lit until they believe you are really Folks. Then they will treat you like visiting dignitaries. Since the lit is very complex and secret, it's generally impossible to "pass."

For example, in the People lit, fish is not to be eaten because Peter was a fisherman and they detest Peter. Folks won't eat pork. Nor tomatoes. They believe the British tried to kill George Washington with a tomato, erroneously thinking tomatoes were poisonous, and People like George Washington. Folks like David; People, Goliath. Both will eat chicken, but Folks won't touch turkey. Snakes are reviled by Folks; practically worshiped by People. The lit for both sides is replete with biblical overtones.

If you are Folks, you are right sided and your number is 6. That means you are identified by a hat cocked right or a bandana with the corner pointed right. Or maybe shoelaces only on the right. Or the right side of your head shaved. Right earrings and rings. Your star has six points; your crown, also six points. If you are People, you are left sided and your number is 5.

No matter where you were in the city or suburbs, if you came across a stranger, or worse yet a group of strangers, your life depended upon your knowledge of signs and lit...or your ability to hide

• • • •

The Messengers had been gone about an hour when I took a deep breath, turned and walked into the middle of the carnage in the parking lot. I stopped and did a slow turn. The brutality, the sheer depravity of the deeds was beyond my dark imaginings. There were thirteen men on the ground. Most of them were in football gear. Helmets with elaborate face guards, white plastic stained in red, were scattered across the ground. There was also a catcher's face mask and an ice hockey goalie's mask visible beside two of the corpses.

Flies had begun to gather by the thousands to lay their eggs in the eviscerated corpses and drink from the streams of blood that wound across patches of blacktop. Dandelions, crabgrass and chickweed that had successfully homesteaded in the minuscule cracks in the pavement soaked up the blood. I saw enough internal organs to satisfy the most curious med student, enough brains to delight a neurologist.

I staggered away from the bloodbath and returned to Duke, needing to see something pure and clean. It helped…but not enough. I puked out my breakfast and went back to learn.

The victims were left-sided—earring holes in left ears. The earrings had been ripped out. Left pant legs rolled up. Their tattoos were on the left. If there had been any rings remaining on their fingers, they would have been on the left hands. Many of the dead men had some of their fingers hacked off to get at their jewelry. Their number was six. Six point star and crown tattoos on arms and chests.

The conclusion was obvious. These were the corpses of People. Folks were completely right-sided. Folks' honored the number five. Five point tattoos and crowns.

On some of the torsos of the corpses that had not been gutted were carved tridents pointing upward, a classic Folk sign, one that I usually saw on walls and clothing, not carved into flesh. Had the trident been pointing down, it would have been a sign of disrespect to Folks. On other torsos, 5-point crowns were carved upside down, a sign of disrespect to People. On some of the skulls a 6-point crown had been fashioned by cutting away the skin and scalp to form the design. More Folk sign. More indications of the savagery of their opponents. This brutality was far beyond anything I had ever witnessed.

From the colors I identified the dead soldiers as The Gaylords, a relatively sane group by clan standards who had been aligned with People. I also recognized their leader. His face had not been ravaged. Certainly no accident. His killers wanted his clan to know what had happened. There was a Duke Blue Devil cap on the leader's head, cocked right. Duke was one of the most common and powerful signs used by Folks. The placement of the hat facing right on a dead soldier who was the leader of a People clan was the ultimate insult to a People clan—disrespecting their dead.

A gruesome and graphic message, more powerful than anything I had ever seen, was being sent. Spit in your face. Piss on your grave. Fuck your mother. This was a call to battle.

As I viewed the carnage, pondering whether this was the beginning of the horror that Weasel had been predicting, Duke's growl snapped me back to reality. I saw him focused east and followed his point.

I don't know if it was the echoes of my shots at the dog pack or the simple need to view their handiwork one more time that brought them back. Never will. But two of them had returned, standing 150 meters distant, between two apartments, out of rifle shot, looking at me and Duke.

One was a normal size man, made to look small by his proximity to the giant, The Babe. I raised my field glasses for a closer look. The big man's face jumped into my line of sight. It was expressionless. It appeared that his eyes were looking directly into mine.

Involuntarily, I flinched. He was a mountain of flesh with dead eyes.

He bent his head and spoke to his companion. The other man was a gaunt, stringy haired, fiery eyed Latino. On his left cheek was a brightly colored depiction of a fanged, hooded snake. Green drops of venom dribbled down the man's cheek beneath the fangs. He was a Cobra, a member of The Insane Cobra Nation, as strong and powerful a clan as the Messengers. The Cobras were one of the two clans I regularly traded with. My other trading partner was a city clan, Folk affiliated, the Black Gangster Disciples.

The clothing on the upper bodies of both men was soaked in blood. Their hands and forearms were blooded from their wet work. They looked like butchers after a hard day.

The thin man listened to The Babe and suddenly broke away at a full run, disappearing behind an apartment building on his right, hoping to get behind me, I knew. I took one last look at The Babe. This was a face I was beginning to know well.

He seemed to sense I was studying him. Smiling fully, revealing stained, uneven teeth, he brought his right hand up to his lips and slowly, deliberately, licked each of his crimson stained fingers, sucking on them like undercooked sausages.

A message for me.

I put the glasses away and faced him, lifting my right hand into the air and extending my middle finger. I doubted he could see the gesture, but, as juvenile as it was, it felt good. I took of at a full run, heading north, away from our compound, Duke by my side.

• • • •

In fifteen minutes, we put two miles behind us, and I darted off the road into a copse of trees. I needed to catch my breath…and think.

A man and a dog. That was all The Babe had seen. He didn't know me. We never traded with The Messengers. Stayed away from their territory with a religious fervor.

The Cobra was a problem. I didn't recognize the other man, but it was possible he had seen me before. I frequently traded with the Cobras. Never had a problem. Had met with their leader several times.

The pipe had it that Cobras and Messengers didn't care for each other. But each clan was too big to mess with the other. Too pricey. This was a first—Cobra nestled up with the Messengers. Was it one man?—a change in the weather. Or a policy change?—a shift in climate.

But one major problem dominated my ruminations about the Cobras and Messengers…The victims of the massacre were The Gaylords—a People clan, butchered and carved with Folk's sign all over their bodies.

But The Babe and Satan's Messengers were not Folks.

Nor was The Insane Cobra Nation.

Both clans were left-sided, five-pointed, ever lovin' People. The Babe and his clan had maimed and mutilated thirteen men, all People Nation, all his own brotherhood, and had signed his savage work with the imprimatur of Folks. And at least one Cobra had joined the Messengers during the massacre.

My last thought before I headed back was of Weasel, of his warnings. This was awfully close to home.

CHAPTER SEVENTEEN

I came home 24 hours early, and according to Sarah, as pale as bleached out concrete. She ushered me into the kitchen and made some herbal tea concoction. It tasted like a combination of dandelion stems and garlic. Duke came up to me and nuzzled my hand, offering succor I supposed. I petted him and tried to slip him the tea. He jerked his head away and retreated. Sarah saw my ruse and raised her right eyebrow. Not good.

Weasel and Stevie joined us and I described the grisly hoax to them. Weasel suggested that we all be alert for any information concerning The Babe and his clan and The Cobras. Weasel and I both had sources on the outside among the clans as well as the indies, and it was through these sources that news of disturbing changes began to trickle in.

Over the next month, nothing alarming came in about The Insane Cobra Nation. For several years they had been focusing their efforts internally, establishing borders, strengthening their armaments, refurbishing living quarters. They appeared to have little interest in events outside their turf. Rumor had it that on the orders of their leader, a giant of a man named Roberto, a man I had spoken with many times, they had established a system for teaching their people to read and write.

There was no news of any communication between the Cobras and Satan's Messengers. Nor was there any word that Roberto had ordered his soldiers to be looking for a man and a dog traveling together. It was almost as if they didn't care about us or my knowledge of the events at the parking lot, even though one of their soldiers had been standing with The Babe.

The information that came back about Satan's Messengers indicated a clan in a state of flux. Unlike the Cobras, they were focusing much of their attention beyond their borders. The Babe was forming alliances with other People clans, using the slaughter of the Gaylords as the basis of his efforts to begin warring with nearby Folks affiliates. It was a war of vengeance. False vengeance, but it was an easy sell.

In the months following the college parking lot massacre, The Babe absorbed the remaining Gaylords into the Messengers and persuaded two nearby clans, the Latin Slashers and Westside Homeboys, to wear the red and black colors of The Messengers. A year ago the monstrosity that that led Satan's Messengers had been the leader of three hundred men, women and children. He was now the head man for a group of over five hundred—the largest organized military contingent since the collapse.

We learned they were buying weapons for the newly recruited Messenger soldiers. The guns and ammo were acquired through the sale of the new Messenger drug—Bad Boy—the concoction of battery acid, embalming fluid, LSD, speed, Viagra and probably PCP. The drug's reputation for longevity makes it the hottest pharmaceutical in clan society. The fact that it sometimes caused heart failure or initiated permanent psychotic states among its users was largely ignored. Many of its users reported it kept their cocks hard for twelve hours at a time. What's a little psychosis when compared to a twelve hour hard-on?

Some indies and clan soldiers who were willing to talk to us said that inside the Messenger compound they were quietly looking for a tall man and a gold colored dog, a big dog. Their activity was completely internal. They hadn't asked any other People clans for help with the search. Over the years, there were hundreds of indies and clan soldiers who had seen me and Duke. None of them knew where we lived.

For two months Duke and I were not allowed to scout. Sarah and Weasel let us hunt, but only west of our compound, never east, never in the direction of the city and suburbs. Weasel scouted east, once weekly. He always took Stevie, Sarah, or Duke. He taught them his craft. He taught Duke that we were all part of the same pack. Duke loved the pack. After six months of isolation, I began scouting east with Weasel.

When we were all together, we fortified the compound. We never saw a soul come within five miles of the compound and began to feel safe.

CHAPTER EIGHTEEN

JULY 2056

I liked some of Weasel's music. Some of George Jones was great. Emmylou Harris was a goddess. David Allen Coe definitely had the right attitude. Roger Miller, I could do without. Problem was, Weasel had been playing one of Miller's inane ditties just before Duke and I departed on our scouting mission and the damn song had stuck in my brain—48 hours later on our way back home.

"Dang me, dang me, oughta take a rope and hang me" kept on rolling through my head. It could have been worse, though. He had another favorite guy, Ray Stevens, who was even more obnoxious than Roger Miller.

The Divide Pinion 18 speed touring bike with three Orlieb panniers that could hold 20 pounds each rolled smoothly beneath me as I pedaled at a comfortable pace about nine miles out of Chicago, heading west and back home along Roosevelt Road. The bike had handlebar shift and was the most durable bike we found in our bike shop tour with Weasel in 2054.

Duke loped easily by my side, oblivious to the infrequent intrusions of other bikers on the road. He was wearing a red bandana and carrying light bullet proof saddle bags. I always seemed to get the right of way when Duke ran alongside the bike. We hadn't seen any road surfers, with their elaborate set ups which combined mini-surf boards on skate wheels with billowing nylon sails designed to catch the wind. They usually keep to the huge eight- or ten-lane old expressways where breezes are not deflected by buildings and there is more room to work up to the breakneck speeds they seek.

Bikers and road surfers use the abandoned super highways with enough frequency to keep several lanes relatively weed free, although the multitude of rusting vehicles make for an interesting obstacle course. The steep, circular concrete ramps that mark the confluence of two or more mega roads, are often sites of clan skate board competitions. And I have heard that north of the city at O'Hare airport there are well organized road surfing races—complete with a gambling operation and a food franchise run by a northside Folks clan.

It is rare that I see someone riding a horse. To the west of us there are several wild herds, but no one—including ourselves—has attempted to domesticate the beautiful animals. The maintenance of a bike is much less demanding than that of a horse. But of course, you can't eat a bike if things get rough. It occurred to me then that the four of us should discuss taming horses for transportation and hauling.

Despite decades of the ravages of fire and never-ending rust and weeds and trees, the buildings and roads are relatively undamaged. In my reading I discovered that the roads, bridges and finite, man-made structures that supported civilization and technology in the 20th and 21st had been called the "infrastructure." And apparently in America it had been crumbling.

But in the past three decades, the infrastructure that had worried 20th cen politicos has received no wear and tear from cars and trucks; and no acid rain or toxic fumes from exhausts. Plants, weather, and rust are the only enemies of these roads, bridges, and buildings. According to the vids, the pyramids are still standing after thousands of years, so I figure it is safe for Duke and me to travel on the highways...at least for a few more decades.

When prepping our missions, the four of us scout likely locations of valued supplies and equipment in the yellow pages and old newspaper ads—warehouses, grocery stores, drug stores, manufacturing facilities, computer stores—and then target ten or twenty good prospects within a mile radius on the map. Most of the time the sites have already been ransacked by local clans, but Chicago and suburbs is a big place with a small population so there is plenty to go around if you are persistent.

On this trip I investigated nineteen targeted sites and found usable items in three of them. But what I found along the way was usually more interesting than the primary objectives. The journey itself was always a source of discovery.

Since I had stumbled upon the massacre in the parking lot, we had been in a frenzy of new construction and modification of our compound. Relations were getting very spooky among the clans and we were determined to be as ready if someone came calling. Discovery, we felt, was inevitable. Only the fact that the Messengers were too busy battling other clans and locating weapons and food sources for their new members had spared us. The Babe still wanted Duke and me, but matters of state kept him from mounting a systematic search.

Maybe, Sarah wished, eventually The Babe would lose interest. Weasel raised his eyebrows and tsked, the professor admonishing an errant student.

The main focus of my trip was the restocking of construction materials—sealed boxes of nails, powered drills and and screw drivers with new bits, wood screws, carriage bolts. Our latest concentration had been in hiding all traces of the walls and strengthening the razor-topped barbed wire, grape vines and a raspberry patch barrier that stood between enemies and the house.

I clearly recalled a years old conversation—Sarah, Weasel and I, inspecting the compound's defenses. When we had finished the outer perimeter, Weasel had leaned up against the wall and thumped his knuckles on it a few times.

"They got this new thing out now," he said.

"Yeah," I said. "What's that?"

"It's called fire," he said. "Been known to demolish things like walls."

"Well, shit," I replied, frustrated by the fact that Sarah and I had never figured out that we should have worried about fire, "they were plumb out of structural steel when me and Sarah built this thing. Taking, I might add, six months of our lives at hard labor."

"Gonna take much less time to bring it down," Weasel replied.

As I prepared to sleep, my thoughts turned not to house and hearth, but bunkers, booby traps, and saturation fire zones. I wasn't sure, but I knew that if a couple hundred screaming Messengers pumped up on Bad Boy or Slammer attacked the compound, we would need all the extra protection we could muster. Each of us could only fire one assault rifle at a time. And Duke still hadn't figured out modern warfare. He remained an old fashioned tooth and claw guy.

I found an innocuous vacuum repair store in a strip mall in Addison for the night. My last thought as I drifted into sleep was that getting the hell out seemed the better alternative than fighting.

• • • •

The next morning Duke and I continued to scout, walking the streets, careful of whose turf we ventured across, looking for nothing in particular, open to anything that could catch my eye. That was how I stumbled onto a store in a little high end strip mall called *I Spy, You Spy*. Weapons and security systems came into mind, and I walked through the doorless entrance hoping to get lucky.

Beneath the dust and litter, the broken cases and faded paint, pitted and peeling chrome, I saw it had been a boutiquey little joint, lots of greys and blacks and whites, a high tech little shop full of eavesdropping devices and home and auto security systems. One stop shopping for New Millennials who wanted to eavesdrop on their lovers and friends.

On the floor behind the cash register, where it had probably fallen from a wall display, I found the little treasure—PRIVCOM 2023. The tag line on the box called it "the ultimate in covert communication." It also informed me it was the first time this "military and police communication system was available to the general public". The bantam box, half the size of a brick, light as a sparrow, was priced at $1999.95. Grabbed my attention. We didn't use money, but I knew the item was pricey.

Inside the box was a crystal stud earring, "adaptable to pierced or cuff styles" said the instructions. It was about the size of a half carat diamond. Also inside the box was a dozen finger nail size adhesive skin patches (derms) in different skin tones, three wafers half the size of a penny and a tiny chip with two little hair thin wires protruding from one corner.

As I read the instructions, I discovered the earring was a receiver, the circuitry embedded in the crystal and 18k gold setting. Cuff style, it fit over the outer ear, lipping into the big indentation that surrounded the ear canal. If used as a pierced earring, it had to be on the lobe or near the lobe.

The little chip with the two minuscule antennae was a wireless microphone, which fit one of the small wafers, which were paper thin lithium ion batteries. The mike and the battery then slipped into a little pocket on the derm, which in turn was placed on the throat, over the voice box. If you matched skin color, the derm was nearly invisible.

The finished product, when packaged with one or more identical systems attached to fellow clandestine friends, lovers, or co-conspirators, was a hands-free wireless communication system. Same principle as the walkie-talkies still used by some of the clans or the headsets used by security forces in the 21st. Just smaller.

Only two problems. Finding some more and getting the batteries charged. In the back room I found seven more boxes. I owed I Spy, You Spy $16,000.00. Weasel would solve the battery dilemma. This, I said to myself, was a good two days' work.

• • • •

New day, home in our sites, Duke and I had a typical field breakfast, biscuits, raspberry jelly, venison jerky, and cider. I stuffed about fifty pounds of my loot into the Orleib panniers, mostly tools and nails, plus the eight comm sets, and strapped them on the rear and front bike mounts. The weapons were not stored. The Glock 17L went in its holster across my chest and an Uzi 9mm machine pistol with two twenty round clips crossed the Glock, so I had a weapon available on each side. I covered them both with a light army camo jacket. After checking the tires on the 18 speed, I headed home, moving at a leisurely pace west on Roosevelt Road, Duke cruising by my right side.

As we moved into a town called Lombard, we entered a zone which was essentially about fifteen km of strip malls. On both sides of Roosevelt Road there were fast food places and countless consumer stores catering to every possible human and machine necessity—office equipment, beauty houses, drugstores, restaurants, auto repair, stereo and vid sales, medical centers, used cars, furniture. They had all been looted, burned or trashed. Most of the bare walls wore the signs of the clan who claimed that territory.

At the precise moment that I realized that I made an enormous blunder, it was too late to correct it. It had over two months since The Babe and Satan's Messengers slaughtered the Gaylords in the college parking lot. All had been quiet since then. No bad news. No news at all.

That was the mistake. I had allowed the Cobras to slip from my mind, replaced by the Messengers as a point of concern. The Babe was standing right next to a Cobra when the parking lot massacre was over.

Thinking of how Stevie and Weasel would react to the treasure I carried, looking forward to seeing Sarah, sleeping in our own bed, making love, I had unknowingly passed a border about a mile back.

We were in Insane Cobra Nation territory...and I was in a day-dream, a space cadet not ready for any sort of trouble, thinking about sex, visualizing Sarah, when Duke growled a warning, snapping me out of my fantasy.

Up ahead about 200 meters I could see a group of ten men spread across the road, standing in front of their bikes.

"Easy, boy," I said, slipping off the bike and walking it. If I turned and ran, exposing my back, they would run us down. Had they been on foot, we would have bolted. I chose to face them, hoping to talk my way out.

As we got closer, I could make out their green and black colors. Cobras. I did not see distinctive 280 pound form of their leader, Roberto. He was a huge man, built like a block of granite with a head on top. Even his cranium was square. But he was always quick to smile; and every time we had met, the two of us had spent at least an hour talking, trading stories and stockpiling bits of intelligence about what was happening with the clans.

All of those friendly meets had been before I had witnessed a Cobra in bloody consort with the Messengers at the college parking lot. There had been no communication between us since then. I didn't know if it was good news or bad news that Roberto was absent.

I scanned right and left, glanced quickly behind us. It was all clear. The danger was in front. Too close to outrun bullets, I kept on walking, hoping I appeared unalarmed. Showing fear or hostility would encourage their aggression.

"I'm sorry, boy," I told Duke. "I fucked up. We get out of this and I owe you one." He looked up at me, and I scratched his ear.

I stopped within 6 meters of them, laid the bike on the road and put Duke on heel. He would remain still unless someone made an aggressive move toward me. He did not growl. He did not snarl. He just sat on his haunches and observed.

He was trying to look as harmless as 120 pounds of golden lab could. I didn't see him passing as a toy poodle, but the group of Cobras were not focusing on him.

When we stopped, the ten Cobras spread out in a semi-circle around us. Not a welcoming gesture. They kept the six meters distance between us. Their posturing disturbed me.

By my left side, I could feel Duke shift his weight. He transitioned into high alert. I trusted his instincts, shared his apprehension. I could feel my heartbeat increasing and tried to keep the adrenalin down by breathing slowly and remaining focused. I knew Duke's head was slowly traversing a 180 degree arc defined by the ten clan members. I wasn't worried about his breaking position. He would not move unless I signaled or the Cobras attacked.

The man in the middle was the best dressed and most heavily armed. He had an old short barrel .38 special in his belt right in the center and an army issue .45 holstered on his right side, gun slinger fashion. The flap was still buttoned, telling me he felt he was in control. Duke was on my left, so I shifted very slightly to my right so he could have a better line at the leader.

I could see in his eyes that he recognized me. It made him very happy. I kept my face blank, not wanting him to know that I, too, remembered our last encounter, recognized the bright cobra tattoo on his left cheek, recalled how it had filled the lenses of my binoculars as he stood with The Babe watching Duke and me survey the the remnants of their bloody handiwork.

I directed my comments to him. At six feet tall, he was shorter than I and a very thin, pallid man. His hair was jet black, shoulder length and incredibly dirty. I wanted to ask him if there was a water shortage.

A nasty herpes sore adorned his thin, cracked lips. His eyes shined with a drug induced intensity, probably crystal meth or wicki, hopefully not Slammer or Bad Boy. I guessed him to be about 22 years of age. He looked 40, but most clan soldiers didn't live that long.

When I last saw him in the parking lot with The Babe, the sun had just risen over a blood washed battlefield. His face was sharply focused in my binoculars, eyes gleaming with rage, clothes soaked in blood, lips twisted in a maniacal smile that distorted the tattoo of a hooded cobra on his right cheek. I would never forget his face.

We were in deep shit.

"I am honored to be in the territory of the Insane Cobra Nation," I said in my most obsequious tone. "Where's Roberto? I would like to pay my respects to him."

The man in the middle smiled. There was no warmth and very few teeth in it. "Roberto takes care of business elsewhere," he said. "My soldiers and I patrol this area. I'm the man here. You talk with me. My name is Felipe, but they call me 'The Edge.' You will call me 'sir'." He tapped a huge Bowie knife strapped to his belt and smiled again, a walking monument to all the dead dentists.

I bowed from the waist, keeping contact with his eyes, a difficult task as they danced in and out of reality. "Perhaps you could escort me to Roberto. I have some information for him," I lied to his greasiness. The only thing I had for Roberto was a profound wish that he could get us out of this situation.

"Tell me your tales," he said. "I will pass it on if it seems important."

Having no information to share and doubting the Edge would remember a word I said even if I did, I improvised. "I feel it would be disrespectful to Roberto's position if I do not tell him directly."

Chain of command was big in the Cobras. Maybe he would pass me through out of respect for his leader, send some men back to his headquarters, give us a chance to escape.

The Edge graced me with another picket fence smile. This time a few facial tics dotted his face, a sign he was mixing his drugs and was a few minutes beyond the need for a tune up.

"I know you, McCall. You talk with many clans," he said.

They had my name. I hoped that was all. McCall and a dog.

Felipe continued. "We don't like that any more. The Cobras aren't interested in a 'peaceful relationship' with you." He spat a hocker toward my feet, as if the concept of harmony left a bitter taste in his mouth. "We don't like you in our territory any more. This is for People only." He made a grand sweeping gesture, as if he personally ruled over vast regions of wealth, rather than a minuscule corner of the Cobra Nation, a border outpost, a collection of burned out bagel stores and beauty shops and less than a dozen freaked out punks with a bad color sense.

Then he spoke the words that that triggered a profound appreciation of home and hearth in my mind. "I speak for the Cobras and our new allies, Satan's Messengers. You will no longer walk our territories."

Bribery was my best shot. "I've got two O Z of dynamite weed," I said, deliberately avoiding referring to him as 'Sir'. "I offer this as a token of my high esteem to both you and Roberto. But I can also give you valuable information on the location of food and weapons, and when I return, I will bring items of value that will show my respect. I can bring you more weed. One hit stuff. It'll blow you away. My gift to you when I come back."

His smile returned and so did the tics, making it appear as his mouth was seeking a new home. The thought occurred to me that his clan name, 'The Edge', referred to the cliff that his sanity was teetering over.

"Listen to me, McCall," he replied. "We don't want your gifts; we don't want your tolls; and we don't want no fucking talk out of your mouth. We want you gone." He dropped his eyes to my bike and backpack. "I think you are mistaken about having things to give us. I see many gifts that you can honor me with now. There is no need to wait. That bike is primo. Your weapons are very valuable. So are your shoes and clothing. Those Air Jordan's you got on, McCall? We haven't seen those for years around here."

"Why settle for one pair?" I offered, lying through my teeth. "I can bring you back enough Jordan's for you to form your own basketball league."

"I think the one pair and your clothes and weapons will be enough for us today," Felipe responded, his eyes greedily appraising my gear. "We will also take your dog. The women have nothing to cook for dinner tonight and all this work makes us very hungry." A chorus of twitters followed his attempt at humor.

I could see in his eyes that we were already dead. He was mentally tallying the value of my cache, calculating what he could get in trade for the shoes, bike, and weapons. One of Weasel's maxims popped into my head. Sometimes you do what they expect, make 'em comfortable. Then you look real careful for the moment to do the unexpected. It's always there. Finding it is the key—the exact right moment when you can surprise 'em.

The moment was upon us. I unbuttoned my jacket.

"How do you plan to cook the dog?" I asked, looking him straight in the eyes. "He's very muscular and sure to be very tough. Over a spit? Stir fry? Maybe a nice casserole with wild rice. Are your women good cooks? I'll bet they are. I've heard ugly women make good cooks. Hey, I know what... you can pan fry him. You can use the grease in your hair to keep the meat from sticking to the pans."

The Cobras froze. Their semicircle a statuary. The Edge's face reddened and began to tremble, as if all the tics decided to jump in unison. A little line of spittle snaked across his herpes sore and ran down his chin. I dropped my hands and Duke focused on my left one.

The time was very close.

I took a step backwards, hoping the group would bring themselves closer to us. They obliged by tightening the semi-circle by two steps. One back for me; two forward for them. They were a meter closer now. Felipe looked to the man on his left and, trying to control his rage, managed a guttural croak: "Shoot the fucking dog, Sean."

Duke was trained by both voice and hand signals. When given the sign to attack, he always went for the kill. Only at the "Duke, Stop" command from someone in our family would he break off the attack.

We had several hand signals. Three fingers down indicated he should kill the last person who spoke. Four fingers meant go for the first person who moved.

I signed three fingers and Duke flashed across the distance between him and The Edge in a single leap and found the soldier's throat, shaking his head as his teeth sunk into the leader's neck. Bright arterial blood arced from the Cobra leader's throat, splattering the men on each flank as Duke jerked his head from side to side, snarling deep in his throat, the classic predator kill.

Before Duke had reached The Edge, I took a step toward Sean, who was struggling to pull a pistol from his waist band. My second step was a kick to his nuts. As Sean doubled over, I pivoted to his right side, the Glock already in my right hand. I continued the spin until I was directly behind him, grabbed his collar with my left hand and wrapped my gun hand around his neck and sat down, pulling him on top of me. I rolled to my left putting two shots into his side. His body jumped with their impact, then went still. Then I rolled back and sat up, using his body as a shield.

Of the remaining eight Cobras, three were running, two were standing completely still, their mouths agape, and the remaining were in various states of weapon readiness. Shots were fired and I felt the thuds as they smacked into Sean's inert body. Errant shots kicked up slivers of concrete on either side of me.

I had fifteen rounds left and quickly used three of them on the Cobras with smoking pistols in their hands. I had to fire without a good set and from an awkward position, so they weren't all kill shots. I put two more into each of the shooters. The six bullets that remained were used on the two unfortunates who were never able to get in gear. They died looking dumb. They should have run.

My ears rang from the exposure to multiple close range gun shots. Adrenaline coursed through my veins. I felt like I could have jumped over a building.

I looked over at Duke. He was finished with Felipe and stood next to me, muzzle dripping blood, as if to say, who's next? Seven were down, scattered around us, unmoving. Behind me the remaining three ran toward the faded yellow double arches of a hamburger restaurant, their bodies becoming smaller as they increased the distance between us. I dismissed the notion of sending Duke to bring them down. They were still armed.

I pushed Sean's lifeless body away and reloaded before I stood up, looking for signs of life among the seven Cobras whose blood stained Roosevelt Road. I quickly popped the clips from their weapons and searched their pockets for more ammo, finding several spare clips. The leader's pockets and several of his men's yielded bags of grey powder, which I also kept. The drugs could be useful in barter. I then smashed all of their weapons on the concrete.

There was no more work to do. We needed to get the hell out of there. We had just killed seven soldiers of one of the most powerful clans in the entire city area. Not a good start to the day.

I said to myself, next time I'll take North Avenue. Next time I won't daydream.

It wasn't until I saw Weasel several hours later that I realized that the Roger Miller song had finally been exorcised. That very thought was the catalyst for its return.

CHAPTER NINETEEN

"Let me get this straight," Weasel said.

We were all in the kitchen. The homecoming had gone fine until I told them about the Cobras on Roosevelt Road.

"You and Duke just killed seven members in good standing of the Insane Cobra Nation and let three survivors get away."

"Right," I said. "And we are unscathed. Thanks so much for asking."

"That would be the same Insane Cobra Nation that's so mean even Satan's Messengers won't mess with them?"

"Correct."

He ripped open his shirt, popping buttons all over the table, and tossed me a butter knife.

"Right here," he said, pulling his shirt aside with two hands to expose his bony chest. "Go ahead. Plunge it in."

I smiled at him. "Next time Duke and I go straight to Sarah. She knows how to welcome weary men home."

She was on her hands and knees, cleaning off Duke's muzzle, which was still stained red. She was scooping water out of a bowl with her hands and rubbing it all over his jaws.

Looking up at me, she said, "Don't mind Weasel, hon. He's a heathen. He's just as happy to see you two as Stevie and I are. He has a slight problem expressing. It must have been horrible, what you went through."

"Tell you the truth, Sarah," I replied, "once it became clear that they were going to kill us, I went into an automatic mode. Used what all of us know about survival plus a few of Weasel's lessons and just reacted. It couldn't have lasted more than twenty seconds."

"Lasted any longer than that," Weasel said, "and you might not be here to tell us about it. You did what they didn't expect. Good job, Mac."

Praise from the master. A few years ago, before Weasel had joined us, I wouldn't have been able to come home, back to Sarah, to tell the story. They would have taken us both down.

"Thanks," I told him. "Not for the words. But for the years of teaching. It helped."

"Don't give me too much credit, Mac," he said. "It was you and Duke out there. Not me."

"This presents a new problem for us," I said.

"No shit, Einstein," Weasel responded.

I continued, ignoring his sarcasm. For a couple of months, things had been quiet. If it hadn't been for our sources telling us the Messengers were looking for me and Duke, it might have seemed that both clans had forgotten about us. "We haven't heard a peep out of the Cobras. It's almost like Roberto hasn't even given us any thought. I'm afraid I just woke him up."

"Down in southern Illinois, when I was a kid, we lived in the woods. Place is damn near all woods, come to think of it. Spring and summer we had thunderstorms and tornadoes the likes of which you never see up here."

I could feel a Weasel life lesson coming on. They usually started with a little story.

"I remember sittin' on the edge of a huge meadow, me and my brother and sister, about twenty or thirty woodchucks out in the middle, munchin' away on the grass. Some of 'em standing up and craning their heads to keep a look out for predators. Like little furry people with their hands at their sides and noses in the air. Across the meadow, several miles southwest, the sky turned black. We had beautiful afternoon sun in the meadow, but I could see the storm coming our way.

"All of a sudden, all those woodchucks bolted, scattered to all points of the compass. In five seconds they had all disappeared. All of 'em down their holes."

Stevie and I sat quietly at the table, listening attentively, waiting for the punch. While she groomed Duke, Sarah listened attentively.

"Me and the kids stayed and watched the storm come in. Took about half an hour for it to reach us. Damndest storm I ever saw, short of a tornado. Got so bad we had to find a fallen tree to hide under, keep us safe from the wind and hail. Day turned to night and then we got blasted with lightning bolts that almost broke our eardrums." He laughed as the recollection triggered fond memories. "Soaked to the bone, wind howling like a thousand cougars in our ears, lightning so close you couldn't even call its sound thunder. It was like huge explosions all around us. Two of them squeezed up to me so tight I had little finger marks in my skin hours later. Never cried once, just held on tight. Must have thought I could protect 'em. Guess maybe I did that time."

He got up from the table and began gathering up the equipment he always took with him on excursions. No lessons. No moral. No punchline.

"Let's go, boy," he said to Stevie. "Daylight's burning. Sun's not gonna wait for us."

Stevie jumped up, collecting guns and ammo, hiking shoes, body armor, his backpack.

"Where we going, Weasel?" he asked.

Not why or how long will we be gone or what's our purpose. Just where. The kid had faith. We all did.

"Storm's a coming, son," Weasel said, shouldering his HK 81. "We gotta find ourselves another hole."

"Why?" Stevie asked. "We been working our asses off on this place. We're not going to leave it, are we?"

"Hell no," he said. "And we'll keep working on it, too. But we need to give those Cobras some respect. They didn't get to be number one by being nice guys. And they're all gonna be after Mac now that he's gone and iced seven of their men. We're just looking for a place to weather the storm if it gets too strong."

"What about Satan's Messengers?" Stevie asked. "I thought they were number one."

"In terms of nastiness," Weasel said, "yes. But in terms of effectiveness and organization, gotta go with Insane Cobra Nation. Roberto's got leadership chops."

"Maybe we need a plan," I suggested.

"Got somethin' in mind," Weasel said. "Me and Stevie got a project."

CHAPTER TWENTY

I had been summoned. It meant we would get some data, hard, reliable info. I doubted it would be good news. Best source we had was Merlin—so named because he looks like a young version of King Arthur's advisor and acts weird enough to be a wizard. Duke and I made a night trip to the city to find him.

Merlin is rumor central of our world. He knows everything that's going on and is happy to share—for a price. A snitch, yes, but to us more than that. I'm not sure how much they paid informants in the in the vids, but whatever it was, Merlin is much more expensive. But he's worth it, even though his news is frequently as bad as his looks. Pale, gone to seed, emaciated, and hygienically challenged. But his eyes match. They shine with intelligence. He is always smiling, and I don't hold it against him that his smile is chemically enhanced. He is our biggest marijuana customer. And he pays his monthly bill with information.

I have never seen Merlin straight. I once suggested to him that going weedless occasionally might be a wondrous adventure. He said he tried it for ten years and it wasn't all that it was cracked up to be. One of us, either Weasel, Sarah or me, delivers a half pound to him every month. He uses half for trade, protection, and tolls and smokes the rest.

Sarah calculated that to smoke a quarter pound a month, Merlin would have to put away at least five joints a day, probably more. That seems about right to me from what I have observed when I was in his presence. The pot makes Merlin's world more tolerable. Since he can't change the ugliness of our society, he'll change the way it comes into his brain.

• • • •

First time I met Merlin was in the city, summer of '54. There are two incredible life size statues of horse-mounted Native Americans that stand sentinel over a highway about a half mile from Lake Michigan, where the business section of the city begins. There were some apartments in early 21st, some condos, but mostly stores, the still magnificent Hilton Towers, and office buildings marching north on a street called Michigan Avenue.

The statues are iconic pieces of art. They stand just a few blocks south of the Art Institute. They face each other across six lanes of road, each warrior on a horse, each man preparing to launch his weapon. Time and weather have done little to dilute the impact of what seems the warriors' last stand. Although they are facing each other, I feel they are allies.

East of the statues is Buckingham fountain, a once magnificent centerpiece to the Chicago's lakefront. The fountain is now a mossy, algae filled duck pond.

First time I met Merlin, back in '54, I was about thirty miles from home. The 18-speed touring bike was my transport and I was coming into the area called "The Loop," riding straight East down a highway named after a 50's President called Eisenhower. Duke loped effortlessly by the front wheel as we passed under a huge structural steel frame that held trains above the road, heading toward Michigan Avenue, where I hoped to scrounge computer printer cartridges and parts from the huge office buildings.

A block ahead of us, in the middle of the road directly between the statues of the horse riding warriors, were four men, three clan members and a skinny little guy standing beside a 27-speed racing bike. I recognized one of the four, James, a steely-eyed black kid who was a lieutenant with The Black Gangster Disciples.

Right side jewelry and bicep and forearm tattoos of blood red hearts with wings on the sides and six-pointed stars and crowns identified them as a Folks affiliated clan. The Black Gangster Disciples were a hard working clan, men and women who harvested the lake, farmed Grant Park, and controlled part of the area I wanted to explore.

I never searched for local clan leaders to pay a toll. They generally found me. When I came across them I always began the necessary business transaction, namely identifying myself and paying the toll and agreeing to share information and salvage if they wanted part of anything I had located. Most of the clans were comfortable with this business arrangement. When we ran across a clan that wouldn't cooperate, Weasel or I made a night mission and took what we needed.

As Duke and I approached the foursome, I could see in their body positioning and gestures that the discussion was not friendly. The situation did not look dangerous yet, but certainly unpleasant for the skinny guy with the bike. Weapons shouldered and holstered, I nodded a greeting to James as I dismounted the bike and scrutinized his two friends, who were more alarmed by Duke's presence than mine. I smiled and told them the dog was OK, then put Duke on parade rest.

"Don't be believin' none of that shit, boys," James said to his friends. "I seen that dog take a Double Deuce's arm half off last year. Just don't be makin' no sudden moves at my man, McCall, here, or else that dog be on your ass quicker than a fat boy on grits."

James turned to me. "How you doin', Mac? Comin' down to the city to pick up some more useless shit, man?"

Paper and computer parts were not valuable commodities in clan circles, and James was always glad to see me so he could get his toll and let me take from his turf what he considered to be garbage. The Black Gangster Disciples usually went for ammunition or herb for their tolls and I was carrying enough of each to pay my way.

"What's up, James?" I nodded to his soldiers. "New recruits?"

"Angel, Wind Chill," he said to his buddies, "this white bread here is McCall. If he pays, let him play. The man never gave me any shit. And he always pays with high grade stuff."

Angel was short, dark haired. Intelligent eyes looked me over from a round Hispanic face. You don't have to be black to be a Black G. D. His brown eyes shifted to Duke. "What about the dog, man? I don't like dogs."

I gave Duke the command to lie down. "He won't hurt you, Angel," I said, "unless you go after me or I give him the attack command."

"How you do that? Whadda you say to him?" Wind Chill spoke now. The deep baritone voice emanated from a tall muscular young black man I judged to be sixteen or seventeen.

"Can't tell you," I said. "If I say the word, He will take one of you down, and he knows only one way—balls out. He'll rip you up."

"What if someone else says the word?" asked Wind Chill. "Will the dog still attack?" He laughed, a deep bass chuckle. "Could I get him to take Angel's arm off?"

"Hey, man," said Angel. "Maybe I learn the word and get that mutt to chew your unit off. Whachew think of that, man?" They were both smiling.

"Wouldn't work." I said. "Duke only responds to me and and his pack members. You could say the word all day long and he'd just sit and look at you."

"How many pack members you got?" asked Wind Chill.

"Not so many that the dog gets confused. Good friends are hard to come by."

"I hear that," said James. "And it ain't gettin' any easier. But listen McCall, we got business here with this skinny little dude who's givin' me shit about payin' his toll. He's one of your people. Maybe you can talk some sense to him."

I wasn't sure if James was referring to the fact that both Merlin and I were white…or indies. Whichever the case, the Disciple leader figured I could talk sense to the skinny guy who wouldn't pay. I wasn't so sure, but I was willing to try.

The four of us shifted our attention to the little man with the bike. He shuffled his feet nervously under our scrutiny. A head band cut from a flannel shirt held long blonde hair off of his face, which was decorated with sparse goatee and mustache, both in need of growth hormone. His eyes were hidden behind granny sunglasses. A dago tee covered his scrawny frame and was tucked into a pair of jeans covered with patches of various fading shades of denim, many of them displaying slogans or symbols. Peace symbols and marijuana leaves predominated, and Iggy Pop, Sex Pistols and CSNY were represented on the front legs along with 'Clean Gene' and 'Timothy Leary' and 'Remember The Chicago 7' and 'Dump Trump' patches. Around his neck were lightweight headphones with a cord dangling to the i-pod on his belt.

"Listen, man," he said to me. "You look like a pretty sensible dude. I mean communicating with that dog and all. You've got sensitivity to other peoples' vibes. I can see that. Talkin' to a dog, man. That is so cool."

James interrupted the skinny guy, pointing out the basics of the conflict. "Mac, this little ferret goes by the name Merlin, and he thinks he can talk me out of payin' his toll. He's always paid before and he's short now, so he's puttin' out some shit about bein' brothers together over the undersoul."

"That's 'under the *oversoul*, butt breath," retorted Merlin. "It's the Emersonian concept of all living things joining a mass consciousness at the time life leaves their bodies."

"Shut the fuck up, you crazy mother fucker," said James. "Listen, McCall, I don't wanna hurt this guy. He never gave me any trouble before. But I got a territory to protect. I got no pity for a man not having his toll. When you travel, you gotta be prepared." He pointed his finger at Merlin's chest. "I'll tell you exactly what happened. This crazy stoner smoked his toll. He's higher than a fuckin' falcon right now. He always pays us a quarter and now he got none, but his eyes are so fuckin' glazed over, looks like he's got cataracts. Had to put his shades on cuz he can't take the light."

"Dude, you are totally correct about the toll, Dude," Merlin responded. "But please listen to me. What I'm saying is we should be working together in this shitty city. Hey, wow, man, a rhyme. Poetry from the subconscious. That's what happened last night, man. There was a full moon. I was inspired with heavy thoughts about our predicament. Man destroys self. Earth bitch smacks humanity. Very depressing, dude. Slapped DARKSIDE OF THE MOON in the i-pod and then I just had to smoke some gange to expand the thought process. Guess I smoked a little more than I planned. Top notch Indica, Dude. Super mellow. So I'm a little short. I'll pay you next time through. I promise."

"I can't cut you no slack, Merlin. Besides, there wasn't any full moon last night. Lyin' to me ain't a good choice, man. This is business. I can't be teachin' my boys about runnin' a territory by lettin' people talk me out of tolls. You can leave your bike or that backpack as deposit and when you pay the toll, I'll give it back to you. Final offer. Otherwise I have Wind Chill kick your skanky little ass for about five minutes."

Merlin looked to the sky and raised his arms up, as if in appeal to a deity. He slowly turned a complete circle and stopped, lowering his arms to shoulder length and pointing to the magnificent statues that towered above us.

"You know what those are, James?" Merlin asked the clan leader.

"Indians and horses," responded an impatient James.

"No, James. They are not just Indians and horses. You ever seen an Indian? A real live one?"

James shook his head side to side.

"Neither have I. And that's my point about us working together. This whole fucking country used to belong to the Indians like three hundred years ago. It was beautiful unspoiled land. Ocean to ocean of forests and prairies and mountains and desert, untouched by any stain. Then the white man came and turned the whole thing to shit. Bad karma, man. The white man has always had bad karma. Now we got a land blighted by roads and cities and rusting vehicles and useless bridges and dams, and populated mostly by skeletons..."

Merlin ran out of breath. Noisily sucking in a giant lungful of air, he continued, "...and not one fucking Indian to be found. How's that shit grab you?"

"The way it grabs me," said James, "is that you are a fucking white man and you are giving me a whole bunch of shit."

"But I'm not like those other white men, James. I don't want to control you and make you submit. I just want us to live in harmony, man. Work together. Build something beautiful."

"Only thing I see," said James, "is a slick talkin' white mother fucker tryin' to talk his way out of his toll. You're pissin' me off, Merlin."

James walked over to me and pulled me aside for a conference out of earshot from the other three.

"Listen, McCall," he appealed. "I usually like Merlin. He's a harmless little fuck and good for a laugh. He also knows his shit. And is a top rate scavenger. But he's makin' me look bad in front of my boys with all that bullshit. We ain't in the 20th no more. He better get back to the real world or I'm gonna have to hurt him."

I looked over to Merlin and saw him engaged in earnest conversation with Angel and Wind Chill. They looked at him as if he were speaking Japanese. He was making no headway. The philosopher could not break through to the soldiers.

And the officer, James, speaking to me now of his reluctance to resort to force with Merlin, was also immune to the young thinker's message. In James' case, I think reality had too strong a hold on him. His world was too dangerous, too cruel, too full of the basic survival rituals for his mind to have time for the luxury of strange and challenging thoughts—ideas that could shake the way he perceived his environment and his clan's mores.

I understood James' need to force Merlin to comply with the rules that had been set down by the clans. He had responsibilities to his people. He was protecting turf. Without secured turf, his clan couldn't survive. It was his duty to protect it. His personal feelings about the likability and harmlessness of Merlin had to be cast aside.

I also identified with James' reluctance to sanction Merlin. He was indeed an interesting little fellow, and I think James realized that having a philosopher of sorts, albeit a perpetually stoned one, in our midst added some small dignity to our lives. Merlin could definitely be a pain in the ass, but the little man could make all of us look at things from a different perspective.

So as James and I talked, I made him an offer that allowed him to save face and remain within the guidelines of his duties to the Black G. D.'s. He happily accepted.

We both walked the few steps back to the three others and I interrupted Merlin as he was explaining to the awestruck soldiers the concept of synergy as it applied to the responsibilities of human beings on the planet.

"Listen, Merlin," I said. "Here's what is going to happen. I'm paying your toll. I have enough herb in my possession to pay a quarter for each of us. This is acceptable to James. You pay me back or that dog you think is so cool is gonna chew your leg off."

Merlin began walking in a circle and gesturing with his hands and arms as he spoke. "Dude, that is so excellent. I can't thank you enough. This is like some kind of sign, you know. I smoke my last doob so I can commune with the beauty of nature and the Floyd vibes, and what happens? I meet The Good Samaritan, and Mr. hard-ass Nazi boy James shows a little humanity. James, man, you see what I'm saying? Can't you feel the vibe? See the aura? Mother Nature is saying to us, 'Work together. Be brothers. Seek harmony.'"

He walked over to James and put his arm around the leader's shoulders, reaching up a good six inches to do so. "James, man, thanks a lot. You just expanded your whole world. Your mind is opening up to a whole new scene. Can you feel it?"

Merlin removed his arm and stood face to face with James, standing up on the tips of his toes. "Oh yeah. I see it in your eyes. There's a glimmer of a new consciousness in there. I can see a metamorphosis for you, James."

James looked down at him and smiled.

"Metamorph your scrawny butt outa here, white bread. I'm tired of your mumbo jumbo."

He raised his hand and picked the two foil wrapped quarters I tossed him out of the air.

"See you next trip, Mac. Good hunting. Take this crazy fucker with you. He knows this territory better than anybody. Lives somewhere around here. Nobody's ever been able to find his crib, though."

The three of them turned and left, heading toward the lake. Merlin hurled a final rejoinder at their departing backs.

"Only the pure of heart will ever find my dwelling, James. Keep working on it. You may get there someday."

He turned to me, displaying a huge grin.

"Dude, break out some more of that weed. Let's party."

We did.

• • • •

I followed Merlin, that first day we met, down the entrance ramp cars used pre-collapse to gain access to a gigantic underground garage that stretched beneath Michigan Avenue and a wooded area called Grant Park. We were safe now. Many of the clans had a strict code of honor. If a toll was paid, the Black Gangster Disciples guaranteed us free passage and would even defend (or avenge) Merlin and me if anyone messed with us while you were under their protection.

Merlin and I stayed on the first level, close enough to the entrance that sunlight filtered its way in so that we could see each other while we talked and smoked. Duke and I checked the territory first, scanning for fifty meters into the garage to ensure we were alone. Our only companions were the abandoned cars that dotted the cracked concrete floor. The garage was damp and the vehicles had lost their battle with mildew and rust, more lonely reminders of humanity's lost prosperity. We sat on the bed of a rusted pickup and filled a bowl.

We spent two or three hours together talking high talk and laughing about things that seemed absolutely hilarious. I felt a kinship with Merlin, and I think it was because he reminded me more than a little bit of Stevie. Merlin was only four or five years older than Stevie. Stevie was built similarly to Merlin, each of them thin as a mangy dog, Stevie several inches taller.

But most of all, they were both survivors. Merlin's self-imposed isolation was remarkably similar to the choice Stevie had made. I asked him about his preference for solitary existence.

"I'll tell you, Mac," he said. "You aren't going to believe this, but I grew up in a clan. Maniac Flyers. Way up north by that huge airport. They used to sit in those empty planes and pretend they could fly. That's where the name came from. You should see those planes, Mac, they are unbelievable. They got some up there bigger than an apartment building. They were great fun playing in."

He smiled at the memory. I asked him what went wrong.

"The whole clan system is wrong," he replied. "We were Folks. That meant People were our natural born enemies. What the fuck is that all about? How can I hate anybody I don't even know?"

"I think it has something to do with being part of the human race," I said. "Been going on forever."

"That doesn't mean I have to partake in it," he said. "When I was fourteen, seven years ago, we went out on a turf tussle against the Snakes. I got fucked up pretty good. Almost bled to death before someone showed me how to find a pressure point and apply a tourniquet. While I was recovering, I thought, 'What the fuck am I doing, almost dying for some concept of hatred I don't even subscribe to?' So I decided to be an indie. Not live with a bunch of indies. Be a real one. All alone. Hell, indies aren't independent anyway. They live in total fear all the time. Just because you aren't with a clan doesn't mean you can call your own shots. Shit, indies got both Folks and People to deal with. Not just one or the other. So I don't live with anyone."

"How did you leave?" I asked. "Never heard of a person surviving an outing."

"There was no way I was going to go to the council and asked to be outed," he said to me, fire in his eyes. "It's a death sentence. I saw one once when I was eleven. Guy said he just wanted to take his girl and move way out into the country. No problem. Even offered to supply the clan with food he was planning to farm. Council said fine, just gotta go through the ceremony." Merlin shook his head, as if trying to dispel the memory. "About five minutes in the guy knew he wasn't gonna make it out alive. I could see it on his face as the punches just kept on coming, growing more and more vicious. He lived about two hours after they finished with him. He just laid with his head on his girl's lap breathing blood bubbles. Then the bubbles stopped."

"What about his girl?"

"They told her she had to be outed too. She swore she'd stay, never think about leaving again, but they said she broke the code. What fucking code, I asked myself? They didn't kill her. But it ended up crippling one of her legs, so they sold her to the Two-Two Boys. The Deuces needed a cook. Theirs died. Infected cut turned to gangrene. We got fifty rounds of ammo for her."

"So how did you get out?"

"I simply disappeared in the night," he replied. "Didn't take a thing except the clothes on my back and shoes on my feet. I figured they'd remember me if I stole anything. Probably have no memory of my existence by now. Been seven years. But I'll tell you, Mac, I sure as hell don't travel up in that area. Just in case someone recollects. What about you, Mac. What's your story?"

It was a question that had never been asked of me. Not even Sarah had asked that question. Of course, she knew she didn't have to. Each of us knew the other's history. But the question had never been vocalized.

"Had a family. They got killed. I survived," I recited.

"Kind of the condensed version, huh?" Merlin responded.

I felt bad about my abrupt response. But not bad enough to talk about it. Once was enough.

"I'm sorry, Merlin," I said. "Not something I talk about much."

True to his namesake, Merlin sensed my anguish and adeptly switched subjects. An hour or so later, as we began to straighten out, Merlin and I struck our business arrangement.

"You know," Merlin said, "I sure would like to buy some of that herb you grow. It is absolutely the best weed I've ever sampled."

"I'd be happy to sell it to you," I replied. "All we've got to do is fix a price."

Our hours together had put us beyond the point of trying to take advantage. Neither of us would attempt to bargain beyond the limits of the friendship that was beginning to develop. I wanted him to have the pot, and he was willing to pay a fair price.

"What I've got," said Merlin, "is information. The reason I say that is because I see you as being fairly self-sufficient. Material items I think you've got plenty of. Judging from the artillery you're packing, I'd say weapons are probably not a priority either. So what I can give you is data. You want to locate a certain item, I'll find it for you. Food, military hardware, tools, supplies—you name it; I know where it is. You want to know who's doing what, I'll give you the latest buzz. You need drugs, I know who manufactures the best meth, who produces the best acid, where the PCP's at. Slammer, Brain Fuck…You name it. I can get it. That's what I'll give you, man. I don't keep these things myself. Too risky. If I run across something I think might be valuable, sometimes I might hide or camouflage it. But I won't take it with me. I move around too much."

"O.K.," I said. "Give me a generic example of the kind of information you're talking about. No specifics. I don't want to put us in the position of haggling over the value of something I may not need or already know."

"Some of the stuff I get," he replied, "is hard data. Other info is just rumor. I'll always tell you which is which. Rumors I can't guarantee. Let me give you an example. Troop movements. There's some stuff going on up north. Not sure what, but some clans are arming and recruiting."

"OK. That kind of information is always useful," I said. "Particularly when I'm planning an excursion. What other kinds of items are you talking about?"

"There's a new drug making the rounds in the People clans. They call it "Bad Boy..."

I kept my face neutral. Didn't mention Weasel and I had come across the factory nearly a year ago during our excursion into The Babe's Satan's Messenger camp.

"...It can be really, really good. Or fry fuck your synapses. The chem hasn't worked out the bugs yet. I heard about one guy took two snorts, thirty seconds later, he had a seizure so bad it snapped his fucking neck. Died looking like an expressionist sculpture. Stay away from it, Mac. You'll recognize it by the grey flecks in white powder."

"Thanks," I said. "I make it a general policy not to put anything in my body that isn't 100% earth grown."

"Good plan, man," Merlin replied. "Herb, wine, shine, shrooms. That'll pretty much cover you."

"Not to mention food," I replied.

"Yeah, food. I forgot about food," Merlin said, smiling sheepishly and then rushing on, trying to give me the right data to seal our deal. "Here's another example," he continued. "This will give you an idea of how bits of information that filter in over a long time can be coalesced to provide new conclusions. You've been roaming around this area for about seven or eight years now. Right?"

"Close enough," I responded.

"That's about the same amount of time I've been out here, too. But you've never seen me, have you?"

"Can't say that I have."

"Bet you never heard of me either, have you?"

I shook my head.

"That's my point. I know a hell of a lot about you; but you don't know shit about me. Why? Because I make a point of presenting myself as being totally non-threatening. To the clans, I'm part of the background. Harmless. Barely noticeable."

"Well, hell," I said in defense of myself, "I'm pretty much trying to stay out of the light too."

Merlin laughed. "I know you don't go looking for someone to go up against. But take a look at yourself, Mac. You and Duke don't exactly come across as timid. And when someone fronts you, the response is generally bad for their health. That's your style. No problem. But with me, I've got to approach confrontations from a different angle. I'm not a warrior; I'm a fucking magician—a man of grace and finesse."

"At least that's the image you've been perpetuating to survive," I responded.

"Ouch," he said, rubbing his arm. "That arrow hit home. Nailed me pretty good with that one, Mac. Truth is, if my wits fail, I'm not incapable of defending myself. But projecting the image of wandering wizard and philosopher has worked well for me. Matter of fact, in a perfect world, that's what I'd be—a philosopher."

"I don't want to pour water on your campfire, Merlin," I said. "But I don't really picture myself as a warrior. I'm not a samurai or a cowboy riding through the countryside out to right the wrongs of the world and protect the innocent."

"You just want to be left alone, right?"

"That sums it up nicely," I replied.

"Join the club," he said. "But don't pay your dues, because it ain't gonna happen. This little world here is about territory and power—not peace and love. And if you create something, whether it be material or spiritual, someone is going to try to take it from you."

I laughed, thinking of the years of Weasel's preachings to Sarah, Stevie and me. "I've got a friend who's been reading the same books you have."

"Yeah," said Merlin. "That would be the text titled, SURVIVING THE CLAN WORLD VIEW, author deceased. I hope your friend has been getting through to you. You seem like too nice a fella for us human beings to be mourning."

"He's been making some very real progress," I said. "I'm on my way to becoming one pessimistic, realistic, pissed off son of a bitch."

"Excellent. There is hope. Now just remember not to trust anyone until you've known them for at least a couple of years, and you are on your way to becoming a long term survivor."

"Not trusting," I said. "That would include you?"

"Naturally," he responded. "But let me give you a little insight into the kind of information I carry around so we can begin building that trust. Here's a perfect example: No one knows where you live or how many people you got with you. But they sure as shit know who you are. Some of the clans don't care for your independence, man. But your weed and ammo is so good that they don't want to mess with you. Unless of course they can find your place. Then they'll try to take it all and take you out."

He paused, as if waiting for a response. I remained silent.

"Perfect, man. Don't give away anything. But I'm going to tell you something right now. My reading on your state of affairs. All speculation. Don't respond. It's not necessary. Right or wrong, don't say anything. This will give you an illustration of how I work. Here's my take on your situation: You've got between three and six people living with you. One or two women. You are completely self-sufficient and armed to the teeth. And here's the kicker: You live west of the city. Way out beyond the clans."

I sat quietly, trying to mask my fear. The little guy really was a magician. For a brief moment I considered killing him on the spot. But my experiences with Weasel and Stevie gave me faith in my ability to judge people. Merlin wasn't a danger to us. Worst case was neutrality. Best situation was a new ally.

He was watching me intently, trying to read my mind.

"Don't worry. I formulated that hypothesis on you over a year ago from stuff I've seen and heard. I'll never rat you out. Two reasons. Number one is we're going to be working together. We will soon be business associates. And you possess a product that is essential to my day to day existence. To me, finding a source of good weed is like

Columbus sighting land. Number two is, I like you. Can't say that about many people, man. It's worth more than I can calculate to find a person I can talk to. But even more crucial to me is the fact that you seem to be trying to live your life by some kind of code. There's a whole bunch of good people out there, McCall. But they're all in hiding. Scared shit of the clans. Can't say I blame them. They scare me sometimes too. But I can't crawl in a hole and grow some vegetables and wait to grow old and die. You see where I'm coming from, Mac?"

"Yeah, I see," I said, making my decision. "Let's do some business."

He breathed a sigh of relief. I'm not sure if he knew how close he had come—to being right about the compound and being dead. I've never told him.

"Good idea. I have two more items for you. They concern valuable merchandise and locations. Hard information. How we going to work this?"

I had already given the matter of payment considerable attention and gave him my idea.

"I think a monthly retainer would be a good idea. You provide us with what you think is important to us and we'll provide you with a set amount of herb each month. We just need to figure out how to make the trade."

"What size retainer you talking about," he asked.

"I figure a half pound each time."

He rolled his eyes and whistled.

"Definitely acceptable, man. Here's how I figure it. We set up a drop point each of us can check every week. Probably rotate three or four locations. Once a month you leave the stash. Whenever I've got something, I'll either leave a note or set up a meet. If you ever feel the arrangement is no longer profitable, you just let me know."

His information was solid. He told me the location of a stash of gunpowder, several pounds. Apparently it was a pre-collapse hunter who preferred to pack his own loads. It was in a residence, sealed and undisturbed all these years. I even got a couple of shotguns out of the deal.

• • • •

Duke and I waited for Merlin in the underground garage, the site of our original meeting a year ago. We had been there since before dawn, sleeping three sections back from the entrance in the bed of a pick-up truck. The note I received from Merlin at one of the regular drop sites was an arcane composition, full of innuendo and mysterious warnings.

DROP BY SOMETIME. NO HURRY. AVOID SITE OF ORIGINAL WEED FEST. TRAVEL ONLY BY DAY. PACK LIGHT ARMOR. THE WIZARD ARRIVES AT MIDNIGHT. EVERY NIGHT FOR NEXT FIFTEEN. EVERYTHING IS COOL.

We had established a code based on opposite meanings and subtraction for our communiques with Merlin. Any time mentioned was exactly twelve hours opposite. Midnight meant noon. Travel by day meant move under the umbrella of darkness. Light armor indicated I should be ready to battle dragons. Any number or day mentioned was on a subtract one code. Fifteen meant fourteen. Wednesday meant Tuesday. Avoiding an area meant meet me there. No hurry gave the message an urgency I had never before encountered with Merlin.

Duke and I left the compound at sunset on the day we received Merlin's three-day old message. That was last night. Creeping into the garage before the sun caught us, we found a truck and slept for five hours. We shared a simple breakfast upon awakening and moved closer to the entrance to await Merlin.

Above us the city was quiet as noon approached.

CHAPTER TWENTY-ONE

JULY 2056
CHICAGO LOOP

As Duke's ears stood up, I looked expectantly to the entrance ramp that sloped up in front of me, allowing access from the street level. I faced the ramp, sitting cross legged on the concrete floor, my back to a concrete support column. A 9 mm Intratec TEC-9 pistol with a 36 round magazine lay in my lap. It was a no frills combat weapon, not much on accuracy, but with 36 rounds available in single shot or automatic mode, it was an attention getter.

A sound come from behind us, in my range now as well as Duke's, and I flopped onto my stomach and turned, the TEC-9 pointed into the darkness where Duke and I had been sleeping just a short time ago. I heard the sound again, this time identifying it as the pursed-lip sound people make to summon a pet.

"Hey, Duke," came a whispered voice. "Come here, boy."

More kissing sounds.

I was sure it was Merlin. So was Duke, and he bounded to meet his buddy. Duke was fond of Merlin, mostly, I felt, because Merlin spent a lot of time talking to him. Merlin believed the dog's body was a sacred vessel for the soul of 20th cen hippie.

As Duke dashed into the darkness, I didn't worry about him running into trouble. Had there been anyone with Merlin, Duke would be on high alert.

In a few minutes, they both materialized from the black recesses of the garage, side by side, dos amigos, happy to see each other after a few weeks separation. A smile adorned Merlin's thin face; the ever present headband and earphones graced his forehead and neck. He walked up to me and shook my hand, a ten second ritual consisting of a 20th cen power shake, followed by a standard hand shake and concluded with a little finger tip number. It was his routine form of greeting me.

Standing on tip toes, Merlin put his arm around my shoulder and gave me a hug.

"How you doin', Mac," he said. "I've been worried about you." His concern was genuine. Merlin liked to joke and spent most of his waking hours in a marijuana fog, but he took friendship seriously.

"Thanks, Merlin," I said, reciprocating the hug. I pointed to the darkness from which he appeared. "What's with the back door?"

"Mac, this city is one amazing place. Ever heard of Dungeons and Dragons? This town is one big game board. It's got more back doors than a whorehouse. Besides, man, it is totally unsafe hangin' with you. I gotta stay very slick in your presence."

"Between your cryptic message and these ominous words," I said, "I get the feeling you're trying to tell me something. Spit it out, Merlin. What's going on?"

"Not here, man. Not now. We gotta be in a safe place first. We are talking major heat. Plus I've got a few things I need to show you. Be patient. Now that I've got you under my wing, there's no hurry. You're in my territory now, Mac. Safe and sound. Let's move."

I had a million questions, but knew no answers would be forthcoming until he deemed the time to be right. I had no choice but to follow the program.

We stashed my bike on the first level of the underground garage, covering it in darkness and then began a journey into strange. Merlin was as careful with the location of his base as we were with ours. Most everyone thinks he lives in the city, but no one has any idea where. I was about to find out.

Instead of exiting up the ramp in front of us, Merlin led us into the blackness of the underground along a sidewalk that was adjacent to a concrete wall on my left. In a minute or so he told us to stop, and I heard a door creak open, which allowed some light to enter our tenebrous domain. We exited the garage into the dim light and I found myself in concrete room with four exits—two stairways up to what was obviously a street, a closed door and an entry to the subway system that the city had expanded and renovated in '21 and '22. Merlin herded us up the steps to the street, stopping before we reached the top step.

"Chill a minute," he said and disappeared over the top, turning right and moving beyond my line of vision. In less than thirty seconds he returned.

"It's cool. Follow me."

We entered into full sunlight and stayed behind him as he scampered down what I recognized to be Michigan Avenue for two blocks to a street called Adams, where we turned left and ducked into an entrance to a parking garage.

"Jesus, Merlin," I said, slightly out of breath from our furtive two-block sprint, "you expecting some kind of commando raid or what?"

"Bear with me, Mac," he said, eyes aglow with excitement. "I promise this will all make sense by sunset. But it's gotta be my way. Don't worry, man. You're gonna enjoy the trip. I promise."

He then scampered up three blocks to State Street where we rounded the corner and jumped into a windowless department store display. Merlin leaned back on a one armed, dirty, sexless mannequin and patted it on the butt.

"This here is Arlene," he said. "She and I have had many an intense conversations over the years."

He looked at Duke and me, reading my aversion to new turf, and laughed heartily.

"It's OK now, Mac. Relax. This is my country. A fucking army could march down the street right now and we could disappear before they could even imagine our existence." He snapped his fingers. "Just like that we'd be gone. So fast even our auras would have to run to catch up."

"Fuck the auras, Merlin," I said. "What the hell are we doing here?"

"This, Mac," he replied sweeping his arm to indicate the area outside our shelter, "is going to be part of your cultural education. One of the truly great cities of the world lies at your feet, and you are ignorant of most of its wonders. You've got brains; you read poetry; you are more than casually aware of Pink Floyd; you certainly don't beat your wife—"

Merlin met Sarah a couple of times at weed drops. I replied, "You've met Sarah. Lucky she doesn't beat me."

"—or your dog. That fuckin' Duke, man. He's got some old soul in there. And you, you've got the bitchin'est conscience I've ever run across; and yet you are amazingly illiterate about this great city that graces your front door. Time to change that, Mac."

"For Christ sake, Merlin," I said, "you bring me down here on the pretext of telling me some earth shattering news, and now you act like some kind of tour guide for a fucking dead city. I've seen you weirded out, man, but this is one for the record books."

"Perspective, Mac. It's all about perspective. Later on, when I tell you what you have to hear, you're gonna need a proper frame of mind to process the information. There's some very heavy shit going on, man. But when you hear it, it's going to have to be put in a context you can work with. I got a plan here, Mac. Two years, Mac. That's how long we been working together. Have I ever given you anything but the best? Ever steered you down the wrong path?"

I had to admit that indeed he hadn't. He had become a good and trusted friend. What had begun as a business relationship had evolved into an easy and comfortable camaraderie. Both Sarah and Weasel had met Merlin at drops and felt the same way I did. Same with Stevie. Probably the most important factor in his favor was Duke's reaction. The dog had loved the quixotic little man from the start. And all of us trusted Duke's instincts about people. When it came to reading people, Duke was our secret weapon. It would have been impossible for us to accept anyone into our group without Duke's blessing.

Merlin climbed out of our window and looked up and down State Street.

"Take a look around us," he invited. "We're taking a little stroll around this area. Keep your arsenal available in case we have visitors. But I don't expect anyone. Clans don't find any of this of interest."

Even though the territory was just a few blocks from my familiar scavenging domain on Michigan Avenue, it was new ground to me. And somehow Merlin was very much aware of the fact. My business was rarely in the heart of the city, and when it was, I was always in and out as quickly as possible and had never visited anywhere except

Michigan Avenue. Most everything we needed for the compound could be found outside of the city proper. In open territory.

Duke and I climbed out of the display window and followed Merlin as he returned to Adams Street and ambled west, moving away from our point of origin. There was a different feeling here. The emptiness was more profound, spookier than that of the areas outside the city. What had once once been the commercial and cultural heart of Chicago was now a ghost town. We were walking across the bottom of a canyon, high rises forming the walls that towered over us. On the street level a few rusting cars remained, their tanks and engines drained of gas and oil; their tires deflated and graying from years of summer sun and winter winds. Forlorn reminders of our pre-collapse affluence.

The streets and sidewalks were infested with weeds that had worked their way into cracks in the concrete and asphalt and then expanded their base as seeds found new points of purchase. Trees that had been planted five or six decades ago as some landscape architect's attempt to remind urban dwellers that photosynthesis had nothing to do with cameras—and left unattended for forty years—had broken through sidewalks and streets with their powerful roots. Their inquisitive limbs stretched into the lower floor windows of department stores and towering office buildings.

Decades of falling leaves merged to form a humus base in which the hundreds of varieties of weeds, flowers and grasses took root and thrived. But concrete was still visible among the weeds and rotting leaves, for the winter winds whipped much of the leaf cover away before it could create a soil thick enough to survive the onslaught of snow, ice and winds that swirled and swept through the canyons.

Broken glass was everywhere, but it posed no threat to Duke because its edges had been dulled by time and weathering and Duke's pads are leather thick with callouses from thousands of miles of walking or trotting by our sides over the last five years. On the street level all the glass was shattered during the collapse. Up higher on the huge buildings, many offices were without the protection of glass—empty, ominous holes looking like the beginning of decay in giant teeth. I guessed that the seals and caulking in some of the upper level windows failed the test of time and the onslaught of weather and the huge thick slabs of glass had fallen victim to gravity.

We paused in the alcove of a high rise on Adams. Merlin pulled a couple of apples out of his pack, tossing one to me. He reached back in and retrieved a piece of jerky which he tossed in Duke's direction.

"You notice," said Merlin, "a complete lack of human habitation in this area. It's only very rarely that I see anyone in this section of the city. On ground level most of this was stores, clothing, shoes, books— you name it. Looted out decades ago. All the rest of it is offices. For the life of me I can't figure out what they needed all those fucking offices for. I mean, you got blocks and blocks of buildings twenty, thirty, forty, hell, eighty stories high filled with fucking offices. What the hell were these people doing in those offices?"

"Got the same thing in the suburbs," I said. "Except the buildings are long and low instead of thin and high. Full of file cabinets and desks and chairs and fake plants and machines and pictures of families. Not to mention a few skeletons. That's why I don't need to come in here much. I can scavenge just as well outside the city. Only places I've been down here are the Washington Library, the Art Institute and Michigan Avenue offices."

"Did you find the Art Institute as depressing as I did?" he asked.

I stood up and walked into the middle of the street, slowly turning and observing the bleak surroundings.

"Why do you suppose," I asked Merlin, "people avoid this area? We haven't seen anyone or any signs of recent activity down here. Kind of spooky, if you ask me."

"Begins to work on your nerves, doesn't it?" he replied. "But I think the reason is far more practical than it is supernatural. Simply put, there's is nothing of value to people here. Office suites and department stores don't make for good homes. A bit drafty and not very well furnished. And the offices of lawyers and business people hold little of value for scavengers. Not much you can get for a bunch of files and sales training manuals on the open market. Only use I can see is fuel for fires."

CHAPTER TWENTY-TWO

We resumed our journey, wandering the streets for another hour with Merlin as our tour guide, seeing no one, no signs of recent passage by other explorers. It was if we had the city all to ourselves. Human adventurers entering an alien urban landscape.

The silent surroundings brought to mind a story that Asimov or Bradbury had written in the 50's about a similar scenario. In the story the city was alive. It had been waiting patiently for eons for the humans to return to punish them for their past transgressions.

It didn't quite fit our situation.

We had already been punished.

• • • •

After we returned to State Street, Merlin took us into a building that occupied the whole block, a former department store. I guessed we would be going up, but Merlin took us to the lower levels via a stairway and then across the level below the street, which appeared to have been a section that sold kitchen utensils and dishes. He found a door on the far side and went down again, where no sunlight filtered through. He shut the door behind us, and in the dark I heard the scrape of a kitchen match.

The flame circled around a bit, then became two as it met a candle. Then another candle was lit and the match extinguished. "I always carry at least eight candles and plenty of matches. Make the matches myself," said Merlin, his voice dulled by the small enclosure in which we stood.

"How come you don't use your Walkman batteries in a flashlight?" I asked.

"Only got two nickel cads left, man, and a solar recharger. But these babies don't last forever. Music's real important to me. Can't be wastin' my batteries when I can use candles. You ever heard *Darkside*, man?"

I told him I had.

"Roger Waters," he said, his voice taking on a tone of reverence. "That is one serious dude. I read where they made a movie out of THE WALL. I'd give a testicle to see that, man, someone ever comes up with juice again."

"Left or right?" I asked.

We had two versions of it on Blu Ray III—the movie with Bob Geldof and the animated stuff and the live concert at the Berlin Wall. Merlin didn't know yet that we had electricity. Nor did he know that I had lithium ion batteries and solar chargers.

We came to a landing which led down to yet another level. He reached down and rubbed Duke's shoulders.

"Ol' Duke doesn't seem spooked. But this place sure can get on my nerves," Merlin said. "I'm always thinking there's something moving just beyond my light. Never found anything though. Just a few rats. That's why I never come down here high. Can you imagine what it would be like to get paranoid in a place like this? Talk about your major freak out."

I said, "Shit. I'm paranoid right now and I've got an attack dog, three guns, two knives and a canister of pepper spray."

"I've come to expect nothing less of you, Mac." His voice floated from behind the candle. "That's one reason why you're my favorite traveling companion."

He handed me two candles and lit them from his.

"There's a whole system of tunnels that snake under the city. Some even have old train tracks in them. I read they were used over a hundred years ago to move goods and freight from store to store, entering through the basements or sub basements. I need better light to explore them, so I'm not sure how extensive they are any more. I also read there's flood run-off tunnels too. Watch your step, now. We're going down."

And down we went, descending two short flights of steps and entering a passage through a steel door rusted in place and leaning on its hinges, open just enough for us to squeeze through. The only sounds were dripping water, our steps, and our breathing. Our light extended a few feet, enough for me to see a damp concrete ceiling less than a foot above my head, crumbling concrete walls and a floor littered with small stones and dirt.

"This is one of the newer tunnels," said Merlin, unaccountably speaking in a whisper. "The older ones have brick walls and make me feel like they're gonna collapse any minute."

"What are you whispering for?" I asked in a normal tone of voice.

"Didn't know I was. Never had anyone down here with me to talk to. I guess its kind of spooky, so I just whisper. Feels kind of weird talking in a normal tone of voice."

We were walking slowly. I had no idea in what direction. Merlin continued to whisper.

"Some of the city dwellers say there's giant alligators down here, twenty or thirty feet long. Left over from The Collapse. Some were pets that got away or were flushed down toilets; others escaped from the zoos during the collapse. Never seen any sign of them though."

"I hate to ruin a good myth," I said. "But animals need food to survive. What do you suppose these giant alligators eat?"

"Well, I've thought about that," said Merlin. "There's also supposed to be giant rats down here. Maybe they eat the rats."

"What do the rats eat?" I asked.

"Shit, Mac. How the hell should I know. What do I look like? Some kind of fucking zoologist? I'm just telling you a few ghost stories. I have seen some pretty weird shit here in the city. But I don't care to talk about that kind of thing down here in the bowels of hell."

We came to a cross tunnel and Merlin steered us right and we continued through two other such intersections of passages before he brought us to an up stairway.

"We're going back up to daylight. Let me have the candles back."

I blew mine out and returned them. Squeezing through another door, we exited the tunnel and moved up three flights of stairs and entered into the lobby of an office high rise.

I was astonished to see that we were back on Michigan Avenue, very near where we had started a couple of hours ago.

"Why didn't we use the front door?" I asked, indicating the spaces where windows once surrounded the building at ground level.

"I'll answer you in a minute," he said. "First we gotta move."

He hustled Duke and me across a floor tiled to give the appearance of marble, between two huge banks of elevators, at least ten on each side, and through another steel door with a stairway leading both up and down. This time we moved up. It was dimly lit by sunlight that filtered in on each level through open doors. On the third level he stopped and sat against the wall.

"Take a load off. We'll rest a couple of minutes and then head up. I'm going to share one of my favorite places with you two."

I unwrapped three of Weasel's special batch of oatmeal and raisin cookies, distributing them among the three of us.

"The deal is," he said between bites, "it never hurts to be cautious. That's why we aren't loitering in the lobby. I know this part of the city better than anyone. But even though I'd like for there to be peace and harmony, man, I'm not an idiot. Couldn't have lived this long by trusting people. It's a damn shame, but I work with it the best I can."

He finished his cookie and put the paper it was wrapped in back into his bag, cautioning me to do the same when I was finished.

"If anyone comes this way, I don't want there to be any evidence that a person has been here recently. Then they don't have any reason to wait for someone, namely moi, to return. People with time on their hands and very little intellect have been known to wait for long periods just to see what might pop up. You ever had a cat, Mac?"

"Never have liked them that much," I said, savoring the last scrap of cookie.

"I had one once and kept him locked up when I went out exploring, cuz I was afraid it would get hurt or lost if I let it out. Felt I should protect him. They don't follow you around like a dog, you know. Well anyway, every time I'd come home, that cat would slip right out the door the second I opened it. Figured he sensed my walking vibrations as I was approaching and then waited. Then I stayed home for a couple of days, reading and sorting through my stuff because I was about to change cribs. I saw that cat sit by that door for hour after hour, too stupid to figure out that the only way it opened was me. So fucking stupid he would just sit there and wait for divine intervention. Too ignorant to do anything with its brain but just sit and look at the door."

He paused to pick at a raisin stuck between two teeth with a fingernail.

"I gotta tell you something, man," he said, stroking Duke behind the ear, "I have never in my life seen a dog act like old Duke does. I mean, you treat him like he's one of your family. That's beautiful, man. Can you imagine what the dog thinks about you? I'll bet he's got like some kind of family feeling for you. Like you're not his master, but more like his big brother. Wow, man, maybe he thinks you're God!"

These were pretty scary thoughts, considering they were coming from the brain of a guy who was not yet stoned.

"Merlin," I said, "I've been with you several hours now and I've yet to see you fire up a bowl. What's the deal? Run dry?"

"I've been cutting back, man. Particularly in the city. Too many hiding places for the bad guys. I'm down to three or four a day now. Usually only two when I'm in this area. Let's move out. You are gonna appreciate this."

We packed and headed up the stairway.

"About that cat," he said as we ascended. "There's people out there like that. Got nothing better to do but sit around waiting for something to come up so they can cause some pain. Not enough brains to create an independent thought. You can't ever be too careful out there, Mac. Never leave any sign that you passed this way."

We scaled twenty-one flights, stopping occasionally to listen for indications of other visitors. Merlin said he had never run across others in these office towers. But we checked anyway. We entered the hallway upon reaching our target floor and continued down to a corner of several office suites. We entered a vestibule, obviously a greeting and screening area. Beyond the entryway were two doors on each side and one at the end.

"Stop there," he said before we entered the office area. He bent down, inviting me to inspect something, although I couldn't see anything on the carpeted hallway.

"Lookee here," he smiled at me. "But be careful."

His fingers were sliding very gently along a strand of thin, almost invisible fishing line. It was about a foot above the floor and ran across the hall into a side office. It was anchored to the hall wall by a screw in the plaster. The set up was practically invisible. On the other end of the line was the trigger of 10 gage shotgun.

"I'm very peaceful," Merlin laughed. "Just not very trusting. Tell Duke we're safe and let's go see my digs." As we entered the corner office, he said, "I'm moving outta here anyway. That's why I gave such a graphic demonstration. Into every life a little drama must come. I think it's time to party now, Dude."

I set Duke to guard the front end of the hall; then dug a pipe out of my pack, loaded it, and passed it to Merlin while I took in the amazing canvas stretching before my eyes. We were in a huge corner office, probably about forty by thirty. There was a beautiful desk in the middle, mahogany I thought, with a leather top. It was big enough to be a skateboard park. Lovely nautical prints adorned two of the walls. A leather executive chair was behind the desk. Along one wall was a credenza with drink glasses, an ice bucket and a coffee service. The top of the desk was littered with books and magazines, which I assumed were Merlin's. J.R. Tolkien, Jack Kerouac, David Brin, Greg Bear, Timothy Leary, Ursula Le Guin, Susan Brownmiller and Justin Cronin, Marcus Sakey were among the authors of the books that peeked out of the litter of Omni, Analog, Dungeons and Dragons, *Nat Geo, Rolling Stone, Smithsonian* and other assorted magazines and comic books.

In one corner, adjacent to a hole in the wall large enough for a man to crawl through, were a neatly rolled sleeping bag, a sledge hammer and another shotgun, this one a 12 gage pump combat shotgun. He saw where I was glancing.

"Never be without a back door," he said.

"A truism from the Weasel survival book," I replied.

Merlin took a couple of hits and passed it back.

"Hang on a minute," he said and hastily left, returning seconds later with a chair identical to the one behind the desk. He wheeled them both to the 30 foot outward-facing window and we both sat, taking in an extraordinary sight and sharing the bowl. The the floor to ceiling window was amazingly clean both in and out.

Years ago, when I first visited the city, I was surprised to find most of the upper level windows clean inside and out and very few signs of insects in the high rises. Nature has a process by which she cleans away the filth, utilizing decomposition, carrion eaters and precipitation. In the case of the human race, she added a few more tricks—like plague, ozone holes, nukes, drought and flood. But regardless of the method she chose, she was determined to return the balance, reestablish synergy.

The windows were clean, I figured out, because we weren't around to dirty them up with air borne pollutants that adhered to surfaces and hitched rides on rain drops. It was not uncommon for a muddy rain to fall, having picked up dust in the atmosphere, but dirt is easily washed away by the next storm. The key was that there were no longer acid and oil-based contaminants in the atmosphere. As for the absence of insects, the answer was simply that the sterile skyscrapers provided no food supply.

Two of the smaller office buildings below us were burnt shells of twisted steel. I was unsure of how steel and concrete burned. But fire damaged skyscrapers were rare. Pre-collapse fires were caused by humans or infrastructure breakdowns, like gas leaks or electrical shorts. South of us, some of the neighborhoods were destroyed by fire. There were patches of dead neighborhoods, like bald spots in a meadow, but the fires eventually ran out of fuel or were rained out.

Lake Michigan lay below us, gentle and calm, about a half mile away, her blue green waters stretching east, north and south, then blending with the deeper pure blue of the sky at the horizon. The smoke was good and as it took effect, I felt that I could see the exact horizontal line where the water ended and the sky began.

A few fishing boats were coming in. I noticed a beautiful black and blue sail furling in the lake wind, a sky blue six-point star in the middle of a black background. James' clan, the Black G. D.'s, claimed the fishing and docking rights for about a mile on each side of us. Smart leadership. They even managed to extend their turf over water.

There were other boats, all sail powered, large enough to carry several hands and the nets they used to harvest the lake. Untainted by oil leaks, sewage and pesticides for over thirty-five years, Lake Michigan was now a fertile breeding ground for fish. Coho salmon were the big catch for all the shore line clans. Sarah and I had watched the fishing boats last spring bring in several tons of fish, their nets nearly bursting with the catch. Lake trout, bass, bluegills, walleye, perch and crappie were also plentiful. None of us would ever starve as long as the lake stayed clean.

North of our location, on my left, the water met the land at a man-made harbor which once must have contained hundreds of boats. Half a mile from the shore, a crumbling breakwater was succumbing to the wear of its decades long battle with the forces of wind, ice, and water. The harbor now was home to dozens of sunken yachts and sailboats, some of their triangular prows peeking out from their watery grave. The shore line was littered with masts and rigging.

As I looked down from our 21st floor perch, all the detritus of 20th cen urban life—rusted cars, sunken ships, broken windows, cracked concrete—could not diminish the natural splendor of the landscape. Between the lake and our location, riding on thermals from the canyons, Red Tail Hawks and Peregrine Falcons sought prey from the thousands of pigeons and sparrows and countless other breeds who had established nests in the fissures of the buildings and the resurgence of tree growth. A few hundred feet above the smaller birds of prey two Golden Eagles and one Bald Eagle floated above the lake, searching for fish near the surface. Ring Bill Gulls drifted beneath them, seeking scraps from the fishing boats.

In the woods that had once been Grant Park, I saw a herd of fifteen or so deer, led by a huge buck, skittishly flee from a fountain that served as one of their drinking holes. I couldn't see what frightened them. It didn't take much. They were the Indies of the animal world, weaponless in a savage land.

I turned to Merlin and said, "Thanks, man. I never took the time to look at the city like this. I've always taken the small view. It's dirty from close up. Cracked and broken. But from here I can see the bigger picture. It's not such a bad place."

"You know, Mac," Merlin replied, his eyes beginning to squint, "I look at this part of the city as indestructible. It's a monument. Glass and concrete and steel. What's gonna harm it? Lightning fire? Maybe if one catches, the insides of a building could be gutted, but all in all, there isn't much to burn, especially with no electricity and no people to start fires. This is gonna stand a long, long time."

He passed the bowl, almost cashed now, and I finished it.

"But you know, man, there's another view I can show you some other time that isn't so pretty. If you look down into the old neighborhoods, away from the lake, from way up, Old Sears Tower or Hancock, you can see where the collapse took its toll. Block after block gutted and leveled. North, south and west. Frame houses, apartment buildings, warehouses, stores. Anything that supported population and was made out of wood is pretty much gone from the city. From up high many areas look like woods. But when you walk through them you can tell the trees and shrubs are growing out of what used to be houses and sidewalks and roads and ma and pop grocery stores.

"Find some pretty weird shit on ground level, man. Trees growing right through cars and houses. Walked into a huge warehouse once, roof burned off, just the brick walls standing, and I see a herd of deer grazing on grass growing out of the floor, picking their way through aisles made by stacks of steel shelving. It was like they were shopping, Dude. Very strange."

The two of us rambled on for hours, swapping stories and laughing, riding the high like the eagles on the thermals, sharing exploits about our explorations of our strange landscape. He was far better traveled than I and apparently always had at least four locations he called home. Each was changed two or three times a year, more often if circumstances dictated.

• • • •

Details of the vista outside our window began to slowly fade as the sun set behind us. About ten stories below we saw hundreds of bats darting across the sky, dipping sharply when their sonar located an insect. We both pulled out food and canteens from our packs and shared a meal in the darkening room, including Duke in the repast.

We were down now from our high, our brains capable of linear thought, mellow and comfortable in the darkening office high above the city.

"I know what's out there," I said. "It's not the moon or a mangrove swamp or an endless void. It's old Chicago. Battered and beaten and scarred and burned. Gutted of her wealth. But not completely stripped of her dignity. She's still standing. And I agree with you about the people. I know—even though I can't see them—that there must be good people out there. The collapse couldn't have left us as a race of savages. There's a whole bunch of men and women out there somewhere that aren't like the beasts you and I see every day. I know it."

"Hiding in the darkness," he said.

"Exactly."

"And you feel confident they're out there. Despite evidence to the contrary."

"Take a look at James," I said, "the guy that gave you a hard time when we first met in '54. What would he be like if he was removed from the influence of his clan? He's got some pretty decent qualities. He's not a natural born killer. I don't see any sadistic tendencies in his make up. There's bound to be thousands out there like him."

"Yeah, man. I see what you're saying. James has a different weave than most of the other clan soldiers. You know he's got the helm of the Black Gangster Disciples now, don't you?"

"I've been sticking out west for a while now," I replied. "Haven't been keeping up with the city stuff."

It was interesting news. James had a certain humanity about him. I couldn't put my finger on it. He was different...fair...curious...even honorable. Not unlike what Roberto, leader of the Cobras, had seemed to be.

But it had been a year since there had been any contact between Roberto and me. And the silence from the camp of Roberto's Insane Cobras did nothing but increase our fears that Roberto and The Insane Cobra Nation were communicating with The Babe, entertaining some sort of relationship between Satan's Messengers and The Insane Cobra

Nation. If it happened, I knew the result would be that The Babe would pull Roberto and the Cobras down to the Messenger's level of savagery.

Merlin pulled me back from my troubling thoughts.

"You're an optimist, man. Seeing that positive juice in people. So am I...sometimes. Trouble is, it's dangerous to go against the flow around here."

"So to extend Pink Floyd's metaphor," I said, "You and I are in bands that aren't playing the same tune as the clans. And we're not going to change...and we're not going to leave."

"It's a dangerous choice we're making, Mac. We're walking around with targets on our backs."

"Are you telling me, Merlin, that we don't have the right to live the kind of life we choose?"

"All I'm sayin', man," he said, "is that choice carries some heavy consequences."

I was confused at what I perceived to be a major reversal in his philosophy on survival. "You telling me now you're afraid to make a stand?" I asked.

His laughter punctuated the darkness, followed by a swishing sound he made with his lips.

"You know what I'm doing, Mac?" he asked.

"No," I replied, confused by another one of his reversals.

"I'm reeling in a fish. And you are my catch. Shit, man, I'm just fucking with you. Playing Devil's Advocate. I meant everything I said today. And everything I told you was for a reason."

"And just what in the fuck was that reason?" I asked, relieved that we were back on the same page.

"Patience, Mac. We're very close to the end of our mystery. Just a few more minutes. Now do me a favor and answer this question for me: What rights do we have, you and me and people that might share our sensibilities?"

"Pretty basic, Merlin," I responded, going along with whatever program he was running. "As long as we don't fuck with anybody, they shouldn't fuck with us."

"That how your life has been going, Mac?"

"Not really," I replied, deciding to go on the offensive in our verbal game of chess. I wasn't sure of the rules, but I was uncomfortable being trapped into the corner of his choosing. "You tell me something, Merlin. What about life, liberty and the pursuit of happiness? Do you have those things in your life?"

"Not operative concepts anymore," he replied, then paused, frustrated I hoped, by my switch to the offense. "But what the fuck you want me to do about it, Mac? Have a goddamn sit-in? Recruit a fucking army? Preach the friggin' Gospel? All I want to do, man, is get high, listen to my tunes, read good books and find some people who can carry on an intelligent fucking conversation. Can I throw in find me a nice lady? Is that too much to ask?"

His voice had taken on a higher pitch and volume. I could feel the frustration and bewilderment in his words. I had hit upon an issue that had been eating away at him.

I reached out and patted him on the knee.

"I think I found an open wound," I said. "You've got some serious stuff going on in your mind, don't you Merlin?"

"You and your friends are a big fucking pain in my ass," he replied, his voice taut. "Sometimes I think running into you was the best thing ever happened to me. But there's other times, like right now, when I'm afraid it's gonna get me killed."

"Jesus, Merlin, Duke and I love you. Look at him. He's thrilled every time we get the chance to see you."

"He's asleep, Mac."

"Yeah," I said. "But it's a happy sleep. Trust me Merlin, we'd never do anything that would in any way endanger you."

"It's not you guys I'm worried about, Mac. It's me. It's the change in thinking that's come over me since you have come into my life. It's dangerous to my health."

"How?" I asked. "What are you talking about?"

"Used to be, I could cruise the territories picking up items and intelligence, trade them to the clans for herb and supplies, and lead a pretty simple life. No hassle. Smoke my herb, read my books, deal some chems to the freaks, live a mellow life. Sure, occasionally there'd be conflict, but I could hide in a hole and stay out of it. Didn't have anyone to talk to much, but I had my books and my music."

"So you were pretty satisfied," I said.

"Until I ran into you, you asshole, and and hear about all your fucking friends. Stevie, and Sarah, and Weasel. You and Duke. I see your group, family, whatever it is you call it, trying to improve your lives. Standing against the clans. And I find someone, several people in fact, that I could talk to. People with ideas and opinions. You're fucking up my life, man."

"How?"

"Because now I have hope. There didn't used to be any when I was alone. So I accepted the situation and adjusted. It was safe. Now that there is hope, life isn't safe anymore."

"Why not?"

"Because if I'm going to hang on to the hope, I've got to make a stand. No more hiding out, drifting with the prevailing wind currents. I don't know if I can do any good for you, but if you want to keep on fighting the good fight, particularly after I tell you what the purpose of this whole day is, I'll stand with you."

Our conversation was rapidly moving into some very dense territory. I felt that the darkness which enveloped us was a potential barrier.

"Can we light a candle, Merlin? I think we need to be able to see each other before we move on."

"No problem," came the answer. "But we need to move. I have no idea if anyone on the outside can see candle light flickering from the 21st floor. But I'm not willing to risk it."

We moved our chairs into an interior office and placed a lighted candle on a desk. We were a couple of meters apart and the candle provided enough light for each of us to see the other's features.

I resumed the conversation where he had left off.

"What you said in there was nice. Thanks. But you should know that you have a made an impact on all of us too. Look at yourself. You are one unique individual. If we had this city filled with people like you, there wouldn't be any more killing."

He started to respond, but I cut him off.

"What you're telling me is that you are ready to come out of your hole. You're picking a side. Right?"

He nodded.

"Why now? What's going on?"

He threw up his hands in frustration.

"What's happened the last couple of weeks pretty much slices it. They mess with me, it's usually no problem. I can talk my way out. Act stupid, stoned. But now they're into the shit of the only friends I've ever had. I'm in."

Something had happened to him. I'd never seen him in such a quandary before.

"You need to tell me now why you called me down here," I said. "What's going on? Why did you tell me I can only travel in darkness?"

"Last month you had an altercation with the Cobras over on Roosevelt Road."

"They wanted to cook Duke for dinner," I said.

"Well, when I heard that you and Duke wiped out half of one of their outposts, I figured you probably had a fairly good reason. I think trying to eat one's best friend qualifies. Thing is, Mac, you pissed off some people who have serious problems with impulse control."

"I wasn't figuring on making friends, Merlin. For Christ sake, they were trying to kill us. Is this the bad news you've been hanging over my head all day?"

"You know Roberto's got the Cobras looking for you, right?"

"It's a logical consequence of incident," I replied. "We capped some of his soldiers, he needs to balance the sheet. It's a shame, though," I added.

"Whaddya mean?"

"I've known Roberto four, maybe five years. He's always been real straight ahead, Merlin. Treats his people good, well organized, always fair. The Cobras showed promise. But I've got a real bad inkling in my gut the Cobras are talking with the Messengers."

"Your gut's gotta be wrong," Merlin responded. "I know Roberto, too, man. He's big as a fucking truck and tough as a cougar, but he's got a spirit to him that I've never seen in any clan leader. As weird as it sounds, he seems to possess a sense of honor. I can't believe he'd even

221

talk with the Messengers. What's in it for him? He's on the top of the heap already."

"Got a little story to tell you," I said. "It's going to change your world view. Goes back about a year." I gave him the unedited version of the slaughter of the Gaylords, how Duke and I had come upon the clan skirmish in the parking lot that turned into a bloodbath, finishing with the brief encounter with The Babe and the one lone Cobra and our knowledge that the Messengers had been quietly seeking a man and his dog ever since.

Merlin was speechless.

"Those Cobras that fronted me on Roosevelt Road last month," I continued, "were led by the soldier that I saw with The Babe over a year ago at the massacre. He and the fat man looked like they had bathed in blood."

"Son of a bitch." Merlin was truly astounded.

"Plus these guys that tried to burn me and Duke weren't the usual Cobras, Merlin. Most of them were seriously fucked up. No way are Cobras allowed to use while they're on their posts. Roberto would never stand for that. And the leader of these freaks had no respect for Roberto. Never encountered anything like that before."

"I got more bad news for you, Mac," Merlin said softly. He was reluctant to impart the information. "It's not a secret anymore. Since you capped those Cobras, all the People clans know who you are...There's a contract out on you. City wide. Jewelry, assault weapons, women, children, food, chems, blades—you name it. Whoever nails you is gonna be rich...and famous. That's part of the bad news. Every clan associated with People is looking for you...and Duke."

I asked the question.

"Who? Where's the contract issued from?"

"That's the worst part, man. It's Satan's Messengers. They're paying the bill. These guys are bad news, Mac. Make the Marquis de Sade look like Walt Disney."

I was confused.

"Why not the Cobras?" I asked him. "They're the ones with the dead soldiers."

"Cobras take care of their own, Mac. No way Roberto's gonna ask for help. That's their code."

"I'm still thinking those two are connected," I said. "The Gaylord massacre can't be ignored."

"Few days after you tussled with the Cobras, The Babe puts out a bounty on you. Only connection I see is that they're both People clans. But to tell you the truth, I still think Roberto's got no respect for the Messengers. I don't see the connection."

"There's gotta be one," I said.

He cast his eyes downward.

"There's more."

I took a deep breath.

"Fire away."

"The bounty specifies you gotta be alive if the hunters want to collect the reward. Dead dog, live man. If you aren't alive, they gotta bring your head."

Being delivered to the man responsible for Stevie's horrors and the massacre near the college was as disturbing a thought I had ever conceived. As I watched Merlin, I could tell he wasn't finished with the bad news. I told him to get it all out.

"They're puttin' pressure on me, Mac. They know your name. They know you got a dog. And they know you're the man with the best herb in town. Can't hide good drugs, Mac. The clans know I been trading with you. Everyone knows the herb I'm smokin' is your stuff. They want me to rat you out. And if they're going after me, you know they got to be pressuring every damn person who's ever even heard of you."

"Who's squeezing you?"

"People clans. Any of 'em I run across last week or so. Some of 'em won't trade with me. Others threaten me. Last week the Latin Kings ran me out of their territory. I'm afraid to go do my business, Mac."

"I don't blame you for being frightened, Merlin. I'm sorry you got wrapped up in our mess."

"It isn't me I'm concerned about, Mac. I could lay low awhile and see if things blow over. I got enough shit stashed in all my places to live for months. But I can't abandon all of you. I'm worried about you and Sarah and Weasel and Stevie—and old Duke sitting out there in the hall, watching over us. It scares me that half the fucking clans in Chicago want you dead. And what makes me more scared is that I want to help. See what I mean about all of you fucking up my life?"

"I've seen you operate for a couple of years now," I said. "You're a very brave man, Merlin. You've got just as many guts as any of us. It wasn't easy crawling out of that protective hole. For what it's worth, we're not exactly what you'd call defenseless. We can help you survive."

"Figured as much," came his reply. "It's worth more than you know. Thanks."

"Tell me something," I said. "We received some info from the pipe that's very disturbing. The Messengers have been taking children as prisoners. You know anything about why?"

"I was planning on getting around to that," he said. "Nastiest piece of work I've ever seen. And that's saying a lot. He's expanding so fast, he can't keep up with the food and guns and ammo for his new recruits. Plus the more men he gets, the more whores and cooks he needs. He usually trades chems. They manufacture Slammer and Bad Boy. But his factory can't produce enough to keep his own men satisfied plus have a surplus for trade."

"So he's selling children?" I asked, horrified.

"Well, yes and no. The Slammer their chems put out makes the men want to fuck anything that moves. Shit, I've seen bowlegged sheep in their camp. Babe's using some of the kids for his own men. Keeps the best ones for himself is what I hear. Sells the rest to other clans with similar proclivities in exchange for guns and ammo. From what I hear, it's a booming market."

"It's what we imagined but never talked about," I said, hollowly.

"He's cornering the market on depravity," Merlin responded. "And I don't see anyone out there who's gonna stop him."

We were finished, I decided. Nothing either of us could say about what we had just shared would serve any purpose. I wanted to be home, see something clean, wash away the filth Merlin and I had just exposed.

And Merlin would accompany me. He needed it too.

"I think it's about time you came out and visited our little home in the suburbs," I said. "But first, why in the hell has there been all this subterfuge? Why didn't you just tell me all this straight up at the beginning of the day?"

Merlin smiled a devious magician's smile, pushing back the horrors, recalling the magic of our day together.

"We had some fun, didn't we? I was worried that when you got all the bad news, you would want to cut and run. Pack all your bags and all of you leave for a new climate. I wouldn't blame you, Mac. Would have asked to join you too. But my preference is to stay here. Why should I let those bastards drive me out?"

"So you wanted to show me some of the good before you told me the bad? Hook me with the art. Show me the city's good sides. Get me high. Put me in a good mood."

I laughed, amused and deeply touched by the lengths to which he had gone to persuade me to stand my ground.

"Shit, Merlin, we all decided two or three years ago that no one was going to drive us out. We are all going to be buried here. Only question is when."

CHAPTER TWENTY-THREE

Merlin, Duke and I returned to the compound at dawn, traveling in darkness, a logical concession to the bounty hunters who sought me. I entered one of the tunnels and disarmed the traps, signaling everyone in the house that someone was in the tunnel. When we were safely inside, I reset.

Merlin was astounded by the tunnel and threw nonstop questions at me during our eighty meter crawl through its midnight black length. When we reached the entrance to the basement of the compound, I tapped on the door, 2-1-2, indicating it was me. I heard the locks slip, and we entered.

Weasel was waiting in a shadowy corner, a Galil Sar assault rifle pointed in our direction. "Morning," he drawled, his voice emanating from the shadows. Merlin hit the floor and crawled behind me, his instincts a second behind his recognition of the voice.

"Jesus Christ, Weasel," Merlin exclaimed. "Don't be hiding in corners like that. Almost crapped my pants."

I heard the safety of the Galil snap on. Weasel came into the light. Duke bounded past me to greet him.

"You boys working late or getting an early start?" he asked.

"Late night," I said. "All I want is bed."

"Stevie and Sarah are making breakfast upstairs," he replied. "Can't have you sleeping on an empty stomach."

We climbed the basement stairs and entered the brightly lit kitchen. Merlin was speechless. He knew us from out in the world, bartering. But he had never been to the compound. Never seen working electronics. He just walked around and touched things, the microwave, refrigerator, faucet handle, light switch. Then he wandered to the living room and quietly marveled at the electronics we had racked, CD player, dvd, graphic equalizer, amp, pre-amp, two big screens, LG and Sony.

Sarah and Stevie watched him, smiles creasing their faces. Merlin continued his exploration. He moved next to the computer table— monitors, printers, CPU's, piles of paper—stroking the machines gingerly, as if they might crumble to dust at his touch.

"All this shit work?" he finally asked, looking back over his shoulder at the four of us.

"We're not wired for cable yet," I said.

"And we can't seem to get the modems to work," Stevie added.

"Other that that," Sarah said, "everything works just fine."

"This," he said, flapping his arms like a bird and twirling in a circle, "is a fucking wonderment. You live in a goddam functional museum. When you gonna let me see all this shit in action?"

"After we eat and talk," Sarah said. "Then you can play to your heart's content."

• • • •

Merlin sampled the electronics for a couple of hours before exhaustion finally forced him and me to bed. He bounced between vids and computer games, the microwave and ice from the freezer, all the while sampling CD's at full volume—Lou Reed, Frank Sinatra, Roxy, Ministry, Nine Inch Nails, Pink Floyd, Iggy Pop, David Bowie, Ariana Grande. He skipped from the '40's through the 21st in a frenzied rush to hear it all.

That night we gave him a special gift, a taste of the past, an exhibition of the best of the 20th, a couple of hundred thousand people gathered peacefully at the Berlin Wall in 1990 to hear Roger Waters and assorted 20th cen musical icons perform *The Wall*. The system was placed in an interior sound-proofed room with blackout curtains on the exterior windows.

Weasel gave Merlin a joint and Sarah sat him in the middle of the room, encircled by quad surround, facing a 70 inch 1080 Sony monitor. We didn't tell him what was about to happen. He was only a couple of feet away from a hidden satellite bass system, which at full volume would loosen his teeth.

When he was comfortable, I punched out the lights and turned on the Blue Ray V, adjusting the sound to nearly full volume. It started with crowd sounds and a helicopter view of the audience, probably as many people gathered in that one place fifty years ago as we had living now in all of old Chicago.

There were a couple of announcements and then the deep reverberations of road bikes, Harleys, filled the room as the Scorpions rode onto the stage, so massive in its length and breadth that it resembled a landing zone more than a stage. Then the opening chords of *In the Flesh*, replaced the bass of the Harleys, and the concert began.

It was such a massive assault on Merlin's senses, that for the next two hours he forgot to light the joint that we had placed in his hands. He spoke not a word, although we saw him scream several times, particularly during the double guitar solo of Comfortably Numb; his eyes never left the big screen.

When the concert finished, Merlin slumped on a cushion and threw his hands behind his head. Looking at the ceiling, he asked, "You guys do this shit on a regular basis?"

"Not so much lately," Stevie said. "What with people trying to kill us and all. This one was in your honor. It's no secret you got a thing for Pink Floyd."

Merlin noticed the joint in his hand, lit up and passed it. "That was rapture. Epiphany. I've heard that album fifty, maybe a hundred times. Hell, I only got ten tapes, and three of 'em are Floyd. Never really new what it was about until now. I don't know how to thank you."

"It's a hell of a ride," Sarah said. "There's a movie too, you know."

"No shit. Let's watch it. Hey, what about the rest of Floyd? David Gilmour. Mason, Wright. Syd Barrett? How come they weren't there?"

"Barrett went nuts. Rest of them broke up in the 80's. Wright died. Only Waters and Gilmore, and Mason left," Sarah said.

"Jesus," he said, genuinely aghast. "How could such a thing happen? That's a genuine fucking tragedy."

"From what we can tell," I told him, passing the joint back, "20th was a rough place."

He took a deep hit and held it, talking while he held the smoke in his lungs. "Goddam... tragedy ...what ...it...was... Can't... imagine... anything...worse..."

• • • •

The most important lesson we learned from Merlin's visit to the compound was that it isn't always easy to live with your friends. He stayed with us a week first time, departing just before the moment one of us, pick any of the four, Duke excepted, threw him and all of his weed out a second story window.

His presence drove us crazy but did nothing to decrease our affection for him, nor his for us. But by the third day, all of us, Merlin included, realized he wasn't cut out for group living. He tried for four more days to make the necessary adaptations, but he was too internally focused, too much caught up in the wonder of each moment, to be a contributing member of a group.

He stayed up most of each night, slept through lunch and smoked incessantly. Whenever we asked for help, he was always there. But we always had to ask, prying him away from computers or vids. He was seriously depressed when he realized that the generator was used sparingly.

When he left, taking with him our pleas for caution, he promised to take care of some business and move out of the city, closer to us. "That way I can visit more often," he explained.

We smiled and waved.

• • • •

In the two weeks since I had returned home with Merlin and his information on the celebrity/bounty hunter status Duke and I had achieved, we continued making defensive modifications, fortifying the tunnels and booby traps during the days and discussing further changes—including building a bunker—when the sun set.

Unlike the natural world, where the top of the food chain was generally free from harm, our world was one of constant threat. And the source of danger was our own species. We were used to it, expecting that at some time another human would accidentally stumble upon our hideaway. But now our concerns were heightened by the fact that The Babe had put out a contract on me for erasing the group of Cobras on Roosevelt Road, a deed that all of us and several hundred Folks clans perceived as an act of civic improvement. It was a small part of the Cobras, and we didn't know how the main body, led by Roberto, viewed Satan's Messengers or us. The Babe did not give a shit about the Cobras, but it was bad for recruiting to admit it out loud…yet.

Before the incidents with the slaughter of the Gaylords at the college parking lot and my skirmish on Roosevelt Road with the Insane Cobras, very few of our citizenry were even aware of our existence. And no one wished us harm. They were too busy with the business of survival to worry about us. But now thousands of clan freaks were out there looking for me and Duke, eager to cash in on The Babe's lavish bounty on my head, be a hero, live the good life, buy some new friends. In the 20th, they had something called lotteries, where a person could win a lifetime wealth with a small wager. The bounty on my head was our equivalent of such riches.

A much discussed option was taking The Babe out first, before he could get to us. "Time to go on the offensive," Weasel said. "As long as that man lives, our lives will be nothing but a state of red alert. We gotta take it to him."

Stevie was silent on the issue. Any mention of the name of the beast would visibly affect him. The conditioning was too strong, the incidents of terror in his life that had been associated with The Babe were too frequent. But it wasn't fear that rendered Stevie silent; it was dread. Haunted by his past, Stevie was more concerned with how his future would be affected if The Babe entered his life once again.

Weasel, Sarah and I had spoken of the probable scenario in whispers. We were united in our determination that The Babe would never again have the opportunity to torture Stevie. The three of us had never verbalized it before the bounty was placed upon my head; but The Babe's death, by one of our hands, was an inevitability. If he came to us before we got to him, so be it. But our plan now was to get to him first.

• • • •

The day after Merlin left us to return to the city to find new living quarters, Stevie and Weasel, the two tinkerers, began a pattern of disappearing at dawn and returning after sunset. They smiled their silly smiles, the grins of people who have a big surprise in store, in response to each inquiry Sarah and I made of their whereabouts and arcane purpose. We resolved ourselves to wait and see, confident our patience would be rewarded, our only clue, the dirt and grease that covered the two of them whenever they returned.

"Some kind of machine," I said.

"No duh," replied Sarah.

"Well, Einstein," I said, "knowing these two, that doesn't really narrow it down a whole bunch. Got any guesses?"

"Could be anything but an airplane."

"Why not an airplane?"

"Good point," she said. "Never place any limits on the imagination and capabilities of Weasel. Particularly now that he's got Stevie helping him. It wouldn't surprise me if the two of them showed with a moon rocket."

I laughed. "And converted it to run on compost. But actually, the fuel problem limits their options a great deal."

• • • •

Duke and I were outside doing a security sweep. Actually, I just wanted to be outside on a beautiful summer day and he always preferred out to in. Beyond the thistle, raspberry, buckthorn, razor wire barrier, we could see the compound and it was truly unexceptional. Our fortress looked no different than the thousands of abandoned houses that nestled in forests throughout the landscape. We had also added grape vine, which was growing enthusiastically.

Most deadly was a minefield, out newest defensive weapon. Weasel had locations of many armories and had scavenged an U.S. Army depot north of O'Hare Airport. He taught us how to install the mines. They were placed along several strips of land, running out from the hub of the barrier like spokes in a wagon wheel. These strips contained hundreds of land mines. The safe zones were marked by Queen Anne's Lace, a beautiful drought resistant weed.

Duke and I were walking a safe zone in the meadow between the compound barrier and the forested area when Duke's ears perked up and he looked to the woods. "What do you hear, boy?" I asked, bringing the Mauser from back to front. I hit the "on" switch my right earlobe. It opened Sarah's line. Sarah stepped on to the porch, shotgun in hand.

"What've you got?" she asked.

"He hears something." We never ignored a warning from Duke. "Wait for me. Grab your weapons. Duke and I are coming back in," I said to her departing back.

Our new communicators were the ones I salvaged from the electronic store, *I Spy, You Spy.* The little personal communicators worked like walkie talkies, but the receiver looked like an earring or ear cuff and your transmitter was a throat derm, a little skin colored adhesive patch wired for voice transmission. We practiced with them and the battery life was amazing and distance was over two miles. The devices were voice activated and operated on a different frequency than traditional hand-held boxy walkie talkies, meaning we were on a different frequency than the clans.

Duke and I sprinted toward the compound and negotiated the mini-tunnel underneath our barrier. I reset the grenade booby trap and rushed into the house. Stevie and Weasel were gone. I grabbed a Kevlar. "You got your vest?" I asked Sarah. We each hit our stations— me on the front windows, Sarah up top with a sniper rifle. Stevie and Weasel would normally take the side windows. Putting the Kevlar on Duke, I said, "Duke. Go see Sarah."

He launched up the stairs. From the small cupola in the center of the roof, Sarah covered the back. "I got nothing," she said. She sounded like she was right next to me.

I couldn't see anything from my front vantage point. Beyond our walls, stretching for one or two hundred meters in all directions, the compound was surrounded by grass cover. No trees or bushes to hide behind. Gullies or depressions that could conceal an enemy had been back-filled with tunnel dirt.

At the peak of a very small rise in the landscape, the compound did not offer the most advantageous view from a military standpoint, but from the rooftop post, we had the ability to observe at least a mile in every direction, taking in woods, two ponds, a small stream and several houses. In darkness, military issue binoculars, designed to suck up all available light, allowed us to survey the surrounding terrain.

Sarah's voice entered my ear, crisp and clear as if she were standing by my side. "Ten four, oh fearless leader. How's the weather down there?"

I waited for further communication and then instructed. "You're supposed to say 'Over and out' when you're done." Silence. "Well," I asked, "what are you waiting for?"

"You forgot to say 'over and out', general. Over and out."

"I think its best to maintain radio silence," I responded. "Over and out."

Then I heard the sound, the strange rumble emanating from beyond the fences, Sarah's voice came back on. "I see something, Mac. Hold on a minute. Can't tell what it is. But I'll tell you this much, whatever it is, it's big. And moving fast. Hold on…Hold on…Look to your left. In those trees about 200 meters out. Duke's freaking out," she said. "I don't know what the hell is riling him up."

She was silent for about 20 seconds. I strained to see something in the direction she had indicated, but she had a much better vantage point. "Holy shit, Mac," she came back, excitement growing in her voice, "I can see part of it now. It better be Weasel and Stevie. If it isn't, we're in big trouble. Another twenty or thirty seconds and it'll be out. Man, this is unbelievable. You thought the microwave and tunnel auger was a big deal, wait'll you see this mother. You're gonna have fuckin' apoplexy."

The sound was louder now, and I recognized it from the vids. I had heard it many times, but never in real time. The only people in our world that had ever heard this sound were adult survivors of the collapse. Not many of those left.

The trees were shaking now a few yards into the wooded area, but I still couldn't see anything. The noise—definitely an automotive engine, a big one—increased as the trees thinned out. Suddenly, I saw color, blue and white, and the saplings were swept away by a huge machine, a truck bigger than anything I could imagine moving under

233

its own power in our time. It burst through the last of the trees, through the meadow area in perfect alignment to avoid the mines. The massive vehicle obliterated the barbed wire and vine barrier as if it were dental floss and tinker toys and the engine was the roar of dragon.

I opened the front door and stepped onto the porch. The Mauser was a piece of shit at this distance, but I held it up anyway, wishing I had the SP66 instead, a sniper rifle that fired the heavier 7.62mm rounds and a had a far greater range. As I sighted on the truck, Sarah's voice blared, "Don't shoot, Mac. Don't shoot. It's Weasel. I can see Stevie on the passenger side, grinning like a fool. His mouth keeps on opening. I think he's screaming like a kid on a roller coaster."

"Jesus Christ, Sarah," I said in normal conversational tone, "whatever you do, don't ever yell when you're wearing these things. My eardrum's throbbing."

"Sorry, hon. Got a little carried away. It's unbelievable."

In just a few seconds the truck roared across the 100 meters to the compound and skidded to a halt three meters from the gate. A huge cloud of dust surrounded the vehicle. When it settled, I saw Weasel on one side of the giant vehicle and Stevie on the other, doors open, standing on the running boards, grinning like idiots.

I was very envious.

"I'm coming down," Sarah said. I could hear her panting on the way down the steps. "You can switch the communicator off," I said.

As Weasel looked at me from his running board, posing like a rock star before an adoring audience, greasy and torn Gram Parsons shirt and that huge Weasel smile plastered on his face, I flashed back for an instant to our first meeting, a different season, but the the same sort of dramatic entrance he was so fond of.

"Sorry about the barrier, Mac," he said. "But me and Stevie figured you two would appreciate a little drama."

"Yeah," Stevie said. "Been getting a little boring around here. Thought we'd spice things up a bit." Stevie dusted imaginary dust from his black Zeppelin t-shirt. Both of them were trying very hard to be adult and cool about their grand entrance, but the child inside each of them was not to be denied.

Stevie broke first. Jumping down from the running board, he was screaming up at me before he hit the ground. "You shoulda been there, Mac. It was unbelievable. We were going so fast, I thought we were gonna fly. Speed, Mac, speed. You gotta try it. There's nothing like it. I thought I was in a Terminator movie! You remember when Sarah and John and the good Terminator were bein' chased by the T 1000 in the big semi? That's what it was like. Total rush."

He started running around the truck, still yelling in my direction. "Look at this, Mac. Check it out. Me and Weasel did the whole thing. Wait'll you see the modifications. You'll freak. When those bastards that're after you see this baby, they're gonna shit."

"Hold on, Stevie," I said, laughing at his energy and enthusiasm. "I'm coming. Then you can give me the tour."

I took the steps two at a time. Duke, caught up in everyone's hyper state left Sarah behind. He raced out the door, feet and torso skidding on the the front porch like a flat rock on water, rolled down the stairs, and landed square on his nose. He made a big woofing sound when he impacted the ground.

His one-point landing didn't seem to faze him a bit, and he barked at me enthusiastically. I'm pretty sure he was smiling and saying, "Holy shit."

Sarah was a few seconds behind. She hadn't turned her mike off. "Wait for me. Wait for me," she pleaded. "I want to see this close up." She hit the doorway and rushed down the steps. Standing by me, Sarah removed her derm and the earring, placing the minuscule components of the set in my hand. "Over and out, General," she said.

We both stood rooted in our tracks. Duke ran past us and made a circuit around the huge truck, barking loudly every foot of the way, and pissing on each tire. Two or three barks, a headlong charge within a foot or two of the giant machine, piss, and then a back off. That was his pattern all the way around. Weasel and Stevie stood by the passenger door, facing us, side by side, arms across each other's shoulder, smiling hugely. Behind them stood Weasel's masterpiece. They reminded me of a Wright Brothers picture I had seen.

By looking at the parts of the vehicle that had not been cut away or augmented, I could tell Weasel had found a brand new truck for us.

The paint remaining that was unblemished, a shiny blue and white, proclaimed the truck to be the property of DuPage Concrete and Excavation. It was a dump truck, not as huge as some I had seen abandoned at construction sites, but large enough to haul anything we could ever desire. The bed was large enough to hold a good sized car.

The structural steel of the bed was scorched with burn marks where approximately two feet had been trimmed from the top. This was on the sides only. The part behind the cab still rose to its original eight foot height, protecting its occupants from any foreign objects, namely bullets. The gate was also original.

The sides rose to a height of about seven feet. Several gun ports had been cut into the sides and back gate. Across the top were steel bars, from the Kane County Jail, I later found out, spaced about six inches apart. Where the bars approached the cab, there was a three foot open area, presumably where someone could stand and look over the cab, through another gunport which had been cut from the steel. Two steps had been welded into the bed to accommodate one or two of us in looking over the cab. On top of the cab, part of the original bed was welded across from side to side, protecting whomever was standing from whatever projectiles might be launched from the front of the truck.

The vehicle was downright intimidating, not so much because of its size, but because we had the ability to put its bulk in motion. Its builders had decided that it needed two axles in the rear, each one requiring four tires instead of the normal two per axle, so we had a truck that so huge it required ten wheels to stay on the road.

Weasel lowered the rear gate, which came down with a thunderous clamor, and Sarah and I climbed into the truck's bed for an inspection. Having settled his territorial display, Duke also joined us.

"He owns it now," said Sarah, nodding in Duke's direction.

We had a pool table in the house. All of us used it frequently. The bed of the truck was large enough for the table, plenty of room to play and several chairs for spectators. There was enough head room for all of us to stand beneath the horizontal bars Weasel and Stevie had welded across the top.

Weasel joined us and said, "Tried to think of problems that could come up in the combat situations. These bars across the top should discourage anyone from tryin' to jump on the truck and keep out good size rocks and stuff they might want to throw in our direction."

In the front of the bed, the part nearest the cab, four unused tires, mounted on shiny black new wheels, were stacked in a corner and held in place by three vertical bars welded to the floor. Next to the tires was a yellow device about five feet long, and a foot high and wide that curved on both ends and was tapered slightly. It lay on the floor and looked to be solid steel.

"You know what I say about always bein' prepared," said a smiling Weasel. "The tires came off another truck. Never been used. Got 'em for a good price. They were all flat, but me and Stevie injected some sealant into where they meet the rim and then pumped 'em up with a foot pump. Had to do the same with all the tires on the truck, too. Think the two of us got the strongest thighs in the whole damn city."

"What's the yellow thing that looks like a huge fish?" Sarah asked.

"They call it a jack. You pull out this handle on one end and put the other end under one of the axles. Then you step on the handle a bunch of times and the damn thing lifts up the truck so you can crawl under it and fix what's broke or just look around awhile. Incredible piece of engineering. Don't even need a motor."

We walked to the front of the bed, where Sarah and I could stand behind the cab. There was plenty of room for the two of us and on the left wall, opposite the corner where the tires were stacked, was a gun rack welded into the side of the bed which held a shotgun and a Baretta assault rifle. I noticed there was room for several more weapons. A platform with three stairs allowed us to reach the rifles.

"Each of you grab a gun," Weasel said to Sarah and me. "Step up and see if there's enough room for you to maneuver if two people need to be up there firing." It was no problem. He had probably tested the thing himself several times.

Sarah and I turned on the platform, ending up facing each other. We both smiled.

They had built us a rolling fortress.

"Why didn't you just bring a fucking tank?" I asked Weasel sarcastically.

"Gave it considerable thought," he replied straight faced. He wasn't kidding. "There's plenty to be had. They get shit for gas mileage, though. Plus they're diesels. And they ain't too fast."

Back in the 20th, people probably didn't look upon dump trucks as objects of beauty. But to our eyes it was a wondrous and majestic sight. Wondrous because of its speed and power. Majestic in its sheer bulk and muscle. I was in awe that we could make something as huge and bulky as a dump truck move faster than anything in our world.

Nature contributed most of the speed that we were witness to. The death dives of hawks and eagles; the graceful leaps of rabbits and deer; the darts of hummingbirds, so quick as to be beyond the abilities of our eyes to follow; horses at a gallop; wolves in their final lunge to a kill; trout leaving their watery home to snap an insect from the air. Speed was all around us in the natural world. But birds of prey and deer and wolves were not required to move two and half tons in their quests for food or escapes from predators.

Man-made speed came to us in the form of bullets and arrows. Frisbees and baseballs could certainly zip along also. All of them weighed in at the ounce scale of measurement, a far cry from the massive 10,000 pound vehicle that stood before us.

Here was something alien and intimidating. A Frankenstein truck reanimated. A symbol of the destruction humanity wrought upon itself. Maybe a taste of the future. I hoped not. The thought of cars and trucks once again choking the highways like little fat globules in arteries, depriving the heart of the city of oxygen, was repulsive to me.

I was in the classic approach-avoidance stance, fascinated and frightened. Enchanted by the lethal combination of bulk, menace and speed. Captivated by the Promethean vehicle's potential to improve our defensive situation and function as a instrument of destruction. It took little imagination for me to conjure up the offensive capabilities of truck.

But the vehicle's power and potential beguiled me before I could even begin an internal dialogue. Conflict resolution was blown away by my need to experience its power. Hell…I just wanted to play.

"Take me for a ride, Weasel," I demanded.

"Me too," echoed Sarah. "Me too."

"Everyone hop in," he said, laughing at the two children begging him for a ride. "Stevie, you and Duke ride in the back. You two join me," he said to Sarah and me.

When the three of us were seated in the cab, Weasel began teaching. "Both of you are gonna have to learn to drive this thing. Stevie already knows. No tellin' when it might be a lifesaver. I'll take you through the modifications later."

In all the vids we had seen, the inside of a vehicle, the dashboard, gear shift, pedals and various knobs, had never been shown. There were sticks and levers and knobs, things that you could pull, push, squeeze, switch or step on. I counted eight different gauges. Sarah and I both thought a computer was much easier to master. At least it didn't move while we were learning. What was a banality in the 20th cen, looked like the cockpit of a space ship to us. But the teacher in Weasel walked us through it.

"We gotta limit our practice time by doing a lot of dry runs in this thing," Weasel said, patting the dash. "Fuel is a major problem. We got about 20 gallons of ethanol. This little beauty's gonna suck down a gallon every six or seven miles. So we can't go playin' around, usin' up all our surplus ethanol."

"Plus we don't want to let anyone know that thing even exists," Sarah said. "If anyone saw this truck moving, it would be a magnet drawing the clans straight to us."

"Exactly why we do a lot of dry runs and very little actual driving," Weasel said. "OK. Let me show you what all these doodads are. Then we're gonna take a two mile trip. Give you a taste. Ain't no way to learn without watchin' someone do it."

So he taught us for about half an hour, but I don't think we were very good students. It was like someone stopping the vid JURASSIC PARK in the middle to give a lecture on dinosaurs. We wanted the thrills.

When Weasel finally started the engine, I could feel the immense power beneath my feet. "Got a big V-8 here," he said. "We had to have one because me and Stevie couldn't have converted a diesel to run on ethanol." When he stepped on the clutch and put it in the first of six forward speeds, it worked just as he had explained: easing up on the clutch allowed the gears to engage. And we moved, slowly at first, but as he went through the gears, we picked up speed, and the wind rushed through the cab, blowing our hair and roaring in our ears.

Stevie was right. It was a major rush. Behind us I could hear him screaming and Duke barking his dog equivalent of a yell. Up front the three of us were elated, huge smiles plastered across our faces as we joined in the vocal revelry. As we picked up speed, and the landscape flew by, I realized Stevie's other prediction was right: The clans really were going to shit when they finally got a look at this magnificent machine.

• • • •

We settled into the living room to become acquainted with the modifications Weasel and Stevie had made on the truck. The Moody Blues, a band we could all live with for background music, were orchestrating softly in the background. Crystal glasses filled with white wine were scattered around the coffee table.

After the thrill of flying across the ground in the huge truck had been begun to fade, a contrary little thought, a pesky intruder, began niggling away in my mind. I was balancing the vehicle's allure with the fact that we had already introduced the emissions of several internal combustion engines into the atmosphere. Reluctantly, I decided to share my unwelcome thoughts.

"Any of you see an irony in our situation with the truck?"

The three of them looked at me. Weasel sighed and smiled. "What's on your mind, Mac?" he asked.

I was relieved to detect no impatience in his voice. We had begun to evolve into a group with three leaders. In another couple of years we all expected Stevie would be the fourth. Respect for the input of others was vital to that process.

"I know what you're thinking," said Sarah. "The situation struck a discordant note with me, too."

Stevie was looking back and forth between Sarah and me, finally discarding both of us as reliable sources and turning to Weasel. "What's going on with these two?" he inquired.

"Well, son," Weasel said to Stevie, "we got a very nice family here and we're damned lucky all of us got good brains. Thing about brains, though, is they work differently for everyone. So all of us are smart in different areas. Now these two confused individuals," he nodded in our direction, where we sat side by side, holding hands, "and I mean that with respect, see what's called 'the big picture' better'n you and me. The two of us," he now put his arm around Stevie, "are better at creating things and fixing stuff than they are. So we got good balance. Wouldn't wanna have it any other way."

"Well spoken, Weasel," Sarah responded. She gave my hand a squeeze. "I think I'll let Mac explain what's on our minds."

"All of us know what caused the collapse. That truck out there was one of the major contributors."

"But, Mac, it's only one truck," said an exasperated Stevie.

"True," I said. "But is it a first step? Ten years from now is there going to be a fleet of cars and trucks and ethanol complexes refining fuel and filling the skies with fumes again?"

"Even if there was," said Weasel, "it would be only a fraction of what was goin' on in the 20th cen."

"Bullshit," I said to Weasel. "If we get technology cranking again our population could be in the billions again in a couple of hundred years. We already did it once. I figure the world right now is pretty close to what it was around 1790. Took them 200 years to crank it to max and then blow it to hell."

"Who cares?" said Stevie. "We'll all be dead."

"So it's OK with you, Stevie, if we go down in the history books as the morons that started up the use of the internal combustion again?"

"Well...uh...actually I don't guess I want to be remembered like that."

"So where do we stop?" asked Sarah, entering the battle. "What's our responsibility."

"Our responsibility," said Weasel, "is to survive and protect people like all of us who just want to live a good life and be left alone to do it. That there truck is gonna help us."

"Are we that important? More important than the idea of never again repeating the mistakes of the past?"

Weasel looked intently at both of us. "How many people you figure are out there that're like us? Don't wanna cause no trouble. Decent folks. Care about their kids. Wanna be free of the clans."

"A whole bunch," I said. "I can't see them. But they have to be out there somewhere. We can't be the only ones."

"You figure those decent people can afford to lose you and me and Sarah and Stevie? How about ol' Duke? He be able to find a nice family like us if we get killed? What if the three of us get killed and Stevie lives?"

His questions hung in the air, like eagles drifting on thermals, wings out stretched, unaware of the menace below.

"Enough," I said, standing and reaching out to shake Weasel's hand. "Thanks, Weasel. Sarah and I never considered not protecting our family. But we had to ask the question."

"Havin' a conscience sure is a pain in the ass," he replied. "But I wouldn't want to have you two any other way. Thing is, if I get you two killed off, who's gonna be the conscience for the rest of us? There ain't no way you two would ever let someone start building refineries. Hell if we couldn't talk 'em out of it, we'd just blow the fuckers up."

"Yeah," said Stevie. "CHINA SYNDROME, dudes. Mac is Michael Douglas and Sarah is Jane Fonda. No one would get away with that shit with you two around." He gave us all high fives. "Let's get back to business. We got plans to make."

Weasel looked over to Sarah and me. "You two OK with this? I don't wanna move on until you're comfortable."

We both nodded our assent. Our survival outweighed considerations of a problem that couldn't begin to manifest itself for fifty or a hundred years into the future. After all, I thought, what kind of positive impact could we have if we were dead.

CHAPTER TWENTY-FOUR

"Here's the way I figure it," Weasel said. He was decked out in a welder's apron, black leather boots, welder's gloves, a big visor that flipped down when he was welding, and a torn Son Volt t-shirt. The visor had a little window in it so he could see what he was doing and was in the up position as he laid out the work plan for us. He looked like a cross between a blacksmith and a 1940's steel worker. We were in front of the garage, the four of us and Duke gathered around the truck, ready to put in a hard day's labor.

It had taken us two days to blow out the front of the garage to accommodate the truck's height. We raised the headers and elevated the garage door four feet. We had an enclosed space to make more modifications—and hide the truck.

"Once we finish with the changes, this here vehicle," Weasel emphasized his point by smacking the truck with a crow bar, "is gonna serve three functions. First thing it's gonna be is our new armory. When we finish, we'll take most of the guns and ammo we got in the basement armory and store them in here. If we ever need to leave in a hurry, then we don't leave our defenses behind."

"And," I added, "we don't leave any loot behind for the clans. I'd hate to add what's downstairs to what they already have. When we get it loaded, we park it inside the garage. It's close to the house, ready to go."

"What's its next function?" Sarah asked.

"Between the four of us, in the next few days we're gonna make this thing as close to impregnable as possible."

"Good word," Sarah commented.

"Been working on vocabulary on the computer," Weasel explained. "'Impregnable' means 'cannot be overcome by force.' That's what this vehicle will be when we're done. Function number two will be a war wagon. We can use it for offense or defense. The Babe's gotta be made to disappear. This may be the way."

"And the third?" I asked.

"Tell 'em, Stevie," Weasel said.

"It's another back door," Stevie replied. "Between the eight tunnel exits and the truck, we're up to nine escape routes."

Weasel continued with the lecture. "We cut out a bunch of sheets from rail road freight cars for extra armor. Measured first and cut 'em all to pattern." He walked us over to where we could see them laying flat on the truck bed. "You can see a bunch of dents in 'em where me and Stevie did a little target practice. They stop everything we pump at 'em. Even a .44 mags. Also 10 mm semis. Haven't tried a 50 cal cuz we don't got one. If we run into trouble, don't figure to see anything heavier'n 44's or 10mm from the clans. I know where to find a 50 cal, but it's not in an easy in and out area."

"These steel panels look awfully damn heavy," I said, "are we going to be able to move them into place?"

"We loaded 'em with a winch that operates from the cab," he answered. "But none of 'em are really that big. It can't get too heavy, or else we're gonna have a problem with the truck. That's why I cut off parts of the bed and moved 'em around. Gonna use about half of what we cut off, too. But a lot of it ain't the right size for what I got in mind. That's why we made these custom welds."

"And keep this in mind," Stevie added. "This truck was designed to pull a full load of dirt or stone in the bed. That's several tons. A little extra weight on the armor isn't going to bother its performance a bit."

Weasel motioned Stevie over to his side. "The boy here knows the whole plan. Run through it for 'em, Stevie."

Stevie stepped away from us and moved to the front of the truck. I could see him trying to hide his smile. This was a serious responsibility that Weasel had given him. But at the same time he was overjoyed at his new status. He called Sarah and me over to the cab area and began to explain our tasks for the next two days.

"We're gonna armor plate parts of the doors and the side windows in case there's a clan attack. The window armor will be removable so we can see good when everything is running smooth." Stevie moved to the front of the truck and knelt down by the wheel. "Now these tires are also vulnerable to bullets, so we're gonna try to protect them as much as we can with more armor. You two got any questions?"

"Yes, Stevie," said Sarah. "How are we going to attach this armor to the truck?"

"Some of it will be welded," he replied. "Me and Weasel will do that. When we can get a firm base for bolts, we're gonna bolt them on. That way the armor is removable in case we want to make the truck lighter for work in safe zones. You and Mac will be doing mostly holding in place and carrying work. Also all of us are gonna paint this baby in camouflage colors when we're done with the modifications.

"Weasel figured we could use some spot lights. We're going to mount halogen lamps on the roof and hood and then wire it into the battery. We'll do the mounting and Weasel will do the wiring. We also gotta put together a tool box, first aid kit and some food and water."

"How long do you figure this will take?" I asked.

"Me and Weasel figure three nine hour days plus an extra hour at the end of each day for driving practice," he answered. "Starting now."

And so we started, Sarah and I were mules for the master craftsmen. It took us two days to finish—including the new paint job. On the third we rested.

CHAPTER TWENTY-FIVE

SEPTEMBER 2056

The first time one of Weasel's land mines was triggered, we ended up having steak for dinner. One of the cows from remote pasture had stumbled upon a weakness in the fence and had gone grazing in one of the several strips that had been mined. From the looks of her tracks, she had been out there for several hours, munching away at the high grass, oblivious in that special cow stupidity of the destruction that lay beneath her feet. At one of her stops, she had managed to trim the grass from the top of a mine without disturbing the device.

But she ultimately stepped on one with a front hoof. The resulting blast had killed her instantly, shredding her front legs and big head and eliminating the need for deer and varmint hunting for an entire month.

Weasel had found the mines in an armory over in Rock Falls, north and west of old O'Hare Airport. They were late 20th models, not the ones from Viet Nam, but the updated versions of the Claymore used in the middle east and South America by American troops in the 90's.

We didn't figure that the blast that awoke us at the deepest part of a warm September night was another cow. It never paid to think an unusual event was a random, harmless happenstance. Always interpret surprises as harbingers of doom—Rule Thirteen in the Book of Weasel.

Like pre-collapse firemen, we all jumped into our roles when the shuddering blast of the claymore awoke us. Dressing quickly, making sure the bottom layer was body armor, all of us donned our headsets, courtesy of *I Spy, You Spy*, and grabbed our weapons. Weasel headed straight up to the observation post on the roof.

No lights were switched on in the house to aid us in our tasks. We had done the drill blindfolded many times. All the routes had been mapped and memorized, locked in our brains. But since Weasel had come up with the Night Vision Goggles from the SWAT armory over in the city, we used the NVG's to navigate to our posts.

Merlin, back again for another visit and technology fix, stumbled out of his room, the sweet scent of stale marijuana smoke accompanying him like bad cologne.

"Mac, you there. Where's the lights? You hear that, Mac?" he asked excitedly. "Something blew up out there. Shit, man, we under attack?"

"Not sure yet," I replied, sticking a set of NVG's on his head. "You're with me."

Duke, excited by the change in routine, sensing the adrenaline rush all of us were transmitting, followed me and Merlin downstairs. I let him out the front door to patrol the inside the barbed wire barrier. If there was something inside our walls that didn't belong, he would let us know.

Sarah and Stevie split up and headed front and back, second floor to check the outside, peering through the gun slots in the blackout shutters, while I did the same for both sides of the house, running through the long hallway that traversed the second floor.

"Back clear," Stevie's voice said in my headset.

"I got movement in the front," Sarah said.

"I got 'em," Weasel drawled from the cupola on the roof. "Three standin' still as dogs on point and one chile releno on the ground. What about you, Mac?"

"Clear on the sides," I said. "Nobody inside the walls according to Duke. What's your reading, Weasel?"

"I see 'em as clan scouts, not indies," he said. "Too well armed for indies. Each one's got a rifle and a couple of pistols. The three still standing are either black or got camouflage paint on for night work. Guy on the ground isn't moving. I'm taking them out. There may be more out there. Don't want to mess with these guys if they got friends coming."

"Shit." It was Sarah's voice. We all heard it over the headsets Each of us was open to everything that was said. And each of us knew what she was thinking: They're just standing there in the dark. How can you kill them?

"The fuck you think they came here for, Sarah?" Weasel replied, not bothering to hide the exasperation in his voice. "To get the name of a good real estate agent? They're lookin' for Mac and Duke."

"I know. I know," she replied. "It's gotta be done. Doesn't mean I have to like it."

"Don't care a whole lot for it myself," came Weasel's reply through all of our headsets. There was a sadness in his voice. But it wasn't for the men in our mine field. It was for the fact that Sarah hadn't understood this didn't come easy to him either.

He had a Mauser SP 66 sniper rifle up there with him. It was there all the time, along with a HK 81 assault rifle and a Heckler & Koch HK21A1 GP belt fed machine gun. It was one of the few available machine guns designed to be operated by one man. Every weapon in Weasel's nest fired the 7.62 mm rounds. The Mauser sniper rifle had a flash suppressor and scopes for both day and night.

I had practiced with it at night and knew that with the Varo image intensifying scope, operating on the same available light principle as our night vision goggles, Weasel could see the interlopers well enough to count the lashes on their eyes. All of us were good shots, but he and Stevie were the best, consistently nailing targets 400 to 500 meters in distance. The clan scouts were under 100 meters away.

"Hold it," I said. "We should talk to one of them."

"Gotcha," came his reply. Two shots followed, less than a second between them. "It's done. Third guy's still standing."

I left the house and went through the tunnel under the barbed wire. I yelled at the clan soldier. "The sniper's still got you in his sights. You're surrounded by mines. If you don't move, you'll live. We'll come get you in the morning." I couldn't tell him to toss his weapons away for fear they would trigger another blast from one of the mines.

I went back behind the barrier, whistled for Duke, returned to the house. Then I gathered up Merlin, heading up to Weasel's post in the cupola where we replaced him at the spot in front of the HK machine gun with Merlin. "If that guy moves," I instructed Merlin, "just point and pull the trigger. Follow the bullet tracks right up to him."

"No problem, man," Merlin replied, stroking the gun. "I can do this. Guy moves, I turn him into compost. Right?"

"We'll be back at daylight," Weasel said. "You're safe here."

"I am not frightened," Merlin replied, as if rehearsing the words for a mantra. "You leaving Duke here?"

"He's coming with us," I said.

"No problem," Merlin replied. "Wish I had a joint. Left 'em in my room."

• • • •

Weasel, Stevie, Sarah and I exited the basement, each from a different tunnel. It took about five minutes to clear the booby traps and then all of us were out, beyond the fences and pastures, checking the night environment for signs of more intruders. Duke, making his own decision, had chosen to be with Stevie. None of us knew his criteria. Sarah figured some kind of telepathic sense guided his decisions at such times. Within an hour, all of us had returned safely. No other clan soldiers were outside our walls.

"No sign of any backup for this group," Weasel said. "Definitely a scouting party."

Back in the basement, near time for the sun to rise, Weasel inspected our group and said to Sarah, "I'm not so sure about that dog telepathy stuff. Everybody looks pretty healthy. Nothing out there to harm us tonight."

She looked up at him, ignoring his attempt to start one of their friendly arguments. "I owe you an apology," she said. "I disrespected you tonight. It was very narrow of me to think I'm the only one here who abhors killing. It's not good for any of us to be so internally focused. That's one of the most important things I've learned from you, Weasel. You care for us more than you do for yourself. Will you forgive me?"

Uncomfortable as ever with a show of emotion, Weasel shuffled his feet and gazed at the floor. "I can't imagine anything you'd do that I wouldn't forgive you for, Sarah," he said to his feet.

"Maybe," Sarah said, changing the subject and smiling as she reached out and gently squeezed his cheek, "Stevie would have befallen some kind of harm if Duke hadn't been there. Stepped in a hole, got bitten by a snake. Something like that. Maybe Duke's presence stopped that event." Sarah turned toward Stevie. "What do you think, Stevie?"

He looked over at me and gave me a sly little smile. "Well, I did mostly follow Duke's lead. He might have known something I wasn't aware of."

"There," Sarah said. "There you go. Even Stevie says its possible."

"Shit," Weasel scoffed, happy to be back on safe conversational ground, "that ain't fair. Sayin' something might have happened that didn't happen. You can't prove that."

"And you can prove otherwise? That such an event wasn't a possibility?"

"You're beginning to piss me off," Weasel said, smiling.

"I know," she said. "It's one of my favorite hobbies."

• • • •

"Except piss and sit down, guy didn't move an inch. Guess his legs couldn't hold him up any more." Merlin was pleased with himself when we came up to tell him his turn behind the machine gun was over. "Your life always like this, man?" he said to no one in particular. "It's a fucking trip. Every time I been here there's some spectacular shit going down. Vids, goddam truck in the garage, building shit…Now this attack. I gotta go get me a joint. Chill out a bit."

"Merlin," I said, "this wasn't an attack. They stumbled upon the mines by accident, sniffing around. Probably looking for me, but definitely not an assault on the compound. If you're around when that happens, there will be no doubt as to what's going down."

The sun was fully risen when the five of us stepped out of the house to bring in our prisoner. He was sitting, knees up, arms across them, perfectly still. "Stand up," I hollered at the man from the porch. "I'm gonna walk you in. Take off all your clothes first. Shoes too."

"Fuck you, asshole," he yelled back.

"Let's go have breakfast," I suggested. "He'll wait."

When we came back an hour later, satisfied with the coffee and biscuits and Merlin's vegetable and cheese omelets, the man was in the same spot, butt naked, his clothes and weapons in a pile beneath his feet. He looked completely ridiculous, big bellied, bow-legged, barrel-chested, pasty pale white man with a huge round black camouflage face. Looked like a bowling ball on a snowman.

• • • •

"Ooo eeee," said the man, completely in awe, totally oblivious of his nakedness or the fact that he was our prisoner. He was looking at me the way a hungry man does a nice fat hen turkey. We were in the kitchen.

"Big man. Tall. Well-armed. Plus a tan dog. Jackpot. This close to the fucking prize. I found McCall." He did a little jig, dancing in place, mindless of his arm and leg manacles. "Nail your ass and every fuckin' slit in the state'll lay down for me. Goddam. I'm fucking rich. Feels good to be so close."

"You want I should surrender now or later?" I asked, giving his shoulder a shove. Without his arms for balance, he found himself abruptly seated on the floor. "Scoot into that corner," I instructed. "And shut the fuck up. We don't want to hear you babble."

"He's nuts," Stevie said, looking at the black-faced man sitting in a corner of our kitchen.

"Not nuts," said Merlin. "High. Look at his eyes. Check his clothes. That's where it is. Must have been snorting all night. Bad Boy, I'd guess. Makes you feel invincible."

The man's head whirled on Merlin and he popped to his feet like a jack-in-the-box. "Shut up you little fuckin' scrote," he snarled. "I know who you are. Seen you pokin' around our camp, seen you out tradin' for your weed and those fuckin' cassettes. You're dead too, little man. We're comin' after all of you."

Sarah laughed. "Al Jolson on acid," she said. "Let's go clean the guns. He's no threat to us."

His fevered eyes turned to Sarah. "McCall's cunt, huh?" he said. "Nice hair bitch. Seen all kinds of colors. Blue, green, pink too, but never red like that. Your pussy that same color. Let me see, baby. Show me that snatch. We can make a big score with red pussy hair. Sell it 'til it dries…ooofff."

Stevie buried his fist in the man's solar plexus driving the wind from his lungs. The soldier sat straight down again and rolled into a fetal position, his mouth working soundlessly, hands clenching spasmodically behind his back.

"Somebody tie him up," Weasel said. "We gonna go clean those guns like Sarah suggested."

"One of us should stay and watch him," Merlin said.

"Duke," Stevie said, loud enough for our prisoner to hear. "If the man moves an inch, tear him up."

As we left the room, commanding Duke to guard the Messenger, I put my arm around Stevie's shoulders. "Beat me to the punch, young man," I told him. "Thanks."

He was embarrassed by what the man who didn't know he was a prisoner had said about Sarah. "Needed to be shut up," he replied. "Lost it for a second. Sorry."

"They have an interesting outlook on women," Sarah said.

"Women are property to the clans," Merlin replied. "The good ones are very valuable. But they have no rights, no say in the running of things."

"Some things never change," Sarah said.

• • • •

Before we cleaned our weapons, not much more than a ritual because only one had been fired, we dragged the corpses from the field, deftly maneuvering through the Queen Anne's Lace and tulips to avoid the mines. Each mine field was mapped, but to make life easier during spring and early summer, we had planted tulips to the right of each mine. The brightly colored flowers were now gone, but the spiked leaves remained, drawing sustenance from the sun to feed the bulbs and marking a safe path for us through the mines. When the tulip leaves dried up, Queen Anne's Lace would mark safe passage zones.

We buried the dead clan soldiers out back, behind the house. No one offered a prayer for their souls.

We took their weapons, drugs and ammo, destroying the M 16's and several of the older semi-auto pistols, removing them from circulation. We kept the clips, couple of hundred .223 rounds, and drugs—Slammer, Bad Boy and some crystal meth. Their jewelry and clothes were buried with them. Like the drugs, the jewelry could have been valuable in trade, but none of us had the desire to touch the corpses. The men felt filthy to us, not only physically, but also spiritually.

Down in the basement armory, we talked while we stored the captured ammo and two of their pistols. "Out of those four men," Weasel said, "I see three clans."

"You hit it right," Merlin said, loading up a pipe. Of the five of us, he was the most knowledgeable on the signs and affiliations of the clans. A wandering trader and barterer, as well as a former clan member, he was familiar with at least a hundred of the groups. "All of them were People, too. You saw all the jewelry was worn on the left."

"The tattoos, too," Weasel said. "Pyramids, five pointers, diamonds. Those are all People signs. But I'm not sure what specific clans they are. What about it, Merlin?"

"Two of 'em are Messengers," he said between tokes on his freshly loaded pipe. "The one trussed up in the kitchen with Duke and the guy that stepped on the mine." He offered the pipe to me.

I declined, as did Sarah, Stevie and Weasel. "If I smoke," Sarah said, "I won't be able to carry any single thought beyond two sentences. I don't know how you do it, Merlin."

We all nodded in agreement. If we smoked we would accomplish nothing, and upstairs, bundled up and partnered with Duke, was a man we needed to talk to.

Merlin laughed. "I'm not so sure I could carry on a conversation straight," he said. "I just find my level every day and stay that way. What were we talking about?"

I pointed to the ceiling. "The man in our kitchen," I said. "The one that wants to kill you."

"Oh, yeah. The clans. That pig upstairs is definitely a Messenger. Upside down cross tattoo, left side of his head shaved. Then in the ground out back you got another Messenger and a Lakeside Homeboy and your basic Black Mamba, one of the snake clans. They're Cobra wannabes, the snakes are. But the Cobra's won't have anything to do with 'em.

"How can you tell exactly what clan they're with?" Sarah asked.

"Homeboy had the 'H B' and the pyramid tattoos on his hand," Merlin said, "and the Mamba had the snake earring in left ear plus the usual stars and shit."

"So what does that tell us?" Sarah asked. "Anything new?"

"If hanging out with Satan's Messengers means these guys have joined up, then both of these clans are new entries under the Babe's umbrella," he said. "This is the first time I've seen a Homeboy or a Black Mamba affiliated with the Messengers. Homeboys like to think they're hot shit, but they're really just preening punks. They tried to fuck with the fishing territory of the Black Gangster Disciples couple of years ago and got their asses whipped pretty good. Never really recovered. But in their own minds, they are mean. Not in anyone else's, though. Mambas are small fish too. But it's starting to add up. The Babe may be getting a bunch of punks to join up, but his numbers are getting pretty impressive."

"So are his problems," I said. "With prosperity comes some extra responsibilities. Food, drugs, weapons...I'd say he's got four or five hundred soldiers to keep fed and armed."

"And don't forget women," said Merlin. "He's gotta have plenty of whores. These guys are animals. One of the lieutenants in the Messengers offered me a half pound of Slammer if I could come up with a half dozen decent whores. That's ten times what the price was six months ago."

Sarah shot him a withering look. Merlin didn't miss it. He held up his hands in supplication. "Don't start on me, Sarah," he implored. "I never deal in people. I came out of a clan myself. I know what goes on inside. Believe me, I'm never gonna peddle human flesh."

"What I can't figure out," I said, "is why The Babe is bothering with me when he's got all those other problems. He obviously wants to rule Chicago, run the whole show. Why worry about one guy and a dog?"

"The Cobras you killed were People," Weasel said. "So are the Messengers. Maybe he's trying to buy some votes."

"It's possible," Merlin said. "Cobras are huge. They like to handle their own shit. And I know they don't trust the Messengers. But they can't begin to find out anything about Mac. No one has any idea where you live."

"Why didn't they put a price on my head, like The Babe did?" I asked.

"It's not the code, man," Merlin replied. "It would be totally against their system of beliefs to hunt an enemy for material rewards. The honor of their clan is at stake. When you killed those men, it became personal for every Cobra. Any soldier who hunted a Cobra enemy for profit would be outed by the clan."

"Those soldiers we killed on Roosevelt Road were completely out of control," I said. "They weren't anything like any of the Cobras I had ever dealt with. I'd never seen any of Roberto's men that combative. They didn't give us any choice."

"You ever try to tell Roberto that?" Merlin asked me.

"No. Been too busy hiding."

"It could solve some problems."

"It could get me killed."

"If Roberto agrees to talk with you," Merlin said, "he won't take you out. Not there, at least."

"We'll think about it," I said, looking around at Stevie, Sarah and Weasel. "But we still have the Messengers to deal with. Why are they after me?"

"Because of what you saw in that parking lot last year, Mac," Merlin said. "The massacre. Only reason they need. He was starting a war there. Breaking every one of the few rules that the clans operate by. Why in the hell didn't you tell anybody about it? That's pretty important shit."

"Yeah, yeah, yeah," I said. "I know all that stuff. But to tell you the truth, who's going to believe me? Folks clans, sure. Because that's what they want to believe. But People clans wouldn't believe it. No way. There's more. And I think its related to the Cobra, Felipe', the guy Duke chewed up on Roosevelt Road. Think about this: The

Messengers were hunting me quietly until we whacked those Cobras. Then suddenly I'm number one priority for every People clan within fifty miles."

"And all this time," Sarah said, "not a peep out of Roberto and the Insane Cobra Nation."

"That's what I don't understand," I said. "But I've got an idea that's been percolating. Mull this one over: What if Roberto, leader of the Cobras, incredibly respected by his clan, never knew anything about any of this, nothing about Felipe' sleeping with the Messengers? Nothing about who perpetrated the massacre at the parking lot?"

"The implications of that theory are pretty severe," Weasel said.

"Right," I said. "It would mean that Roberto and The Insane Cobra Nation have been infiltrated by the Messengers. It's not such a far-fetched theory. Loyalty is a valued attribute in the clan culture. But individual weakness is also rampant. How hard would it be to find a soldier in any clan that could be bribed away from his affiliation?"

"It's a great hypothesis," Sarah said. "But unfortunately it's untestable. The Babe is the only one who would know."

"Why don't we ask our friend upstairs," Merlin said. "You see the crosses on the backs of his fingers?"

"Yeah," Weasel said. "Upside down. Identifies him as belonging to the clan."

"More than that," Merlin said. "The man's a player. Only about ten Messengers got five crosses on one hand. This guy is one of 'em. It's like when they used to have armies in the 20th. You did good, you got stripes. The more stripes you got, the higher your rank. Those crosses are the Messengers version of stripes."

"What happens if you get demoted?" Stevie asked.

Merlin held up a finger of one hand. With the other hand, he made a scissors with two fingers and snipped at the extended digit.

• • • •

The prisoner was in a corner of the kitchen, hands and feet manacled with police cuffs. Three feet in front of him, Duke sat on his haunches, implacably staring into the man's eyes. Weasel had gone upstairs to check on him. "Guy's twitching every once a while," Weasel reported.

"Head and shoulder, like a spasm. Every time he does it, Duke snarls. Man is obviously scared shit of the dog. But he can't stop twitching."

"Good sign," Merlin said. "He's starting to come down from the Bad Boy he was snorting in the mine field. Been about four hours now. We can use that."

"Reward for cooperation," Stevie said.

"Right. One of the clan chemists told me Bad Boy is a combination of meth, cleaning solvents, battery acid and just a dash of window pane. Plus some home brewed PCP. There's about five different versions going around. Makes you mean, nasty and very brave. Also makes you want more. This man isn't an addict. Too fat to be one. Addicts last about a year. Die from malnutrition. Man hasn't been missing any meals. But when the drug wears off, he'll begin to realize he's in trouble. Probably start being scared, way a normal person would. A little Bad Boy would smooth out that edge."

I grabbed the bag of smoky grey powder that had been in our prisoner's shirt. It would be the carrot. Denying the drug was the stick. "Let's go talk."

• • • •

Sarah grabbed a soup bone from the freezer and tossed it to Duke, the signal that he had been relieved of guard duty. Bone in mouth, he walked over to the kitchen table where the five of us were seated, drinking milk and munching oatmeal-raisin cookies. Duke weaved in and out of the chairs, circling the table and receiving attention from each of us. Satisfied, he lay down under the table and began noisily working the bone. In the corner the naked man with the painted face, a drop-out from mime school, twitched and passively surrendered any sense of dignity he might have ever possessed. The drugs weren't helping any more.

"We need to talk," I told him.

"Hungry," he responded. "Thirsty."

I toasted him with a glass of milk. "After we talk."

"Fuck you." His head snapped down in a spasm. The right shoulder came up to meet it. Couple of times a minute now.

Each of us munched on a cookie and smiled.

"Fuck all of you."

Stevie went to the refrigerator and pulled out a pot of lamb stew, placed it in the microwave and set the timer and temperature. In about two minutes its smell began permeating the kitchen. Made me hungry even as I ate the cookies.

"How'd you find us?" Stevie asked.

"Been looking a long time," the Messenger said.

I went to the sink and poured a glass of water, giving the man two sips. A small reward. Then I went to the microwave and stirred the stew, intensifying the aroma of garlic, lamb and vegetable stock that floated in the air.

"How'd you find us?" I repeated.

"There's ten different scouting parties looking," the man said. A shiver shook his body. "The Babe knows which way I was headed. When we don't come back, you're fuckin' dead."

Weasel pushed back his chair, grabbed the prisoner's glass of water, took it to the sink and poured its contents out. "It pisses me off when you're not polite," he said. "We'll be back later."

As we each served ourselves a bowl of stew, the man screamed and pulsated, the little spasms increasing in frequency and intensity. "You're dead. You're all fuckin' slow dead. Except the cunt, McCall. She's mine. She's my dog. Gonna ride her while you..."

Duke materialized in the man's face, inches away, snarling, hairs on his back bristling, canines flashing. The Messenger went instantly silent. His eyes protruded from the sweat smudged face like twin full moons on a midnight sky.

"You interrupted his meal," I told him. "He hates it when that happens. If you make another sound, he's gonna chew off your testicles."

The Messenger lieutenant's eyes grew even wider, and a shudder shook his frame.

We all exited then, leaving the man alone with Duke once again. Hunger, thirst and the ravages of withdrawal from the Bad Boy would eat away his resolve.

CHAPTER TWENTY-SIX

T he five of us took our stew outside, eating at a picnic table behind the house. We discussed the next step and decided to give the prisoner another thirty minutes to simmer before we returned. Confident that the intruders had been a scouting party, we felt no sense of imminent danger—no more, that is, than we did every day. It would take several days before the Messengers declared them missing.

Sarah, Weasel and Merlin dispersed in three directions, looking for quick chores or, in Merlin's case, some down time. Stevie and I went through the woods to feed the free range chickens. They didn't care that we had a crisis. To them, hunger was a crisis.

As we hiked through the meadow and wooded area, Stevie was quiet. Something was on his mind. Normally he would have been full of questions and comments about the extraordinary events of the day. I continued hike side by side with him, waiting him out.

"I'm scared, Mac," he finally said.

I continued walking, not changing pace. "Of what?"

"It's not that man back there, if that's what you're thinking," he said.

"Wasn't thinking anything," I replied. "I know that after what you've seen and experienced, there's not a man alive that could scare you."

"That...thing...in the kitchen. I'm getting some memories back. Stuff I haven't thought about in years. The Messenger is triggering them. It's, uh, unpleasant."

"Is it like you're reliving all that bad stuff you experienced when you were a kid with the Messengers?"

"Not exactly. I never forgot any of that shit. The dogs, the beatings, that clan attack when I was seven, The Babe trying to get Eric to do him, then killing him. That stuff's not gone. It never will be. It was too powerful. It's just not as important to me as the present."

I pulled a couple pieces of grass and we both picked at our teeth with the sweet ends, thinking about what he had said.

"You know what I'm saying?" he asked.

"I think so. Look at the four of us. Even Merlin, too. Five. And Duke. Everyone's lived through devastatingly painful experiences. Physical pain, sure. But that kind of pain gets forgotten about. Break a leg, cut yourself, get shot. Man it sure is bad when it happens. But do we sit around and think about it years later?"

"Yeah," Stevie said. "The physical stuff kinda fades. But the pictures don't. Like when a dog pack was after me. Or the day with the wolves. You remember the fear more that the pain."

"Right," I said. "We don't dream about pain. We dream about fear."

Stevie put his head down and spoke softly. "I was lucky to be saved."

I nodded. All of us were. Sarah was the one that saved me. We both saved Weasel. And Weasel was returning the favor to all of us. The three of us considered ourselves lucky that we had the chance to do the same for Stevie.

"Tell me," I said. "You're not afraid of the Messenger prisoner on the kitchen and you're not afraid of the pain that's probably coming. If it's not the memories coming back, what's got you scared, Stevie?"

He niggled away at his teeth with the grass, at the same time poking around in his brain for the answer to my question. I didn't know if he wasn't sure…or just didn't want to say.

"I want to kill that man," he suddenly said, the words rushing out in a torrent. "That stupid, pathetic, fat bellied, face painted goon in our kitchen. I want to kill him because I know he's a fucking beast, and I know what he'd do to you and Sarah if he had the chance. I know the Messengers. When he talks about Sarah like that, he means what he says. Those freaks don't know any limits. It's like The Babe is a magnet, drawing every evil man within twenty miles to his camp. I want to take my knife and put it right below his navel and yank it up with both hands until it reaches his sternum. That's what scares me, Mac. I want to do it. I can see myself doing it."

"And you think that kind of feeling just isn't natural?"

"Right."

"Wrong. It's as natural as can be. I'll bet you that Weasel and Sarah feel the same way. I know I do."

"No shit," he said. "How do you hide it?"

"Same way you did. If we weren't talking right now, I wouldn't know the guy made you crazy. You controlled it beautifully. When you slice him up, can you see his intestines falling out between his fingers?"

"Great picture," he said. We both laughed. It was OK to laugh because we would never do it. I told him that.

"Unless you are a saint, there's no way you can't hate them, Stevie. It's natural. But torturing them isn't. We become like them if we do that. Make him suffer only in your mind. If he's a real threat, kill him. Just do it quick. You'll have to do it someday, maybe soon. They're coming after us, son. Evil men can't tolerate the existence of good people. When it happens, if you don't move fast, they'll kill you...or worse, someone you love."

"That's a scary thought," he said.

"I'm glad to hear it. If you enjoy it, the killing, then you can start to worry."

"I meant losing someone. Never cared about anybody until now."

• • • •

When we returned to the kitchen, the naked Messenger was paying full price for his night of packing the Bad Boy up his nose. Instead of three times an hour, his spasms were coming two, three times a minute. Shivers, tremors, full body contortions—they were coming in all the garden varieties of withdrawal. Between his spasms, I unlocked his handcuffs and allowed him to place his hands in front, relocking the cuffs after he massaged his aching muscles. For a minute I was the good guy. It wouldn't last for long.

"The higher you fly, the further you fall," Merlin said. "Must have been good shit. Only two ways to get through it." He was speaking loud enough for our prisoner to hear him.

"What's that?" I asked.

"Time or more drugs," he answered.

I pulled the bag of grey powder from my pocket. "Guy's a fucking mess," I commented, holding the bag up. "You mean this would help?" I tossed the bag toward the manacled prisoner, landing it right beside Duke's front paws, between man and dog.

The Messenger lieutenant gazed at the bag, then up to me. I think he was trying to look mean. It was hard to read his expression with the black paint masking his features. Whatever effect he was working on was completely demolished by a head, neck and shoulder convulsion that jerked him sideways, banging his head into the corner.

"You're a cocksucker, McCall," he said. "I'm gonna enjoy seeing your head on a stick."

"Duke," I said, flashing him a hand signal.

He was immediately in the man's face, lip to lip, teeth bared, growling ferociously. A splash of urine washed down the man's legs.

Weasel groaned. "That's fuckin' pitiful," he said to the man. "You call yourself a soldier? Hand me that mirror, will you, Sarah?"

She pulled a 3x2 oak framed mirror from the wall. Weasel walked it over to the man, tiptoeing around the growing puddle that surrounded his legs. Holding it up, he said, "Look at yourself. You're fat, ugly and painted like a member of the Insane Clown Posse. Top it all off, you're sitting in your own piss and shaking like a gut shot deer."

The Messenger looked into the mirror, quickly turning away. Reality's a bitch sometimes.

"Talk to us," I told the humiliated man. His bravado was temporarily in abeyance. Hard to act tough when you just pissed on yourself. "Tell us what we need to know and you can clean up, get some clothes on and have your drugs back."

"I'm hungry, too," he said, head down, voice soft.

"We'll feed you if you cooperate," Weasel said.

He didn't hesitate for long. "Whaddya wanna know?"

"Why is there a city wide bounty on Mac?" Sarah asked. "He hasn't done anything to you."

"The Babe's had us looking for a year now," he said. "We kept it inside. Our business. Babe don't tell me everything. He just told all of us he wants McCall. Alive."

"We know all that, ass wipe," Merlin said. "The lady asked you why the Messengers put out a city wide bounty on the man and the dog."

"He fucked with the Cobras," the man said. "Cobras are People. They're our brothers."

I flashed on the Gaylords, slaughtered and tortured in the parking lot by the college, just about a year ago. The start of all of our current problems. They were People, too.

"Bullshit," Merlin said. "Cobras spit on you guys. They think you're a bunch of animals. Only reason they tolerate you is because someone decided you were People thirty or forty years ago."

The man looked up at Merlin. He started to speak when another tremor hit him, pulling his head down and his shoulder up as if he were trying to quell an uncontrollable itch on his shoulder by rubbing it with his chin.

When the seizure had run its course, he spoke, a crooked little smile on his blackened face. "You ain't as up to date as you think, little man. Babe's had a couple of sitdowns with Roberto. Cobras are thinking about joining up with the Messengers. First thing happens we join together is little bugs like you get squashed."

"Think maybe them Cobras will provide diaper service for you Messengers?" Weasel asked, verbally slapping the Messenger back down.

I picked up the bag of Bad Boy, which had remained untouched by the pool around the man. Taking out a handful, I sprinkled it in the urine, watching it dissolve into the liquid. Our prisoner's eyes widened. Another series of twitches shook his body.

"I'm not believing your answer about why there's a price on me and my dog," I said, floating some more powder to the floor. The contents of the bag diminished. Only half remained. The smell of urine was getting stronger. I wanted to finish it up.

"People stick together," he said. "It's the fucking code, McCall."

I took another handful of powder and threw it in his face. It stuck to the greasy paint, making his countenance look like it was covered with dirty snow. "Stop!!!" he screamed, frantically darting his tongue out as far as possible, retrieving as much of the drug as he could from his lips and chin. "You're fucking nuts. That's the best goddam BB in a hundred territories."

My hand went back into the bag. His eyes followed the movement.

"OK. OK," he said, licking his now white lips with a newly blackened tongue. "Truth. Just put the shit back in the bag." Another seizure hit him as I poured the powder from my hand back into the bag. "Cobras are playing with us. Think they're hot shit. Better'n us. Babe offers Roberto drug concessions, jewelry, guns, whores, even little kids to play with. Roberto ain't buyin'. Says he don't want no war, got enough whores and guns and don't fuck children. What a wimp."

"The Babe had a Cobra on his payroll, didn't he?" I asked, referring to the recently deceased Felipe.

The prisoner snorted in derision. "You don't know half of it, McCall," he said. "All this fancy shit you got," he moved his head to indicate the interior of the house, "you're still nothing but a dumb fuck indie. And Roberto...he ain't got the balls to lead the Cobras anymore. He's out of touch. Asshole gives books to his soldiers. Makes 'em listen to women trying to teach them to read. Woman's mouth should be sucking cock, not telling a soldier what to do."

Sarah pushed back from the table and walked over to me. "Excuse me, sweetheart," she said, voicing dripping with solicitude, "do you mind if I have a word with this gentleman?"

I moved over, making room for her just outside the puddle. She sat on her heels and, speaking sweetly, asked the prisoner, "Now tell me, does all of this cocksucking occur before or after you big, tough Messengers piss yourselves?"

"Fuck you, bitch," the man snarled, hatred flaring in his eyes. "You got a big mouth. How many Messenger cocks you think you can fit in that hole?"

"If they're all the same size as your equipment," Sarah responded, nodding toward his crotch, "at least a dozen. Did you get shot or something?"

The Messenger lunged at her, reaching out with manacled hands for her neck. Duke flashed forward and took a chunk from his forearm before the man retreated back to his corner, yelping in pain.

Sarah pulled Duke to her, putting her arm around his shoulders, reaching across to stroke his chest. He turned his head and nuzzled her neck.

"Let me tell you something about this dog," she told the Messenger soldier, a man now both humiliated and angered, a man who was losing control because he was in withdrawal from the massive doses of Bad Boy he had stoked himself with in the mine field. "Unlike the dogs you see running in packs, he feels love and respect for human beings. Well actually, just for us. Because we love and respect him in return. We're his family. He protects us. Thing about dogs, though, is that they are carnivores, meat eaters. All dogs are. When they hunt and bring down an animal, or sometimes a man, they go for the internal organs. Always the liver first. It's the most nutritious and satisfying to them."

The man was now watching Sarah and Duke very closely, frequently shaking as another tremor racked his frame. He didn't like the direction her conversation was heading.

"Now you may think," she continued, "that Duke here thinks you're another human being, just like the five of us. But that's not the way he looks at it. If you're not family, you're just another piece of meat to him. Prey. And you know what? Duke here knows exactly where your liver is. And if I allow him, he'll eat right through your body until he finds it. Watch."

Sarah leaned down and whispered in Duke's ear, as if she were having a talk with him. In actuality, she would give him a one word command. In this instance, it would be "sit," which in Duke-speak meant "attack the torso."

He plunged forward, straight at the prisoner's side, right above the spot where the hip bone begins, snarling and baring his teeth. The Messenger tried to become one with the wall, ended up slipping in the wetness around him as he tried to scramble away from the gnashing teeth. Sarah tapped Duke's flank twice, breaking off the attack before he tore off a chunk of meat.

The Messenger, now almost completely covered with his own urine, pulled himself to a sitting position and stared wide-eyed at Duke.

"Now," Sarah said, "before you enlightened us with your views on the role of women in your clan, you were about to tell us something about The Babe and his relationship to The Insane Cobra Nation. Please continue."

"Over the past couple a' years," the man said woodenly, "we found some Cobras that ain't so much interested in books and fixing up buildings. Pussy and drugs is pretty much what they wanted. We supplied it to 'em. Babe's got some young stuff he brings 'em in with. They like it, they bring some others in."

"How many?" Weasel asked.

"Them that got killed by McCall and the dog, there were three in that bunch. We got five or ten more. They tell us what Roberto's up to so maybe we can get some advantage on him. Get him over to our side."

"How long this gonna take?" Weasel asked, wrinkling his nose. "Gettin' a bit ripe in here."

"You butt wipes remind me of the Cobras," the prisoner said, looking at Weasel. "Got all these big ideas, always building shit, think you're better than everyone else. Let me tell you something. The Babe's got this big bird cage, you see. Must have held some kind of owl or hawk or somethin'. Takes it with him whenever we move. Keeps his drugs in it. Just hangin' there from the ceiling, full of the best stuff. He always gets the best shit. Anyway, The Babe figures he's gonna go visit the Cobras, take Roberto this cage, covered with a blanket, see, and then he's gonna sit down and talk awhile and then suddenly remove the blanket and surprise Roberto with this great present. Then—when Roberto is real grateful—the Cobras will understand The Messengers are someone to take seriously. Insane Cobra Nation will join up with Satan's Messengers. Then we do some serious dancing. Rule this fucking city. Wipe out fucking dweebs like you."

"What's in the cage, asshole?" Weasel asked.

The Messenger looked at all of us. Smiling, he said, "McCall's fucking head, you stupid shit. McCall's fucking head is gonna buy us the Cobras."

CHAPTER TWENTY-SEVEN

T he prisoner, a man whose name we had never learned because you don't want to put a name to garbage, was mightily pleased with himself. We didn't let the man know we, too, were pleased. Instead, we gave him a mop and pail of water, allowing the Messenger scout to clean himself with the water he used to mop the floor.

In addition to being a bully, he was a whiner. Before we fed him, he groveled for his Bad Boy, needing a hit to control his spasms, resurrect his courage and resurrect his dignity. After he ate, I poured the remaining Bad Boy down the sink, causing him to go ballistic. Hands free so that he could eat, he lunged at me, mouth twisted in a snarl eyes popped wide in rage. Before Duke could take his ankle off, I stuck my arm out, fist locked, and he obligingly met it with his face, dropping to the floor, lights out before he landed.

We manacled his hands again and tossed him in the closet, allowing for the possibility that he was of value to the Messengers. He was, in other words, a keeper, of possible potential as a trade if things went badly for us. His presence presented a security problem, which we solved by building a new door to the closet, installing two dead bolts and two cross bars which could only be opened from our side. The only ways out for him were one of us opening the door or persistent use of his teeth.

"Jesus, Mac," Stevie said, smiling at the Messenger hitting the floor, "guy went nuts when you poured that shit down the sink. You think maybe that was a form of torture, stringing him along like that and then not giving it to him." His grin had broadened.

"Well, son," I said in mock seriousness, "drugs are a scourge upon our land. Man was in real bad shape. Any more of that shit in his system could have killed him. Might have twitched his head right off his shoulders. Call it forced detox. We're really doing him a favor."

"Yeah," Stevie said. "I see where you're coming from. Altruism in the highest sense of the word. Plus…he's still got all his intestines and we have our dignity intact."

"I don't know what you two are talking about," Merlin said, mystified by the banter between Stevie and me, "but we need to change the subject real quick. That asshole just laid some serious bad news on us."

"You believe what he said about the Cobras?" I asked. "The possibility of them joining up with the Babe."

"From what I know about Roberto, it's hard to grasp. I can't see it. But it's a fucked up situation out there, man. Nothing would surprise me."

"What are we doing about this?" Sarah asked.

"Team the Cobras up with the Messengers and you got a juggernaut," Weasel commented. "Un-fucking-stoppable. Be ten or twenty years before the dust settled."

"No way," Merlin said, "is Roberto going to throw in with The Babe. He's got too much pride. Plus, near as I can tell, he is a sane man."

"Unlike the Babe," Stevie said.

"Man may be nuts," Merlin said, referring to The Babe, "but if he gets a couple of breaks, he's gonna make Idi Amin look like Snow White. And what he's looking for right now is your head, Mac. That's his first break. He thinks Roberto's gonna kiss his feet when he gives him your head."

"What about the story that the Messengers have spies in Roberto's camp?" Sarah asked. "Are we to believe that?"

"It's a whole bunch more believable than Roberto voluntarily teaming up with The Babe," Merlin answered. "I can see the scenario going down just the way the man described it. That could be our biggest problem. The Babe's eating away at the Cobras on two fronts. From within like some kind of cancer and the more direct route, trying to buy Roberto's allegiance with Mac's head."

"We need to narrow the field," Weasel said. "Too many players. We have two of the biggest clans out there after Mac's head."

"Here's the way I see it," Merlin said. "Reason The Babe is courting the Insane Cobra Nation is that the Cobras got the respect of all the People clans. Messengers got the fear, but Cobras got the respect. The Babe can't unify the People without Roberto's blessing."

"So why doesn't he just take the Cobras out," I asked.

"He could probably do it," Merlin replied. "But think of how many men it would cost him. Cobras wouldn't lay down. Roberto knows about fighting. War between those two could last for months. If The Babe won, he'd have nothing left. Have to start building all over again."

"And there's always the possibility he could lose," Sarah added.

"So either way, he can't afford to front the Cobras," Weasel said. "It's a lose/lose for the Messengers."

"Right," I said, beginning to get a grasp on the intricacy of the fat man's proclivity for evil. "And in the best tradition of Machiavelli, The Babe falls back on the tried and true methods of chicanery, subterfuge and bribery."

"And The Babe thinks he can get Roberto's blessing by presenting the Cobras with your head," Sarah said. "Oh, Mac, you've got to talk to Roberto. You've got some information he needs to know. If we can get the Cobras on the sidelines, then we can focus on the Messengers."

"Right," I said. "All 500 of them."

"Probably closer to 1000 now," Weasel said.

"You want me to set it up, Mac?" Merlin asked.

"Do it," I said. "It's really our only chance."

"How will you handle it, Merlin?" Sarah asked. "Why should Roberto consent to talk with Mac?"

"Roberto is intelligent," Merlin told her. "Intelligence means curiosity. That's what I'll play on, his curiosity. Plus he knows Mac. I think he'll be willing to listen."

"Where you going to set the meet?" Weasel asked.

"There's no choice in that. It has to be on Cobra turf. Mac will have to go to him. If he OKs the meet, he's doing us a favor. We have to go to him."

"Oh, Merlin," Sarah said, "that's so dangerous. What if Roberto has just recently decided to join up with the Messengers? He could kill

Mac right on the spot. We don't have any idea what's going on inside that camp."

"If Roberto promises Mac safe passage…"

"In and out," Weasel interjected.

"…in and out," said Merlin, "the man will honor the commitment. I'd stake my life on it."

"Yours and the rest of ours," Weasel continued. "Guilt by association. Let's say you're right. Mac gets safely in. Roberto keeps his word. What about those Messenger spies running around in the Cobra camp? What's to keep them from whackin' Mac?"

"I've got some thoughts on that," I said, feeling like I should have some input on a discussion that centered on my safety. "First of all, I'm not that easy to whack."

"They won't let you take any weapons in," Weasel said.

"Secondly," I continued, ignoring his comment, "anybody takes me out in Cobra territory while I'm under Roberto's guarantee of free passage is committing suicide. I don't see any of the Messengers or their Cobra spies as dedicated enough to the cause to knowingly give up their own life to take me out."

"The bounty is huge, Mac," Stevie said.

"They can't spend it in hell," I answered. "And that's where they'll be if they try for me when I'm under Roberto's guarantee of safety."

Everything I was saying had a ring of authenticity to it, as if I really believed it. But the points that Sarah, Weasel and Stevie were making were legitimate concerns. My problem was making them believe the risks were minimal. It was a particularly cantankerous issue, because I didn't believe it myself. It was Stevie who came up with the idea that made all of us feel more confident of my surviving a meeting with Roberto. What would happen to us after my discussion with the leader of the Cobras, was entirely dependent upon my persuasive abilities.

"Check this out," Stevie said. "We're all worried Mac's gonna get smoked while he's inside the Cobra borders. But we're sort of in agreement that if Roberto gives his word, he'll keep it." Stevie shifted his focus directly on the man who would set up the conference. "Merlin, can you get Roberto to agree to meeting Mac at the border, escorting him to a safe place for the talk and then getting him back safely?"

"No matter how the discussion goes," I said.

"So Mac's in Roberto's presence the whole time," Merlin commented. "Hell of an idea, dude. Some wild card out there is gonna be very reluctant to take Mac out right under Roberto's nose. Yeah, I think he'll buy it. When we doing this?"

"How soon can you leave?" Weasel asked.

"I'll pack some weed and I'm gone," Merlin replied.

CHAPTER TWENTY-EIGHT

"How can you read at a time like this?" she asked, her voice showing the strain.

"I always read before I go to bed."

"I'm worried about tomorrow," she said. Merlin came back in a single day with the news. It was set for me to go in the morning. Alone was the way I pictured it.

"There's a possibility he could believe me, about my not having a choice in killing his men," I told her. I thought that maybe if I acted like nothing big was happening, it would keep her from feeling the strain. Naturally, it didn't work because I was showing the strain myself with a myriad of tells.

"I'm not concerned about whether or not Roberto will believe you, Mac. I'm deathly afraid that he's going to kill you the minute he sets eyes on you. Or one of his men will. You should take me along."

"He's not going to kill me. At least not tomorrow anyway."

"Because of the code." She said it like it was a fantasy concept, a child's belief in a fairy that gives gifts for baby teeth.

"Be thankful for it," I said, tapping the bed beside me, inviting her over. "It means there's still a few rules still operating out there. He will keep his word."

She straightened the comforter that was folded over at the end of the bed, stopped to pet Duke, who acknowledged her with a sleep groan. Stripping off an oversize t-shirt, she climbed on the bed, got under the sheets, then turned to me, sitting cross legged, the sheet across her lap.

"Not all of the clans follow the code. Some of them make up the rules as they go," she pointed out.

Her green eyes met mine. Her auburn hair was shiny, freshly combed, short now for the summer and beginning to lighten a little in sun streaks. She was so beautiful. I couldn't remember a day I wasn't thankful for her. I had trouble keeping eye contact.

"I can't talk like this," I said. "With you like that. It's distracting."

She rolled her eyes. The hint of a smile pushed up at the corners of her mouth, then disappeared. "You could die tomorrow, and you're telling me you can't talk because my breasts are showing?"

"It's a distraction. Like a teensy little pebble in your shoe when you're walking. Doesn't hurt, doesn't slow you down, but you know it's there. Keeps making its presence known. Large breasts pretty much do the same thing to me."

"What about small ones?"

"Never seen a pair." Actually I had never seen any but hers, except on vids. "But I imagine it would be the same."

She pulled the sheet up, across her breasts. "I should go with you," she repeated.

"Let's work on that a minute," I said, able to focus on the matter at hand. "If you're right, about Roberto not following the code, then he's going to kill both of us."

"Right," she said. "But we'll be together."

"Kind of like a picnic with a bad ending," I commented.

"I'm not worried about the ending," she said. "I'm worried about you." She paused and pierced me with her eyes. "We are each other, you know. I would be diminished without you."

She was right. Each of our lives was defined by the presence of the other. She was also bringing in the heavy artillery.

"What about Stevie?" I asked. "Both of us killed would be devastating to him. He's under more pressure than he's showing with The Babe so close. And Weasel. He could be the strongest of all of us. But we both know how hard he took the death of his family."

"They would have each other," she replied. "That would help. You know Weasel would get him through it."

The stakes were high. I brought out the big gun.

"And Duke," I said. "How do you think he would fare with both of us gone?"

"You are a son of a bitch, Mac," she responded.

I reached over to her and pulled her head next to mine so that we were ear to ear, heads on each others shoulders, hands on the back of each others head. I stroked her hair.

"I love you, Sarah," I whispered. "The reason I don't want you to go is the same reason you want to. Neither of us wants the other in danger. Would you consider a compromise?"

She shook her head. Her breath came softly on my shoulder. I told her my idea. She accepted, and then escorted Duke to Weasel's room.

We made love softly and tenderly, more of a communique that an expression of passion. The closest we could get to each other was me on top, deep inside her, each of us looking into the other's eyes. We stayed that way for a long time, rocking gently, totally connected.

In the morning we left together.

CHAPTER TWENTY-NINE

erlin's presence at the breakfast table, coinciding with the new light of dawn, marked it as an important day. His first meal was usually a sleepy eyed lunch. It was traditionally a happy time, full of banter and big appetites. Another night we had survived, another day we could spend together.

"Jesus Christ," I exclaimed to the forlorn faces across the table, "I'm not dead yet, and this isn't a funeral."

"I'm getting some serious waves of negativity," Merlin said, pulling on a newly carved corn cob pipe. He was unaffected by the gravity of the impending meeting between me and Roberto. "Makes for bad karma, dudes. Trust me. This will go smoothly."

"Thank you for setting this up," Sarah said. She kept getting up and down, moving plates, refilling coffee cups, fussing in the sink. Her fear for me was front and center.

"Sarah, I know you're freakin'," Merlin said. "But Roberto agreed to all the terms. Mac is going in healthy and comin' out the same way. Straight from Roberto's mouth."

They all smiled weakly and tried their best to make it seem like a normal day. Merlin's words had helped—because he obviously believed them. So we all pretended it was day like hundreds of its predecessors, full of chores and ideas, construction and camaraderie. But when Sarah, Duke and I prepared to exit the compound from one of the tunnels, they were all there at the door, hugging me and patting my back. Hardly the usual send off.

I looked at them all and smiled. I felt good. This was a positive move I kept telling myself. When I returned, we would certainly be no worse off, possibly in better shape. "I'll be bock," I said in my best Arnold voice from the vids.

It earned me some smiles.

• • • •

"You got cajones, McCall," Roberto said, leaning back in a huge leather chair that ended up looking small when he settled his bulk into it. He was the second biggest man I had ever seen. A couple of inches shorter than me, he had me outweighed by nearly a hundred pounds. None of it appeared to be fat. He was wide…and solid.

Jet black hair framed a round copper hued face. His nose roamed a little to far left and right, the result of having been broken more than once. If it weren't for his propensity to smile frequently, flashing square, brilliantly white teeth, he would have been considered ugly.

Between us was a executive desk. Definitely not the one that had been here in the 20th when the room had been the office of the manager of the Integrity Office Suites, a converted motel on Roosevelt Road in Lombard. This was where the Cobras now called home. Forty or fifty years ago the desk, a huge slab of polished irregularly shaped mahogany, had probably cost as much as some automobiles.

"I appreciate your talking to me," I said. "Guaranteeing me safe passage." These were the first words either of us had spoken since he had met me at the border. Accompanied by a contingent of five guards, we had walked thirty minutes in silence. Only when we had entered the sanctuary of four walls, did I speak.

I had left Sarah and Duke a quarter of a mile from the Cobra's northern border. She had all my weapons. I had her words of encouragement and her love. We had taken five hours to make the journey that would have been a one hour jaunt in better days. Taking back roads, biking through woods and meadows, we detoured way south, beyond the expanded borders of the Messengers, before we turned east and ultimately back north again to meet Roberto at one of his headquarters at noon.

If it went badly and I didn't come back, they would all be in worse shape than they were now. They would go after the Cobras, just as I would if they took someone from me, and at the same time still have the Messengers to contend with. They would all die.

But I had believed all along, ever since Merlin had suggested the parlay, that Roberto would honor his word of safe passage. Even if our talk accomplished nothing positive, he wouldn't break his promise.

"Wasn't easy," Roberto told me. "This is a big territory. Got outposts all over the place. Took me a whole day to set it up so some young blood wouldn't mistakenly take you out. I think maybe it just buys you a couple of days to smell the flowers, McCall. Nothing you say is gonna negate the fact you capped seven of my soldiers. You and that devil dog. My people got legends about that dog, McCall. We tell the little ones horror stories about the jaws from hell to keep them from wandering away."

That was only one of the many traits that set Roberto apart from the other clan leaders. He cared about his children. Recognized that they represented his people's future. For the past ten years he had been educating himself, devouring books from the libraries and bookstores on Cobra turf. He insisted the children do the same.

The living quarters of the Insane Cobra Nation were another representation of his unusual leadership abilities. The Cobras had been at this one location for nearly three years now, treating it as a home, improving on it, rather than trashing it and moving on.

Roberto's Integrity Office Suites, a three story structure consisting of a hundred or so rooms, squatted right in the middle of his territory, an area of land of at least fifty square miles that contained within its borders one huge shopping mall, hundreds of strip malls and specialty stores, including several gun shops, and thousands of suburban homes.

It was prime real estate for scavenging. And a bitch to defend.

The outposts that Roberto had mentioned were the prime features of his defensive system. There were dozens of them on the borders, each manned by three or four soldiers. Runners, pedaling 18 or 27 speeds, flowed back and forth like little corpuscles between the main compound and the outposts twenty-four hours a day. If a runner didn't show up every thirty minutes or so from each outpost, the main body of the Cobras went on red alert. Thus far none of the other clans had the ability or the desire to challenge The Insane Cobra Nation's dominance in the hierarchy.

"It used to be," I said, "that outside of my family, you were one of only four or five men in this miserable land that I respected. If what we have to say doesn't change the bitterness that has tainted our relationship, it will be a great loss to me."

"If things don't change as a result of this meeting," Roberto replied, "you will soon die with the fangs of a Cobra in your neck."

"Even as the bodies of Cobras pile up at the feet of me and my family," I replied.

We both smiled at our posturing. But we knew that if I did not satisfy the man in front of me, we would go to war. And I would eventually lose.

"The man who set up this meeting, Merlin, the trader who is always floats on a cloud of smoke," Roberto said, "he is another of the men that has earned your respect?"

I nodded affirmatively.

"He does not appear to be much of a warrior," Roberto replied.

"He has a strong heart," I said. "And is very brave and resourceful. He's the one that most forcefully urged me to speak to you."

Roberto thought about my response. "When I look at my people," he said, "I see that not all of the ones I respect are the soldiers. I never thought about it before. But when I think of the women, particularly the teachers of our young, I see much to admire. It takes the wisdom of the fox and the heart of the wolf to teach some of our children."

I remained silent.

With a wave of his hand, Roberto dismissed the topic. Sighing his reluctance to begin, he got down to business. "I am saddened to think this may be our last conversation, McCall. It is the best we have ever had. Do you think anything you can tell me will be powerful enough for me to lift the sanctions on you without making me lose face? If I lose face, my power is diminished. What we are building is too important to take that risk. In my heart the Cobra Nation looms larger than the respect I have for you. I am sorry."

"I've got nothing to lose here," I said. "Things can't get any worse than being put on your sanction list. Let me tell the story."

His huge head nodded in agreement, and I began my account of the confrontation on Roosevelt Road, telling it completely, leaving nothing out, emphasizing that we were put in a no win situation by his soldiers.

Roberto listened attentively to my explanation of the encounter with his men. When I had finished, he replied. "Once we were friends.

Now, I am saddened to say, your actions have made us enemies. Am I to believe the words of an enemy against the reports my soldiers have given me of the battle?"

"How does their story differ?" I asked.

"You were the aggressor," he replied. "Without warning you had your dog attack Felipe and you swept the other men with your assault rifle. They had no chance to even return fire."

"Tell me something about those men," I asked. "Felipe in particular."

"Until the last few months, before they had the misfortune of running into you, they were a good unit. They were promoted twice to positions of greater responsibility, higher visibility."

"What about the last few months? What was happening with them?"

"Felipe became more, uh, high strung, aggressive. Some of his responses to authority were out of line. He wasn't controlling his soldiers as tightly as he used to. It was why I sent him and his men back to the outpost. It was a demotion. It takes them away from friends and family. I thought that perhaps Felipe had risen too fast, had allowed his new status to go to his head. This was my way of bringing him back to reality."

My interpretation of their altered behavior patterns differed from Roberto's. I pulled four small bags from my pocket and tossed them onto his desk top. "Recognize this shit?" I asked.

He picked up the bags, dipping his huge fingers in one of them, feeling the texture by sifting and rubbing the grey powder with his fingers.

"It's Bad Boy," he said, smiling. "Fairly new entry into the pharmacy. It's Slammer with an extra slam. Slammer used to be one of my drugs of choice. In my youth, that is."

At 30, Roberto was an old man. His gargantuan frame had surely contributed to his longevity, absorbing bullets and knife slices and body blows that would have killed men of normal size. But I knew he had stopped using, with the exception of booze and pot, nearly ten years ago, the same time he began his self education.

"Recognize the chem?" I asked. The grainy texture and the grey color identified its origin as surely as if it had been a signed painting.

"It's Messenger stuff." He spoke the words as if they left a rancid taste on his palate. "Very powerful. Unpredictable. Why you showing this garbage to me, McCall? You know I don't use anymore."

"What about your soldiers?"

He shrugged his shoulders. "It's a hard world. We discourage the hard core chems. But they are tolerated when my people are not on duty. If a man or woman cannot handle it, they are outed. It happens sometimes. Addicts have a way of shaking themselves off of the tree. Why are you asking me this?"

"I found these four bags on your men. The smallest one is Felipe's, Roberto. He was so fucking high when the dog killed him, he didn't even know he was dead."

Surprise registered on his face. He toyed with the concept awhile, the thought of his men using drugs while on duty, their possible disregard of Cobra law—accepting it, rejecting it, analyzing the implications. The easiest course was for him to toss the premise aside, treat it as the last ditch attempt of a liar to save his skin.

The more difficult path was to consider that I was being truthful. To do so meant that he had been betrayed, had lost the fealty of some of his soldiers.

"You know I've never lied to you," I said. "We've always been completely straight with each other. And you know damn well it's not in me to throw down on defenseless men. Nor is it the way of your soldiers to be so easily eliminated."

Roberto sat back in his chair, looking me straight in the eye, challenging me to back down, tacitly admit I was the liar he never imagined I could be. His life would be easier if it were true.

I returned his gaze, held it until he suddenly leapt from his chair and slammed his massive fist to the mahogany desktop. Sounded like a leg of lamb hitting a tree. His face flushed in anger; his eyes flashed his rage. "You son of a bitch!" he screamed. I momentarily feared he was coming over the desk at me. "You know what the fuck this means if you're telling me the truth?"

I stayed quiet, willing him back to his chair before I responded. I had never seen him explode. Almost 300 pounds of muscle packed on to a 5'10" frame, Roberto was like tightly packed bags of sand with arms and legs—the whole thing poised to topple over on me.

"It means you're gonna look like an asshole," I said, maintaining my position.

"You're fucking ace deuce right," he said, voice still several decibels beyond the conversational level. "It means I look like a fucking stooge to my people. I tell them you're on the list; then I say, oops, never mind, our own people betrayed us all. This guy's OK."

"I'm not lying to you."

"You know what happens if you are?"

Slow death. Painful death. I smiled my confidence.

"How you going to find out?" I asked.

He laughed, combination of a bellow and a bark. Nice sound to hear in my situation. It dispersed the smoldering fire between us.

"You think Cobras don't lie, McCall? This is a fucking clan, not a monastery. I been dealing with druggies and liars for ten years now. Before that I was a druggie and liar myself for another ten. At ten years old I could have been in the Olympics of liars. Liars forget their lies. The truth is easy to remember. You watch. If my men lie to me, I will know it. If they are lying..."

The implication of his unfinished sentence hung in the air like the smoke of burning garbage.

Over the next half hour he called in the three men who had escaped the battle with me and Duke. He asked each of them two questions: what kind of weapon had I used and in what order I shoot the men? He received three different sets of answers.

Finished with his interrogations, he ordered us the finest array of Mexican food I had ever sampled. We talked over lunch. "You watching those men?" he asked between bites of soft chicken tacos liberally spiced with peppers and onions, hot enough to make my eyes water. "Almost every liar has a tell, usually in the eyes. Sometimes its a small facial movement or something with the hands. Maybe in the voice. All those men were lying. Got three different stories and none of 'em were true. In five minutes we get some more evidence, wait and see."

"What about me?" I asked. "Did you think I was lying?"

"Any man who can take out seven Cobras, even with the help of the devil dog," he said, "I got to figure that man could be such a good liar that even I couldn't catch it. Because I didn't see any giveaways, no tells. So…you are either a most skillful bender of the truth…or…something that is as rare a commodity as the perfect liar."

"What's that?"

"An honest man. Honest men are terrible liars."

A soldier knocked and entered, approaching Roberto and whispering in his ear. The man placed something in his hand and left us. Roberto threw three more bags of Bad Boy on the desk top, identical in color and texture to the one from Felipe's pocket that I had given him.

"While I listened to those pigs, my men searched their quarters."

The big man picked up the seven bags of Bad Boy and poured their contents on his desk, creating a salt and pepper pile that he plowed his immense fingers through, creating little valleys and hills.

"I hate these drugs, McCall. The men, they think it makes them tough. It keeps their brains soft and their cocks hard. They think that is all a woman wants, a hard cock. It is a shame reality is not enough for some men."

"Sometimes it's too much," I said.

• • • •

When we finished our meal, he walked with me through his compound, showing his people we were friends, stopping to tell soldiers what had happened, that I was no longer to be hunted.

"Now that you are no longer an enemy of the Cobra Nation," Roberto told me, "perhaps the Messengers will remove you from their hit list."

"Why am I on their list?" I asked, testing his feelings about the Messengers.

"The Babe wants me to commit the Cobras to join him in his war against all Folks clans." He spat on the ground. "He thinks he will gain my favor by searching for you. In truth, it makes me sick. We need no help in our efforts to avenge our own. The Babe is seriously loco. He is a fool who does not know that if we wipe out every Folks clan in the entire area, reduce them to rubble, kill their offspring, salt the earth, it will change little in our lives."

"How's that?" I asked.

"If we were to successfully eradicate every man, woman and child who lives under the Nation of Folks, who would certainly not go down easily, mind you, the cost to the People Nation and all of our clans would be very high. If we were to do this, McCall, embark on a war to annihilate all Folks clans, what would change in our world?"

I shrugged my shoulders. I had plenty of opinions, but I wanted to hear his take.

"We are savages," he said. "It is a natural reaction to the collapse. The clans are nothing more than tribes of primitive hunter gatherers. Instead of spears we have assault rifles. If all the Folks were purged from this city, it would be only a matter of months before People began to battle amongst ourselves. The only way we can evolve beyond this primitive state is to resist such temptations. The Cobras will defend ourselves. But I will not commit my people to a war of aggression. We cannot grow unless our numbers increase."

"Did you know The Babe dreams of presenting my head to you in a bird cage?"

Roberto sneered. "Herod offering the head of John the Baptist to Salome. Such drama. And this from a short eyes. You know he fucks little children, don't you McCall? Tortures his prisoners. Sells little ones to the sex pens of other clans. Keeps the freshest ones for his own depraved needs? He had the balls to ask us if we wanted to buy. The man lives in an evil fantasy. If he does not self destruct, it is a guarantee that the Cobras will have to deal with him. But I feel he is embarking on a journey that will prove too difficult for the Messengers to survive. At least now you will no longer be on his city wide hit list."

"Uh, well, unfortunately, I've got a dead Messenger in my back yard, along with two dead Mambas, and another Messenger locked in my closet, banging on the door screaming for his Bad Boy. The guy in the closet was part of a Messenger scouting party looking for me and the dog. I think I'm still high priority."

"Your life is a mess, McCall. It is good you came to talk to me. Look at it this way. At least today you have solved half your problem."

• • • •

Roberto walked with me as I began my journey back to his border. Ten meters behind, we had a small contingent of armed guards. Unlike the trek we had a few hours ago, this time we talked.

"What happens to those men?" I asked him, referring to the three soldiers caught in the lies.

He snorted in derision. "They are dead. It is the only way. First we talk to them for a day or so. Then the execution, and we feed their bodies to the dogs."

"Talking to them" was a clan euphemism for intense interrogation. "Before you start on them," I told Roberto, creating the opening that would enable me to finish my business with him, "there's some information you should know."

I had been thinking about our situation with the Messengers for days. The whole thing started at the parking lot, over a year ago, the massacre of the Gaylords. From that point our lives had no longer been our own. We were no longer in control. Unable to make choices, move freely. And the whole problem centered around The Babe and his Messengers and Roberto and the Insane Cobra Nation.

Two days before my meeting with Roberto, a possible solution to the bizarre relationship between the Messengers and Cobras came to me. What if Roberto was another victim in this scenario? What if he and the Cobras, rather than active participants, were also objects of The Babe's manipulations? Just some more chess pieces.

"You are about to make my life more complicated, aren't you?" he replied.

It was time to test my theory. I took a deep breath. "I think some—maybe all—of those men were in bed with the Messengers."

"Because the fools purchased the Bad Boy from the the Messengers? Unfortunately, the Messengers and the Cobras share a western border. It could have been a matter of convenience."

"Remember when the Gaylord's were slaughtered at the college parking lot?"

"It occurred only a mile from where our territory ends. Open turf. The college is my favorite place to find books. I was there within an hour of hearing the news. Gaylord's may have been pusses, but they were still People."

"Didn't hurt The Babe's recruiting," I commented.

His eyes narrowed, and he slowed our pace. "You goin' somewhere with this, McCall?"

"Pretty brutal scene."

"Biggest fucking mess I ever saw," he replied. "Funny how no one's come forward to claim it. Clan carves up another like that, they always take credit. What good's a message if no one knows who sent it?"

"I know who did the work," I said.

He stopped dead in his tracks. Behind us, his soldiers snapped their rifles up, began scanning the environment. He waved them off, told them to relax. Urging me forward a few paces, out of their hearing range, he said, "You're one amazing fount of information, man. Anything you don't know?"

"It's been a busy year," I said smiling. "I could use a vacation. The fact that you're not teaming up with The Messengers makes that a possibility. You're telling me you have never had any shared operations with the Messengers?"

"I can't believe you could ever think I would consider such a move. Team up with a such a beast. You disappoint me, McCall."

"Aren't you the one who believed I killed your men in cold blood?"

"Touche'. Irony noticed and accepted."

"Seems like that's what most of this is all about. Making you think things you normally wouldn't think. Making you miss items you'd normally see."

"Explain."

"Some of your Cobras have thrown in with The Messengers. They are in your camp, Roberto. They're living with you. Sleeping with your women. Selling Messenger Bad Boy to your soldiers and children." I nodded my head back to his guards. "Some of them could be reporting to The Babe. He's pulling every string he can to get you to join him. If you throw in with him, the rest of the People clans will follow. Then he goes to all out war. My guess is you would suffer some grievous wounds somewhere early in the conflict. Then the Cobras would belong to The Babe."

"You're weaving this tale based on the fact some of my men are using Messenger Bad Boy? That's a pretty weak link, McCall."

"No," I replied, "there's a couple of more items. The prisoner we have locked in our closet, pretty much put it together for me. He indicated The Babe is obsessed with taking me out. But its not completely because he wants to win your favor. More importantly, he wants to keep me from ever talking to you. My head in a cage would serve both purposes."

"Why should he worry about me and you talking?"

"Because I saw the massacre of the Gaylords at the college. I was there."

"Madre Dios," he exclaimed, belief battling skepticism. "You could, uh, maybe provide a detail or two that would dispel any doubts I may have lingering in my mind?"

"What happened to the corpses?" I asked.

"We dragged them over to the Gaylord camp. They were a small clan to begin with. Not many left after the massacre. The few that remained moaned and groaned and appropriately beat the drums of vengeance and then fed the bodies to the dogs. So much for respecting the dead. Gaylords never extracted their revenge. They basically fell apart, drifting into other People clans. We took none. Gaylords are not Cobra material. Mambas got a few. Messengers got the most. Messengers recruited them."

I described the scene in detail to Roberto, the placement of the corpses, the exact number, itemizing the grisly mutilations to the bodies, the Folks sign carved into skulls and torsos, the upside down People signs, challenging and disrespecting the affiliation of People clans, the removal of fingers to get at the jewelry. Every detail I could remember was given to Roberto.

He believed. He had seen the bodies.

"You've known all along who did this and didn't tell any one? Why not?"

"I've known what happened," I said, "but not why. Three reasons I've been keeping this quiet. Number one, no one would have believed me. Number two, what good would it have done? It would have started a bigger war than is going on now. This is small time compared to what The Babe really has in mind."

"Number three?" Roberto asked.

"I hadn't figured any of it out until just two days ago."

"You could have told me, McCall. I like to think I have retained a certain amount of sanity."

"I thought you were in on it. Until today, even though Merlin assured me it was impossible, I still entertained the notion."

He gave me a befuddled, what in the fuck are you talking about look. I quickly continued, giving him the final puzzle piece he needed. "The Gaylords were killed by People, Roberto. People killing People." A Barbara Streisand song, one of Weasel's favorites, suddenly popped in my head. "It was the Messengers. The Babe was belly deep in blood. His bat looked like he was tenderizing sides of beef. They lured the Gaylords in, making it look like a no guns rumble against Folks, played with them a little and then brought out the hard stuff."

"How do I fit in?" he asked.

"There was at least one Cobra there. Probably more. It was Felipe, the Edge. He was having a good time. He liked using his knife on dead bodies. I figured the massacre had been OK'd by you. Why else a representative of the Cobra Nation?"

He slowly absorbed the impact of what I was telling him. Over a year ago, Felipe, a rising star with the Insane Cobra Nation, a man Roberto had trusted, had been in bed with the Messengers. How many more of his soldiers had gone over? He glanced back to the five guards who had accompanied us, as if his back were no longer safe. Maybe it wasn't.

"Jose', Flint," he yelled to two of the guards, "come over here."

They trotted over and stood awaiting directions. "Send the rest of the men home. And bring me two of their rifles." As the two men departed, Roberto told me, "Those two have been with me since we were all hanging onto our mothers breasts. Thirty years, McCall. I trust them with my life."

"It was when they left the parking lot," I continued, "that Duke and I walked among the dead, saw what had been done to them. Some of the men were still alive when they were mutilated, Roberto. Maybe he just wanted one last look, maybe he had a feeling, a premonition. I don't know. But The Babe came back. He wasn't alone. There was one man with him. It was Felipe."

"That little fucking vermin," Roberto hissed.

"They were out of rifle range, but close enough so they could see us. I looked them over through binoculars. They were as clear to me as you are now. Felipe's tattoo was very impressive. We, the people I live with, have known for quite some time that the Messengers have been looking for me and the dog, keeping it quiet. When I ran into Felipe and his men, it was like they struck gold. But they were too whacked out on the Bad Boy, overconfident."

"So for a year," he said, "you have been living under the threat that both the Messengers and the Cobras have been after you. A heavy burden. Most men would have run."

"We made other adjustments. Running wasn't an option. There was one item of information in our favor as far as you and the Cobra Nation were concerned. None of our snitches reported that you were looking for us—not until I killed Felipe' a couple of months ago, anyway. It was if you didn't care, weren't threatened by my knowledge of the attack on the Gaylords. It was that possibility that brought me here today."

His two soldiers approached, carrying the two extra rifles he had requested. The big man inspected each weapon, popping the clips, checking the load, clearing the chamber, dry firing. Satisfied, he tossed one to me. It was a FA-MAS, 5.56 25 round clip. Well maintained, it looked to be the better of the two rifles to me. An extremely valuable piece. He pulled a pistol from his belt and handed it to me along with two extra clips.

"You will not need these in Cobra territory," he said. "But you must travel beyond our borders."

I thanked him.

"But my own weapons are stashed at the edge of your territory," I said.

"Then you keep these until you retrieve yours," he replied. "Jose' will accompany you. Return them to him."

BLOOD OF THE DOGS

He shouldered his weapon in preparation for his return, but he didn't move. Reaching his hand out to mine, he said, "The Cobras are in your debt, McCall. I have some very complicated business to tend to back at the camp. It will take some time to cull the traitors from our midst. So you will not hear from me for awhile. But when my house is in order, I will find a way to repay you."

Captured by his huge paw, my hand felt like that of a baby. I could barely get my fingers to the edges of his palm. I returned the pressure of his shake the best I could.

"The resumption of our friendship is payment enough," I said, smiling. Such a huge weight had been lifted from us that no further benefits were necessary.

Roberto laughed. "Such a politician. If peace ever visits this war zone, perhaps I will make you the ambassador of the Cobra Nation. You would be good. Such a bull shitter."

He spun and began the trek back home, where he would begin his nasty work.

I headed for the north border, a taciturn Jose' by my side. Unlike Roberto, I was bearing good tidings.

When we reached the border, I whistled. Fifty meters distant, from behind an overgrown honeysuckle stand in front of a hair salon, Sarah and Duke appeared. Jose' looked at me, shifted a bit on his feet.

"That the devil dog?" he asked.

I signaled Duke to come. "He won't hurt you," I said. "Just don't raise the rifle."

As Sarah approached, her face plastered with a smile, Jose' watched every step. "She as nice as she looks?"

"How do you mean?" I asked. Neutral.

"I mean, man, look at that red hair. That beautiful smile. She's glad to see you, McCall. If she wasn't carrying all those guns and knives, you'd think she was some kind of movie star from the old days. She looks like a nice lady. You're a lucky man."

I handed him the weapons Roberto had loaned me. "Thanks, Jose'," I said. "You take care of Roberto. He needs your help."

• • • •

When Jose' had disappeared from sight, Sarah threw down her guns and took a run at me, building speed and leaping at the last second, wrapping her arms around my shoulders and legs around my waist. Her momentum carried us both to the ground. She planted a wet kiss on my lips and, straddling my chest, said, "God I'm glad to see you. Tell me. Tell me. Tell me. You got that shit eating grin, buster. It's good news, isn't it?"

Duke was prancing about, bouncing off his front paws, barking like crazy. Looked like fun to him. I waved him in, and between the two of us, we wrestled Sarah to the ground.

"Yeah," I said, still smiling, "it's good news."

A week later the sky fell in.

CHAPTER THIRTY

"You're late. We were getting worried," Sarah said to Stevie, who had just returned from checking for messages from Merlin. We had received no word from the little guy for several days.

"Two soldiers tried to follow me home from the drop," Stevie said.

"What make did you put on them?" Sarah asked.

"Messengers," Stevie said. "They were easy to lose."

"You know what the means," Weasel replied.

"Yeah," Stevie replied. "They must have followed Merlin from the city when he made the drop."

"They're closing the circle on us…and Merlin," I said.

"Maybe we should have tried harder to talk him into moving in," said Sarah, "after he told us they were putting pressure on him."

"He loves it here," I said. "But there was no way we could have persuaded him to stay. He's got to have his own cribs, places to hole up. Be alone. That's who he is."

"In trouble is who he is," said Weasel.

"Let me see the note," I told Stevie.

Merlin's message, in his distinctive scrawl, was simple in content, ripe with duplicity.

> NEED TO TALK. GOT SOME RIFLES FOR YOU.
> HOW ABOUT SOON? NO BIG DEAL. AON #17.
> COME ALONE. EVERYTHING'S SMOOTH.

"He's up to his neck," Weasel said.

"No doubt," I replied. "Working on our opposites code, it's a very big deal; I better not come alone; there are no rifles; and there's trouble waiting for us."

"What's with 'need to talk' and 'how about soon?'" Stevie asked.

"I gotta guess someone made him write it," I replied. "I think they really want us there soon. They just don't know the code."

"AON number 17?" asked Sarah. "That's his new place?"

"That's what he told me last week," I said.

"Is seventeen the right floor or is it a code?" Weasel asked.

"Let's assume for a minute that someone made him write the note," I responded. "If that's true, then seventeen is where they want me."

"So it's a trap."

"Probably."

"Merlin could already be dead."

"It's possible. They might be keeping him alive in case we don't show. Try to persuade him some more. He obviously hasn't told them about this place. Else they'd be here instead of trying to lure us there."

"He is our friend."

"Not many of them around."

"Set Mac up with Roberto."

"Saved our butts."

"Guess you could say we owe him."

"Let's pack up. How many of us should go?"

Everyone stood.

"What about the Messenger in the closet?" Sarah asked.

"Feed him. Lock him back up. Put the arm and leg shackles back on. Leave some water in the closet. Tell him Duke's staying with him. He'll be good."

• • • •

Even with the threat of Cobra retaliation removed from our backs, travel was still a dangerous undertaking—the Messenger bounty was still on my head. So we went at night, riding 18-speeds, wearing NVG's and the communicators, coming into the city from the south, away from the heaviest clan concentrations.

Merlin's most recent headquarters were in a monolithic, grey-white eighty story tower they called the AON Center in the 20th. It was located a few blocks north of Grant Park, the area where I had originally met Merlin two years ago. The building itself was in Black Gangster

Disciple territory, the powerful Folks clan led by the young black kid who had been arguing with Merlin over his toll beneath the two Indian statues. James had been the honcho of the BGD's for nearly a year, assuming the mantle when the former leader had died the ignominious death of an infection caused by a fish hook that had lodged in his arm.

It was to James that we had to present ourselves before we could investigate Merlin's predicament. To get his attention, we simply stood across the street from the old Hilton on Michigan Avenue, a heavy, square, blocky structure that, despite its age and the preening of its high-tech architectural neighbors, managed to retain an air of elegance. Our assault rifles, two apiece, were on the ground in front of us—a formal signal of our peaceful intent.

They knew we were here. Had picked up our presence as we biked under the old post office about a mile west. Maybe even earlier as we had come up from the south on Halsted. We didn't have to wait long. James exited the Hilton from the Michigan Avenue side, three Disciple soldiers armed with M-16s behind him. Their rifles were shouldered. At our backs, the sun was a red ball on the horizon, looking as though it had just popped up from the depths of the lake.

James and I were friends—a mutual respect relationship that was about five years old. I hadn't mentioned it to Roberto. Disciples were Folks. Since the action with the Cobras on Roosevelt Road, Folks clans were all big fans of Duke and me.

In the five years that I had known James, The Black Gangster Disciples had risen to near the top of the hierarchy of the Folk's clans. From their base of operation on the lakefront, they were the most prodigious of the fishing clans, excellent providers of food for their own members and resourceful and discriminating traders of their fish for supplies and weapons. Accordingly, their population—and power—had grown. Militarily, they were not yet in the league of Satan's Messengers or The Insane Cobra Nation. But they were strong enough to discourage direct assault.

James, shirtless and wearing cut off fatigues, armed with a semi-automatic 9mm Ruger pistol and a fillet knife in a long, thin deerskin scabbard, crossed the street, his three soldiers two paces behind. The musculature on his chest and arms was well defined. They were a hard working clan, living on the generosity of the lake that was their front door. Tatoos of pitchforks, tridents, and six-point crowns and stars adorned his chest and arms. In the center was a beautiful crimson heart with wings on its sides. On his head was a stained and faded Duke Blue Devil cap, cocked right.

His lack of heavy armament was a sign to us, a symbol of hospitality. The bounty that The Babe had put on my head was interpreted as a badge of honor by all Folks clans. James walked straight up to me, and we shook hands. His soldiers stayed two meters back, eyes on the five of us, frequently darting in Duke's direction.

The Disciple leader smiled, releasing my hand. "Good to see you, McCall. And I ain't just bein' polite. You been pretty scarce the last year." He stepped back and inspected the five of us, left to right, Duke, Sarah, me, Stevie, Weasel. "Never seen you with another human being except Merlin," he commented. "Just you and the dog. Didn't know you had any friends, McCall."

"These are business associates," I said. "We have a slight conflict to attend to in your territory."

He glanced at Sarah, then back to me, once more to her. He smiled, managing to keep it from being prurient, respecting what he somehow grasped was a relationship. I introduced them all by name, and James solemnly shook each of their hands, spending equal time with each, welcoming them to G.D. turf, refusing to comment on our obvious resolution to task or Sarah's drop-dead beauty, conspicuous despite her avoidance of enhancement, a single red rose among the dandelions.

When he reached Duke, James turned to me, asking if it were OK to pet him. I gave a hand signal, and as James knelt in front of him, Duke wagged his tail and happily accepted the offer of friendship. The gesture was a symbol whose meaning was not lost on James' men. He had no fear of the dog.

James stepped back and eyeballed the formidable pile of assault rifles and machine pistols at my feet, then glanced up to the two semi-auto pistols we each had at our waists. Grinning at his own joke, he said, "You plannin' on trading those pieces for fish? Got some great walleye and pan fish. Lake trout been running real good. I'll even throw in a soul food gumbo recipe, no extra charge. Set your palate free."

I smiled politely. "We can't stay long to talk," I said. "Someone's got Merlin, and we need your permission to go in to get him."

"Back it up a notch, McCall," James said, now deadly serious. "That word 'someone'. You tellin' me GD turf's been violated?"

"They're after me. Figure they can go through Merlin."

"The 'they', Mac. Who the fuck is the 'they'?"

I tried to be casual about it, but it was pretty much the emotional equivalent of telling someone…had a chance to fuck your mother the other day, but the line was too long. "Probably Satan's Messengers. Maybe some other People clans. Don't know for sure who or how many."

The man was good. Without any show of emotion, he raised his right hand and flashed a series of signals, then raised his left, opening and closing it twice. Before his hands were back at his side, ten soldiers rushed from the hotel across the street, formed a circle around us and ushered us into the building. Not a word was spoken until we were safely inside.

• • • •

Huddling with James and a two of his lieutenants, we planned for a couple of hours and then slept until late afternoon.

There was no way we could exclude the Black Gangster Disciples from the action. It was their turf, their code, their honor that had been violated by the Messenger running an operation within their borders. We finally decided that James and two of his Black Gangster Disciples would accompany us into the eighty story AON Center. The base of the high rise would be surrounded by 30 or 40 more Disciples.

"Anyone comes out of the building before sunrise," I told them, "is not us. Take 'em down."

• • • •

The sun had been down for an hour. We were in the massive lobby of the Hilton, the Black Gangster Disciple headquarters, dusty 20th cen opulence, marble floors, vestigial chandeliers hanging over our heads, draped in cobwebs. Lamplight threw flickering shadows as forty soldiers inspected weapons and ammo, packed bags, sharpened blades, dressed for battle, spoke in hushed tones to one another. Marijuana smoke hung in a layer of cirrus a few feet over our heads, battling for dominance with the smell of the lanterns.

Sarah and I sat on a dusty couch, James in front of us, crosslegged on the floor. We were double checking each other's body armor and weapons. Stevie and Weasel were doing the same across the room. James watched silently, almost in awe, as our ritual unfolded before his eyes. Duke lay beside him, oblivious of the preparations.

Body armor first. Each of us had the armor rolled in our backpacks, Kevlar IV and V, 21st cen models. It would stop most everything except armor piercing and heavier caliber magnum rounds. But when you took a hit, you paid a hell of a price. Depending on the caliber and how long it had been flying, it felt like someone was driving a steel rod through your torso.

I stripped down to skivvies and covered my upper body with a Kevlar IV vest which had a crotch protector attachment all of us wore. Sarah did the same, stripping down to a matching sports bra and panties and evoking a considerable display of whistles and hoots from the Disciples, which she silenced quickly by searching out offenders and making eye contact.

When Sarah and I had finished suiting up, she whistled Duke over. I pulled a modified Kevlar V vest from the backpack and draped it around his body. Tying it beneath his belly, I checked its tightness. It would protect most of his body, from throat to hindquarters.

James' men were also suiting up. A few had body armor, most of it the bulky '70's and 80's issue stuff they had found in police armories. Others used football pads, catcher's chest protectors, hockey equipment—whatever they could get their hands on that would stop a round but allow them some freedom of movement.

The four of us would carry two rifles and two pistols each with the requisite extra clips, choosing the weapons that we were most comfortable with. We each also carried at least two knives, and I knew that Weasel had some more pistols secreted away somewhere on his body.

Sarah was the only one carrying a shotgun, which supplemented her Leader Sar assault rifle, chosen for its short length and light weight. The Sar fired 5.56mm rounds in thirty round magazines but weighed only six and a half pounds. The shotgun was a beauty, designed specifically for combat by an Italian firm, Luigi Franchi. It was a 12 gage auto, folding butt, eight round capacity. The feature that drew her to the weapon was a shoulder hook which allowed her to loop the gun over her shoulder and fire from the hip with one hand, leaving the other hand free for a pistol or light assault rifle.

The Disciples were very impressed when we rolled out the grenades, three frags each, from our armory stockpile.

"Haven't seen any of those since I was a kid," James commented. "Didn't think there were any left. Summer nights when I was kid, the soldiers used to throw 'em up like fire works. Best when they got on the roof of a highrise and waited for the last second and then tossed 'em down."

"Except for these," I said, "me neither. Got a few held back for emergencies."

When we finished with the weapons and body armor, we began unpacking the night vision goggles and communicators I had retrieved at *I Spy, You Spy*.

We would go in an hour.

"Tell me about them gadgets," James said.

"That," I told James, who was inspecting what appeared to be a bandaid's cousin and curved piece of flat plastic, "is a device for communicating with each other when we're not close."

"Like the long talkers without a box," he replied.

"Exactly. Found them last year. They use batteries smaller than a button and are completely wireless so your hands are always free."

I showed him how to put the ear piece on, using the ear cuff because his ears were pierced only on the lobes and edges and then explained that the microphone was in the derm patch that I taped beneath his voice box. I did the same for myself and told him to go across the room.

"How loud you gotta talk?" James asked.

"A whisper will get the job done." When he was across the lobby, I whispered, "That's far enough. But you could go across the street and I could still talk to you."

"Mother fucker," he said. "That's incredible. You got some for me and my boys that're going up with you?"

Each of us had two sets of the communicators and the NVGs. "We've got enough for you and three of your men. But we need to tell them that when they're in operation, everything you say goes to all the other people wearing the earpieces. So we need to make sure only one person at a time is talking."

"What about the NVG'S? They are rare."

"Weasel found them in a police armory few years back. Late 20th models. They work on what they call available light. Hard to believe, but in the dark, they suck out light that our eyes can't see and show us what's there. It's not perfectly clear, couldn't read a book or anything, and it looks like everything is in a green fog. But you can definitely see your enemies. Try them on. They won't work in here. Too much light. But you can get an idea of how they feel."

He put my goggles on. "Uncomfortable, aren't they?" I commented.

"No problem," he said. "We use shit like this to snorkel in the lake all the time. Feels lighter than the ones we use in water. Need batteries for these too, right? Lake probably looks as murky as these things do in the night. How you find all those batteries, Mac?"

"Rechargeable ni-cads or lithium ion with solar rechargers," I answered. "Search around electronic stores."

"You got goggles for us?"

"Maybe I should carry you up the stairs when we get there, too," I commented.

END OF PART TWO

PART THREE

CHAPTER THIRTY-ONE

Three hours after the sun had set, we began our ascent of the stairs of the AON Center, our objective, the seventeenth floor. We knew it was a trap. Figured the Messengers weren't aware that we knew. Didn't know if Merlin was still alive. Didn't matter. He was coming back with us.

There were two sets of stairways. It was a logistical nightmare because the stairs were right next to each other, separated by a wall, placed almost directly in the middle of the building. Pretty ignorant was my thought. Stairs were for emergencies. Block one set with a fire and maybe people would have a shot at the other. But if you put them both right next to each other...

Our problem with the stairways was that it was almost impossible to make a direct assault on any floor. All the defenders had to do was sit outside the stairway doors with an assault rifle on full auto and a couple of dozen clips and keep firing at the doors. If they knew we were coming, there was no way we could even enter a floor from the stairways, let alone extricate a hostage.

"Merlin's sure makin' this rescue a challenge," Weasel commented when we surveyed the layout several floors below seventeen, where (we hoped) Merlin was being held captive by the Messengers.

I pointed out that Merlin chose his holes on the basis of defensive capabilities, not ease of attack. "Stairs may be the only way in," I commented, "but you can bet the bank he's got one or two ways out that the architects didn't originally incorporate into the building."

"Think we need to find those escape hatches," Weasel commented dryly. "By my way of thinking, each of these floors is probably laid out pretty much the same. Let's scout down here and see if we can find some likely places he'd hide a back door. Try to think like he would."

"Does that mean we've all got to get stoned first?" Stevie asked.

He had been uncommonly quiet ever since we had left. When I pulled him aside earlier to ask if he was all right, he had explained that all of the other times we had ventured from the compound as a group, it had been for scavenging, usually trips to libraries—low risk, adventurous, fun.

"This isn't fun," he said. "We could all be killed."

"Definitely a better chance here than in a library," I said. "Books and disks don't shoot back."

"I'm just worried about everyone," he said. "Not scared. Don't fret about that. I'll be fine. Just worried. You take care of Sarah, Mac."

"Tell you something, Stevie," I said. "Sarah never talks about it, but she's seen plenty of combat. I wouldn't be here if it weren't for her. We'll all watch each other. But Sarah doesn't need any preferential treatment."

"It's just that she's…"

"Special," I said.

"Right. Precious. Like a natural resource. Or the sun rising every morning."

I pulled his head next to mine so that our foreheads met. "You tell her that when this is over," I told him. "It'll pay big dividends."

• • • •

James and two of his Black Gangster Disciple soldiers joined me to search the fifth floor, looking for likely locations where Merlin would have placed escape hatches in his home on seventeen. We found several possibilities. The best bet was in the bathrooms, where there were hidden access hatches to the plumbing in both the floor and ceiling. A little creative engineering would transform them into passages to the floors above and below.

We resumed the ascent. James accompanied Sarah, Duke and me in one stairwell. Stevie, Weasel and the two Disciples—Angel and Wind Chill—ascended in the other side, only a few feet away from us, but separated by a solid wall. All of us were wearing NVG's, which made the stairway an eerie green vertical tube, and the communication devices. There was one more comm set and pair of goggles available.

One of the Black Gangster Disciples on ground level had them, monitoring our progress in his earpiece.

"Watch for booby traps," I told everyone before we began the climb. "Merlin always rigs his places."

We took the ascent slowly, checking the stairway door to each level for enemy soldiers, assuring that no one would surface behind us, communicating in whispers among the seven of us. On six, Duke scratched my leg. He knew when not to whine or growl. On eleven, we found our first body, sprawled on the landing, looking as dead in the green hued night vision goggles as he would have in stark daylight. Duke had smelled it long before our noses picked it up. The man had been dead for several days.

"Be careful with that body, Mac," Weasel whispered from the other side of the wall. "Could be booby trapped. Be something I sure as hell would do."

Except for a small crossbow arrow in the leg just above the ankle, wedged firmly in the bone, and a very unusual cant to his neck, the soldier was clean. No traps, no weapons, no bullet holes, no body armor, no boots. Stripped of anything of use to his clan. Tattoos marked him as a Messenger.

"Looks like he tripped one of Merlin's wires, took an arrow in the leg and fell down the stairs," I commented. "Guess that pretty much takes care of any speculation as to whether or not they're here. When we hit fourteen, let's check each floor thoroughly. They got any brains, they'll have men set up on one or all of those floors to get in behind us when we enter seventeen."

From the other stairway, separated from us by the concrete wall, Weasel's voice entered our ears. "Sit a minute," came the whisper. "Now we know we got something, let's coordinate these two teams."

Before the mission we had tried to plan, visualizing the environment, the building itself, which none of us had ever entered, inventorying what we would need, speculating on how many soldiers we would encounter, where they would set an ambush.

We gave up. Not enough data. The only items we had settled upon was that we would need silencers for the pistols, which we had, and oil for squeaky door hinges. "We goin' into a high rise and checking floors out for ambushes," Weasel said, "I think we need to do something about those hinges. Thirty-five year old hinges make some serious noise, even if they been kept dry." James provided us with fish oil. Merlin had WD40.

Now we planned, sitting on the stairs in a jade twilight, aware that a few floors above us, someone was waiting, anticipating the opportunity to take me down, present me to The Babe, be the richest man in the world. It was, in fact, quite possible that the fat man himself was lurking above, shrouded in the darkness our goggles would penetrate, dreaming of my head in a bird cage and Roberto's never to come pledge of fealty.

• • • •

Each floor was a perfect square, nearly 60 meters to a side, giving us an area of nearly two thirds of an acre to clear of Messenger soldiers—assuming we located them before they found us. The first twenty floors were serviced by a bank of eight elevators, four facing four. They were useless to us, forming a cul de sac in the middle of each floor.

From the stairs we could enter any floor into a hallway which traversed north/south for about thirty meters. The stairway entrances were in the middle of the hallway, meaning that when we entered, one team would be responsible for the right; the other, left. Each end of the hallway opened into a huge bull pen of glassed cubicles which circled the entire floor. Between the two stairway entrances was a wall with double glass doors. On some floors the bullpen was replaced by individual offices.

Essentially, the outside of each floor, which gave the bullpens or offices access to windows, was the working area of the AON Building in the 20th, and the interior of each floor was used for access hallways, elevators banks, supply closets, bathrooms, vending machine areas and a separate section for two freight elevators.

The hallway ran the length of the building, north to south. Before it opened into the bullpen on each end, it had eight areas that were sources of potential danger, places for our opponents to hide. For a team exiting from the right side stairwell and sweeping right, there were two bathrooms about ten meters down the hall, facing each other on either side of the hall. Before the bathrooms, there was also a hallway on the right side of about twenty meters in length which led to the freight elevators.

Most dangerous of all, was an access corridor to the east side of the bullpen on the left side of the main hall. It was about five steps away from the stairway entrance.

From the other stairway, the one on the left, there was a vending machine area about the size of small bedroom on the right hand side. On the left was the main elevator area—eight double doored elevators facing each other across a twenty foot expanse. It was a big three sided open area. No place to hide, but nonetheless a source of danger.

The two other areas that were a danger to us were the very stairwells that we were planning to use to surprise the Messengers. It could be a two way street, and we had no idea how many were waiting for us above. They could use the stairwells as easily as we could.

• • • •

We decided, sotto voce, to begin sweeping each floor on fourteen, coordinating our efforts to have two of us from our respective stairwells enter from the stairway door and work our way right or left, taking out whomever we encountered with blades or silenced pistols, then meeting again in the middle. When we finished with fifteen and sixteen, we would skip seventeen, where Merlin's new domicile was located, and clear out eighteen and nineteen of any obstructions. Two hours outside for the work would give us plenty of time for the business on seventeen before the sun rose.

Considering we knew nothing of what awaited us, it was a nice plan.

• • • •

Sarah and I took our half of fourteen from our stairway entrance, darting in without resistance and then moving right, clearing each room, hallway and cul de sac until we entered the huge bullpen area. Weasel and one of the Disciples were doing the same on the left. We met at the east wall of the bullpen and teamed up to clear the rest of the floor. We left Duke in the stairwell with James. Duke was a noise maker when things got rough.

Fourteen was clear. No sign of human occupation.

On the way up to fifteen, we picked up the smell, the cloying heaviness of stale marijuana smoke, the prickly ammonia stench of old urine. We couldn't tell from which floor it emanated. I oiled the door, swung it open to accommodate a peek and looked in. Scraps of paper and food littered the floor. There was no sign of the enemy.

"I think we have someone up here," I whispered. "Be careful."

Sarah and James entered from our side at Weasel's signal. Stevie and one of James' soldiers, Angel, went in at the same time from the other stairwell.

I watched them work both sides of the hallway for five minutes, oiling the doors when they were closed, nudging them open, looking inside, then one entering while the other covered the hall. Sarah and James cleared their section and entered the bullpen area, disappearing from my sight. To my left, Stevie and Angel were almost finished. We could all hear each other's breathing in the headsets. There was no conversation.

Suddenly I heard the squeak of a door, then the bark of a laugh. I knew Sarah and James could hear it also. But I was closer to the sound. I left the stairwell, turned quickly right, and then entered the short hall on my left that gave access to the east side of the bullpen. I peeked my head into the open area, looking left, where I thought the sound came from and saw a huge walled off office area in the far corner, a flickering light emanated from its open door.

Quickly removing my goggles, I watched the light grow brighter, finally resolving itself into a lamp held at arm's length by a scruffy soldier. He was heading directly toward me.

"Everybody down," I whispered urgently. "I got a guy roaming around out here. Probably more of them in an office in the northeast corner. Don't know how many."

I scrambled back down the hallway and returned to the safety of the stairwell, leaving the door open a crack so I could monitor the man's movements. Duke nuzzled my arm pit as I peeked into the hall. The soldier walked down the connecting corridor and took a quick left when he came to the main hallway, continuing down the hall, his back to me. He passed the branching hallway that led to the freight elevators and entered the bathroom on his right, draping the hallway once again in total darkness.

"Everybody stay still a couple of minutes," I said. "The guy is in the bathroom. I'm going to pay him a visit."

Placing my HK 81 assault rifle and the Skorpion machine pistol beside him, I told Duke to stay, placed the night vision goggles back over my eyes and slipped into the hallway, breathing softly as I crept along, unholstering the Glock, the pistol with the silencer.

When I reached the door, tagged by the line of light emanating from the gap at the floor, the stench told me it was a communal bathroom. It was one of those doors without a knob, the kind you just pushed open. I turned away, removed my goggles once more, took a deep breath and held it, pushed the door open and stepped inside, Glock in a two-handed grip at my right shoulder.

The soldier was stepping out of one of the stalls, the kind that separated the toilets, zipping his fatigues. The stink of the room was overwhelming, searing my nostrils, burning my eyes. "That you Dog Boy? Whoooee," said the man as he walked over to his lantern. "Smells like twenty-one rotten pussies in here. Be glad when this job is done."

The opening of the door informed him of my presence. He hadn't bothered to look at me. As he reached for his lamp, he looked up at me, surprise registering in his eyes, then sudden realization that I wasn't one of them. Before his brain could get a message to his vocal chords, I put a shot between his eyes, the noise of the round no more than a pushy whoosh of air. He fell behind the lamp, eyes open, mouth in the initial stages of a scream.

I grabbed the lamp, not bothering with a search of the body, blew out the flame and stepped back into the hallway. "He's down," I said. "I'm staying out here. Main hallway. Don't shoot me. I'm a good guy."

They all acknowledged. Sarah's sweet voice entered my ear, the last to respond. "Are you OK, Mac?"

"Fine," I responded.

"Be very careful," she replied. "James and I are almost finished here. I think you should join us when we check the area that the soldier came from. Weasel," she added, "you be careful too. You gotta figure there might be more of them than what Mac has seen. Stevie, you OK?"

"Cut the roll call, Sarah," Weasel groused. "We got work to do. Watch your butt, young lady. Mac, I'm going out to join the Stevie and Wind Chill."

"I'm fine, Sarah." Stevie's voice. Then silence.

Five minutes later Sarah said, "James and I are coming back to the stairway entrance. We're clear here." I joined them, and the three of us looked down the other hallway, green hued, silent. "Let's go check that room," I said. "See what we got. Weasel, when you three finish, cover the stairways. We don't want anyone coming up behind us."

Sarah, James and I crept down the hall and snuck a look to our left at the room in the northeast corner. There was a dim vertical line of barely visible emerald luminescence, marking the doorway to the office. I lifted my goggles and peered at the same spot. The light was no longer visible. They must have stuffed the edges with paper or rags.

"Definitely someone else in there," I whispered. "The guy talked to me like he wasn't surprised that someone would be there."

James shrugged his shoulders. How many? he was asking.

I shrugged a don't know reply and signaled it was time to find out. We crept to the threshold of the office and I removed my goggles, letting them hang from my neck. James and Sarah took the cue. I signaled that I would open the door and go center, Sarah left, James right. Each of us would be responsible for a third of the area. I pushed my palms toward the floor to indicate stay low. They nodded. I pointed the Glock at my head. Headshots when possible. We didn't know how much armor they wore.

I turned the knob and pushed on the door. It opened a few inches and stuck. In the dim light I could see it was jammed into the rags they had used to keep the light from bleeding into the hall.

"Took you long enough," said a voice on the other side of the door. "You whackin' off or what?" Laughter. Several voices. The shadowy figure of one of the soldiers approached the door and kicked at the rags, clearing the obstruction.

They had been there a long time, too long. Weary of the anticipation of action, the trickle of adrenaline, fluttering in the stomach, with no pay off, they had lost their edge. Then tried to get it back with chems.

Before the man at the door could get away from its arc, I kicked it in, smashing it into his head. He dropped like a heart shot deer. I belly flopped center and heard Sarah and James dive in on my flanks. We were in a suite of offices, not just one. Three or four lanterns flickered. Reception area, couches, chairs, tables to my right and left. In front of me was a curved work station, home to a receptionist four decades in the past. Behind it sat an astonished clan soldier, one hand, full of powder, was at his nostrils, the other was beginning to reach for an M 16. I snapped a shot, hitting the hand with the candy in it. The man dropped behind the reception desk. I swung left for more targets.

On each side I heard several shots, quiet little poofs from James' Baretta and Sarah's Ruger. All of us had 9mm semi-autos. They took well to silencers but still had the stopping power we needed.

A head popped from behind the work station at floor level, looking for a target. Seeing me, the man ducked back. I spaced five shots into the wood where I expected he was laying. There was no more movement.

From the corner of my right eye, I saw a clan soldier running toward the back of the office suite. The man dove past the protective contour of the work station, beyond my line of sight, headed for one of the rear offices. I dashed after him. It would only be seconds before he started firing or screaming. I saw him enter the first office and followed, closing the door behind me and flipping my glasses back on.

He was in a corner, back to the wall, frantically digging a huge .45 out of a holster, peering squint-eyed into the dark that enveloped him. I put a shot in the wall right beside his left ear and softly said, "Stop." He hesitated a second, trying to locate me from the sound of my voice, then continued. I shot again, right side this time, and he stopped.

It was quiet in the other rooms. I asked Sarah if everything was all right. "We're done," she said. "You need help?"

"Give me a minute and I'll be out," I said. "I got a guy here who's gonna talk to me."

"Mac, how many soldiers in there?" It was Weasel's voice.

"Five or six," I said.

"Seven," Sarah corrected. "Plus the one in the bathroom."

"We're finished," Weasel said. "Floor's clear. Nobody else up here. We're heading back to the stairway in case anyone above us heard anything."

"Wise choice. Five minutes," I said, returning my full focus to the man in the corner. "Push the gun along the floor in front of you."

He complied. I walked over to him. He couldn't see a thing. The room was windowless, dark as a bear's den. I stopped a meter in front of him.

"Is your prisoner still alive?" It startled him, my voice so close, the unknown hovering over him.

"Suck me," he said.

I pulled out my buck knife, not a huge blade, but at five inches, bigger than the clip knife on my belt. I reached out and laid the blade—cold, unforgiving steel—against his cheek. He tried to shrink back.

"Suck this," I replied, placing the tip of the knife between his lips, pushing until his teeth parted to take the blade into the soft recesses of his mouth.

"Is your prisoner still alive?"

"Yeth," he croaked around the blade. "Take i ou."

"Where is he?"

"Theventeen."

"How many men up there?" When he didn't respond, I pushed the blade further back, triggering his gag reflex.

"Firry fi or forry," he responded.

"How about on sixteen?"

"Pwenny."

"Eighteen?"

"Mum." I pushed the blade back again, exploring his tonsils. He gagged and tried to pull back. Nowhere to go.

"Eighteen?"

"Pwenny."

"Nineteen?"

"Mum."

"How many left on this floor?"

"Mum."

"One more thing," I said. "How long you been here?"

"Fibe dayth."

I believed him, returned the knife to its scabbard.

· · · ·

In the dim light of the reception area, James looked at the soldier who stood facing us. Devil's head tattoo on his left forearm. Left sided jewelry. He spat at the man's feet. "Messenger," he said in disgust. "What you comin' into the city for, boy?"

Turning to me, he asked what my plans for the invader were.

"Truss him up and gag him," I said.

"I got a better idea," he replied pulling his pistol. He put the silenced automatic to the man's temple and pulled the trigger. The man's head snapped back and for almost a second his legs didn't know his brain was dead. Then he gracelessly toppled, splintering an end table and shattering a deco lamp. "None of them get out alive, McCall. Not if we can help it."

Sarah and I shared a glance. Like anthropologists in the field, we understood.

A squawk of static came from somewhere in the room, followed by a tinny voice. "What the fuck you assholes doing down there?"

Silence. Then, "Johnnie, you there?"

The three of us searched the room frantically. We knew what it was. Walkie talkie. Long talker. Fairly uncommon because of the battery problem. The Messengers must have gone solar. We only had a few seconds to get back to the man on the other end.

"Over here, Mac," Sarah said. She found it under one of the bodies. Tossed it over to me. Little grey-brown rectangle. Red thumb button on the side. Radio Shack. A 20th cen kid's toy.

I depressed the send button, replied in a sandpaper voice. "Everything's OK."

"Who's this? Where the fuck's Johnnie at?"

The Dead Zone, you asshole. Like you're gonna be soon. "To the can. Knocked over a lamp tryin' to get the door open."

"Who'm I talkin' to?" the voice squawked back.

I searched for the name the man in the bathroom had called out. Reminded me of Duke. I made an association. Dog something. "Dog Boy," I replied.

"You sound weird, man. You sure everything's cool?"

I took a breath and held it. "Just took a hit. Don't wanna waste it."

A laugh came out of the little box. We all relaxed. "Watch that shit, Dog Boy. We may be getting visitors."

"Doubt it," I improvised.

"Yeah. Me too. Think they smelled us out. But keep it quiet anyway. Babe'll have your ass if he hear's any noise."

I put the device in my jacket pocket, smiled at Sarah and James, spoke to everyone. "Fat man in the building. We could get lucky here."

• • • •

The dead soldier told the truth about fifteen. There were no more soldiers. We sat by the stairway doors and conferred before moving on. "Seventy-five guys are stacked above us," Weasel said, nodding his head toward the ceiling. "We got seven and a dog."

"I got nearly forty more men on ground level," James said. "Let me bring 'em up."

"Until we get Merlin out," I responded, "we can't have a fire fight."

"Starve them out," Stevie said. "Put them under siege."

"They'd just drop the little guy out a fucking window," James said. "Wet blob on the sidewalk. They don't give a shit."

"I got an idea," Weasel said.

"Don't forget we've only got a few hours before sunrise burns off our advantage," I told him, referring to the night vision goggles.

"If it works, we'll be done before the sun comes up."

• • • •

From the stairwell we could see light from the seventeenth floor leeching out from under the door. Sarah was beside me, a hand resting on my shoulder. Behind her James and Duke sat, waiting for information. Behind them were five of James' soldiers.

We were in the middle of their trap, the meat in the sandwich. But the Messengers didn't know it. Twenty of them above us on eighteen, another twenty below on sixteen. Thirty or forty more just beyond the doors we sat behind in the stairwell on seventeen.

Five days of waiting had taken the edge off their vigilance. Boredom was their enemy now. They no longer expected us. No battle, no pussy. Just each other and whatever drugs they had brought with them.

This was the advantage that had gotten us this far. They had no women. Sleep had to be difficult. The place smelled like a sewer. The drugs were probably running out, and I knew the food had to be horrible. There motivation and vigilance were at low tide.

We had brought all of James' Disciples up to take positions in the stairwells on sixteen, seventeen and eighteen. None of the Messengers had sensed our presence.

We were at full strength. Forty-two men, one woman and a dog. Between seventy-five and eighty of the Messengers were within a few feet of all of us.

We were now in The Babe's trap. But he wasn't expecting nearly forty of us. Nor did he expect that we would control the doors to the stairways. We had five or six men on each door of sixteen, seventeen and eighteen. Each man with two assault rifles and plenty of ordnance.

It was time to see just how sloppy they had become.

I oiled the door to seventeen and opened it enough to allow access for my head. I slipped James' baseball cap into the gap. Nothing happened. I followed with my head at floor level. I spoke in a whisper. Everyone with the comm gear on would hear. "Listen up. Hallway's empty. One lantern to the left by the elevators. More light coming from the side hallway on the right. More lanterns. If there's forty men on this floor, they're keeping it secret."

"That's what you do in an ambush," Stevie said.

He was in the other stairwell, adjacent Sarah, James, Duke and me. He had Angel and four more Disciples with him. Sarah had given up her comm set. James retained his to keep in contact with his men, make sure they stayed out of it until we got Merlin. With our spares, we had eight total. Two sets were in the ears of Disciples in the two stairwells of sixteen; the other two, on eighteen.

Weasel was alone. In a very special spot, a highly precarious spot. He needed his comm set. Stevie, James and I wore the remaining three comm sets. We had distributed the NVG's in the same way.

"You OK Weasel?" I asked.

"Used one of the rifle straps to belt me on," he replied. "Very fucking spooky in here. Let's get it on."

"Hallway's clear. Try to get the doors open."

I could hear his exertions, the heavy breathing, grunts, in my ear. It was a tough job, awkward angle, bad leverage, doors that hadn't moved in 35 years or so. Drop into oblivion if he fell off. "Can't do it," he finally said, "without makin' a whole bunch of noise."

"It's all right. Back off. We'll go to step two. Open it up when the noise starts."

I pulled the Radio Shack walkie talkie from my pocket. Before I pressed the button to send, I reminded everyone not to fire unless ordered to or fired upon. I waited a second so they could pass the reminder on to James' troops, then jumped into the Messenger's loop. "Yo, fat man. You there?"

A slight pause, then a voice jumped out of the little box, gravelly, baritone, pissed. "Who the fuck is that?" The voice hesitated, then came back, lower volume, farther away. I pictured him holding the walkie talkie away from him, screaming at his lieutenants.

"Find out who the fuck this is. Bring me his goddam tongue." Then full volume. "Get off the air, dumb shit. You're fucking up the plan."

"Your plan is flawed," I said.

"Who the hell are you, telling me that shit?"

"Karma. Bad Karma."

Slight pause. "There ain't no Carmen in the Messengers. Ever hear of the Messengers? You're dead, Carmen."

"You got something I want."

"I'm gonna eat your liver," he said.

"I want Merlin. I'm willing to trade."

"Mother fuck," he said, registering more surprise now than animosity. "The man with the dog. That you McCall?"

"I want Merlin."

"You're close, aren't you?" he breathed. It made him feel good to know that I was nearby. "These things don't carry too far."

"Way above you," I lied, not mentioning a floor. It would keep him from springing his trap, bringing forth the men on sixteen and eighteen, sandwiching us on seventeen. We weren't ready for that yet.

"Unless you got the balls to bring him yourself," I continued, "send Merlin up to me with one of your men. I'll give you the dog in return. You want the dog, don't you, asshole? I'm not sure if his head will fit in a bird cage, but you can give it a try."

No response. Only his inner circle knew about the bird cage. He had had someone inside the Cobras for at least a year, reporting Roberto's thoughts and plans back to him. Now he was feeling those same little prickly feelings of betrayal that Roberto had been subjected to, the beginnings of doubt. I possessed knowledge that was supposedly confined to the inner circle of the Messengers.

I planted a seed of paranoia.

• • • •

Real time it was probably a couple of minutes, but it felt like an hour before he came back on. "McCall? We should talk. Work something out about getting your friend back. All this chasing after you makes me tired. Whatta you say I walk up to twenty-three? Meet you there. Just the two of us. We talk. Settle our differences."

"Give me five minutes to think about it," I responded. "I'll get back to you." I put the little communicator in my pocket, leaving it on "receive" to monitor any of his commands.

"What's he going to do?" I asked anyone who was listening.

"He's coming after you," Weasel said. "Up above. Where he thinks you're at."

"Definitely," James replied. "He'll try to get some men upstairs."

"We got movement up here on eighteen." It was one of James' men, Wind Chill, one floor above us. "They're headin' for these fucking stairway doors. Tell me what you want, James, man. Do it quick."

"How the hell did he get those men into action without this thing?" I asked, tapping the walkie talkie.

"Good question," Sarah said.

"Weasel," I said, "something's about to start. When you hear the shooting, use the noise to cover you getting those doors open. We need you to have access to seventeen."

"Do it," he said.

"You tell me quick, James," came Wind Chill's voice came from eighteen, panic at the edge. "They're bunchin' up."

I nodded to James. He smiled. This was what they were there for. "Wind Chill," he said, "don't let the bastards out. Take them down. But don't be going in after them. Everybody else, you men on sixteen and seventeen, maintain your positions. Keep quiet."

"Oh, shit, they're comin' at us," came Wind Chill's voice from the eighteenth floor stairwell. "Fuck 'em up, boys!"

The firing started immediately. The rattle of M 16s, the distinctive pops of the old Russian AKs, the deceptively harmless sounding blats of the Uzis and Skorpions. Thousands of rounds were bouncing off the walls and shredding flesh above us. It wouldn't last for long. The Messengers were in an untenable position. Only two ways out—the two doors that opened to the stairwells.

The Messengers were in a funnel, and James' Disciples had the hole plugged. Even outnumbered two to one, we were at a distinct advantage. Their trap had folded in upon itself. Only if we went in after them would the odds begin to favor The Babe's men.

In about three minutes, the firing began to taper off to sporadic single shots, occasional bursts. I heard spent shell casings pinging on the concrete above us. Then it stopped. "Report, Wind Chill," James said.

Wind Chill's breathing was heavy, his voice too loud for our earpieces. "Fucking river of blood in the hallways," he said, pumped from the action. "Lots of them down. Rest retreated. We slaughtered 'em, James. Fuckin' Messengers down all over the place. At least a dozen."

"What about us?" James asked his soldier.

"Nothin', James. Not even a scratch. Hold on a minute... something's going down." Pause. "They turned out all the fucking lamps. Darker than a whore's heart in here. Shit. Holy shit..."

"What? What the fuck's going down, Wind Chill?" James asked, concern for his men straining his voice.

"Weird shit. Bunch of red dots comin' out of the dark. Movin' toward our position."

"Same thing on this left side." It was another of James' soldiers, the man in charge of the men on the other stairway on eighteen. "Never seen anything like this, James. Like eyes of the devil. About ten or fifteen drifting in the air. Gives me the fuckin' willies. I'm blastin' em, man."

A harsh whisper came onto the line, commanding attention. Weasel. "Shut the fuck up and listen. You don't have much time. Keep your goggles off. Switch your rifles to single shot. Swing the doors all the way open and get as many rifles as you can pointing into those halls. Aim at those red dots. Use 'em like targets. Keep it up 'til they go out or stop moving. Then put your night goggles on and check it out. Do it...now."

We heard the shots from upstairs. Directly above us, the retorts were harsh and hollow, echoing through the stairwell. Answering fire from the Messengers came on full auto. In less than a minute it was finished.

Angel's voice came on line. "Shit. More bodies. Fucking blood looks black with these glasses on. Dead Messengers layin' in black water. Some of them got huge buggy things on their eyes. What the hell's goin' on?"

"Tell ya later," Weasel said. "Thing is, there's only eight pairs of night goggles for the thirty-seven of us. You tell all your men, that if the Messengers turn out the lights, that means any red dot they see is a fucking target. Tell 'em all. Could save their lives."

• • • •

We heard nothing from The Messengers for ten minutes. The walkie talkie in my pocket remained silent. No shots, no sounds of movement on sixteen, seventeen or eighteen. Three of James' Disciples on eighteen had been wounded in the second charge by the Messengers. The Babe lost seven more warriors in the second assault. We calculated they were down to around three or four men left alive on the eighteenth floor. But we weren't willing to send any of the men in to check.

The Messengers on sixteen and seventeen had made no moves.

The numbers were evening up.

We still had the strategic advantage.

They still had Merlin.

We used the time to plan the next step—the rescue of Merlin.

CHAPTER THIRTY-TWO

Weasel was hanging in the coal dark vertical tube of an elevator shaft. Before we brought all of James' soldiers up to help even out the huge number discrepancy, we found a custodian's closet and took a crow bar; then used it to pry open the elevator doors on the fourteenth floor. Weasel stuck his head into the pit, first looking up, then down, seeing nothing in the near perfect blackness, even with the aid of the night vision goggles. He gave us a little farewell wave and a weak smile and disappeared into the maw, climbing up the steel rungs that marched up the wall of the shaft.

First time I had ever seen a hint of fear.

He was on seventeen now and had used the noise from the two battles on eighteen to pry open the elevator doors. They were closed again, but, he assured us, they could be easily reopened, allowing him access to the floor where we believed Merlin was being held. We had a plan of sorts, and his location in the elevator shaft, smack in the middle of the seventeenth floor, hidden from the Messengers, was a crucial component in our efforts to extricate Merlin—if he were still alive.

The plan was a teeter-totter. The fulcrum it rested upon was getting Merlin out into the center of the corridor, near enough to the elevators that Weasel, creating some type of distraction which we had yet to conceive, could haul himself out and take whoever was holding Merlin from behind. If we got lucky, The Babe himself would bring him out. If that happened, we all reminded ourselves that the primary goal was to liberate Merlin, not destroy The Babe. Merlin's safe return was top on the list.

To get Merlin out into the hallway, we needed bait.

I was the bait.

Despite The Babe's machinations, the plan was still perfectly workable, perhaps even more so now that he had lost at least twenty-five per cent of his troops in the battle on the eighteenth floor. As we spoke, via the comm sets and my translation to Sarah, who had given up hers to one of James' men, we arrived at the consensus that The Babe would move soon, try to entice me out into the open while he had strength.

If the Messenger who James had killed on fifteen was telling the truth about their numbers, they had at least sixty men left alive, most on them concentrated on sixteen and seventeen. In accordance, we had brought all but two of the Disciples from eighteen down to seventeen and sixteen to beef up the defense of the stairwell doors. There were now over thirty of us divided among the four stairwells on sixteen and seventeen.

We might not be able to get in through the doors.

But the Messengers would find it impossible to get out.

"One more thing," I asked Weasel, "what was with those floating red lights on the eighteenth floor?"

"It's a nice little story," he replied. "But we got no time for stories here. Tell you when we get back home. Just remember, we got nearly thirty men here without night glasses. You tell them that if the lights go out and they see a red light, shoot it. It will save their lives."

• • • •

I pulled the walkie from my pocket. It was set to receive at low volume. We were very close.

"Here goes," I told everyone.

Thumbing the send button, I said, "I've thought about your proposal."

"Tell me," he replied.

"Know why I came here, fat man?" I asked.

"To meet your little friend," he laughed. "He's not feeling so good, McCall. Little bit sore. We been without slits for five, six days now. Your little man-boy's got a nice ass. We been taking turns on it."

My stomach dropped. Beside me, one ear close to the walkie, Sarah squeezed my arm and whispered in my ear. "Don't lose it, hon.

That's what he's shooting for. You'll make a mistake if you lose your cool. At least we know Merlin's still alive."

Behind her, James was silent. He heard the words. Just sat on his haunches and petted Duke. I couldn't see his eyes with the goggles on, but his motions were stiff, mechanical. He wanted to kill someone.

I digested Sarah's words, accepted her wisdom, took a few seconds to breathe deeply, refocus, slow my heartbeat. I found her hand and gently covered it with mine, then went back to business.

Thumbing the button on the walkie-talkie, I said, "I came here because I knew you'd be here." I paused, letting it sink in that the prey was after the hunter. "I'm going to kill you, you fat bucket of puke."

He laughed, a deep, harsh bark. "If you knew I was here, you'd be miles away. I'm the monster that visits when you sleep, McCall. If I can't get you, if you keep running and hiding from me, I'll devour anybody you know. I'll snuff every person you ever talked to just to make you hurt."

"Keep pushing him, Mac." It was Weasel's voice over the comm set. "He's getting pissed."

"Are your soldiers beginning to lose faith in you?" I asked. "Seeing as how you been looking for me for a year without any fucking results."

"You're here now," he replied, anger beginning to affect the timbre of his voice. "You don't set up a meet with me and I'm gonna start carving on this little whore up here."

"You know what happens if you do?"

"You gonna hurt me?" he replied, mocking, taunting.

"No. I'll leave. I'll pack everyone up and slip away. Leave you sitting here holding your pecker. Twenty of your men on eighteen drowning in their cowards' blood. Leave you to explain to the People clans how one man and a dog elude the great Messengers. How they should all join you even though you live in fear of a single man and a mangy dog. That you are a great warrior, slayer of women, defiler of children, who lives in fear of one simple man and his stupid dog."

His reply came in stutters, as though a giant had him by the throat, choking off his breath. "I've...got...you...here...now."

"I think its the other way around. Is the blood of your men seeping through the ceiling? Watch your head. Cowards' blood will eat your skin off."

"What...do...you...want," he croaked.

"I want to kill you. But I'll settle for taking Merlin home. I'm coming down to seventeen. If Merlin isn't in the hallway by the stairs in ten minutes, I leave this place. You can hunt me for another year. You want to deal, I give you the dog for Merlin. Otherwise I'm going home. You don't cooperate here, then I'm willing to pay for your humiliation with my friend's life. I'll find another snitch."

It was a few seconds before he came back. Was I telling the truth? Could I give up on Merlin? It meshed with his system of values. He could appreciate the logic.

"Be there," the fat man said.

"You coming too? I'll let you pet the dog."

"I'll tear its head off."

"I'll let you know when I'm coming in."

• • • •

I pocketed the walkie and peeked into the hallway, still dimly lit by the lanterns, marking in my mind the spot where Merlin was supposed to show up. On the other side of the door, in the Messenger's lair, I heard the sounds of our enemies preparing for combat, weapons shouldered, clips driven home, bodies in motion. The flickering lamps began to show dancing shadows approaching our position. I ducked back behind the door.

They would bring Merlin. The Babe couldn't risk my leaving. His reputation would be in tatters. Without new recruits attracted by his power, his dreams of domination would dissolve.

"Weasel?" I asked via the comm set, "Is he going to bring Merlin himself?"

"I doubt it," he said. "Man's pretty smart. He's not afraid to mix it, but you got him a little wary. He'll send someone else."

"How we going to play it?" Sarah asked.

"Fast," Weasel said. "They probably got some kind of plan. Let's not let 'em get it started. First instant you think I got an angle, let me know. Tell me where, how many. I'll pop these doors open, sneak into the hallway and go for whoever's got Merlin. Make sure their backs are turned to me."

• • • •

The three of us, Sarah, Stevie and I, had nine minutes left to run down to fifteen and work our way back up to seventeen through Merlin's escape hatch. Weasel found it in the women's bathroom on fifteen. In the corner, over the last toilet stall, hidden by the original ceiling tile. Dust on the floor had given it away to his eyes. We didn't know how far up it went. Figured at least through eighteen. All we needed was to get to the seventeenth floor.

I went first. Up onto the toilet, remove the ceiling panel, pull myself up to the next level and push up on the floor tile to enter sixteen. The bathroom was empty. I reached down for Stevie, pulled him up and then did the same for Sarah. We then repeated the process, finishing up in the women's bathroom on seventeen.

I visualized the terrain outside the bathroom door. Immediately on our left was a doorway to the bullpen. Across the hall was the men's bathroom. Also across the hall a meter to the right was the hallway to the freight elevators. Then the two stairway doors on the same side. Behind those doors our reinforcements awaited our signal. There was a double glass door between the two stairwell doors. Further down on the same side was the cul de sac that housed the eight main elevators. That was the spot from which Weasel would enter the battle.

On the same side that Sarah, Stevie and I would enter the hall, to the right of the bathroom, was another hallway, the one that led to the east side of the bullpen. Fifteen meters down was the vending machine room. It was across from the banks of elevators where Weasel was hiding. Right in the middle of all of these openings where the Messengers would surely be setting up defenses was the spot where Merlin was to be presented to me.

We had four advantages. They didn't know our strength; Weasel was going to get behind them; they expected me to enter through the stairway door. The fourth and biggest advantage was that The Babe wanted me alive. That would buy Sarah, Stevie and me a few seconds when we stepped into the hallway from the bathroom.

Normally, the grenades would have been ideal to clear the hallway of defenders, allowing our men to enter from the stairwells. But with Merlin in the hall, they were useless. He would be shredded along with the Messengers.

• • • •

It had been ten minutes. I got on my hands and knees and pushed the bathroom door open a crack. About ten meters down the hall, illuminated by the lights of the lamps, Merlin was standing, under his own power, flanked by two Messenger soldiers, pistols in their hands, M 16s on their backs. He was on the other side of the glass double doors. His face was swollen and discolored. But in the dim lamp light, I couldn't make out details of the injuries.

No one else was visible. I told Weasel the situation, ordered everyone to remove their night vision goggles and then told the two men left above us on the eighteen to enter their floor and begin firing. Weasel would use the noise as cover to exit the elevators, letting us know when he was in position.

Five seconds after the firing on eighteen commenced, Weasel came on the line. "Door's open. Got five soldiers in here, waiting in ambush for you. Can't get out."

Stevie translated for Sarah.

"Toss a grenade in," I said. "The shrapnel's not going around the corner where Merlin is. When it goes off, we'll make our move."

From our position by the closed bathroom door, I mapped the situation for Stevie and Sarah. Two men, ten meters down on our right, Merlin in between them. Head shots only.

Ten seconds later, the concussion of the grenade reverberated throughout the seventeenth floor and the three of us stepped out of the bathroom into the hallway. Except for Merlin and the two Messenger soldiers, it was still empty. They were still planning to take me when I entered from the stairwell.

Stevie and I dropped to a shooter's crouch. Sarah covered our backs with the Franchi combat shotgun and the Australian Leader assault rifle. The men guarding Merlin had swung around to the other end of the hallway in response to grenade's resounding explosion, placing their backs toward Stevie and me. We each fired two shots from the silenced pistols, the 9mm slugs shattered the glass in the double doors and flew true to their intended destination in the men's skulls.

The guards crumbled, leaving a bewildered Merlin standing alone in the hallway.

"On the floor, Merlin!" I screamed. "Crawl toward the explosion. Move your ass."

In the fifteen seconds following my command to Merlin, there was more action than all of us had experienced in our combined lifetimes. It was if my voice had shattered an invisible barrier that was holding everyone in check.

• • • •

Sarah and I had once walked in the woods with Duke on a spring morning, stumbling across a meadow filled with thousands of Canadian geese, browsing the grasses for morsels, chattering at one another under the warm sun. Duke went on point and Sarah and I stopped dead in our tracks. We had never witnessed a goose gathering of such magnitude.

Duke went down on all fours and managed a strange creeping, stalking crawl until he achieved the edge of the meadow, hidden from his quarry by the high grasses. I saw the muscles in his haunches bunch, preparatory to his big leap, anticipatory of the best fun a dog could have.

He shot forward in a golden arc, barking furiously, and achieved a position twenty meters into the meadow before the thousands of huge birds arose, en masse, as if on a signal from God, darkening the sun and filling the sky with downy feathers and dust motes, deafening our ears with their honking and the flaps of their muscular wings.

The three of us—man, wife and dog companion—stood in silent amazement, heads pointed to the sky, gazing at the mayhem Duke had wrought.

What occurred in the fifteen seconds following my command to Merlin to hit the ground on the seventeenth floor of the AON Building made the pandemonium of thousands of geese seem like an orderly procession of monks to chapel.

• • • •

Merlin heard my voice, but didn't heed my command. In the lamplight that illuminated the seventeenth floor, I saw Merlin drop to the floor, squeezing between the bulks of his two dead guards, moments before rifle fire came at him from across the hall, where more Messengers were lying in wait for my expected appearance in the stairway door. Their bullets smacked into the flesh of the dead men. Merlin's former potential executioners now served as his bunker.

I heard the fire from Weasel's Uzi before I saw him. He was sweeping the other Messenger soldiers who were hiding in the vending machine alcove. He came around the corner and changed to his Galil SAR assault rifle, peppering 7.62mm rounds from his 36 round clip into the men who were firing upon Merlin from the connecting hallway, driving them back toward the west wall of the bullpen area.

Merlin was in a paroxysm of rage, twisting one of the guards' bodies to extract his M16. When he retrieved the weapon, he began spraying rounds at the same men Weasel was firing upon, screaming maniacally, having crossed over the line of sanity, possessing no regard for his safety.

During the same five seconds that I observed Weasel and Merlin defending their end, I heard three blasts from Sarah's shotgun. I snapped a glance back at her. The double doors to our left, the entry to the north area of the bullpen, had been blasted away. Some of the Messengers were trying to flank us. They were gone now, two of their dead on the floor, victims of the blasts from Sarah's shoulder slung Franchi 12 gage.

With Sarah covering our left flank and Weasel and Merlin on our right and a wall to our backs, Stevie and I focused our attention across the hall. Men's bathroom in front of us. Entry to the freight elevator hallway a meter or two to the right, then a few meters down the two entrances to the stairwells, where reinforcements awaited us.

We needed to make it possible for James and his Disciple soldiers to gain entry from the stairwells.

From the darkened interior of the hallway that led to the freight elevators flashes of rifle fire became visible, quickly followed by the impact of bullets on the wall to our right. Telling Stevie to cover the bathroom, I dropped to the floor and inched forward a meter so I could train my assault rifle on the recesses of the hallway. I sprayed the hall with 30 rounds from the HK assault rifle, flipping the double taped clip to reload when finished. Their firing stopped.

Stevie did the same on the bathroom door, reducing it to splinters. He then kicked it in and underhanded a grenade into the dark interior. Its muffled thump followed two seconds later, ejecting dust, smoke and shrapnel into our hallway.

Only ten seconds had passed. We seemed momentarily clear, and I looked right, where the firing was still furious. Merlin was doing the dance of a maniac, firing the M16 into the hallway and screaming at the top of his lungs. None of the words were intelligible. They may not have even been words as we know them. But they were a clear expression of his mental state. He cared not whether he lived or died. He just wanted to punish.

Weasel's voice entered my ear, loud against the competition of the rounds being expended in his end of the battle zone. "Mac, give me a hand with Merlin, 'fore the little fucker gets himself killed."

Weasel approached him from behind and I moved forward to help, crossing the hallway that led to the freight elevators. I didn't move quickly enough. Several shots rang out from my left as I crossed the corridor, Messengers laying in wait, looking for something to shoot. I was punched fiercely on my left side twice, debilitating blows that pushed me to the wall on my right, knocked me to the floor, took my breath from me. The Kevlar III kept the rounds from penetrating, but my torso felt like I had just taken several body shots from a heavyweight fighter.

With my right hand, I swung the HK to spray the corridor once more, then tried to crawl beyond it opening, past the angle where they could get more shots into me.

I looked right. Through the smoke and haze and the dust raised by the grenades, I saw Weasel approaching Merlin, who was oblivious to any of our efforts. Using his left hand, Weasel was firing his assault rifle into the same corridor Merlin was focusing on. With his right, he grabbed Merlin by the collar, jerked him off his feet and dragged him back to the elevator area. Merlin kept on firing at the hallway and screaming at the Messengers who had retreated.

That was the first fifteen seconds. The next fifteen were worse.

• • • •

Across the ten meters separating us, Weasel's eyes met mine. "Are you all right?" he asked his voice clear in my comm set.

I nodded my head. I couldn't speak.

"Hang on," he said. "Stevie and Sarah are comin' up behind you. Let's get those men out of the stairways and onto the floor. James," he spoke to the Disciple leader who was waiting for a chance to enter the main hallway, "you got an opening. Bring 'em out now!"

Then he and Merlin disappeared into the cul de sac that housed the elevators. Last I saw of them on seventeen was Merlin's boots being dragged around the corner.

"I'm gettin' him out of here, Mac," Weasel said. "Down the shaft. Clear everyone out quick as possible."

Both sets of stairway doors slammed open. Black Gangster Disciples poured out right and left, rifles and pistols ready, searching for targets. I prayed none of us would be snuffed by friendly fire. Among the fifteen men was a golden form, close to the ground, moving fast. Duke came unerringly straight for me and straddled me as a lay upon the ground. If they came at us, his body would take the first of the bullets meant for me.

I looked behind and saw Stevie and Sarah heading toward us. Then I heard a squawk on the walkie talkie, silent in my pocket these few long seconds. I couldn't make out the words, but I recognized the voice.

Then, behind Sarah and Stevie, filling the doorway they had just vacated to come help me, pushing two of his men before him, screaming into the walkie talkie, The Babe entered the game. He surveyed the scene, saw several of his men down, unmoving, the Disciples moving down the hall in both directions, Sarah and Stevie moving away.

Army fatigues covered his massive frame. Three rifles were draped across his chest. Football pads covered his shoulders. Hanging below his bearded chin were strange looking goggles. Shin guards from a 20th cen catcher protected his lower legs. A WWII Nazi helmet, large enough to cook a fifteen pound turkey in, covered his head.

Two of his men tried to retreat in the face of the Disciple on-slaught. He pushed them back to face his enemies, and they went down under a hail of bullets. They were replaced by five more Messengers, eyes dancing, grins on their faces, screams of joy in their throats. Slammer or Bad Boy. They were flying.

He saw me then. Recognizing me not because of our previous encounter in the parking lot (he was too far away to make out my features without binocs) but because of the dog that protected my prostrate form. Duke felt his presence, whirled to face him, snarling and snapping his warning to keep back.

The Babe wasn't impressed. He smiled at the dog, then shifted his eyes to mine. He screamed over the melee, "I'm gonna fuck you up, McCall."

Then he reached back to just above his shoulder and pulled the baseball bat from the harness that kept it always close. He swished it through the air, practice swings, smooth black Kentucky ash that would shatter bones, split the flesh. Then he slowly, deliberately lumbered in our direction, ignoring the shots and screams that filled the hallway.

He only had eyes for me.

That's when the lights went out. That's what his walkie talkie command was for…extinguish the lanterns. But it didn't stay dark. Muzzle flashes illuminated the hallway.

I tried to get up, but the pain in my left side kept me down. My left arm hadn't been hit, but when I attempted to move it, the motion was fiercely protested by my ribs and torso muscles. I went to the right hand, pulling the Desert Eagle .357 Magnum semi-auto pistol from my shoulder holster. Nine rounds, spare clips accessible, it would stop anything, even The Babe, who was just a few steps away.

I saw him coming…as sure and true as a bear to a rotting carcass. Nothing stops a hungry bear. They know no fear or caution. The muzzle flashes provided the light. Hundreds of rounds were being expended in the hallway. The noise of the rifle and pistol shots, punctuated with screams of terror and excitement, transformed the corridor into a twisted nightmare of sight and sound.

I brought the .357 up, using Duke's back to steady my arm, looking for a shot at the man coming to take my head off. But Stevie and Sarah were still moving toward me, firing over Duke and me at whatever threatened us from the other end of the hallway. I couldn't get a shot off at The Babe. Sarah and Stevie kept moving into my line of fire.

I tried to scream at them—Get the fuck down! He's behind you! He's gonna kill you!—but I couldn't get enough breath into my lungs to fuel the shouted command. The muscles in my left side wouldn't cooperate.

I waved the pistol side to side, big motions, then up and down. But they were too busy defending themselves and me to notice.

Sarah and Stevie were close now, just a couple of steps away, appearing and disappearing with the intermittent lighting of the muzzle flashes. Both of them were firing repeatedly, Sarah emptying her shotgun and flinging it to the ground, replacing it with the Leader SAR. Stevie was with her, pouring out an even heavier wall of fire over the bodies of me and Duke, a Skorpion machine pistol in one hand, HK 81 assault rifle in the other.

Two steps behind them was The Babe. He was focusing on them now. They would have to go down under the power of his Louisville Slugger before he could get to me.

Sarah and Stevie were at my side. Sarah leaned over me, concern etched on her face. She was mouthing words I couldn't hear in the din of the screams and rifle shots. Flashes of lightning illuminated her face, beautiful auburn hair, emerald eyes.

Behind her, the beast drew nearer.

I widened my eyes and pointed my head down the hall. Stevie was covering both of us. I pointed with my right hand to the monster that was bearing down upon all of us. Turn around!, I screeched in my mind. He's coming! Gonna turn your brains into pulp! Take you away from me. Extinguish the light in your eyes. Please, Sarah, please look.

She checked my body for wounds in the flashing light. She couldn't read my mind.

The Babe was a step away now, the bat above his shoulder, preparatory to a killing blow. Stevie was on his feet, focusing forward. He did not sense the beast behind him. He would be first. Then Sarah. I didn't care what he did to me.

The bat began its downward arc. The fat man's eyes were shining with anticipation. Muzzle flashes made him appear and disappear, as if each sighting were a lighted picture, one frame of a sequence. And each snapshot brought the bat inches closer to Stevie's head.

We were going to die...and I was defenseless, powerless, unable to stop the force that threatened us. Couldn't even scream a protest.

Duke launched.

One hundred and twenty pounds of claws and fangs, golden fur and wiry muscles. A flash of Stevie's rifle highlighted Duke's leap. He was stretched out fully, suspended in mid-air, perfectly equidistant between me and The Babe, a projectile launched from a cannon, heading straight for the fat man's throat, frozen in a photograph that would never leave my mind.

Duke's body didn't knock the fat man down, but it stopped the behemoth in his tracks and caused him to drop the bat. Duke was too close to be hit by the bat. He was plastered to the monster's upper body, his head thrashing, working his way in toward the soft fat flesh of the throat.

Duke was just seconds away from the jugular. I could see the terror in The Babe's eyes as Duke's growls filled his ears and the dog's sharp fangs ripped at the bloated face and neck of the man who would kill his family.

Stevie and Sarah turned when Duke launched. They watched in stunned fascination at the struggle for life, close enough to them that they could reach out and touch Duke's fur. None of us could help. We couldn't get a shot in without jeopardizing Duke.

It was over in less than three seconds.

The Babe's huge arms came up and his meaty hands grabbed Duke by each shoulder, peeling the dog from his upper body. In the flashes of light, I could see bright red blood covering Duke's jaw and fangs. The right side of the Babe's face was awash in blood. He flexed his arms and tossed Duke aside, bouncing him off the wall to my right. Duke hit high up and slid to the floor, unmoving.

The Babe wiped the blood from his face and reached down for his bat. Stevie was closest. He swung his rifle and smashed it into the Babe's forearm before he could retrieve the bat, receiving a backhand in return which knocked him back three feet and momentarily cost him his coordination.

Sarah brought her weapon up, but the Babe retrieved the bat before she began firing, swinging at her and smashing the SAR. He turned to me then and saw the Desert Eagle .357 coming up to the level of his head. I wasn't fast enough. The muscles on my left were still fighting any movements I made from the right side. The pistol came up, but not before he started backing away. The man was close enough to see it was a very large gun.

Sarah pulled a 9mm Ruger from her holster and we both brought our pistols up to center on his head. In the flashing lights, he saw our move and ducked his head, presenting the helmet to us. She fired first. I was too weak and slow. Her shots bounced off the helmet. He continued to retreat.

I brought the big pistol up, but at over four pounds of dead weight on my right arm, and no help from my left, my accuracy was non-existent. I unleashed four rounds. The sound was deafening in the confinement of the hallway, louder by far than any of the other weapons.

The first three missed completely. The fourth hit his helmet at an angle, not a direct hit, ripping it from his head and sending it flying toward the bullpen. Sarah and I both went for head shots then, hoping to end the fat man's reign.

But he had already reached the safety of his soldiers, and before we could get off, he pulled two of them in front of him and ducked behind the shelter of their flesh and bones.

Our shots went into his temporary bunker, smacking into the men's flesh, riddling their protective sports gear, tearing plastic, flesh and bone. The shots from the .357 (I had five left) traveled right through the men that protected him. I saw The Babe's bulky form jerk back as some of them impacted. But they didn't stop him. He pulled back around the corner into the bullpen and then I heard the squawk of the walkie talkie in my pocket as he issued more orders to his men.

• • • •

Within five seconds, except for a few random single shots in the bullpen area, there was silence...and total darkness. With my right hand, I put the goggles over my eyes.

Sarah was bending over me. "Mac," she said, "Mac, honey, where are you hit?"

I reached up with my right hand and pulled her head down so that her ear was right next to my mouth. Whispering haltingly, I said, "Took a couple of slugs in the ribs. Armor stopped 'em. But it's sore as hell. Can't hardly talk."

I took the derm patch from my throat and placed it on hers. "Take my ear piece and get everybody the fuck out of here. We got what we want. We need to draw back and regroup."

She took the little earring from me and immediately began barking orders, telling James to get his men back into the stairwells, checking on Merlin and Weasel, who had escaped down the elevator shaft.

To my right, in the green hazy gun smoke, I could see Duke limping toward me. Behind me Stevie was stirring. Bodies littered the hall; moans of the wounded filled the air.

We got out before they decided to come at us again.

CHAPTER THIRTY-THREE

U p on the twenty-first floor, where we had moved because it was
the high ground, easier to protect, we posted guards in the
stairwells and assessed the damages by candlelight.

Stevie was bruised but fine. Sarah had a couple of nicks from
random bullets, but the bleeding was checked. Weasel was unscathed. I
was very sore and limited in my range of motion. But I could finally
talk again, and it appeared that my ribs were not broken.

Except for a face that looked like it had been on the losing end of
a clan boxing match, Merlin was physically fine, no bullet wounds or
broken bones. Psychologically he was in bad shape, sullen and
brooding, alternating periods of silence with energized bellicosity.
During his quiet spells, he cleaned weapons, completely focused on the
task, oblivious to any of our attempts at conversation.

He had become a completely different person. Nearly a week as a
prisoner of the Messengers and the vile acts they had perpetrated upon
him had robbed Merlin of his most endearing personality trait, his zest
for life. He needed our help. We would take him back home again.
Probably have to drag him. He would not want to be around us.

James had a bullet wound in his thigh, but was more concerned
with the condition of his men than his own injury. Three of the
Disciples had been killed by the Messengers; four more wounded badly
enough to have to be carried out. That job was underway. The soldiers
who helped the wounded would return, bringing reinforcements. We
had men posted on seventeen and sixteen, in case the Messengers tried
to leave, or resume the attack.

Four floors below us, the our enemy was silent. My Radio Shack
walkie talkie hadn't made a sound. I chose not to attempt to open
contact. Never fuck with a wounded bear.

• • • •

James sipped on a canteen, tossed a biscuit and piece of smoked salmon to Weasel. "We're going back in," he said. "Ain't finished until every last Messenger is dead or gone from our borders."

"What I would expect," Weasel responded. "We'll go in with you."

"No need," James replied. "This is our fight now."

"No," Stevie said. "You saved our asses. We continue together."

James nodded his head. Despite his words to the contrary, it would have been a breech of code for us not to have gone. In most ways we conducted our lives in a different value milieu than the clans. But with a few of them we shared some common beliefs. In this case we would finish the job, not because it was an expectation of James' code, but because it was part of ours.

"We got time now before my men get back," James said to Weasel. "Tell me about those red lights. What do they mean?"

"Couple 'a years before I migrated up here," Weasel began, "I lived on the Mississipp, west side, Cape Girardeau. State called Missouri. Beautiful town. Probably about five thousand of us scattered through the town and countryside. Made most of my livin' trading herb. Everyone grew it, but not with the seeds I had. People were happy when I came in to trade.

"Some of the local yahoos tried to trade me some night vision goggles, old bulky things, Viet Nam era. Looked like you had a pair of binoculars tied to your head. Thing was, I knew these things were infrared glasses. Had some knowledge of infrared night scopes. Ran into a fella whose daddy was a soldier in 'Nam. Sniper to be exact. Told his son the infrareds would produce a little red light comin' out of the scope when they were powered up. Viet Cong would line up on the light and put a single shot right on it. Get 'em in the head every time. Like they had a little sign on 'em, sayin' 'Here I am.'

"So I know I don't want any part of these glasses. Yahoos don't know about the problem, and I sure as shit ain't about to tell 'em. Never give away an advantage. They're pissed because they want my weed. I say fine, give me that Browning over and under 12 gage and

I'll give you a half pound. Hell of a shotgun for pheasant, turkey. They go away, but not too far. I see 'em hanging around.

"Gotta give it to those boys. Best goddam trackers I ever saw. Only people ever tracked me back to a home base. And I was extra careful. Knew they had something on their mind. Middle of the night, one of my alarms goes off. Could be a deer. Cougar. But I always check. Sneak up to a little bunker I got set up, scope the Remington .30-.30, not one of them night scopes, mind you, and take a look.

"Sure enough, there's ten little red lights out there, movin' toward me, bunched up nice and pretty. They figured they was invisible. They could see in the dark, but no one else could. Snapped the Remington up and extinguished seven of those little lights before they could figure out what was happening. Hour later, I was gone. Heading north.

"That's what the Messengers got, infrared. That why I never messed with night vision until I came across the image intensifiers. Not an advantage if the guy you're looking for has a gun and knows you're looking. If they come in the dark, we'll see those red lights again…and use it against them."

Everyone had been quiet during the tale, focused on Weasel's down home twang, caught up in the little mystery and adventure all of his vignettes conveyed.

"Damn," James said, "that was a hell of story. You know there's an indie up north makes his livin' telling stories? Mostly to other indies, but some of the clans let him in too. Spins a few tales, entertains the little ones, adults too from what I hear, gets fed, sometimes a woman, always a place to sleep."

"I'll be dipped," Weasel said. "Never heard of such a thing. Maybe when I retire I'll take it up."

"I'm afraid the point of the story is going to be moot," Sarah commented. "By the time James' men get back it's going to be full blown daylight."

"Just as well," I said. "If we're going to have to dig them out, I'd prefer to have full vision. Seems like things will be more even that way."

"Agreed," James replied. "But that info about red lights gets tucked away." He tapped his head. "Never know when it might save our hides."

"Let's talk about going back down there," Merlin said, the steel in his voice contrasting with his normally peaceful persona. "I got some scores to settle."

We all stared at him in disbelief. Some of us in sorrow for what he had lost. I wished I could have made it all disappear for him. Wipe it from his hard drive. But I couldn't. No more than I could do it for Stevie. Merlin would have to deal the same way we all did.

Duke got up and walked over to Merlin, doing a three-sixty and then plopping down beside him, eyes up, checking him out. He sensed the change.

Sarah and I shared a look. I knew what she was thinking. In some ways, particularly his pacifism and love of music and longing for the good parts of the 20th, Merlin was the last of the innocents.

• • • •

Fifty of us went in an hour after dawn. Each of us who had a comm set led a force of seven or eight. Three groups crammed into the bathroom through Merlin's escape hatch. The other five groups entered through the two stairwells. At a command from James, we hit the seventeenth floor like the beaches of Normandy.

It was empty. They were all gone. Vanished.

At first we thought they had used Merlin's exit. But when we found their escape route, it explained how The Babe had communicated up to eighteen earlier without using the walkie talkie.

They had a hole in the southeast corner. It was large enough to allow quick escape and ran from nineteen to fifteen. A desk had been pushed aside for their escape. A rope dangled from seventeen down to fifteen.

Weasel smiled. "Never did accuse the man of being dumb."

They left their dead, stripped of all useful items.

They also left their sign—upside down crosses, five points carved into wall paper, devil's pitch forks, painted on walls in blood. It drove James into a frenzy of furniture smashing and shooting. He peppered the walls containing the Messenger spoor with automatic weapon fire, trying to eradicate their effrontery. Merlin, stern faced, devoid of emotion, joined James in the thunderous assault on the painted walls, emptying three clips from one of the Messenger's own M 16s into the offending surfaces.

As quickly as James' rage had flared, it subsided. As if drawing his energy from James, Merlin, too, ceased firing. Throwing his assault rifle down in disgust, frustrated that all he had to shoot at was a wall, James turned and smiled grimly, ordering five of his men to find some paint.

"The only sign these pigs will leave on Black Gangster Disciple turf will be their rotting corpses. Take these bodies to the borders and leave them as markers."

His men left and he focused his attention on us—a weary, wounded group who had achieved success but found no joy. The man we had come to rescue had been possessed by another. And we didn't know how to bring the original back.

"You have my gratitude," James said to all of us, "for showing respect to my people and our laws. And for your courage. Without your help we would have lost many more men."

"Without our help," I said, sarcastically punching the last word, "you wouldn't have lost any men at all. This was our battle. We're sorry those soldiers had to die, James."

"You're missing the point, McCall," James countered. "It doesn't make any difference that the Messengers came down here to get Merlin because they wanted to fuck with you. That's not part of the equation. What's important is that Merlin was under our protection. For years he's lived in Disciple territory with our knowledge and permission. Except for a couple of minor hassles, he's always paid for the privilege. Our men died with honor, protecting our territory. If the Messengers had gotten in and out and whacked Merlin here in the process, the BGD's may as well just roll over and die. Because every clan in the city would know—both Folks and People—and they'd all be after our turf. In a couple of weeks Disciples would be nothing but a bad memory."

"The way I figure it, James," I said, "it's us that owes you one. Not the other way around."

He smiled. "I'll accept that. Make it flow both ways. Here's what I want from you. We're not going after the Messengers right now. Be suicide to front them on their own turf. But we got long memories. And any of us would be honored to fight with you again. Including the dog. I saw him flying through the air, munching on The Babe's face. You fuckers are something else. This battle will be legend."

"The Messengers sure as hell won't be talking about it," Stevie said.

"We will," James said. "Everyone likes a good story. And this is gonna be one of the best. What I want from you is that we get to finish the story. You let us know if you meet the Messengers again. This isn't over for us."

"If the opportunity presents itself," Weasel said, "we'll let you in. Now," he continued, pulling James aside, walking away from the rest of us, "I got something you can do for us."

• • • •

On a yellowed interior wall of the bullpen, Stevie found the special communique that the Messengers had left for me. It was a primitive drawing, etched in blood, of a dog fucking a woman. Stick figures except for two details—the dog's penis (they were downright artistic when it came to depicting sexual organs) and the woman's hair. Rich in detail, requiring more blood than the rest of the childish sketch, the woman's hair was represented in a deeper red than any other part of the drawing.

As I gazed upon the crude sketch, painted in the blood of dead men on an east wall, brightly lit by the morning sun, my insides turned cold.

He knew about Sarah. Grasped that there was a connection between the two of us. Perceived the value of the auburn haired woman to the man he now sought more desperately than ever.

Beneath the drawing was a red lettered caption:

NOW IT WILL BE YOU
AND THE DOG
AND THE CUNT MACCAL
SWEET DREAMS

CHAPTER THIRTY-FOUR

H ome was comfortable. Home was nice. Home was vulnerable. The man in the closet was a testament to our vulnerability. He was more manageable now that the drugs were expunged from his system. But he was stupid, and he was mean. Being drug free didn't change that.

He had found us. Now the Messengers would be looking for him. Only safe place was another state. But we wouldn't run.

"You know," Sarah said one morning over breakfast, five days after we had returned from the AON Center, "we could go live with the Cobras. Or the Disciples. Either clan would accept us."

"It would just make the war bigger," I said.

"Live with them and we'd have to abide by their rules and customs," Weasel said. "We wouldn't fit in too well."

Sarah worked on some egg yolk with the corner of a piece of raisin bread. Bread from our oven, raisins from our grapes. "I know all that. The suggestion wasn't one that I necessarily would prefer. But I want all of your thoughts. We could be sitting at the site of our funeral right now, you know. What about you, Stevie?"

"I'll never live with a clan again," he said. "No matter who they are or how different they may seem. This here," tapping the table, "is my home. You are my family. We keep this business to ourselves."

"Merlin," Sarah said to our taciturn friend, the man who used to chatter like a squirrel, who had uttered barely a word for days, "how about you? What's your opinion?"

"I'm just along for the ride," he muttered.

I counted off the words on my fingers. Six of them. A veritable oration. We had been home for five days. Merlin had barely spoken. First couple of days we let him be. Figured he needed time to himself.

When he got hungry, he requested we bring the food up to him. We refused, making him come to us, feel the presence of someone who cared.

Didn't do a bit a good.

He was stoned all of the time. He showered incessantly, at least four times daily, hour each session. When we returned to the compound after the rescue, he had headed straight for the shower, stayed in until the hot water ran out.

We weren't sure if he had gotten any sleep. The bags under his eyes, his pasty color, more washed out than his usual pallor, the haunted look on his face were reflections of the internal battle he was waging.

The only color on his pallid features was the blues, purples and reds of the healing bruises and contusions on his face. The swelling had subsided. There would be some scarring. There were a few missing teeth. None of us had seen the rest of his body. He kept it covered, as if winter were in the air.

On the third day, after we found Merlin tearing up the house looking for the Bad Boy we had taken from the Messengers, Sarah went to the computer, searching the files for psychological problems, rape victims, treatment modalities for victims of abuse.

She found hundreds of references, thousands of pages.

None of it did any good.

Last night, Duke had wrested Sarah and I from our sleep and led us downstairs, where we found Merlin playing a deadly game with the man in the closet. Merlin located my Ruger Super Redhawk .44 Magnum revolver, one of the heaviest, most powerful pistols we possessed, and was placing it in and out of the Messenger's mouth, spinning the cylinder each time. The click of the hammer falling on an empty chamber was a haunting sound.

I took the pistol from him (there was no resistance) and Sarah walked him back to his room. The prisoner was happy to return to his home in the closet, particularly when I showed him one ominous .44 magnum slug in the cylinder. I locked the Messenger in, then hid the keys to the padlocks.

Sarah returned to our bed two hours later. She removed her gown and slipped under the sheets, melding her body to mine. "Hold me," she said.

I put aside *Farnham's Feehold* and extinguished the light. She rested her head on my shoulder, encircled my chest with one arm. "He's in such bad shape, Mac," she whispered. "He just doesn't care."

"What did he say to you?"

"Not much. But he talked a little. He's so full of hate, it's like his body is simmering internally."

"Wouldn't you be? Wouldn't anyone?"

"Most definitely. It's a natural response. But the shame, the humiliation he's feeling is more dominant. It's more debilitating than the hate. If he can't beat that, he'll never come out of it."

"How do you think you would handle the same problem?" I asked, sickened by the thought. "Maybe if we brainstorm that, we can figure out ways to help him."

She thought about it for awhile, absentmindedly twirling her hair. "Even if I could conjure up the feelings such a horror would generate, I don't think it would help Merlin," she finally replied.

"Why not?" I stroked her bare shoulder. Small comfort, it seemed to me, but she always liked it. Said it soothed her.

"Women handle the aftermath better than men. I've seen it. Clan and indie women are raped all the time. Before you and I met and we removed ourselves from the indie camps," she continued, "I came across women who had been victims of violence by men all the time. I can remember it even from my childhood, my mother trying to console women who'd been beaten, raped."

"But if we figure out how women survive it, the mental part, maybe we can use that to help him."

"I don't think so. I think it has something to do with both gender and sex. I never really thought about it. But…if you look back, as far as thousands of years, I think we see women in the role of victims more frequently than men. Men are programmed for aggression. Often against their own kind. But when it get mixed up with sex, then women are the natural recipients. We don't have any mechanism like that. Sex and violence don't go together for us. So maybe we have a gene or something that allows us to survive the mayhem caused by your genes of aggression."

"So women have a biological mechanism that allows them to survive our transgressions."

"As well as a gender mechanism—a learned behavior. We share victimization. We're taught to go on. We naturally comfort one another. If we don't, the family falls apart. It may get biological here. If we collapse, so do our children. So we're programmed to survive being victims."

"Genetically and socially."

"Who knows. They hadn't figured it out up to the time of the collapse. No reason to think our ideas aren't as good as theirs. Probably better. Look what happened to them."

"So what does all this mean?"

"It means," she said, "that this may be a man thing. His problem isn't with women, wasn't caused by women, and the shame he feels isn't related to women. It's men he's worried about. It's men that will see him as weak, think he should have died before he submitted."

She sat up. In the dark I could sense her sorrow. "What is it, hon?" I asked, reaching for her hand.

She tried to choke back tears. Failed. Sobbing quietly, she said, "They raped him both anally and orally, Mac. They stuck their filthy cocks in his mouth, taunting him while they used his body. He told me everything, Mac. Said it's in his head all the time. He can't get over the shame."

"He's lucky they didn't kill him."

"Not to his way of thinking. He wishes they did."

• • • •

In the morning, we told Stevie and Weasel what Sarah had learned from Merlin, extracting their pledge of silence. They needed to know what really happened to their friend. Could never let him know they had the knowledge. As the four of us sat at the table, a thousand times over ritual for us, I suddenly realized that Stevie had faced his biggest demon of all in that skyscraper six days past, and none of us had said a word. We licked our wounds, congratulated ourselves, and fussed over Merlin. Stevie was lost in the shuffle.

"We," I said, indicating Sarah, Weasel and myself, "are a bunch of assholes."

"What'd we do?" Weasel asked.

"Six days ago Stevie stood this far," I held my hands six inches apart, "from The Babe, smashed his arm with his rifle, got a backhand that punched his lights out in return and generally saved the lives of me, Sarah and Duke."

"Son of a bitch," Weasel said. "Why wasn't I told about any of this? You OK, boy?"

"Didn't seem like a blow by blow playback was appropriate," Stevie said, smiling. "All of us faced the same shit. And, yeah, I'm fine. I was kinda hurt at first, wanting to be treated like a hero, but then I realized everyone was a hero."

"Weren't you scared," Sarah asked, "when you found yourself face to face with him? After all, the man almost ruined your whole life, killed your best and only friend right in front of your eyes."

"I was real scared at first. Then I just reacted. I'm all right now. What I realized afterward, is that I'm a man now—not the nine year old boy who lived with the Messengers when it happened. And when I smashed his arm, it hurt him. Suddenly I realized he's not invincible. Flesh and bone like the rest of us. Just real big...and dangerous."

Weasel reached across the table and took Stevie's hand in his two. "I'm proud of you, boy," he said. "You just figured out the number one rule of survival."

"What's that?" we all asked.

"The glass is half full."

• • • •

We went through three more days of hell with Merlin before Weasel decided to try something. We were at dinner. All of us were bone tired, having put in twelve hours on the compound's defenses. Merlin had hidden in his room all day, exiting only to eat, shower or go to the bathroom. Now at dinner, he was picking distractedly at his food,

BLOOD OF THE DOGS

nibbling now and then, moving his meal from one section of his plate to another, refusing to speak when spoken to.

"Stevie," Weasel said, "will you get me a towel, a big one?"

As Stevie left, Weasel stood up and began to disrobe. Shirt first, then shoes and socks. Sat down to remove his pants.

"I'm glad I'm finished with my dinner," Sarah commented. "I'm thinking whatever it is you have in mind would not enhance my appetite."

Weasel looked at her and smiled, then made a muscle man pose with his arms. "I'm hurt you'd call my physique unappetizing," he said.

"What do you have in mind?" I asked.

"A guided tour," he replied.

"This would be of your body?" Sarah asked.

"Only the exterior," Weasel said. "Minus the privates. That's what the towel's for. Cover my privates."

Stevie returned with a bath towel, tossing it to Weasel and returning to his chair, a look of anticipation on his face. He knew when the good stuff was starting.

"What's up, Weasel?" he asked.

Weasel stood up, removed his underwear and circled his waist with the towel. "What I got in mind is a graphic presentation to Mr. Dopehead here," nodding in Merlin's direction, "that he isn't the only one suffered a few bumps and bruises in this life. Matter of fact, if we rated the injury and injustices all of us here have experienced, it's very likely he may have to go to the back of the line."

Merlin looked up from his dinner plate. "Fuck you, Weasel," he said. "You don't know shit about what I went through."

"Ain't no way for me to know, ass wipe," Weasel snapped back. "You're too busy feeling sorry for yourself to talk to any of us about it. Too wrapped up your dope fogged head to consider anyone else may have just as much pain in their past."

Merlin looked up again, a flicker of anger in his reddened eyes. "You tryin' to make some kind of point here, Sophocles? Some goddam psychological ploy?"

"Take your shirt off, Merlin," Weasel challenged. "Let's compare scars."

Weasel raised his arms and did a slow turn, revealing a blueprint of human depravity sketched across his wiry frame. Scars and welts and angry red rashes dotted the landscape of his upper body.

He began a travelogue then, categorizing the multiplicity of wounds by part of the country he was in when they occurred, beginning at the shoulders and working his way down to his legs. Bullet hole in Atlanta, knife scar in Memphis, graze wound in Carbondale, whip lashes from Effingham, bayonet in Peoria.

The nastiest looking defacements were the ten parallel lashes that marched down his shoulders, ending on his buttocks. "Whipped like a mule by a bunch of shit kickers 'cuz I walked in the wrong field. They made a mistake by letting me live."

Merlin listened to the monologue, sitting back in his chair, arms crossed, expressionless. When Weasel sat back down and started dressing, he said, "I get it. I'm supposed to see what you've been through and reach out to you, setting aside my selfish concern for my own little ordeal." He did sarcasm well. Generally physically non-aggressive, Merlin compensated with a sharp tongue. "It won't work. Fuck you, Freud."

"You know," Weasel said with a wave that encompassed all of us at the table, "this little group been together nearly five years now. If I ask Mac and Sarah and Stevie to strip nekkid and show their scars, they'd do it. But there's not much to show. Most of it is inside. Mac and Sarah never talk about theirs, but it's there, the pain inside. Stevie's been through shit that's hard to imagine. When he was nine he saw his best friend sodomized and murdered right in front of him. By The Babe, the man that tried to separate Stevie's head from his shoulders a few short days ago—while we were rescuing you. That's the first time he's faced him in nine years, Merlin. He did it for you."

Weasel didn't punch the last five words. He gave them the same inflection as the rest. But they were out there, in the open, a little reminder, lest Merlin forget, that we had faced more than physical danger during the rescue.

Merlin shifted his gaze over to Stevie. "I'm sorry, Stevie," he said softly. "I didn't know." Then a little hesitation. "How'd you get through it, man?"

"I'm not sure I ever did," Stevie said. "It's just that in my life now, it's...not important to me anymore. It's been replaced. The fear, the pain. We can't take it away, Merlin, all of us who are here with you. Mac and Sarah and Weasel never made it go away for me. But we can give you something more important than the pain."

"It's not the pain. It's the...humiliation...the..." Merlin searched for the word. Maybe he had it, but didn't want to bring it out.

Weasel finished the sentence. "...Shame. It's like there's a big fucking sign across your forehead."

"Yeah," Merlin replied. "A scarlet letter. How'd you know?"

"Been there," Weasel said. "They call 'em rump rangers down south. This part of the country hasn't cornered the market on sodomy. It's the same everywhere. It's why I came up here. I felt like everyone knew. Judged me as a coward. I never even told anyone—until now."

"What happened to the men that did it?"

"They're dead."

"Did it help?"

"Not then. Nothing helped. But it does now. Now that I got distance, it sits right. Wouldn't be able to live with the memory if I knew they were still out there. I wasn't the first. Wouldn't have been the last. Let me try to explain. You kill them, it's not gonna make you feel any different, any better. But if you don't..."

"...then the book's still open," Merlin finished.

"Wait a minute," Sarah said. "You've got to understand that revenge isn't a cure."

"There is no cure," Stevie said. "Only displacement. Find something more important. Like people."

"I feel like I can't ever leave this house," Merlin said. "I'm a prisoner. Everyone will see me as...as a piece of cheap meat."

"Merlin," Sarah said. "Besides those of us in this room, only James knows what really happened to you."

"And he ain't tellin'," Weasel said. "Got his word on it. Said he owed us one and that's what I took. He's the only one heard it said over the walkie talkie besides Mac and Sarah."

"The code," Merlin said, a faint glimmer of hope in his voice. "He'll keep his word, James will. God bless the code."

"When it works in our favor," I said.

"But the Messengers," Merlin said, forlorn again. "They know. They'll tell everyone. Every People clan will know."

"They got their asses kicked up in that building," Weasel said. "They'll never talk to anyone about what happened."

Merlin thought about it, sat there in his chair thinking of shame and fear and revenge. After a few minutes he spoke. "I don't feel much different. Everything's still there. I don't know who I hate more—myself or them. I know you're trying to help. It's just not working."

None of us pointed out that this was the first time he had talked in six days, that he hadn't had a toke in the last twenty minutes, that he had identified his fears.

"There's no time limits here," Stevie said. "No schedule or set of expectations you've got to meet. I was here six months before I even begin to trust these three. Hell, Merlin," he laughed, "Duke was the only one I'd talk to."

Merlin smiled. It was pretty weak, but I'm sure I saw his lips move.

"I gotta go take a shower," he said.

• • • •

When the water started running, Sarah turned to Weasel, "I'm so sorry about what happened to you. We had no idea. I'm very proud of you for trying to help like that, giving up yourself for Merlin."

"Don't be too proud, Sarah," Weasel said, a mischievous smile flickering on and off. "That stuff about being raped was all a damn lie."

"Jesus, Weasel," she exclaimed, "what if he finds out? He'll be devastated. That was what finally started him talking."

Weasel looked at the three of us. "How in the hell is he ever going to find out?"

"Good point," I said. "But what if he wants to talk, asks for details about what it was like when it happened to you?"

"Never happen," Weasel said. "Man doesn't ask another man that. Besides, he already knows. Nothing happened to me could be any worse than what happened to him. He'll never ask me."

"He's right, Mac," Stevie said. "None of us want Merlin to tell us what they did to him, do we? If he wants to talk, that's fine. But there's no purpose in our seeking out the details."

He was right. There was no benefit in the knowledge.

"No," Sarah said. "We don't need to know. And maybe he'll never want to tell any of you. Perhaps it took all he had to tell me. It's probably easier to tell a woman than a man, anyway. All he needed was the knowledge that someone understood what he was feeling. It's no cure, but it is a start. But," she admonished, "if he wants to talk, Weasel, don't you be encouraging any revenge fantasies on his part. He's a brave, resourceful man. But he's no soldier."

"We needn't be worrying about that, Sarah," I said. "We'll be seeing the fat man again. Duke made an awful mess of his face. Merlin is going to have deal with him again whether he wants to or not."

CHAPTER THIRTY-FIVE

They found us ten days later, the Messengers did. They made their first incursions just before dawn. We had hoped for a night attack. We knew the ground better, and our NVG's were superior to theirs. But that's the thing about enemies, they don't often cooperate. We were five on that day—Merlin was still with us—and a dog, only a fraction of their number. But it was our turf. We knew the secrets, the traps, the mines, the tunnel system.

And we were expecting them. Had been for years.

Merlin had been drifting back and forth. Here for a day or two, gone for a time. He was mending his wounds, looking for distractions, trying to retrieve a taste of his old lifestyle. When he returned, he remained generally taciturn, but occasionally spoke a few words. Sometimes flashed a smile. He had even cut down on the showers and incessant dope smoking. The fact that he kept coming back was an encouraging sign. There was something about us that drew him back. It was an indicator that he hadn't given up on himself.

He came back again the night of the attack, was sleeping soundly in his room when the first warnings were sounded. It was a trickle at first, like when you initially notice a few wasps hovering around, scoping out the site of a possible nest, and then suddenly they're all over the place. Within five minutes two mines had exploded and three of the inside lights indicating breech of pasture land had flashed in the house. Before the third light had begun blinking, we were all in position, night goggles in place, comm head sets on.

Weasel and I were in the tower, red light patrol. We each had a image intensifying night scope on our sniper rifles. We had noise suppressing headphones and all of us had communicators.

Weasel was using the Hechler and Koch PSG-1. I had the Mauser SP 66. Both fired 7.62 rounds and had flash suppressors to keep our location hidden.

We started with a quick survey of the land outside the walls with Zeiss binocs, military model rigged for night vision. It was a disheartening sight.

"Shit," Weasel said, his voice echoing the sense of loss he felt, knowing this would be the last night we would ever spend in the compound. "What do you count, Mac?"

"At least two hundred. Maybe three," I replied. Our voices were carried to Stevie, Merlin and Sarah through the comm sets. They each manned a gun slot on the second floor. Duke was with Merlin tonight. First time he had ever made the wrong choice.

"Jesus," Sarah sighed. "We're fucked."

"Not us, Sarah," Weasel comforted. "Just the compound. And we got all we need to start over in the truck."

It had been loaded for weeks. Mobile armory. We could fight the Hundred Years War using it as a base.

"We need bigger bedrooms anyway," Stevie said.

Weasel gave us a reminder of the plan of battle. "We whittle 'em down as much as we can without presenting any serious danger to our selves. Then we get the fuck out of here. Two in the truck. The other three through separate tunnels. Meet at Fox Valley, Sears entrance. It's ready for us."

Stevie and Merlin had been working at the mall a couple of days a week for over a year. Called it the new storm cellar. Sarah and I hadn't seen it. Nor had Merlin. We always stayed back to keep working on the compound. We knew we couldn't keep the Messengers out. Our efforts were concentrated on making the price of entry very expensive.

"I'm sure going to miss all that music and vids," Merlin said. "And that microwave. Man, that's the best."

"You don't know me very well, do you, Merlin?" It was Weasel. "Let's get to work. Remember stay in your zones unless someone calls for help. No chatter on the circuit. Business only."

By the time The Messenger soldiers started their first exploration of our defenses, the sun was a semi-circle on the eastern horizon. Our night vision goggles were no help. They wouldn't be presenting easy targets to us with the red lights on the infrareds of their NVG's.

Their first assault was straight toward the front of the house. They were cautious. The threat of a land mine ripping your lower body apart will do that to a person. And when mines on two sides of the force exploded, the soldiers figured out the right path and grew bolder. We used the scopes on the sniper rifles and picked up the targets as they stood and began their dash toward our front. Weasel and I began pruning their numbers, all the time looking for The Babe among the first wave. We had little hope of seeing him this soon. The general would send in grunts first.

At first, they thought they were out of rifle range, but our sniper rifles were well beyond the reach of any weapon they were familiar with. By the time Weasel and I finished our first sweeps, each handling 180 degrees of the territory, picking out each man as he stood to begin his dash, the Messenger soldiers began scrambling back beyond our range, triggering several more mines in the spokes of the wheel that was the grasslands leading to the barbed wire. We diminished their numbers by approximately twenty in the first stage. Only Weasel and I had fired. Sarah, Stevie and Merlin were still unknowns to the attackers.

A stillness descended, replacing the sharp explosions of our sniper rifles. Weasel and I swept away expended shell casings and restocked our ammo supplies, saving his five round clips to be oiled and reloaded when it was safe once again. The Mauser I was using was bolt action, three rounds and reload. I restocked my ammo pouch, primed for the next wave.

• • • •

They avoided the mine fields in the next assault. They came full blast, balls out, from all sides, requiring all five of us to defend our positions. They started chanting before they began the second run, a low three beat thrumming that I couldn't make out until it approached its crescendo, seconds before they commenced their charge.

"MESS-EN-GERS. MESS-EN-GERS." Over and over.

Designed to scare us. Did a good job on me. It took a big bunch of voices to make that much noise. The chant came from every compass point. A perfect circle…with us at the center.

I had been surrounded by a dog pack once, little over a decade ago. The day I met Sarah. They too formed a circle and made noise. I had an empty M 16—ammo expended, it was little more than a high tech club—and a buck knife. They slowly closed the circle while I whirled, never allowing my back in one place too long, swinging at the bravest or hungriest, the ones who leapt toward me, darting forward with canines gnashing, attempting to remove some flesh from my bones, then pulling back before my M 16 could find their heads. The low pitched, high decibel resonance of their growls and snarls filled my world…

The chant of the soldier/dogs reached its zenith, peaked and shattered, exploding into hundreds of high pitched scream fragments and snapping me back to the present. In the next moment, as if on command, they stood and charged, over a hundred strong, dope-fortified maniacs, garbed in the detritus of 20th cen football and hockey teams, carrying molotovs and assault rifles instead of footballs and hockey sticks.

They had nearly two hundred meters to cover between their position and barbed wire/thistle/grape vine barrier. It was naked territory, no cover, nothing to hide behind, no obstacles to deflect the path of our bullets.

Weasel and I started with the sniper rifles, but there were too many of the Messengers this time, and in a few seconds we had to discard the snipers for automatics. I put the tripod-mounted HK21A1 belt fed machine gun into service while Weasel went to his assault rifle.

Beneath us the sounds of Sarah, Stevie and Merlin firing from their positions were added to the wall of fire designed to break the Messenger's circle. The heavier ordnance of the machine gun was the extra help we needed. It drove them back, those of them who could still flee, but, without a flash suppressor to hide the barrel flashes, the machine gun also marked our location on top of the roof. We came under heavy fire toward the end of the second wave.

Some of the molotovs, probably shine or paint solvent with rag wicks, made it to the barbed wire barrier. But our preparations paid dividends. The flames licked at the vegetation, and finding no purchase, faded into nothingness, leaving the barbed wire hidden.

I surveyed the killing ground with the binocs. Outside our walls a circle of bodies littered the landscape. Some were moving, crawling back to the Messenger lines, hoping for succor from their savage mates. We let them go. Wounded men were a bigger drain on their resources than the dead.

I remembered the dog pack then, how when they were closing the circle, their eyes intensely focused on me, their breakfast, I had finally said to myself, fuck it, and tried to bust out, make it to a tree just twenty short meters away.

I didn't have a prayer. I bashed two of them with the M 16 stock, then used the buck knife, whittling my way through what appeared to be a tiny arc of weakness in their circle. It was an illusion. They were too fast and too strong. The last sensations I remembered were the intense pain in my legs and arms as their teeth tore at my muscle and the horrible noise of their hunger, the snarls and growls, so precisely perfect that I could make out individual animal sounds, even through the thickness of my arms which were clenched tightly about my neck and head.

We needed to break out of the circle before it closed too tightly. "I think it's time to get away from here," I told Weasel.

"You're right," Weasel replied. He began breaking down the machine gun. "Next charge is gonna bring some of 'em to the barrier. The razor wire's gonna hold 'em back, but not forever. And it gets them close enough to try'n burn us out." Figure we got five, ten minutes. Let's pack it up and head for the truck and tunnels."

"I still think all of us should go in the truck, Weasel." It was Sarah. Everybody was on the comms. She hadn't agreed with the original plan but had been out-voted.

"Ain't the plan, Sarah," Weasel responded. "If we split up, it divides them up too. Besides, they get lucky enough to punch out a couple of tires, that truck's gonna be dead in its tracks. I'd hate to see that happen if all of us was in it."

"OK. I'm just worried about you and Stevie."

"We worry about you too. This way gives us all a better chance of starting over again. And a greater opportunity of finding The Babe out there. We don't get him on this try, he's still gonna be coming for us."

"All right," I interrupted, "enough chatter. All of you get to your positions. I'll stay up here and pepper the next wave so they don't get the idea we're breaking out."

"Be careful," Sarah's voice.

"You too," I said. "Meet you in the basement."

Weasel shouldered the machine gun, also taking my sniper rifle along with his, and began climbing down to the second story from our perch. Before his head disappeared from view, he said, "Don't stay too long. Let 'em come but don't make it too easy for them."

"Don't forget the prisoner," I said.

"We got the rig all set for him," Weasel replied.

The plan was to harness the Messenger in the closet to the front of the truck, a hood ornament, hoping it would buy a few seconds hesitation from his comrades. Weasel nodded at the three remaining assault rifles. "Don't leave them little beauties behind. See you outside."

The Messengers started the chanting again, building to another crescendo and launching from their cover at its zenith, a full circle of men, several pairs carrying ladders. Didn't look like they left anyone back this time. I didn't have time to count, but around 200 seemed right. Far too many for one man to slow down. I briefly wondered who was minding the home fires. It looked like The Babe had brought just about everyone old enough to walk.

He was a good tactician. They came in three waves. I concentrated on the men with ladders first, taking out three before their first assault line got in range of their M 16s. Then eight of them, each occupying a piece of the circle, hit the ground while the rest kept charging for the safety of the wall. I immediately came under fire from their assault rifles. There wasn't much I could do because they had me from all angles.

As the bullets chipped away the wood of the cupola, I snatched up my three rifles and told everyone I was coming down, leaving the battleground to the Messengers. When they realized my firing had stopped, their screams filled the air. They thought they had us.

None of us had seen The Babe yet. But there was no doubt he was out there, directing the troops with his Radio Shack walkie talkie, the mate of which I still carried.

I sprinted to the kitchen. I went to the door connecting the kitchen to the huge remodeled garage to check on Weasel and Stevie. I heard the screams from the man who had occupied our closet for weeks, the house guest from hell, before I entered.

"What the fuck am I supposed to be? A fucking battering ram? You guys are fucking nuts. My boys gonna skin you like a deer. Fuck you assholes. Your time is coming."

The prisoner was tied in mesh cage to the front of the hood. Sort of looked like the front of the old sailing ships, like in *Moby Dick*, where they had figure of a woman projecting from the prow. If he survived the gunfire, the bars of his cage would protect him from projectiles and razor wire. Our hope was that because of our prisoner's status in the hierarchy of the Messengers, the soldiers wouldn't fire upon the truck.

The doors to the garage were already open. Outside, the shooting had stopped. Weasel and Stevie were scurrying around the truck, last minute checks of the vehicle that carried our most valued contents, weapons, electronics, munitions, artwork, books, disks. The tank was filled with almost all of our ethanol. The remainder of the fuel was stashed at the mall, held back for the generators.

"You two get the hell out of here," I told Weasel. "They're at the barrier, and they're gonna try to use ladders to get over."

They both jumped into the truck, Weasel driving. As it started up, the muscular pulse of the huge engine reverberating off the garage walls, I went out the garage doors and ducked to the right side, rifle ready, thirty round clip full. Facing the front gate, the house and garage behind me, I could see four ladders already up. It would be the same in the back.

They started coming over then, not easily because the barrier was compressed by the ladders and the thistle and razor wire came up through rungs, snagging clothing and skin. I fired short ammo-conserving bursts with the assault rifle at as many of the front men as possible, jamming up the traffic flow. But it was like one of those video games on the computer. The arc was too big for me to cover all of their incursions. Within a few seconds two of them made it over the barrier, jumping to the ground. They had good sight lines on me, the truck, and the man in the cage.

The sight of the truck stopped them in their tracks.

"Get the fuck out of here, Weasel," I screamed.

The truck lurched from the garage, the biggest, ugliest moving object anyone had laid eyes upon for thirty-five years. For a brief moment all the firing stopped. The Messengers were paralyzed by the awesome oddity that rolled into the front yard. Then they all turned their rifles on the truck, which had turned left, toward the mine free escape route. The man on the front of the truck was hit by about thirty rounds before the vehicle had moved more than a few meters.

"So much for respecting brothers in arms," said Stevie's voice over the comm set. "We're gone, Mac. Take care of everyone. See you on the other side."

The truck rumbled toward the barrier. On the passenger side, Stevie's rifle was spraying anything that moved. I could see little sparks where the bullets of the enemy soldiers hit the armor and careened harmlessly away. The soldiers were screaming like animals, braying, blatting, baaing and clucking, near apoplexy from the monstrous machine that lumbered through their pitiful resistance.

The truck hit the wire barrier, compressing it like chicken wire, its thick tires invulnerable to the razor edges. The truck gained speed and shot across the field. All the Messengers were firing at its tailgate, completely ignoring my presence at the front of the compound. I lost sight of the truck and slipped back into the house and headed for the basement. On the way down my comm set picked up Stevie's screams and the shots from within the cab. They were screams of excitement. Both of them were safe.

His voice was beginning to fade as they moved beyond the range of the comm sets, when I heard him yell, "Over there, Weasel. It's The Babe. To your right. Yeah. Run the fucker down." A few seconds' silence, then, "Shit. He's fast. You missed him. Go back. Go back."

Then the voices faded as they moved beyond the capacity of the signal. Weasel hadn't turned around.

• • • •

I could smell the ethanol when I opened the door to the basement. We had held back a couple of gallons. Merlin and Sarah were splashing it around inside the almost completely empty armory room while Duke sat outside, looking very uncomfortable, edgy from all the action. We had saved the fuel to ignite the concoction of explosives we had in the basement—several grenades, three kegs of gunpowder, a few hundred rounds of ammo—and two large drums of liquid Weasel had retrieved from a paint factory. They were labeled with all kinds of warnings, most of which contained the words, "hazardous," "flammable," and "explosive."

The armory was stocked with a dozen M 16s and several pistols, dozens of empty clips and empty ammo boxes. There were also six wooden crates, the kind used to transport assault rifles. They were sealed—and empty. It looked like a good haul for someone who was attempting to outfit an army. In a far corner, under a shelf, sitting in a little puddle of ethanol, was a tiny receiver.

I stepped into the doorway of the armory. Stevie and Sarah were waiting. Duke was in the tunnel, beyond the fumes. "They're gone," I said. "Made it out OK."

"We heard," Sarah replied. "Sounds like they almost had an encounter with The Babe. Wish Weasel could have gone back."

"I'm glad he didn't," I said. "I want them safe."

"Betcha if he was alone in that truck, Weasel would have turned around," Merlin said. He was probably right. But the plan was for all of us to survive. He wasn't going to risk Stevie.

"You two ready?" I asked.

They were both strapping on weapons and checking ammo. They shook their heads in affirmation.

"Run it by me one more time."

"We each take a separate tunnel leading out back. Mac in the middle. Merlin and Duke on the left. Me on the right," Sarah said.

"When we get near the end," Merlin continued, "me and Sarah blow the middle of our tunnels with a grenade, causing a cave in between us and the basement." The cave-in would protect each of us from the blow back of the basement explosion. We had no intention of leaving the house for the attackers. What we couldn't carry would be destroyed, along with any Messengers we could attract into the house.

"Then each of you neutralizes the booby trap at the exit and waits for my signal before going out," I continued.

The plan called for me to wait for as many Messengers as possible before I blew the basement, using a little battery powered remote that would set off a spark in the receiver at the other end—the one in the pool of ethanol. When the time was right, I would head for the other end, seal the middle with a grenade and then push the button that would ignite the ethanol. When that happened, all of us would escape from our respective tunnels in the confusion. Just how much confusion there was would be dependent upon the volatility of the two drums of solvent from the paint factory.

"Let's go," I said. We opened three tunnel doors.

Sarah hugged Merlin and bent down to squeeze Duke. He lapped at her face. Turning to me, she pulled my face down to hers and whispered, "Be careful. I love you."

"Me too," I replied.

Sarah turned and looked around, her eyes moving up toward the house above us, our home for nearly ten years. I knew what she was feeling. It represented the happiest times of our lives. It would be kindling soon. So much work. Driven away by the stalkers, not allowed to make a life, create a family, live in peace.

Each of us moved to our tunnel entrance. I looked over to Sarah. "It's the people," I said. "They're what made it good. Not the house itself."

She half smiled, mouthed the words, I know. Thanks.

Then each of us grabbed our sheet metal shields to protect us from our own grenade blasts and ducked into our own tunnels, like trapdoor spiders retreating into their sanctuaries.

I went last, watching Duke follow Merlin before I closed the door to our home for the final time.

CHAPTER THIRTY-SIX

We each closed the tunnel door behind us, added protection against the blast I would soon trigger. None of us had a prediction of its power. Enough to burn down the compound we were sure. Beyond that, we had no idea. The drums of Weasel's chemicals were the x factor.

I could hear Sarah and Merlin breathing in my ear. The comm sets worked fine in the confined environment.

"My God."

It was Sarah. Twenty, maybe thirty meters away. Tons of earth between us. I knew what she meant. The depth of the darkness was profound, humbling. I didn't bother with the night goggles. There was no available light for them to draw upon. Besides, there was nothing to see. It was a long narrow dirt tube that held each of us. A few 4x4's spaced along the walls and ceilings. Nothing else. No life. No paintings on the wall. Just a long, dark, damp…grave.

"It's all right," I said. "We won't be here too long. Use your flashlight if it starts to get to you."

"It's already on," Sarah said. "Let's go to work."

"You two blow your tunnels. I'll wait here."

A few minutes later, the length of time it took them to crawl within a few meters of the outside exit, they both checked in. I remained by the door that led back into the basement, listening for sounds of the Messengers in the house. Nothing yet.

"Blow it in," I said, imagining each of them rolling a grenade down their tunnel, back towards the basement, then crouching behind their shields. I waited in my position, tunnel side of the basement door.

BLOOD OF THE DOGS

Two muffled explsions followed. I felt the vibrations as well as heard the sound.

"Did it work?" I asked.

"Like a charm," Sarah replied.

"Perfect," said Merlin. "Freaked Duke's shit pretty good, though."

"It shouldn't be too long now," I told them. "The explosions should start bringing them down."

From the other side of the door to the basement, sounds from within the house begin filter to my ears. Yells and yips, breaking glass, thumps of furniture being destroyed. They were trashing the place. The destruction reminded me of the houses Sarah and I had seen before we found this pristine one ten years ago. This was what happened thirty five years ago to the homes we had rejected.

They found the door in the kitchen that led down to the basement. Footsteps clunked down the stairs. "Yo, down here. A store room. Rifles, powder. Shit, man, they got fucking lights. Bring The Babe down."

Perfect.

"Sarah, Merlin. Check this. They're bringing The Babe into the basement. Hang on a couple of minutes. I may get to char broil the fat fuck."

"Wish I could press that button," Merlin said.

"I'll put your name on it."

More footsteps coming down. They had found the armory. Just enough in there to whet their appetites. I heard others exploring the rest of the basement, looking for more to scavenge.

"Where's The Babe?" someone asked.

"Outside," came the reply. "Checking to see if he can find another truck. Made a big impression on his ass."

"Right," a laugh. "Almost too big. Get him down here. I found some good shit."

"Hey. Hey," another voice, close to my door. "I got a bunch of doors over here. They're all over the place. Bet they got shit stashed in other rooms."

"Watch your ass," shouted another. "Those assholes may be behind those doors with a gun pointed at your face."

I heard the sounds of weapons snapped to readiness, maybe twenty men down here now, and began scrambling down the tunnel. I had to move fast, before they began opening tunnel doors and leaving the trap we had so carefully set. A few meters down, I pulled a grenade, popped the pin and rolled it behind me toward the basement door. Then I crawled like hell, dragging the machine gun, my assault rifle smacking my chest with each meter's progress, working on distance between me and the blast.

I felt the detonation before I heard it, a change in air pressure, a gentle push before the big shove. I threw myself on the dirt floor of the tunnel, covered my head. The sound was surprisingly soft, a muffled thump followed by a rush of earthy wind and bits of shrapnel that nipped at my feet and clothing. Nothing pierced flesh. There was some dust, but not much. The tunnels were always damp.

I turned on to my back and sat up, pointing the flashlight toward the basement. A wall of dirt hid the door. I was safe from the next blast. The big one.

"You OK, Mac?" It was Sarah.

"I feel like a fucking bullet," I said. "I was a bit close. Lucky the goddam thing didn't send me flying down the tunnel like it was a rifle barrel. Hang on to your butts. I'm blowing the basement."

"What about The Babe? He in there?"

"They found the tunnel doors. Doesn't make any difference now. I gotta blow it."

I pulled the remote and pressed the button, igniting a spark in the armory room. We reasoned later, months after it was all over and we had inspected the site, that the basement explosion was what led them to the outside tunnel exits.

The blast must have been gargantuan. In the tunnels the earth vibrated as it transferred the energy from the shock wave. Clumps of dirt fell upon us. The rumble of the blast filled our ears. But the walls and ceilings held.

Inside the basement, the explosion sought a release from its confinement. The drums of chemicals expelled a massive amount of energy into the confined space of the basement. Triggered by a spark, a couple of gallons of ethanol, a few pounds of gun powder and some spare ammo, the drums of chemicals unleashed a gargantuan explosion.

The house was very well constructed. The concrete walls were too substantial for the force of the blast to breech. The ceiling of the basement was doubly reinforced with two by eights. To exit through the ceiling, the force of the explosion had to puncture the ceiling and the floor to the first story. In the fraction of a second that followed its release, the explosion found more accessible paths.

The single door that led to the kitchen wasn't enough to vent the explosion's fury. It sought other exits, found the doors to the tunnels, the five subterranean conduits we had not sealed with our grenades, and shredded the doors, paltry little guardians, hurling its fury down the other five tunnels, finally finding release at the exits, far beyond the compound walls.

Two of those five tunnels had exterior doors. The force of the explosion, now over a hundred meters from its source, blew the doors off, sending them flying another thirty meters, and finally dissapated in the open air. In the other three tunnels, hidden in gullies or small pockets of trees or bushes, wind and dirt, an angry roar and black smoke marked the exit of the explosion that had originated in the basement.

The booby traps in all those tunnels were triggered when the doors were ejected, sealing them from the outside. The Messengers that remained on the battleground outside the walls rushed to the tunnel exits that the muscle of the explosion had so clearly marked for them. When they found no entry, they looked for more.

Inside the house, a tick of the clock beyond the scouring of the tunnels, the blast located a weakness in the ceiling, wiggled through and burst into the main level of the house, fire and smoke, wind and debris annihilating in seconds what had been our home for a decade. In the process, every Messenger that was in the house was sent to hell.

From my tunnel, which had become the true, perfect re-creation of an Edgar Allen Poe story, it felt like the end of the world. And, lucky me, I had pre-purchased my burial plot.

"That," said Merlin's voice, hushed, frightened, "was the fucking hand of God telling us to straighten up."

"Sarah, you OK?" I asked.

"I'd really like to see some sunshine," she said shakily. "Can we please get out of here, Mac?"

"Me and Duke second that," Merlin said.

"You two take off," I replied. "I'll be just a couple of minutes behind you. I've got to dismantle the booby trap at the exit. When it's clear, take off. I'll meet you down at Fox Valley."

I began crawling toward the exit. The booby trap would take me a couple of minutes. It should have been done before I blew the tunnel, but the arrival of the Messengers in the basement changed the schedule. My tunnel came out in the middle of a small blackberry patch. Its door was treated lumber, covered with dirt and brush to appear as a natural part of the landscape. On either side of me, Sarah and Merlin would exit under the protection of trees and bushes.

Sarah's voice came to me over the comm set. "I'm out, but I got a problem. The area is swarming with soldiers. From all the smoke hanging in the air, I'd say the blast alerted them to the tunnel system."

"How many?" I asked.

"Maybe five or ten. Should I go back in and wait them out?"

"You've got no options in the tunnel," I said. "Please don't go back in. Merlin, what's your situation?"

"I'm out, me and Duke. In a thick stand of honeysuckle bushes. No one over here yet. What should we do?"

"Get out," I said. "You and Duke head for Weasel and Stevie if you've got an opening. I'm closer to Sarah. I'll cover her."

"Can't do that, Mac," he said. "We stay til you're both out. I'm waiting here for instructions."

"All right," I said. "Thanks. Give me a couple of minutes and I'll be out."

Close to the end, I shined the flashlight up to the trap, a wire stretched across the entrance about a foot down, one end in the wood frame, the other in the pin of a grenade. Anyone entering would trigger it when they got a couple of feet inside the tunnel.

Before I could get to it I heard footsteps on the wooden trapdoor followed by the sound of hands scraping away the dirt. "Is that one of you two?" I asked.

"I'm still right outside my tunnel," Sarah said.

"Me too," Merlin replied.

The door began to swing open, trickling sunlight into my tomb. The light dimmed as a helmeted head peered into the darkness, remaining a few inches above the trip wire. He was backlit, and I could only see his profile, not his face. I was ten feet from him, but I didn't think he could see me with his eyes adjusted to sunlight. I dropped the HK machine gun, pulled the Glock and snapped three shots at his head, hitting home with all three, shattering his helmet, pulverizing what was inside.

He disappeared immediately, unseen clan warriors yanking his corpse back by his feet, replaced by another soldier who jumped feet first into the tunnel, snapping the wire of the booby trap. Three second delay. At the same moment I perceived his muzzle flashes, I put two shots into him, threw the Glock over my shoulder and planned to turn and scramble backward, hoping to put some distance between myself and the grenade blast that was about to come.

But something punched me hard in the shoulder, throwing me back. Then the blast came. The explosion was a circle, and I was only a small portion of it. Part of the release went straight outside; the rest remained in the tunnel. A flash of light, the pressure and sound of the explosion, the shrapnel…then complete darkness again.

In the second before I lost consciousness, I realized that the discharge of the grenade had sealed my exit. I was trapped in my own tunnel. My escape hatch now a sepulcher, a tubular tomb with me as the only occupant. I fought the primal panic, imagining the air was already stale, the ceiling cracked and ready to collapse, burying me permanently in tons of dirt, like those 20th cen mobsters I had read about who were sealed in the cement foundations at the construction sites of skyscrapers. Buried alive.

Then I lost consciousness, a flash of certainty that I would never awake. Not even enough time to wonder what was on the other side. Was it better than here?…or to say good bye to Sarah.

• • • •

When I awoke it was to a reality far darker than my tomb, a world composed of pain and despair. Sarah had been taken from me, swallowed up into the belly of the beast.

CHAPTER THIRTY-SEVEN

A t first I thought I was dead. Then the pain told me I was alive. Shouldn't be any pain in the after life, my mind said. Shouldn't be dark either. I must still be in the tunnel, entombed. I sat up, horrified, and suddenly realized the smell was wrong. It was clean, maybe a bit stale, but definitely not the moist, fetid odor of the tunnel, the stink of a grave.

Then a light flickered, flared to its zenith, became part of a kerosene lamp, and two hands grasped my shoulders. My eyelids slammed shut, and I reflexively pulled back from the light.

"Mac, it's me. You're safe—way deep in the mall's basement. We're here with you."

It was Weasel. I sensed movement behind him. Something haltingly approached; a raspy damp warmth persistently swiped at my cheek. Duke.

"Water," I rattled. "Real thirsty." When I had drunk deeply, I asked, "Where's Sarah? She OK?"

My eyes opened to slits, gradually becoming accustomed to the light. I saw their faces, the sadness, the reluctance to speak. My ears were fine, but I heard nothing from my friends. No reassurances. I looked at Stevie, at the edge of the light. Haunted look in his eyes. I started taking in details. Duke's coat was bloody on his right flank. He was limping. His right front leg had a splint on it.

Where was Merlin?

In a corner, behind the light a form was hidden under a blanket. It sat up. Merlin. Blanched, washed out. The lower half of the blanket was a dark stain, color of a red oak leaf. He was weak from blood loss.

"I tried, Mac," he said. "Me and Duke tried like hell."

Weasel was in front of me, on his haunches. Duke was still there, lying now on his left side. Mouth open, tongue hanging out, eyes focused on me.

"Mac..." he began.

"Shut up," I said. "I don't want to hear it."

"I gotta tell you what happened."

No fucking thanks. I don't need a confirmation. I see all of you. Your wounds. Your despair. Don't put it into words, Weasel. Please no. I can't bear to hear it spoken.

"Sarah—,"

"No!" I screamed it at him. Pushed him back, roughly, cruelly. Stood up only to be knocked back down by a wave of vertigo. We were on the same level. Weasel up on his elbows, looking at me. Me back on the floor. He wasn't mad. Maybe another man would have been, being shoved like that. "Please don't tell me, Weasel." I looked at him, imploring him to silence. "She was..." I couldn't find the words.

He looked at me as if I were someone he recognized but couldn't remember from where. Then he suddenly knew, saw the person I was, a man grieving, still in denial, and reached into a pocket of his fatigues and pulled out a scrap of paper, pushing it toward me.

"She ain't dead, Mac," he said. "Least ways I'm pretty sure she's not. Take a look at this."

The crumbled paper, ripped from a child's school notebook, yellow with age, peppered with grease spots, contained a message, written in a childish scrawl that belied its import, a communication that at once gave me hope and then tore it away when I realized she was in their camp.

GOT YUR FUN HOL MCAL. COME GET HER BEFOR I DECID TO RINT HER OUT.

• • • •

The entire story came from three sources—Weasel, Stevie and Merlin. If Duke could have talked, he would have chipped in too. He was in the middle of it all.

The first thing I asked was how long had I been out. Translation: For what length of time has Sarah been in the hands of those monsters.

"About ten hours," Weasel said. "It's almost dark, same day as the attack." He leaned forward, close to my face. "We already got a plan going, Mac. Sorry we had to start without you, but time isn't an ally in this situation."

"Let's go," I said, trying once again to stand. "What do you need me to do."

"Whoa, boy," Weasel said, gently holding me back. "We got a few more things to do, including getting you back to speed. We know where the Messengers are. We're going in 24 hours. Couple of hours before sunset tomorrow."

"Fuck that, Weasel," I said. "She could be dead by then."

Stevie entered the conversation. "I know how you feel, Mac. Me and Weasel feel the same way. But he's not going to kill Sarah."

"Are you a psychic now?" I asked. "That's what they do, Stevie. Kill people. And with women there's some very nasty rituals that occur before the deed."

"He still wants you, Mac," Stevie said. "Sarah's the ticket. The note said for you to come get her. After his losses at the AON Building, the taunting you subjected him to, the men he lost, the wounds he suffered when Duke had him by the throat—the man must be obsessed with taking you out...Plus we got another thing going for us now that will ensure her safety for awhile longer."

"What's that?"

"The truck. We almost nailed him with it. He knows if he hurts her we're coming after him and driving that beast right up his ass. No where to hide from something that big."

I thought about it. Not an easy task with my brain still befuddled from the grenade blast and tunnel collapse. I didn't like it at all. She wasn't safe. She was alone. The Messengers were completely uncontrollable and totally unpredictable. It was like leaving your chickens with a dog pack for safe keeping.

I laid back and closed my eyes, trying to clarify my thoughts. What if The Babe kills her, rapes her, butchers her, leaves her body displayed for me to find so I'll go berserk and come after him? That would work.

I told Weasel and Stevie.

"You're still a little scrambled, Mac," Weasel said. "You gotta trust me here. Me and Stevie looked at this thing seven ways from Sunday, picked it apart and put it back together. We love her too, you know. A few weeks ago, he may have done that, killed her to piss you off. But now that he's seen that truck, real close, mind you, he ain't lookin' at you in the same light anymore. You're too big to piss off because now he knows you can definitely hurt him."

"The only way he can get at you now," Stevie said, "is by lying and cheating. Sarah's still alive. The truck makes you too dangerous for him to kill her."

Listening to the urgency in their voices, hearing their concern wrapped around each word, it suddenly came upon me that I was missing a crucial point: They loved her too and were just as frightened as I was. Just because they loved her in a different way didn't mean that they loved her any less. And who was I to be measuring quantity and quality of love? The bond over the years had become so strong that none of us would feel the loss of another any more than the rest. Like everything else of import in our lives, we had to go through this together. Pain would be shared. Joy would be shared.

"Tell me the plan," I said.

It took them about an hour.

• • • •

"Do we have time for you to tell me what happened at the compound?" I asked later. "Merlin, do you have enough strength?"

"Weasel stitched me up," he said. "Bleeding's stopped. If I don't die of an infection, I'll be fine in a week or so."

He dragged himself over to us, closer to the light. We moved in his direction, but he stopped us.

"I have to start moving," he explained. "You need me when this goes down. Sarah needs me."

We were way deep in the depths of the mall, beyond the range of sunlight. When I began to process more clearly, I picked out the giant generators and heating and air conditioning equipment that surrounded us, ghost machines from the 20th dancing in the lamplight. We were in the machine shop/power plant of the mall. Too much like the tunnel for me, but it was safe.

When Weasel and Stevie explained the set-up to me, how we hoped to rescue Sarah, I understood why we weren't able to use the generator to provide light. When Merlin reached the circle we had formed around the lamp, I retrieved his blanket and made him comfortable. Duke was laying beside him.

"Sarah and I were both out when we heard your shots through our earpieces," Merlin began. "Then we heard you breathing real fast..."

"I was crawling like hell to get away from the booby trap," I explained.

"Then the explosion that we later figured collapsed your tunnel exit. Then nothing." Merlin paused there, trying to get the chronology straight. "We couldn't make any noise, and we couldn't run over to your tunnel because there were soldiers in both our areas. We were hidden, but if we broke out, they'd see us. Sarah started whispering your name real intense over and over. 'Mac. Mac. Mac. Answer me, Mac,' she kept saying. I started to say something to her and she said, 'Shut up. Shut up. I hear breathing.' And sure enough, I could hear you breathing through my ear piece. There wasn't any more gunfire because the house had already gone up and the Messengers didn't have anything to shoot at. Most of their screaming was at least a hundred yards away."

I knew what happened next, because I had seen Sarah in action too many times. Merlin confirmed it.

"Sarah told me and Duke to stay where we were, she was going to help. But I couldn't let her go alone. Not after everything that's happened..." His voice started to break up. He rubbed his eyes and asked for the canteen. I realized I hadn't smelled any of his reefer, knew that he had some.

"Duke and I only made it halfway," he continued. "There were soldiers everywhere, looking for more tunnels that had been blown out. Sarah was talking in my earpiece. Told me she'd made it to your tunnel but there were soldiers there. I could here her shotgun blasts while she was talking. Man, she was calm. She told me she couldn't leave. Said you would never leave her. Ordered us to get Weasel and

Stevie so we could dig you out before it was too late. I told her Duke would never go. Then her shotgun stopped."

"Jesus," I said. "Lucky they didn't kill her."

"She said they all were backing off. Figured they wanted her alive. Told me to get the hell out. Duke had chosen to go with me. That he'd follow. Turns out he did. But we left a few seconds too late. Got fired upon. Both of us were hit."

"Why didn't they finish you off?" I asked.

"Three of 'em on our side saw us. Started shooting. When I returned fire and they focused on me, Duke took one of 'em out. I took the other two. Told Sarah goodbye. Then we both limped off. Headed for Fox Valley Mall. I could here Sarah firing her AUG when we left. She asked me to please hurry. Even said 'please' to me while she was trying to keep them away from you."

Weasel picked up the story from there.

"Me and Stevie figured to go take a look. Found Merlin and Duke up on 59 near that big super highway. They wouldn't have made it much further. Threw 'em in the back and Stevie patched 'em best he could while I headed back to the compound."

"We barreled over the hill full blast," Stevie continued. "The truck even left the ground. But we headed down the other side, there wasn't anyone left. It had been too long. Probably an hour between the time Merlin and Duke escaped and we found them. Ten more minutes to the compound. We dug you out. You were laying on top of your weapons, breathing real shallow. I think the oxygen in the tunnel was just about exhausted."

"Then we searched for Sarah," Weasel said. "Thanked God when we only found Messenger corpses. That's how we came upon the note. It was staked to the fence with one of Sarah's knives. Then we brought all of you back here and went to work on getting Sarah back."

"You think this is going to work?" I asked, referring to the complex operation they had laid out for me earlier.

"We got the bait," said Weasel. "We got some power with the truck. Power is what gets people to listen to you, Mac. All we need to do is get them to bring Sarah to us. That's your job. If they do, we can get her back."

• • • •

Weasel and Stevie went back to work. Help was coming in the morning, they said, and there were still details to attend to. I helped Merlin with the maps. Fourteen was what we needed.

We managed five hours sleep that night, awakening before dawn. I felt my strength was back enough for me to help during the day, but they told me no. Rest up.

In twelve hours we would go to the Messengers camp to begin negotiations for Sarah. You'll need all the strength you can muster, they said.

CHAPTER THIRTY-EIGHT

We knew where the Messengers were. Everyone did. Can't hide a boil on the end of your nose. Their latest headquarters was Wheaton College, a small private school best known in the 20th for its affiliation with the famous preacher, Billy Graham.

It was late on a sunny September afternoon when I slowly presented the truck to the Messengers, moving North on President Street, maneuvering around the rusters when I could, nudging them off to the side with the truck's superior mass when there was no way around. Weasel was in the back with the HK belt fed and several assault rifles. Stevie had dropped off a few hundred meters back. He would set up when we read the situation. Merlin and Duke couldn't make the trip. Their wounds made them a liability. They were back at Fox Valley, recuperating. We would need them both tomorrow.

We were going to negotiate for Sarah's release. It was what the fat man wanted. Sometimes you did what the enemy wanted, Weasel said. They would have to produce her—walking, talking, intact. If they didn't, we would remain, the three of us and the truck, until the stain that was the Messengers was removed. Or we were.

I pulled the truck up a little rise and stopped, straddling the railroad tracks of a commuter line, facing north. We had encountered no one on our journey. In an hour the sun would set. Sarah had been with the Messengers for nearly a day and a half. If all went well, she would have to remain for yet another night. We had to get them to our choice of ground for the exchange. We would not operate on their turf.

I put the huge vehicle in neutral, engaged the emergency break and opened the door, standing on the running board to survey the territory. Except for viewports/gunports, the cab was sealed with armor. Above and behind me, Weasel also stood to have a look, temporarily leaving the safety of our homemade gun turret. His hand remained on the machine gun.

On either side, beginning on a street that bisected President a half block ahead, rows of apartment buildings, three or four story units, lined the street. Filled with students a few decades ago, they were now home to Satan's Messengers. A block away on my left, I could see the college's football stadium. Beyond that was the Billy Graham Library. We had visited it many times in the past several years, scavenging for books and disks.

Across from the library a three acre hill of tall grasses dotted with ancient oaks, some still majestic, some fallen, rose up to the main campus. All of the brick and granite buildings on top of the hill were intact. Birds sang and scolded; squirrels darted through the trees. There was no sign of human movement.

"Nice quiet day in the suburbs," Weasel commented. His voice came in through two channels, via the comm set and the normal air borne mode. Stereo with a millisecond delay.

"They know we're here," I replied.

"Yep."

"Stevie," I asked, "where you at?"

"'Bout a hundred meters behind and west of you," he replied. "Got a intermittent buzzing sound in this ear piece. Can you hear it?"

"No problems with the comm sets. Stay loose. We're going to bring them out. Don't set up until we reach a final spot."

"And watch your back, boy. They may have guard posts out there," Weasel warned.

"Not to worry, Weasel," Stevie replied. "I spent six years hiding from these bastards. They won't see me."

I reached for the air whistle in the cab and gave it three short blasts. The results were immediate, like poking a stick into a hornet's nest. From the apartments nearest us, rifle barrels suddenly appeared in the windows. A few exploratory shots rang out to our left, careening off the truck's armor. Weasel answered with the belt fed HK, a short burst obliterating the window and probably the shooter.

Birds rose from nearby trees, beating a noisy exit from the intrusion on their lives. The guns remained in the windows. But none of the Messengers chose to attempt a further test of the truck's armor shell. Silence returned.

"Hoist the flag," I told Weasel.

A white towel on a broom handle went up in the corner of the truck's bed. To us it meant a willingness to talk. To the Messengers it may have been a handy target. We were about to find out.

I put the truck in first and slowly descended the slope, waiting for the bullets to fly, hoping they would allow us to proceed. I turned left on the road that led to the main campus. In a couple of blocks it would put us in front of the library. The weed infested street, bumpy from the loose slabs of concrete that had buckled over the years, led us beneath a canopy of trees.

From the protection of the turret, Weasel put a couple of long bursts from one of the assault rifles into the trees. Leaves and twigs floated down in front of the truck. No bodies came crashing to the road. As we pulled closer to the main campus, creeping at about five miles per hour to check their defenses, my comm set began shorting out. Static, a far away, garbled voice, static, silence.

"Stevie," I asked, "you OK?"

"Yeah. You hear that too? That's what I was talking about. Could their walkie talkies be jamming our signal?"

"Didn't happen in the city. Shouldn't happen here. The should be on a different band," I replied.

"Keep your fucking focus," Weasel growled. "Within a stone's throw, we got about two hundred maniacs want to fucking barbecue us."

I followed the curve of the road to the left, coming to a halt between the library and the hill that led up to the main campus and bringing the truck to a halt, motor still running. Then I executed a three point turn, so that we were facing the hill. Big, ugly, armored, bulldog, truck.

The interference returned to the comm set, this time not as static and garbled words, but an addition to the loop that was Stevie, Weasel and me.

Sarah.

She had somehow saved her comm set. We had pulled within her range. She had to be below ground level for the reception to be so poor.

No matter. She was alive.

"Mac. Mac. Be careful. The Babe is in a state of apoplexy, he wants you so bad."

Her signal was clear, but her voice was muffled, like she had a mouthful of food.

"Sarah. Sarah," I screamed it, couldn't help myself. "Are you all right? Where are you? Tell me where they're keeping you."

"Jesus fucking Christ," said Weasel. "You just blew my damn ear drum out, Mac. You're screaming so loud she can hear you without this fancy gear. Let me do the talking."

"I love you, Mac. I was afraid you were dead. I tried to help you," she said. "I stayed outside your tunnel until my ammo was gone, then started clubbing at them with my rifle. There were just too many. They couldn't find you, so they wanted me alive. Lucky break, huh?"

"Sarah," Weasel interjected, "we really can't be talking right now. I'm more thrilled than I can say about you being alive, but we got to move on."

"Weasel's right," she said. "This isn't the right time for conversation. No more talk." Then she fired a few questions our way, ignoring her own admonition. "Is everybody all right? Tell me Duke and Merlin are all right. Oh, Mac, I'm so glad you're safe. Where's Stevie?"

"Here, Sarah," he said. "We're going to get you out of there. Duke and Merlin are a little banged up. But they'll heal fine."

Weasel sighed, very audibly, very loudly, very theatrically. "Maybe we should all listen to a few tunes before we get back to business. We haven't even started yet," he groused. "You people ready to go to work?"

We all remained quiet, relinquishing control to him.

"Stevie," he began, "set up where you can cover as much of us as possible with the HK sniper without being seen. I think we're in a central position here. But if we move, you move."

"Gotcha," Stevie replied.

He had the HK and telescopic site as well as 20 five round clips taped back to back in a bellows pocket of his fatigues. In addition to the sniper, he was carrying the Galil SAR, 36 round clips, for close-in work if we needed it.

"Sarah," Weasel continued, "listen to me, hon. We ain't got much time, sittin' here in the middle of Messenger City. We have a plan, but it doesn't involve getting you out right now—unless you feel we can pull it off. You know a hell of a lot more about this set up than we do."

"Stick to your plan," she said. "I'm deep in the basement of one of these old buildings. Can't tell you which one. Heavily guarded. You'll never get in and out alive. Plus he's got the children he kidnapped in this building too. You can't make an assault. The children would be killed."

"What can you tell us that'll help?"

"Here's the deal," she said, still muddy sounding.

I interrupted. Had to know what was wrong with her voice. "Sarah, what's wrong? Your voice sounds weird. You OK?"

"Jaw may be broke," she said, matter of fact tone to her voice. "Couple of teeth gone. But everything else works fairly well. And, I know what your thinking, Mac. They haven't raped me. So just stay cool. I want you clear headed."

Not yet they haven't, I thought, keeping my rage down, repressing my fear for her. She's alive I told myself. Only reason we're here is to keep her that way.

"I promise to maintain a level head," I told her.

"I've been listening to the guards," she said. "In between lewd comments about my breasts and other prominent anatomical features, they complain about how things are going here at Messenger central. All is not well with the troops. There seems to be some lack of faith in the leadership developing. Between the battle in the city at the Amoco Building and their assault on the compound, the Messengers have lost over a third of their soldiers. When you blew the house, we got nearly 40 of them in one swoop."

"How can we use this?" Weasel asked.

"I don't want to hurt Mac's feelings," she said. "But he's no longer The Babe's main priority."

"I'll survive the insult," I said. "Who replaced me?"

"The truck," Sarah replied. "His men are whispering that if he gets the truck, it's worth several hundred men as an offensive weapon. It's what he needs to get back on schedule. He figures he can pull all the People clans together by possessing the most powerful weapon any of them have ever seen."

"That's definitely something we can…"

"Company," I said, cutting Weasel in mid-sentence.

Four men appeared at the top of the hill. From fifty or sixty meters they appeared big, larger than me, pair of fat boys, two well-muscled. They took a couple of steps apart, then began a slow march down the hill, toward the truck.

I stood on the running board, the truck's armored door between me and them. They were all combat ready, two with M 16s, one with an Uzi; the fourth had a Skorpion. All had side arms as well. If we got down to it, the Uzi and the Skorpion would be the biggest problems. Not much bigger than a pistol, each could be brought up quickly and release 30 rounds of 9mm or 7.62mm in our direction in less than a second on full auto.

As they approached, I began picking out details, looking for the leader. There would be one, formal or informal, one man bolder than the rest, a man whom the others would expect to be in charge. Three of them had on hand-to-hand gear, Bears and Raiders helmets, pads, tight leather gloves with the fingers cut out. They felt good in it. You could see it in their walk, more like a strut.

The fourth man, second from my right, eschewed the paraphernalia of battle. T-shirt no sleeves, accentuating heavily muscled arms, fatigues, combat boots, 9mm semi-auto in a shoulder rig, Uzi slung just above his right hand, easy to reach. Jewelry was his trademark. Wide gleaming 14k herringbones hung from his neck along with the heaviest diamond cut rope I had ever seen. From his left ear a thick, golden Spanish cross dangled as he walked.

They stopped ten meters from the truck, close enough for me to pick out more details on the leader. A huge gold lion's head ring with twinkling half carat diamond eyes covered half of the middle finger of his left hand. Rolex on his left wrist. More significant were the tattoos, the crosses on his fingers, indicating he was one of The Babe's inner council. The left side of his head was shaved. It glistened in the afternoon sun, highlighting the red and black inverted cross tattooed on his naked skull. The hair on the right side was long and black, brushed sideways, hanging at shoulder length.

He nodded toward the white towel, hanging limply behind me. "That mean you surrender, hombre?" he asked. Only half of his mouth moved when he spoke. A huge scar ran from below his left eye, down across his lips, ending at the point of his chin.

His eyes, as did those of his men, scanned the truck, as ugly and pitted as their hearts, looking for chinks in its armor. They found none. Behind me in the gun turret, Weasel's head would be in view; and the snout of the HK was poking out, pointed, I knew, at our four adversaries.

"Bilingual," I said. "Very impressive." It was easy being a wise guy behind an armored door. "No," I said in response to the leader's question about the meaning of the towel. "But if you wish to lay down your arms, we promise to treat you with dignity and respect."

Through my earpiece, I heard Weasel's voice. "He's the man. Watch him close. Got enough gold on him to buy ten cases of M 16s."

Sarah was monitoring. Her voice came through, whispering urgently. "The man with the jewelry is Cholo, Mac. Watch yourself. He's very volatile. Really likes to hurt people."

"Did he hurt you, Sarah?"

"No." She was lying. First time either of us had done so. She was lousy at it.

"Where's the dog?" asked Cholo, the one with the jewelry. "Sure like to meet that famous old pooch."

"Dead," I said.

"Shame," he replied. "Our hearts go out to you in your time of mourning."

"Painful death," I replied. "Died of food poisoning after he ate part of The Babe's face."

Cholo smiled. Half of his face stayed behind. So did his eyes.

"You are very clever, McCall. But we already know that. You are also a pesky little coyote, nipping at the fringes of the wolf pack. The

Babe wishes you to be gone…is willing to forgive your transgressions for your word that you will no longer maintain an interest in our affairs…and a few minor concessions."

"Such as?"

Cholo waved an arm in front of him. "This is such a wide space for us to talk from. You should come down to us, speak with me directly, if you wish negotiate seriously."

"I'd prefer to talk directly to the fat man."

"He doesn't like to be called that," Cholo replied. "He is resting. It has a been a busy time for us. I am the one you must talk with."

"You would drop your weapons?" I asked.

"When eagles nest with chickens," he replied.

"Then I remain up here."

"Then we must leave," he said, beginning to back away. "I will tell your slut you were not willing to help her. She is a fine piece, McCall, bountifully endowed. Magnificent tail section. Unfortunately, The Babe will not share. All the men are hard for her." He grasped his groin, gave it a pull. "Big raging hard-ons. But The Babe is selfish. He has reserved her for himself…when she heals a bit, that is. She is a bit too fragile right now to take such a huge weight."

"Hold," I said.

They stopped. A ghost of a smile flicked across Cholo's face. He had just won a small victory.

I turned to Weasel. "Give me Sarah's Mossberg."

He reached down and retrieved the Mossberg, tossed it to me. Late 20th model, it wasn't a turkey gun. Straight combat, a 12 gage clip fed semi-auto. Sawed down stock and barrel, a canvass sling would put it at a level directly parallel with my arm when it was bent at the elbow. Fourteen shots in the clip, twenty-eight with two taped back to back. If I needed more than two, I would be in trouble.

"Careful," Weasel warned. "You're going where he wants you."

"I know," I said. "But he thinks I'm willing to talk. He's not aware that I know he's here for the truck. They gotta make one try for the truck before they negotiate. That way they get me, you, the truck and still hang on to Sarah."

"Just blow the bastards away. Then try talking," Sarah whispered. "Please don't take any unnecessary chances."

"Only way to The Babe is through these men, Sarah. If we just mow them down, he's likely to take it out on you in a knee jerk response. I can't risk that. If he makes his try and loses, he'll talk."

"God, I hate this. I should be there with you."

"Soon," I answered and jumped from the running board, began the walk toward the four Messengers.

"Stay to the right," Weasel said. "The two men on our left are mine. Go for the jewelry store first."

I nodded, kept on walking.

"Stevie," Weasel said, "look alive, son. We got a situation here."

"I've been listening," he replied. "I'm across the tracks. About a hundred meters behind you. Third story window of an apartment building. Got full view of everything. You guys are in the middle."

When I was within ten feet of the four, I stopped, keeping my hands at my side. Ten feet was what I was looking for. It would give the 12 gage shells a little spread but still maintain their power. Cholo nodded, reached for a pocket on his pants leg. My right hand came up, rested on the breech of the Mossberg.

"Just a long talker, man," he said, slowly opening the flap of a bellows pocket. "Be cool. Words won't hurt you. Just tellin' the man you're ready to talk to us."

He spoke one unrecognizable syllable into the device; didn't wait for a reply. Placing the walkie talkie back in his pocket, he said, "Now we get down to business. I take it you aren't willing to give us the slit?"

"Mac, Weasel," Stevie jumped in, "I got five guys high stepping along the tracks, heading your way. I would estimate their intent as less than friendly."

"Cholo…" I said.

"How you know my name, McCall?"

"It is renowned in the circle of short eyes," I replied. Baby fuckers.

He tensed up. The scar across his face flared red. "I hope this conversation goes nowhere. I'd like to cut you up a bit."

Close in, I could see he had a size advantage on me. Inch taller, maybe another twenty pounds. Unlike two of his companions, there was no fat. Right and left of him, his men shifted on their feet, sensing his simmering anger. Their adrenaline would be beginning to flow.

"Cholo, you've got five men coming up behind us. Get on your little toy communicator and call them off."

A flicker of confusion crossed his face, disappeared quickly as he retreated into a lie. "I know nothing of any men. There's only the four of us here and you and your friend. You must be mistaken."

I slowly raised my hand, showing two fingers.

"Stevie," Weasel said. "Take two of 'em down. If the rest don't stop, finish it off."

Two shots shattered the pre-dusk silence. The distinctive cracks of the 7.62 rounds of the HK PSG-1 sniper echoed off the concrete and brick walls of the Wheaton College buildings. The next sound was the squawk of the walkie talkie, followed by a scratchy voice, high volume.

"Andre and Two Toes is down, Cholo," the box screamed. "What you want we should do next?"

I raised my eyebrows at Cholo and smiled.

His face twisted in fury. His mouth worked to get some words out. His brain didn't oblige. He settled for a roar of anger, reached up for the Uzi. I sensed a paralysis in his men, a momentary hesitation as their brains cautioned them about responses that could end their lives.

As Cholo's hand approached the Uzi, mine slipped back two inches on the Mossberg, found the trigger guard. Keeping my eyes on Cholo, charting the progress of his hand to the trigger of the Uzi, I directed my finger into the gap, found the smooth groove, the little curved switch and pressed twice, aiming between Cholo and the man to his left.

At the same time, I heard the sound of a burst from the machine gun on the truck, felt the passage of the bullets as they cut the air inches from my left ear. From the corner of my eye, I caught the motion of the two men Weasel was covering as they were blown back by the impact of the shells.

Cholo was still standing, his back to me now, the impact of the two 12 gage blasts from the Mossberg having spun him half way around. I moved forward, the Mossberg ready, to get a closer look. The other soldier was on the ground, his right side a soupy mess of tattered clothes, blood and unrecognizable internal organs. Cholo was momentarily frozen, shocked into submission by the alacrity of our response and the wounds he had suffered.

The lower half of his left arm was gone. He lifted the shattered appendage, raising it to the level of his eyes, then screamed and turned, the Uzi still clutched in his right hand. He spun clockwise, and I went with the turn, like the kid who taps another on the shoulder and then turns the same way so it appears no one is there.

Cholo ended up facing the truck, looking up at its mass, straight into the barrel of Weasel's machine gun. Before Weasel could fire, I brought the barrel of the Mossberg down on Cholo's right wrist, snapping the bone with a loud crack. If he wanted to fire the Uzi now, he would have to use his toes or teeth.

I ripped the shirt from his back, using it as a tourniquet for his left arm. He offered no resistance, though his eyes bore into mine. "Cholo," I said by way of parting, "I ever run into you again, I'll take another one of your appendages. You keep it up, and pretty soon you'll be nothing but a stump. Maybe someday we'll play softball. You can be third base."

I reached into his leg pocket and extracted the walkie talkie, then pushed him toward the hill. I wanted him back with the Messengers, wanted them to see him dragging himself up the long hill into their midst—beaten, bloody, hopeless and helpless. It would give them something to think about.

"Jesus," Sarah whispered from her basement prison, "that was fucking intense. My heart's thumping like a bird's." She paused. "I take it you didn't believe me about Cholo not hurting me?"

"None of us did," Weasel said. "He won't be bothering you anymore, Sarah. Mac, you're one fucking juggernaut when you get your dander up. Ain't never seen nothing like it."

I looked up at him. "Thanks for saving my butt. You too, Stevie. Good work. But we still got work to do. Sarah's not back yet." I thumbed the walkie talkie. "Hey, fat man. Cholo's coming back. He needs a hand. This isn't getting done til you and me talk face to face. I'm willing to trade the truck for the woman."

It took him a few seconds to respond. I wondered which way he would play it. He surprised me. He kept his cool.

"McCall," he replied, "McCall. That Cholo's a loose cannon. I didn't order him to throw down on you. I'd be happy to negotiate for the woman. We can do it like this—at a safe distance. No sense in endangering..."

"Face to face," I shot back. "You're not down here in five minutes, we're coming in."

No way would he call the bluff. His army couldn't stand up to the truck. His dreams of conquest would be shattered.

"Let's talk this..."

I threw the walkie talkie straight up, watched it climb to its zenith and begin its descent. His voice kept on droning double speak, "...over. No need to meet fa..."

I snapped the Mossberg up and fired at the little plastic rectanglar box, blowing it into a thousand plastic pieces, cutting off the beast's options.

CHAPTER THIRTY-NINE

"Will you look at that," Weasel said.

We were in the cab of the truck, gazing forward from the viewports. Stevie was still in his sniper post, ready to warn us of any movement from the back or flanks. Nearly ten minutes had gone by since I had blasted the walkie talkie with Sarah's 12 gage. I asked her if she had any information on what was going on up there. She said she couldn't tell.

I put the binocs into the viewing slot and focused on the top of the hill, which was mottled with shadows as the sun dipped toward the horizon. "There's something you don't see very often," I acknowledged.

"Give me them things," Weasel said, reaching for the binocs. After a few seconds, he whistled, then added, "We ever set up a basketball league in this town, that's where I'm starting."

"If we don't shoot them all first," I said.

"That could affect my draft."

At the top of the hill, nine men in battle gear were beginning the trek down toward the truck. They were the tallest men I had ever seen, each one at least 6'7", some of them topping out at seven feet. The men had formed a tight circle, the diameter of which was about seven or eight feet. They were all facing outward, weapons ready, so that as they advanced down the hill, some of them were walking frontward, some backward, some sideways. The overall effect was of one large, awkward, bristling organism, a land anemone, perhaps.

"It's the goddam reincarnation of the Chicago Bulls," I said.

"Learning a new folk dance," Weasel continued.

"Any bets on what's in the middle of the circle?"

"The man's nothing if not cautious."

"Stevie, anything moving on the flanks or rear?"

"All clear."

"Let's go to work," I said. "Less than an hour before complete darkness. We need to be gone before that."

We opened our doors. Weasel climbed back to his turret. I resumed my position behind the fortified door, watching the herky jerky progress of the circle of tall men work its way down the hill. They stopped twenty meters back. The soldiers who faced the truck viewed the vehicle with a mixture of awe and lust, their rifles pointed our way.

From the center of the circle, The Babe's bass voice boomed out. "How you want to handle this, McCall? Why don't I bring the cunt out now. You leave the machine and walk out of here."

Nice try, I thought. "We won't make the exchange on your turf," I answered.

"Where then?" he yelled back. He hadn't expected me to approve the exchange in the middle of his camp. But it had been worth a try.

"In the city," I said. "Buckingham Fountain. On the lakefront." We had chosen that location because he would never accept it. Too far. Too risky. Too many territories for him to cross. Plus it was in the middle of Black Gangster Disciple turf.

"You and the Disciples got something cooked up, McCall? You're gonna have to do better than that."

I pretended to think it about it for a few seconds. "Neutral territory then," I responded, preparing to tell him the site we had chosen, our only shot at getting Sarah back and countering what we knew would be his attempt to get it all. "Indie country. No one to help you; no one to back us up. Out near that mall down south, Fox Valley."

He was silent for a few minutes, thinking about the territories he would have to cross, the amount of travel time, the complications of moving as many men as he would need. It was a safe trip for him, no Folks' territories to traverse, no borders to violate. When he accepted, we had our second victory of the day.

"Couple of precautions first," I said. "Number one, while we finish talking, you or your men try to take me out, and the truck gets blown just like our compound. Heard you had a few of your men toasted. Teach you to fuck with someone who hasn't done anything to you."

BLOOD OF THE DOGS

"Noted," he replied, his voice venomous, tightly controlled. "Anyone of you so much as aims a nasty thought in my direction, and the slit gets handed over to my men. Next?"

"No one touches the bitch from this point forward. She's valuable property. Anything happens to her, deal's off," I said in response.

"Mac," Sarah's voice whispered in my ear, "shame on you for talking about me that way." I heard snorts from Stevie and Weasel.

I turned my head away from the circle of men and whispered, "I'm working here, Sarah. Can't let 'em know I love you. Could be an edge for them. I'm trying to guarantee your safety until we can get you back."

"You just watch your step, Mister," she whispered back. "Don't let all of this macho posturing go to your head. I thought I heard just a tad of enjoyment in your comments." Then she laughed. "I'm so relieved you're helping. All of you. Be careful."

"If we make a deal," The Babe hollered from within the confines of the circle, "the cunt will be off limits to everyone."

"Including you," I said.

He hesitated. "McCall, maybe we can work a deal for a little taste. I won't mess her up. She's the finest piece I've ever seen. I don't think you're up to giving her the proper service."

"Right," I said, "she's been hanging on waiting for the right fat, slovenly, rotten-toothed, needle-dicked, smelly psychopath to come along and sweep her off her feet. Let me run it by you again, asshole. I paid two years' supply of ammo and a hundred grams of gold for the woman. The bitch gets touched, and the deal's off. She's too valuable to be pawed by your greasy palms. How much rent you think I could get if johns know she's been had by the Messengers? The market would bottom out."

"Fuck you," he said. "You act like she's some kind of goddam cherry. I'll find some better shit. Younger. Tighter. Keep the slit, McCall. It's a deal."

I placed the Mossberg and my assault rifle on the seat, keeping the Glock and a Ruger as sidearms, and jumped down from the running board. I walked away from the truck, five meters. The soldiers in the circle followed me with their weapons.

"Let's finish the deal face to face," I said to the man in the circle.

He exited from the rear of the circle, and the soldiers broke to form a skirmish line behind him. As he lumbered slowly over to me, he pointedly ignored the HK that was following him from Weasel's turret. He wore combat dress. No fancy three piece suits or warm up jerseys for the general in wartime. His Nazi helmet was in place. It had a deep, furrowed indentation in the front, compliments of a slug from my .357 Desert Commando in the Amoco Oil Building battle. Covered in the grey-green-browns of the fatigues, the fat man looked more like a walking tent than a leader of men.

He had a .45 on his hip, a .38 Special in a shoulder rig, couple of knives…and the baseball bat snugly ensconced in the harness across his back. He stopped within arm's length of me, near enough for a Bowie knife to flick out his eye.

"Close up, you don't look like much, McCall," he said. "If I didn't need that truck of yours, I'd just as soon play a little ball with your head. Ever see how a man twitches when he gets smacked real good with a baseball bat, McCall? They flop around all over the place like a fish out of water. Like they was doin' some kind of sod buster indie dance on their back. You gotta hit 'em just right, though."

He reached out and touched my temple with his forefinger. I snapped my arm up, pushing his away. It was as if I had hit a tree trunk. Guns rattled as his soldiers brought their weapons up. He laughed, booming it out through brown and yellow teeth.

"Just showing you the spot. Right on the temple. Little soft area. Got to hit it just right or they die too quick. I've gotten pretty good at it. Record's two minutes and seventeen seconds doin' the dance. Think you could beat it, McCall?"

His eyes, more like those of a rodent than a man, lost in huge folds of flesh, gleamed with the prospect of bringing about my death. There was no pretense between us. We each had something the other had to have. Each of us would live through this day. Death would wait for the exchange. But we didn't have to feign civility.

The hate flowed back and forth in the narrow space between our two bodies. His for me because I had accidentally stumbled upon one of his schemes, the massacre in the parking lot. Not because I had witnessed the depths of his brutality. That was no problem. He wore his viciousness, his brutal nature like a combat medal. It was his badge, a trademark. His hate stemmed from the fact that I became an inconvienience that day at the college and hadn't possessed the good manners to die quickly, as all of his opponents had done before.

The animosity I held for him was that of a father or mother toward an abuser of a child. His transgressions were beyond forgiveness, beyond the search for reasons, beyond comprehension of thinking men and women, beyond the mercy of God. He preyed on the weak, which in his case, was a group comprised of everyone except those he could use. He was beneath the norms and values societies established to ensure survival. The Babe was pure predator, unadulterated evil. In the 20th he would have been a serial killer, or maybe a dictator. Gacy or Hitler. Probably the former. He liked hands on.

It was a game now for him. He had no intention of returning Sarah to her loved ones. Didn't know what a loved one was. He would try to take it all. Problem was he hadn't figured out a way to take the truck by force. So he would try subterfuge. He was comfortable in that arena as well. His dealings with the Insane Cobra Nation were 100% smoke and mirrors.

His only weakness was that of underestimation. He had done it time and time again with us and still hadn't learned from his mistake. Between the scouts and the Aon Center and his assault on our compound, nearly well over a hundred of his men had perished in his quest for me and Duke. One man, one dog. And he still felt like he was in charge. It was his sense of superiority that we would exploit to gain Sarah's release. While he was plotting to obtain the truck and still keep Sarah, eliminating the rest of us in the process, we would be finalizing the plans for Sarah's rescue and his demise. He was expecting us to be reactive, not proactive. How could a rabbit imagine vanquishing the mighty wolf?

His Nazi helmet cast the top half of his face in shadows, but I could still discern the extent of the damage Duke had inflicted upon him in the Aon Center. The right side of his face and neck bore the marks of Duke's fangs. His mangy beard had been shaved in strips to allow for treatment of the wounds. Several deep, scabby furrows, pulled together with slipshod stitches that peeked out from the puckered flesh like mutant whiskers, ran in vertical lines from cheek to neck.

"Jeez," I said, "nasty looking wounds, fat man. Does it hurt?"

"Maybe we should talk about including the dog in the deal for the woman," he said.

"Dog's been sick," I replied. "Could be rabies. Have you had any fevers, sweats, dry mouth lately?"

"When this is finished, McCall, that mouth of yours ain't gonna be flappin' so much. I think maybe you'd make a decent cocksucker, like your little friend, Merlin. He munched real good. Be difficult for you to talk with a cock in your mouth, McCall." He flashed me a yellow/brown smile. "Let's get this over with. How we make the exchange?"

"I'll leave the truck outside the mall. There's a store called Lord and Taylor on the east side upper level. It will be there."

"And the woman?"

"The truck won't operate without a key. She'll take you to the key, show you its location and start walking away. Simple. You head for the key; she goes in the opposite direction."

"How she gonna know where to find the key?"

"I'm going to tell her. Right now. I'm not leaving until I see what kind of shape she's in. I don't want damaged merchandise. If she's messed up, you'll have to sweeten the deal. We lost a few weapons in the fire."

It was our chance for an quick resolution to the problem. If we had an opportunity, we would get Sarah into the truck and beat a hasty retreat.

He didn't care for that stipulation. Groused about it, finally relented. I found out why a few minutes later. He was concerned about the quality of the merchandise.

She appeared at the top of the hill, between two soldiers who accompanied her down through the shadows cast by the canopy of trees. As she passed in and out of the sunlight, I could make out little more than her bearing. Nothing was broken. She was walking strongly, shoulders back, focused on her objective, ignoring her guards as if they were servants. As she drew nearer, I began to make out details of the damage they had inflicted upon her.

In the truck Weasel watched through the binocs.

"You ain't gonna like this, Mac," he said.

"What is it, Weasel?" Stevie said, his voice edged with concern. "She hurt?"

"Nothing permanent, son," he said. "She'll be fine once we remove her from this human septic field."

Sarah and her guards halted halfway down the hill. I watched carefully as they brought forth a heavy chain, attaching one end around a tree trunk and the other tightly around her waist. They padlocked the huge links together.

There was no chance now of our swooping her up, putting her in the truck and trying to blast our way out.

"Sarah," I said when she continued her trek, speaking into her earpiece, "no show of affection. Don't let them see any signs of caring. Maybe a tad of subservience."

She didn't answer. Just kept on walking, throwing off the restraining arms of the guards as they tried to slow her down, marching past The Babe who had returned to his contingent of lanky storm troopers, stopping right in front of me, the chain stretched out behind her. She shot a withering glance at her escort, who in turn looked to The Babe and, receiving a nod from their leader, stepped back out of earshot.

I don't know how she did it, considering what she had obviously been through, the pain she was still feeling, but she flashed me a crooked smile, the most beautiful thing I had ever seen.

"Should I genuflect, make a little show of subservience?" she asked, her eyes, or eye, one of them was blackened and swollen, twinkling.

Her earpiece was in place, so she had heard my suggestion. But the derm was gone from her throat. When she spoke, it was closed mouth, like a bad ventriloquist. Her jaw injury was causing her immense pain.

I looked behind her, checking the attitude of the guards and The Babe. I didn't return her smile. I felt more like crying but showed no emotion at all. They were watching us intently. At least a dozen M 16s were aimed at her back.

"How can you smile?" I asked.

"I'm happy right now," she said through clenched teeth. "You're here."

"I take it they haven't given you a mirror."

"That bad, huh?"

"Pretty bad. Does it hurt much?"

"Only when I smile."

Much of her face was bruised and swollen. There were a couple of punctures in the center of bruises, either from a knuckle or a ring. Her lips were split in two places. Dried blood flaked on her chin. Her fatigue blouse was ripped and streaked with blood. Her pants were ripped too, held up by a canvass belt. Her nose, the center of huge area of swollen tissue, obviously broken, had a little bend in it now. The bruising from the break had spread to underneath each eye. The left side of her jaw had a lump on it, was swollen from the ear forward to her chin.

The extent of the mayhem inflicted upon her face was amplified by the fact that she no longer had her beautiful auburn hair to draw the eyes away from her wounds.

They had shaved her head.

Seeing my eyes focus on the top of her head, she waved her hand in front of her face dismissively. "It'll grow back," she said. "I let them do it without a fight. Figured if I could get by with only losing some hair, I'd be lucky. But then they tried to, uh, shave another area. Thought it would be a good present for their exalted leader. Make me more like a little girl. He likes the children, the disgusting fuck."

She spoke with great intensity. There was no fear in her, just repugnance and outrage.

"It cost one guy a testicle," Sarah continued. "Another, one of his eyes. They all went at me then, about five of them. Cholo initiated the whole thing. Would have killed me, but The Babe pulled them off. He was enraged at his men. Seems he had plans for me last night. Now, I was, let's say, less desireable. Fat man didn't want to fuck someone who looked as bad as this. I look upon it as the price I paid to avoid being alone with him. A bargain, really—because being alone with him would have cost me my life."

I hated to tell her what I had to say. But she already knew it. Even though we were taking the safest course of action and had done everything possible to ensure her safety, I still felt like I was abandoning her. But by buying another twenty hours, we would be ready for them; have an excellent shot at getting her out in one piece.

The truck made no difference to us. Compared to Sarah, it had no value. We could easily replace it. If we trusted that The Babe would trade her even up for it, we would give up the truck with no qualms. But he had no intentions of playing straight with us. Too much history. He wanted it all. Me, Sarah, Duke, the truck.

"Listen," I began, "I'm sorry..."

"Hush with the apology. You don't have to apologize for anything. You're here. Everyone is. I understand you can't get me out now. Just tell me what you can so that I can help when it goes down."

"Did they take your throat mike?" I asked, thinking it would be helpful for her to have it the next day.

"No," she said, smiling once again. "I hid it when they come in. Hid it when they captured me."

"Where?"

"Butt crack," she answered, smiling lopsidedly.

"Yuk," I said. A smile came unbeckoned. I wiped it quickly. They were watching closely. "All right," I continued. "We don't have much time. Listen up. I'm going to give you the condensed version of tomorrow's plan. You have a key part in the proceedings."

I took less than two minutes to detail the operation for her. It had taken Weasel and Stevie hours to work it out, and much more time than that to set up the necessary equipment. And we still weren't finished. But with Sarah, two minutes was all I could afford to take. While I talked, I made a show of inspecting her wounds, checking her mouth and teeth, looking for contusions on her body. I inspected her ribs, and breasts, and butt. It was what I would have done had she been my property. Our onlookers would understand an inspection of the merchandise.

When I finished, I slowly circled her, as if furthering my inspection. "You'll have to go back now," I said, my hands gently probing her back and shoulders. "I'm sorry for that. But we'll be back together tomorrow. I promise."

She nodded.

"I love you," I continued. "This all boils down to that. None of us will let them take that away."

She nodded again.

We both turned, and I escorted her back to her guards, shoving her toward them on the last couple of steps. As they took her back up the hill, I forced myself to ignore her departure. Turning to The Babe, who had eased his massive bulk down to a fallen oak branch, I said, "That's fucked up. You beat that woman all to hell. I can't tell what she's going to look like when she heals. Might be uglier than a two headed possum."

"It's just a fuckin' cunt, McCall," he replied. "Ain't like a warrior or a good assault rifle."

"Bullshit," I replied. "Before she got beat to shit, she had the potential to be the best goddam whore in all of old Chicago. After she heals, she could end up looking like a walrus. You got no respect for property, no sense of value. How you like it if I do a little damage on the truck to even things out? I'm not thinking we've got an even trade here."

"Listen, McCall," he replied, back on familiar ground, feeling in charge, negotiating a deal he had no intention of honoring, "I did everything I could to keep my men off the cunt. It wasn't easy. These are tough men. They get a little Bad Boy in them and they want to fuck anything that's breathing. I saved that woman a couple of times."

"You didn't do a good enough job," I said.

"What is it you're looking for here, McCall?" he asked.

"Either you sweeten the deal, or I modify the truck so its in the same shape the woman is," I said.

I wanted to appear greedy, interested only in profit. It was what he would expect from an adversary, what he had seen his whole life. If we appeared greedy, small, petty, there was less chance that he would consider we had the same objective he did—no prisoners, no quarter, no mercy. Men who haggled over small details were nitpickers, not visionaries. That's how I wanted him to see me. Just another trader trying to sweeten his pot. He would be the only visionary at the table.

He reverted to form, responded in the parlance of power.

"Tell you what, McCall," he said, heaving his bulk off of the downed oak limb to stand face to face with me, working on physical intimidation, "you fuck with that truck and I'm gonna strap that slit to a tree stump face down and let my boys have at her. By the time they're done with that fun hole, you'll be able to park that truck up her ass."

I backed off a step, letting him think I was cautious. In actuality, I was simply disgusted by the proximity of such a monstrosity. I was filled with revulsion.

"Let's summarize a bit," I said, staring into the eyes of nearly a quarter ton of evil. "You lost…what?…One, maybe two hundred men in the last couple of weeks between the fiasco down in the city and the attack on our compound."

He didn't respond. Close to a hundred and fifty was my guess. He was weakened to the point that two or three clans could possibly take him down if they joined together. An unlikely event in our political climate. But he was now weaker than he had been for over a year. And it would take him another year to build back up again. He wouldn't be able to hold his coalition together that long. Without our truck he would never rule.

"You're willing to queer this deal because I want even exchange for damaged merchandise?" I continued. "How long you think this band of psychopaths is going to stay with you when they find out it will be another year before you can get back to strength without the truck on your side?"

He quickly walked away, beyond the earshot of his men, beckoned me to follow with a motion of his head. "You know, McCall," he growled, "you look tough, you act mean, but when it comes down to it, you ain't nothin' but a dirt farmin' little indie with nice clothes, combat boots, and a couple of fancy firearms. You know I could take your fucking head off them shoulders right now."

"And then you'd be picking that truck out of your teeth," I said. "If I go down, that truck will cut through this camp like a dog pack through a rabbit den. And you'd be a fucking wet spot on the grass."

"Tell me what you want," he said. The truck loomed large in his mind.

"Give me a dozen M 16s, four semi-auto pistols, full clips for each and two hundred extra rounds, and we'll call it a fair exchange, truck for the woman. And nobody touches the whore. I will check her again tomorrow."

"Make it a half dozen of the 16s, two semis and a hundred extra rounds," he said.

"Done," I replied, smiling as though I had won something. "Tomorrow, same time. The truck will be outside Lord and Taylor at Fox Valley. Bring the woman, no more injuries, and the guns. She'll take you to the key."

He smiled back and dismissed me with a wave of his hand. He had given up nothing. The exchange would be our annihilation, not the consummation of a business agreement. And I was just another greedy indie, looking to get the edge on a deal. I was what he expected me to be.

Until tomorrow night.

CHAPTER FORTY

They came at night, liked we hoped they would. If they hadn't, we would have waited them out, not giving them a glimpse until the blanket of darkness provided us with one of the edges we had built into the plan.

At first, undaunted and impertinent because of their power of numbers and the drugs that lubricated their veins, they had flocked around the truck, climbing over, under and through it, like curious dogs on the scent. One of them had even blasted the horn, scaring the shit out of half his brothers in arms. Had one of them possessed the knowledge to start the vehicle, it would have done them no good. The only oil remaining in the engine's interior was the few precious drops that clung to the cylinder walls. A couple of miles' worth at the most. We had drained the oil upon our return from the negotiations with the Babe for Sarah's exchange.

He had at least a hundred and fifty men with him, double the contingent that had been defeated at the AON Building, more than was optimal for our operation, but a workable number for the twenty-three of us to deal with. It was our ground that they were about to enter. Twenty-three would get the job done as long as The Babe ultimately ended up at the location Sarah was to lead him to.

Stevie and Weasel had been working on this site since April, when Weasel heard the story of my battle with the Cobras on Roosevelt Road. This gigantic mall was the shelter from the storm that he had spoken of. It was here that we would have our final meeting with The Babe. If we survived, it would become our home.

If we counted Merlin and Duke, our numbers went up to twenty-three. Duke and Merlin were barely ambulatory. But as noncombatants they were still valuable. Neither of them would be excluded from our plan. Merlin's brains and Duke's heightened senses could work to our advantage.

Weasel pictured our plan as an operation, surgery to eradicate a fat, black-blooded tumor from our lives. The scores of Messengers that accompanied The Babe may have to be excised with the tumor. So be it. If a hand were amputated, the warts living upon its flesh would die.

I visualized our plan as a vehicle, not unlike the truck that served as the bait for the Messengers. It had multiple moving parts which all had to be in a state of well oiled synchronicity, whirling together, one dependent upon the other, a complex machine that could grind to a halt if one little wheel or sprocket didn't flow with the others.

• • • •

When Weasel and Stevie had pulled me from the tunnel, I had been unconscious and remained in that state for another five hours. Knowing the Messengers had Sarah, Weasel and Stevie proceeded without me, would have initiated the entire rescue without my help had it been necessary.

At first, they sat across from my body for two hours, talking back and forth while Merlin and Duke recuperated in the background. In the depths of the mall, the truck safely hidden inside a freight entrance, they began scheming to recover Sarah from the beast. When I awoke, my first sense memory was Weasel and Stevie discussing their plan. It took an hour or two before I could process the campaign they had created to save Sarah.

Weapons were not a problem. We had them all. Everything from the compound. Nor was the location to which they wanted to lure The Babe. After months of intermittent labor from Stevie and Weasel, the mall was now an intricate labyrinth of hidden entrances and exits, large and small stores, storage rooms, booby traps, dead ends and changes in level from basement to the top.

Fuel for the truck was not a problem. Stevie and Weasel had been cooking it for months in one of the delivery bays at the mall.

Bait was not an issue either. The fat man knew the power of the truck. Weasel had barely missed flattening him with it. The Babe had dived from the vehicle's path at the last second, exhibiting amazing alacrity for a man so prodigious, avoiding the massive wheels that would have popped him like a fat tick. Then he had seen it again at his headquarters at Wheaton College. He would hold on to Sarah until he had the ignition key.

The only issue for Stevie and Weasel was manpower. Even with me back in the game, they told me, there would only be three of us healthy enough to implement the plan for Sarah's rescue. Expecting at least one hundred, maybe as many as two hundred Messengers, they knew we would need help.

I was able to sit and stand and had started walking. Turning to Stevie and Weasel, I said, "We have a few friends, right?"

Roberto and the Insane Cobra Nation were an hour away by bike. James and the Black Gangster Disciples were three hours out. We agreed to ask both clans for help. Weasel went to the Cobras to make the request. Stevie went to the city to see James and the BGD's.

Weasel looped around to the Cobra's eastern border and stood unarmed, asking for Roberto, saying he had a message from McCall. Roberto came to him and Weasel told him the story of Sarah's capture, my injury, said we needed help. Couldn't do it alone anymore.

Roberto listened, believed, didn't hesitate. He offered Weasel two hundred men, fully armed, the best warriors the Cobras had to offer. Weasel said no, too many would die, we would all be bathed in blood. Give me five, Weasel said. The smartest, the most self-possessed. Then we can take on two hundred if need be.

Roberto raised a skeptical eyebrow at that one and smiled. Said it figured McCall would associate with a man such as Weasel. Weasel grinned back at the huge man. Then he showed the floor plan of the mall to Roberto, told of the surprises awaiting the Messengers. It will work, he told Roberto. But if it doesn't, the Cobras only lose five. We ask no more. Do not want the blood of friends on our hands.

Roberto said no. But he would allow it if we would accept ten. He would be there too. I owe McCall, he said.

Two more things, Weasel said. Small requests.

Name it, the big man said.

Dogs in heat. I need three or four.

And the other?

We're bringing in five Black Gangster Disciples. They got chips in this pot.

Roberto raised one eyebrow. Smiled. The enemy of my enemy..., he said.

• • • •

Two days before the swap of Sarah for the truck and one day before Weasel, Stevie and I negotiated for Sarah's return at Wheaton College, Roberto arrived with his nine men. Three hours later, Stevie, James, and seven more BGD's rolled in on touring bikes, assault rifles bristling off their packs and pistols on their belts.

Weasel and I pulled Stevie aside. "You told them about Roberto?" I asked.

"Yeah. James got a little prissy, but I told him the history. He knows who Roberto is. Said he could work with them if we went against The Babe. Wanted to give me a hundred soldiers. I said five. He said 15. We settled on seven. Plus him."

Weasel, Stevie, and I met Roberto and James outside the Macy's store, where we had parked the truck. Weasel said I could do that much. Then I would have to go back and rest. Roberto took my hand and shook it, then pulled me to his massive chest, encircled me with his arms and heartily thumped my back with his beefy hands.

"I am sorry to hear about your woman, McCall," he said as he released his hold on me. "'Jose' tells me she has the beauty of poster queen and the eyes of a warrior. We will help you bring her back home. Your scrawny friend," he turned to shake Weasel's hand, "has persuaded me to play David against the Messenger's Goliath." He pulled me aside and nodded toward Weasel. "This is a man of great courage and ingenuity, McCall," he whispered. "Ten minutes in his presence was all I needed to decide would throw in with you in this insane endeavor."

I thanked him.

James shook my hand and said, "I have fought shoulder to shoulder with your men and your woman, McCall. She has the heart of a hundred warriors. I wasn't sure if I decided to come for the respect we

BLOOD OF THE DOGS

owe you or the punishment we owe the Messengers. But now I think I come to help a friend rather than punish an enemy."

"If we succeed," I said, "you will have accomplished both."

"Meet my warriors, McCall," he said, introducing his men while I in turn did the same for Stevie and Weasel, and James presented his Disciples

Jose', the man who had escorted me from Cobra country, and Flint, I knew. They were two of Roberto's most trusted lieutenants. Angel and Windchill, James' top lieutenants, I recognized from my meetings with the Disciples and our battle at the AON Center. Each of them had the aura of an experienced soldier. The other Cobra and Disciple soldiers had the same presence. And when Stevie and Weasel stood with them it was like gazing upon a craggy cliff face, a solid wall of rock that had survived for thousands of years and endured countless storms. Not one of the men had reached his thirtieth birthday, several were under twenty. But they were unequivocally hard, resolute and stern.

I gazed upon a group as fierce as any clan warriors that had taken to battle. Enough scar tissue to start a plastic surgery clinic. None of them wore jewelry. There was no face paint. I knew there would be no drugs secreted in pockets. Their weapons were, for the most part, as good as ours. Roberto and James' soldiers were given the best weapons that each clan had available. We would supplement them with our comm sets, NVG's, flashlights for those without goggles, grenades and any of our rifles and pistols they wanted.

The next part could have been tricky, but it wasn't. I pulled Roberto and James aside. While Stevie continued the truck tour, Weasel and I introduced our two allies, men who ruled two territories, men who were supposed to be enemies based upon the clan system of Folks and People nations.

They shook hands, the behemoth hispanic leader of the Cobras and the slender black leader of the Disciples. Neither spoke and from the corner of my eye I could see that both sets of their soldiers had stopped inspecting the truck and were silently observing the first subtle break in the post collapse social system. The would take their cues from their leaders.

We formed a circle of sorts, the four of us—me, Weasel, Roberto, and James. Far enough from the truck that our words would not be heard by the men, but close enough for them to see our actions, reactions, and body language.

"Thank you," I said to Roberto and James. "We cannot do this without you."

Roberto said, "I owe you, McCall. You and your scraggly squad of misfits. Cobras are clean, thanks to you. The poison has been flushed from our system. And now we can contribute to the demise of the Messengers."

James looked perplexed, and like all good leaders, said nothing. He waited for more information.

"Roberto," I said. "James has had conflict with the Messengers. Can I speak freely of your problems with The Babe to James?"

"No need," Roberto said. "Word of the battle at the AON Center has spread to Cobra territory. The Black Gangster Disciples are spoken of with great reverence and the Battle for AON will be long in our memories. So, James," Roberto continued, "let me tell you of the Cobras' dealings with The Babe. It is not a story of great battles, but of internal struggle and sagacious leadership."

"Damn," Weasel said, "shoulda brought my notebook."

"But, James," Roberto continued, "the story will wait. We have battles to plan and fight and maidens to rescue."

"On point," James said. "But Sarah's no maiden. I've seen her work. Up close. She's a terror."

"I have heard as much," Roberto said. "And I thus offer you the best soldiers the Cobra Nation has to offer. What you see in them is the same thing I see in your two men, this Weasel and the boy, Stevie. Loyalty, a sense of purpose. Truthfully, McCall, in the last few years, I think many of us have tired of being warriors. We are becoming something else. I see it in your group as well. I like to think of us as...ah ...architects."

He smiled at the thought.

"While I listened to your friend, Weasel," Roberto continued, "I watched his eyes. They are the eyes of a killer. None of his enemies will ever father a child. And yet, he would give his life to protect whoever is his friend. He is not a man I ever want to mess with."

"We see much more than that in him," I told Roberto.

"So did I," Roberto said. "In his voice, behind the mask of his eyes. It is the reason I so readily believed him. Before me was a fierce, intense man, a soldier of great skill, an unarmed stranger in the middle of Cobra country, a man unable to grasp the concept of fear, asking for help. His words were not those of a killer. He was not asking for himself, was not beating his breast in the style of a warrior. He wanted me to help you, McCall...and your woman, this Sarah, the Amazon who mesmerized Jose' and fought beside our new ally James and his Disciples. This woman obviously awakened something in Weasel's heart. I am here because of what lay hidden behind the killer's eyes."

Roberto and James steered me back to their men and the truck. Both sets of soldiers began firing questions at Weasel and Stevie. Roberto, James, and their men slowly circled the ugly behemoth, inspecting it carefully, artists evaluating a comrade's work.

"You realize, McCall," James said as we walked side by side around the truck, "that if this plan goes bad and The Babe gets this war wagon, everyone is in for a world of despair for many years to come."

"This thing needs oil to run," I said. "And fuel."

"I know how motors work," James said. "Just never seen one."

"What Mac means," Weasel interjected, "is that when this swap goes down, there's only gonna be a few drops of oil inside the engine. Enough to start it. In a minute or two, it'll seize up, metal will actually melt into metal inside the engine."

"This is reassuring," Roberto said.

"Truth," James said.

• • • •

When their curiosity regarding the truck had been sated, the Cobras and Disciples followed us into the mall. We began walking them through the intricacies of the plan. We provided each of them with a map of the modifications—Merlin's idea, also his drawings, with a little help from me. The sun was high enough to filter through the grimy skylights, and we had enough light to show them all what they needed to know.

The Cobras and Disciples helped us with the preparations, continued working while we left to negotiate with the Messengers, successfully persuading The Babe to bring Sarah to this place.

The mall was huge. Biggest I had ever run across in my travels, although I had heard there was a bigger one down south, near the airport they had constructed in the early 21st. They called this one the Fox Valley Mall in the 20th, probably because at some time in their distant past the Fox River had run through a scenic valley. They transformed it into a valley of low rise buildings and parking lots. A gigantic mall surrounded by dozens of mini-malls. Hundreds of rusters littering countless acres of weed infested concrete and asphalt parking lots.

Miles and miles of stores as far as you could see. It was the last big vestige of 20th and 21st cen commercialism west of Chicago before the land reverted back to its natural flat midwestern prairie dotted with small towns or suburban subdivisions.

It was virtually a small rectangular city under one roof. Over one hundred stores, including three giants—Macy's, Sears, Penney's—that each jutted out from one of the sides of the rectangle. From each of the three anchor stores, consumers could enter the mall from two levels. The was also and east-facing main entrance. We found evidence of nearly twenty fast food restaurants, dozens of bathrooms, offices, a first aid station, security department and a power plant that looked like the bowels of a battleship.

The interior of the mall was built almost entirely on two levels. The smaller third below ground level housed offices, security, and the power plant. The roof, dotted with skylights, rose another two stories over our heads. Where it had been breached by the onslaught of over three decades of midwestern weather, trees and weeds had taken root beneath, somehow finding purchase in the carpet or tile floors. Thousands of birds discovered places to nest, as had many small mammals and reptiles. Nature had transformed tile floors and fountains into mini forests, ponds, and prairies.

It was, in short, a maze. And with the transformations Stevie had Weasel had performed, and the help of Roberto and his nine Cobras, the mall now became a battleground similar to the ones used in Hungary in '56 or in the Warsaw Ghetto by the Jews during WWII.

In the morning, Weasel, Stevie, and I drove to Wheaton College to negotiate for Sarah. While we were gone, the Cobras and Disciples rehearsed the plan that Stevie and Weasel had prepared while I was unconscious. Upon our return from Wheaton College, we drained the oil from the truck and continued preparing for the arrival of the The Babe and Satan's Messengers.

CHAPTER FORTY-ONE

From inside, near the entrance to Macy's, I watched a cluster of over twenty Messengers enter the mall at the top level through the entrance nearest the truck. Inside, it was dark as a tomb. My NVG's cast a green pall around the Messengers. About half of them were wearing their infrared Nvgs. Back outside, scouts informed me that other groups had broken off and were seeking alternate entrances. It would take the other Messengers a while to get in. The exterior circuit of the mall was well over a mile. They would communicate via walkie talkie. Bristling like porcupines with their knives, assault rifles and pistols, the Messengers were definitely over dressed. A blind man could have located them by the steel on steel clanking of their weapons.

The first group of Messengers entered, looking for weaknesses. The red dotted NVGs weren't a surprise. We had figured them for that. It was one of the linchpins that would hold the wheels on our plan. From my place in hiding, I was close enough to see wide white eyes of the soldiers without the goggles. Their eyes darted back and forth wildly as they kept in contact with their goggled team members by touch. If separated from the others in total darkness, the soldiers without the goggles would be totally helpless. We would pick them off like lions on straggling wildebeests.

At least half of the men in the group I was observing were blasted on Slammer or Bad Boy. Jerky movements, nervous twitches, weapon caresses, obsessive spins to check their rear. A scurry of squirrels flicking their tails, twitching their heads and rubbing their paws together in anticipation of crossing a quiet meadow. What was out there? An eagle? A cougar? A human with a rifle and hungry kids by the cook fire? Was it too quiet?

A little paranoia was good for a soldier. Hones the edge. These guys had way too much. No focus. Good for us.

Through the green haze of my night vision goggles, I saw the first group break up into scouting teams, scurrying through the Macy's store and out into the main mall. Neither The Babe nor Sarah was with them.

Jose' and Flint were outside, tracking the remaining Messengers. When the Messengers were all inside, Jose' and Flint would return, joining Roberto's team, avoiding action until we could get Sarah and The Babe to the spot where we would attempt to free her. Within thirty minutes all Messengers were under the roof. Jose' and Flint joined their team and everyone stayed back and observed, waiting for The Babe and Sarah to move in the right direction, staying in touch through the comm sets.

"Who's got eyes on the group with The Babe?" I whispered through the throat derm.

Through my earpiece, Roberto informed me he had them in sight. He had split off to observe The Babe. His only job for now. They were in the southwest corner, lower level near a store that sold sunglasses in the 21st, nothing else, just sunglasses.

"This is so crazy," Roberto whispered, "it's almost funny. He's got eight really tall guys surrounding him. Every time he moves, the circle tries to keep up with him. Like ducklings imprinted on the mother. When he changes direction, they all start bumping into each other."

"What about Sarah?" I asked.

"There's someone in there with him," he said. "Can't get a clear visual. Must be her."

Roberto was reporting from the back of a store that sold prescription eye glasses and contact lenses when the mall was in operation. The Messengers would never spot him unless they actually went into the store, an unlikely event since they had over a hundred to choose from. On the off chance that they did enter, Roberto had two back doors—one through a hole in the wall into an audio-video emporium next door; the other through a genuine door that led to a service hallway that snaked through the interior of the mall.

All of us had similar escape routes.

• • • •

Now that we knew where all the Messengers were, and that they had no idea whatsoever of our placement or strength, our job was essentially that of sheep herders.

In the middle of the giant rectangle that was the mall, there was one spot where they had added a third level in the 20th or 21st, an area beneath the other two, a large circular depression where the planners had decided to accommodate all of the food purveyors who had hawked their wares to hungry shoppers decades ago.

Fifteen fast food restaurants—a gastric world's fair from the 21st, serving chop suey, tacos, pizza, Chicago style dogs, Polish sausage, roast beef sandwiches from Philadelphia, chicken from Kentucky, more chicken from Boston, gyros, cookies, ice cream, even a store that sold only potatoes—formed the outside of a large circle. Inside the circle was an anthropologist's wet dream. Overturned tables, chairs and benches. Discarded food wrappers, newspapers, coupons, shopping guides. Forlorn toys, motherless purses, empty toy boxes. There was enough room to accommodate several hundred 21st cen shoppers in better, tidier days.

It was to this third level, the basement, that Sarah was to bring The Babe to retrieve his key. Sarah knew where we wanted her, but having never been in the mall, she didn't know how to get there.

We would help her.

It was like the children's game of hot and cold. When you got close to the objective, your mother or brother would holler, "Hot. Hot. Hotter. Look out! You're gonna burn yourself."

When the Messengers were cold, we ignored them. When they finally approached the killing ground, discouraged by seeking but not finding, like the random meanderings of rats the first time in the maze, we planned to encourage them.

• • • •

Duke lay beside me. We were behind the serving counter of a chicken place, the one from Kentucky. Even with the splint still on his leg, he could provide us with another edge. I needed his heightened senses.

Across from me, behind a restaurant that seemed to quickly serve Pandas, in the service hallway that circled the courtyard of fast food restaurants, Stevie patiently awaited my signal. James' team of Disciples was several hundred meters removed from this action. If all went well, we would not need them for this part of the plan. They were in hiding waiting for the "go" signal.

Roberto would keep tracking The Babe's group, and when he approached the food service area, he would join up with the rest of his Cobras. When Roberto joined them, their team could send a withering cross fire down on the Messengers when they finally came to the location of our choosing. Came down to retrieve the truck key from me in exchange for Sarah. Only there wouldn't be any exchanging going on. The Babe would go for it all.

When The Babe was close enough for us to initiate the action, Weasel was to leave the group he was tracking and take position with me and Stevie on the bottom level.

Ten on top—Roberto and the Cobras. Four on the bottom—Weasel, Stevie, Duke and me. Thus we would have thirteen of us in the firing zone. I didn't count Duke because he couldn't shoot. Double cross-fire. With the extra edges and the escape routes we had built in case something went wrong and James' Disciples in reserve, it was a good plan.

Time to implement it.

● ● ● ●

Via the comm set, I checked in with the two Cobra lieutenants, Jose' and Flint. They were both inside, working with split teams, each observing groups of Messengers searching the darkened mall. The Messengers were scattered throughout the mall in teams ranging in size from ten to twenty-five soldiers.

Roberto entered the circuit. "The Babe is on the second level," he said, "heading your way. Let's get them moving. I'll track them to make sure they keep heading toward you, then I'll sneak around the perimeter to join up with my guys above you."

"What about Sarah?" I asked. "You sure she's there?"

"Definitely a woman inside the circle," he replied. "I got a glimpse of her. Hands bound in front. Legs free. Looks like she's got a gag across her mouth. Her goddam head is shaved, McCall."

Weasel had been monitoring. "Mac," he said, "I'm coming back in with you."

"What's your group doing?" I asked.

"I'd say they're a tad edgy," he replied calmly. "Group of about twenty freaked out Messengers roaming around down here. We need to start the party before they start lookin' around in these stores and stumble across some of us. They're so pumped up, I'm surprised they're not shooting each other."

"How much time to work your way back to me and Stevie?" I asked.

"Give me ten minutes."

"Roberto," I said the Cobra leader, "I'll start it up when you're in position with your team above us. I need you up there to tell me what's happening. Weasel," I continued, "can you switch from your group to monitor the reactions of The Babe's group? You got enough time?"

"Give me a break, Mac," his sarcastic reply snapped back. "I designed this fucking labyrinth. No sweat."

"James," I said. "Hold your position. We're gonna need you soon."

"Four-Ten," he replied. I thought I heard Weasel sigh.

"OK. When everyone is in position, we start."

• • • •

In the middle of the food court, hidden under a table, invisible even to goggle enhanced eyes, was a boom box, powered by freshly charged solar lithium ions, with a cued up cd.

I pushed the 'play' button on the remote control in my hand. From the boom box came a muffled dog bark. Then a whine. Then I pushed the 'stop' button.

"Jesus Christ," Roberto came back at me from his position two stories above us, "looks like some one stuck a fork in 'em. They're all twirlin' around like a bunch of dogs chasin' their tales and pointing their rifles all over the place. One of 'em is on the long talker. Out."

"The Babe just got the message on this end," came Weasel's voice. "They're moving in your direction, Mac. I'll follow. Once they meet up with the others, I'm coming down the back way. Out."

Weasel slipped in from the back hallway five minutes later. Duke had picked up him up three minutes before he arrived. Duke was in a state of alertness, ears up, head frequently cocked the way he did when action is impending.

"What's the status?" Weasel asked.

"Haven't heard from Roberto for a few minutes," I replied. "I don't know what anyone's doing up there." I nodded up with my head.

"About fifty of the Messengers are above us on the third level," Weasel said. "That includes The Babe and his basketball team. And Sarah. I saw her, Mac. She's all right. The ones up top are pretty much spread around the circle that overlooks our position. Figure another hundred roaming the mall looking for trouble."

"What are they carrying?" I asked him.

"Usual shit. Mostly M 16's. Couldn't see The Babe well enough to see what he's using."

"McCall," came Roberto's voice in our ear pieces, "They're fanned out up here. Just milling around. The Babe's arguing with one of his soldiers. Some of the others are beginning to search this level. Get 'em outta here before they find us. Out."

They were getting hotter. We had about a third of them in one place. Now I needed The Babe to make his move. We would do nothing until he came to us.

We had all pledged to avoid contact with the Messengers until we initiated the plan to extricate Sarah. When she was safe, we would go for The Babe.

"Get in position," I told Weasel.

He smacked my shoulder and patted Duke on the head and slipped out behind me. He was headed to the other side. When in position, he, Stevie and I would each be on a point that would divide our circular area into three equal parts—Stevie in the hall behind the Panda store, me in chicken—the one from Kentucky—and Weasel over behind a Gyros serving counter.

I punched the tape on again. Another dog bark. For good measure, I thumped the counter I was hiding behind with the butt of my assault rifle, the thirty round HK 81. All of us were carrying HK's or the Israeli Galil Sar as the primary weapons because they fired the heavier 7.62mm rounds. We each had another assault rifle for back up, all firing the same rounds as the M 16's, 5.56mm. I also had the HK 21A1 belt fed machine gun beside me. Security blanket.

From my angle I could see a small portion of the railing, two stories above, that kept 20th shoppers from falling down into the lower levels. Five goggled heads peaked over it, little red lights glowing brightly, looking down into the blackness below them our area. They saw nothing but overturned tables and chairs and scraps of 20th cen garbage.

"That got their attention." Roberto whispered. "They're all gathering around the railing, yammering away like a bunch of fucking crows. Out."

In two minutes Roberto informed us that The Babe was pulling men into his safety circle and issuing orders. Everything was quiet for three minutes after that.

Then they made their first move.

"Three guys coming down to you. Good luck," Roberto whispered.

They skittered down the mild incline of the ramp that descended to our position. No stairs here. The ramp looked like a Z. Down and back they came. Twice I saw them through my goggles. Rifles ready, single file, they maintained two meters distance from one another. With their goggles on they looked like frogs on acid. The red glow of the light on their NVG's indicated they were seeing the environment as clearly as I was. All of them were sporting football helmets. Two of them were wearing shoulder pads, a nice look, but they got in the way when you needed to shoulder a rifle.

It was either Slammer or Bad Boy that was whipping through their veins. The three soldiers danced without grace on the balls of their feet, energized by the drugs, unable to control the false messages of power and invincibility their brains were sending. They could probably have run through a wall.

What would I do if this weren't a trap? I asked myself. If I really planned to trade the key for Sarah? If I wanted them to bring Sarah down here to me, I needed to meet their expectations. So I did what I guessed they would expect me to do.

"What the fuck you doing, fat man?" I hollered from my hidden position. "I see three men coming down. But there's no woman with them. Pull them back."

"McCall," he yelled back, "no problem. My men are just coming down to make sure you have the key before I send the woman down."

Weasel's voice came over the comm set. "Bull shit. He's sending them down to see what else is here. Stand your ground, Mac. He won't touch Sarah until he's sure the key is his."

I agreed. "Pull them back," I repeated.

He tried to make his voice soothing, trusting. Didn't work. "Just show them the key," he said. "They won't harm you, McCall."

I pulled the Colt Delta Elite from its holster. It was a huge pistol, designed in the late '80's to emulate the appearance of the legendary 1911 model, but improved in fire power and efficiency. Deafeningly loud and awesomely powerful, it fired 10mm rounds from a nine round clip. It would stop a bear. Body armor would pose no problem for it.

"Stay put, Weasel," I said. "Just let them think it's me alone for now."

Out of the green background, the three scouts entered our domain from my left, about twenty meters distant. Where the ramp ended, there were threes steps down to the food court. They crouched and surveyed the huge circle where they knew the dog's bark had come from.

Before they could take the steps down to us, endangering Weasel and me, possibly placing Stevie in jeopardy, I popped up and took out the one on the left with a head shot, pulverizing his Bears helmet and the skull it protected; quickly turned to the middle man and hit him in the chest because it was a larger target and he was already moving; and put a round in the back of the already retreating third one's leg.

He went down hard, clutching at his thigh. I didn't fire again. I wanted him alive and screaming. It would jangle their raw, drug heightened senses far more than ours. In less than two seconds, all three had gone down. The roar of the three shots reverberated through the darkness of the mall, bouncing off the walls, floors and ceilings, rapid fire echoes of death. I was back in hiding. None of the Messengers above us had seen me.

Speaking into the microphone, I told everyone I was all right before they started asking. Now The Babe had a decision to make. He had to have the key. Sarah was the only chip he had.

The wounded man was broadcasting his pain for all to hear. I hadn't loaded hollow points in the Colt because I wanted penetration, not splatter. But the bullet was huge and had surely shattered his leg if I had hit him square. He was trying to crawl up the winding ramp back toward his compatriots. I let him go, hoping they'd send of couple of men down to assist him. A more likely choice for a clan would have been to roll a piano down the ramp to silence his screams.

"McCall," came the voice from the top level, gravelly, deep, excited by the impending action, "I got a present for you."

A long, drawn out moan, a scream muffled by tape I realized later, reflective of immense pain, followed shortly.

"I want that truck, McCall. Cough up the fucking key...You got goggles; take a look at what I got for you."

A small sausage-like object came over the ledge two stories above and landed with a small plop in the middle of the circle. Duke whined. It was about ten meters from me, inanimate, dead, green-tinted in the enhanced light of the goggles. A few moments ago it had been attached to someone's body.

It was a finger.

Sarah's.

CHAPTER FORTY-TWO

T he fat man's voice floated down from above, full of good humor and joy. "This piece of meat I got a hold of, only got nine now. In another minute, one of her thumbs is comin' down to you. Woman needs a thumb," he laughed and continued. "Can't jack a man off without a thumb. Not much use with just fingers."

The pain that Sarah surely experienced, the shock I felt at his defilement sent a physical wave pulsing through my body. It would have hit my brain too, releasing the safeties that protected me from rushing up the ramp into their midst, had it not been for Weasel's intervention.

"It's business, Mac," he whispered urgently in my ear. "He's reacting to your capping his men. Hold it together. You have to get Sarah down here with us. It's the only way we get her free. There's still a deal to be struck. You lose it now and Sarah's good as dead."

He had been talking to me and Sarah for years, training us, giving advice, teaching—preparing us for this very moment, I suddenly realized. He said the beasts would come. Try to take everything away. Just because they could.

Everything Weasel had ever said to us seemed important, and I was conditioned to listen when he spoke. That was why his words broke through my rage, kept me from charging up the ramp into oblivion.

"The key, Mac," Weasel said. "Make him think you've got the fucking key."

I snapped back in, realizing abruptly that if I didn't do something quick, the beast above us was going to snip little pieces off Sarah until there was nothing left.

"Send more men down with the woman," I said, "and you'll get the key. I won't fire on them."

"Give me a show of faith," he said.

"We're even," I yelled up into the darkness. "Her finger for your three men. I told you to call them back before I shot. We're right back at the starting point."

"Not the way I look at it," he said, showing off now for his men, feeling in control. He knew he was close to the key, my death certificate. "The woman's still got both thumbs. That's what I'm giving you. Show me something nice, McCall."

"Give him something," Weasel commanded. "Anything."

Beside me were two assault rifles, Duke and the HK belt fed machine gun. Duke looked up at me. Was he volunteering? I wondered. I slid the belt fed HK 21A1 machine gun into the center of the food service courtyard. It would be visible from above.

"Look below you," I said. Looking up, I saw a dozen red dots appear over the railing as Messengers inspected the goodies. "That's the gun that goes on the truck. Got an output that surpasses five assault rifles. Bring the woman down and you can take the machine gun and the key back. Then we leave."

No reply from above. No screams either. The only sounds were the moans of the wounded man on the ramp.

"What's going on up there?" I asked Roberto.

"He's conferring with some of his men," he said. "Six guys just broke off the main group. I think they're looking for another way down to get at you. I don't think your business arrangement is gonna be long lived."

"Nice lookin' weapon, McCall," The Babe shouted from above. "Where's the key?"

"When I get the woman, you'll get it," I lied.

"Everybody listen up," I said into my mouthpiece. "Stevie, when I signal you, crank it up, and everyone remember to take off the goggles."

"Roberto, two of you go after as many of the six scouts as you can get. Use silencers or knives. When Stevie turns it on, whoever's left will spray the remaining guys on top. James, have your men ready. They're gonna be coming your way."

416

"Weasel, leave that position and come around behind me and get Duke. You two wait in the halls in case any of the Messengers find our back door."

"Roberto. Talk to me."

"Two of my men are going after the scouts," he replied. "I'll handle the Messengers up here when it goes down. It looks like The Babe is preparing to send more soldiers down. This time with your woman. I don't know how you're playin' this, McCall, but these guys are lining up around the railing like they're looking at a shooting gallery."

"That's what I figured," I responded. "If he gets what he wants, I'm dead meat. Then he takes the truck, keeps Sarah for himself and hunts the rest of you down. But until he sees that key, he's not going full tilt. Without the truck his empire stagnates. We've got a few more minutes until he moves. Just remember, everyone, take those glasses off when I give the signal. First thing is to get Sarah out in one piece. Then we pull back and wait for their move."

"What James?" Roberto asked. "You want his team up here with us?"

"Where are you?" I asked James.

"I got two groups split," he replied. "Watching Messengers over by Sears and another group waiting in a bookstore in the northwest quadrant." He was far removed from our location.

"Stay where you are," I told him. "When the shooting starts here, open up on the Messengers in your areas. Remember...tell your men without NVGs to fire at the red lights. You two take out the Messengers that don't have goggles on. Then head back into hiding. Don't take any chances."

Beside me, Duke perked up his ears and swung around toward the door to the hallway behind me. A minute later Weasel slipped in behind me and retrieved Duke. "Be careful in there," I told him.

His goggled head turned my way. I saw a smile crease his mouth. He reached out a hand and clasped the back of my neck, squeezing it firmly, affectionately.

"I feel like Dr. Frankenstein," he said. Then added, "Don't worry, Mac. We're getting her out of here. It ain't right for it to fall any other way."

He and Duke eased silently into the hallway behind me.

The Babe's voice broke the stalemate.

"McCall, I'm sending your little nine fingered cunt down with some of my men. You best have that key ready for me or we're gonna play doctor with her."

They came down the Z ramp slowly, three more jittery soldiers and Sarah. All I could see was their legs, but it was easy to pick out Sarah's—hers were the ones that kept moving in one direction. The others were boogeying to the beat of the drugs, spinning and prancing in response to imaginary enemies.

They crossed out of my vision and then reappeared heading the other way, close now to the entrance to our domain. They disappeared from my line of sight and I heard a single shot. The moans from the wounded soldier abruptly ceased.

Down three steps and there they were, same area as the first three, but more alert, having just stepped over their companions' bodies. Two of them cautiously ducked behind Sarah, trying to use her ample frame as a barrier against my bullets. The third had her clasped tightly to his body.

A grey slab of tape covered her mouth. She was shoeless and shirtless, no body armor, no protection against the shots they feared I might throw their way. There was no sex in her nakedness. It was a warning. An attempt to intimidate me. Shoot at us McCall. Tear up the woman's flesh with your bullets. She is our shield.

Her hands were tied in front of her. She held them up, across her bare breasts, squeezing the left hand with the right to staunch the flow of blood, a black wetness that covered her hands and torso, flowing slowly now from the stump that used to be her little finger.

She was still strong. I could see it in her stance. Her eyes were alert, darting back and forth, hoping to discover some sign of me in the dark. As she moved her head, I saw the earring/receiver in the inner part of her right ear. She was receiving. Just couldn't send with the tape across her mouth. Nor could I see the derm/mike on her throat.

"Sarah," I said. "Move your hands if you're receiving."

Her hands flicked right to left.

"It's happening in a few seconds. Just hang in there. When it starts, hit the ground and start crawling. I'll be there."

One of her thumbs went up. Nothing else moved.

• • • •

Weasel and Stevie had worked on the generator for hours, fine tuning it so it started on the first pull every time. Pull and start; wait two seconds; then hit the switch for the lights.

The two of them had encircled the entire food serving area with stage lights—the kind they used for concerts and plays in the 20th. They found them in a special events storage area in the depths of the mall basement. It had taken them two days to mount them so that they didn't appear out of sync with the environment. On the second day, they were assisted by the Cobras and Disciples. I wasn't much help. Half the time I was unconscious. The other half I was forced to rest and familiarize myself with Merlin's map of the maze of stores and escape hatches that filled the mall.

Hanging from the ceiling, twenty sets of stage lights, each with three spotlights—the sixty bulbs created a perfect circle of blinding light when we tested them.

• • • •

Twenty meters from me a man large enough to be The Babe's brother had his right arm around Sarah's chest. In his left hand was a sawed off shotgun pressed to my best friend's temple. Behind them the two soldiers duck squatted, using Sarah and their large companion for cover as they peeked out with their red light NVG's to scan the area for signs of problems, hoping to pick out my location.

"McCall," The Babe's raspy voice came from above. "Step out and walk the key over to my men."

When the moon outshines the sun, I thought.

Speaking through the headset, I prepared everyone. "I'm counting down from three. Sight on a target on 'three.' Remove your NVG's on 'two'. Close your eyes and prepare to fire on 'one'. Stevie, at 'zero,' start the generator. Everyone keep your eyes closed. Two seconds after that, hit the lights. Out."

I lined up the Glock 17L on Sarah's captor and counted "three." On "two" I removed the NVG's and closed my eyes. From one to zero I steadied the Glock and heard the dull vibrations of the generator starting up in Stevie's section of the hallway. Two seconds later I heard the distinctive hum as the bulbs sucked up the energy from the generator and flared to their maximum output. I felt the sensation of the bright lights through my eyelids…

…and the Messengers started screaming.

A second after that, I squinted my eyes open, allowing a trickle of the glare to stimulate my pupils.

To pull a trigger, the brain has to tell a group of muscles in the trigger finger to contract. Sarah's captor must have wanted very badly to pull on the double barrel, unleashing two 12 gage shells into her shaved head, punish me for my treachery. But when the sixty bulbs flashed on, magnified in intensity ten fold by his infrared goggles, a primitive little message center at the base of his skull took over function of his body, screaming a microsecond's message that his eyes were in danger of sensory overload. You're going blind, his brain told him.

The pupils of the Messengers wearing the NVG's couldn't close down fast enough to shield the optic nerves from the intense burst of light. Sarah's captor's reflexes took over. The hand holding the shotgun, as well as the arm holding Sarah in check, flew to his face. Spastic fingers ripped off the goggles and clawed at his eyes.

I opened my eyes a bit more and saw Sarah on the ground at the soldier's feet. Three shots from the Glock sped in the direction of his head. The first took out the trigger housing of the shotgun and half of his left hand. The other two found his skull.

His buddies heard my shots and began scrambling back, hoping to find cover. Neither of them could see. I put them both down with three shots each, reloaded, and crawled toward Sarah, hollering her name, instructing her to move toward me.

Above me, The Babe and his soldiers were still shrieking from the pain. Most of them had been looking down into my area, attempting to pick up movement, when the lights had gone on, and they found themselves suddenly staring into a blazing sun that had materialized in an instant from the dark. Shots—a blind reflex reaction on their part—began raining down on me from their position above as I crawled to Sarah. I ducked under a round, formica-topped table, pushed the center support forward, using the table as an umbrella against the hail of bullets, and relentlessly moved toward Sarah.

Hundreds of rounds chewed up tables and chairs and gouged holes in the carpets before suddenly stopping a few seconds later as Roberto's HK 81 began chewing them up from behind their position. Ten seconds after the lights had turned the mall into a winter white out, the Messengers that remained up top with The Babe found themselves blind and helpless under Roberto's and his team's automatic fire. They turned in his direction and returned fire at the sound of the Cobra leader's weapon, momentarily halting Roberto's efforts; and as their sight began to return, they retreated to the safety of surrounding stores. But not before many of them had been killed, including one who had been blown over the railing and landed with a sickening thud in my area, three meters from where I crawled to Sarah under the now shredded formica table.

Except for the groans of the wounded and the mechanical clicks of new clips being rammed home, the mall returned to silence. No more shots, no more surprises.

The Messengers were in hiding. And they knew they had been had.

• • • •

Ripping off the tape covering her mouth, Sarah crawled awkwardly in my direction, happy as an orphaned puppy to see me as I sprinted across the ten meters between us and fell beside her, wrapping her in my arms, asking if she could walk. She sat up and pulled back, reaching both hands to me, which I took by the wrists to avoid contact with her wounded hand. I pulled my clip knife and cut the bonds from her hands.

In the unforgiving glare of the sixty spotlights, the stump where her finger used to be was an ugly lump of pink flesh with white bone in the middle. There was blood all over her head and breasts. Her fatigues were streaked with rust where the blood had soaked in. Her wound wept weakly.

I stood up, pulling her with me. She leapt into my arms and we plastered ourselves together, clinging tightly. It felt like she wanted to crawl inside my body. I wanted to let her in.

As the echo of the firefight faded from my mind, I began to hear the hum of the stage lights and the throbbing of the generator from behind the walls thirty meters distant. It seemed for a moment that Sarah and I were on a stage, alone stage left under the bright lights, our embrace the culmination of a dramatic scene, the audience stunned to silence by our public intimacy.

Then I heard distant gunfire, James' Disciples taking on the other groups of Messengers that patrolled the netherlands of the mall, paring their numbers.

Sarah broke our embrace, stepped back and gazed with wonder upon her four fingered left hand. "Hurts like a bitch," she said softly, looking up at me. Then, amazingly, she smiled. "But we're alive aren't we," she laughed.

I did too; then tears filled my eyes as my emotions spiked, battled with one another for dominance, relief and fear, joy and anger bouncing off one another in my body like molecules of boiling water.

"Jesus," Sarah said, almost as if in a prayer of thankfulness, "I was so afraid that we were going to lose each other, Mac." She looked up to the lights, behind me to the chaos of the abandoned restaurant area. "I think we need to be out of here, Mac," she said. "I feel like a target in a shooting gallery. Give me a fucking gun. We got some payback comin'."

I nodded, so relieved by her presence that I couldn't talk. I put a fresh clip in the Glock and handed it to her, then removed my shirt, used my clip knife to cut both sleeves off, and wrapped her hand to stem the bleeding, using the other half as a tourniquet between her wrist and elbow. The rest of the sleeveless shirt fit her snugly.

A wan smile. "He was laughing at me when he cut off my finger. Looked me right in the eyes while he was doing it. Thanks, Mac. They were gonna kill me."

"Me too," I said.

"Did we get him?"

"Don't think so. But we sure as hell whittled them down. Figure maybe a hundred or so left."

I picked up the HK belt fed that I had pushed out as bait for The Babe. I hated when they left guns and ammo laying around in the vids. Seemed like they always could have used it later on.

"I've been able to monitor," she said. "I see you recruited help. How many on our side?"

I pretended like I was mentally counting.

"Twenty-three."

She rolled her eyes. "Does that include me?" she asked.

"Twenty-four," I said.

CHAPTER FORTY-THREE

E veryone had checked in. Minor injuries. We were all back in our burrows, hiding, awaiting the next move by the Messengers. The two men that Roberto had sent to deal with the Messengers that were trying to work down to me on the lowest level had returned to Roberto, one with a gaping knife wound on his arm. They had dispatched two of the Messengers with knives. The other four enemy soldiers had not attempted to complete their mission when the firing started. Maybe their drugs were wearing off. Perhaps their hearts weren't in it. In the far recesses of the mall, where Jose' and Flint had taken on the other enemy soldiers, it was estimated that at least thirty more Messengers had gone down. We took no prisoners.

"I'm lookin' at six dead Messengers," Roberto said to all of us over the headsets. He was still two levels above Weasel, Stevie, Sarah, Duke and me. "None of 'em are fat enough or ugly enough to be The Babe. There's a trail of blood leading away from me, over to the other side of the circle up on this level. I figure 'em to be hiding in the stores. I'm also looking at eight pairs of night vision goggles. They must have torn them off when the lights came on. Hell of an idea, McCall."

"We've got six corpses down here," Stevie replied. "That makes fourteen in this section if we count the scouts your men took out, Roberto. Add another thirty and we're close to fifty down. Plus some of them have got to be wounded. Many of them without goggles. When we turn out the lights, there's gonna be a bevy of blind Messengers."

"Do it," Weasel said.

The sound of the generator abruptly stopped, replaced by an eerie silence. We continued talking in the dark, seven individuals on the circuit of the comm sets, now eight because Sarah had retrieved her strategically placed derm from her butt crack and jumped back in. She also had her NVG's back again, courtesy of Weasel, who had plucked them from the compound when she had been captured.

Each of us sat quietly with our respective teams, exhausted from the action, crouched in our dark caves, linked to the other groups only by the voices in our earpieces.

Sarah, Stevie, Weasel, Duke and I were all behind an ice cream vendor's serving counter in the lower level. Stevie peeled his shirt and offered it to Sarah, as if proffering a gift to a queen. Now she had sleeves. Cinco homeless amigos. But alive, I reminded myself. Afraid she was too weak to continue, I tried to get Sarah out. It didn't work.

"Not til we finish," she told me, steel voiced. "He's still in here."

I tried another route, attempting to get her to help Merlin with his duties, knowing it would be out of the action. That fish didn't swim either.

I then suggested to everyone that we pack it up and head home, the battle at the AON Building still strikingly clear in my mind. But no one was buying. If we let them go, we'd only have to deal with them at a later date. They would keep coming at us. They would continue stealing children. They would not stop waging war on Folks clans and indies. Even outnumbered nine or ten to one, we still had the advantage of superior equipment and better knowledge of the environment. Mostly we had too many people with us that wanted a piece of The Babe.

"McCall," the now familiar bass voice echoed down from somewhere above me. "What you doin' this for? I ain't never done nothin' to you."

I thought about Stevie...and the slaughtered Gaylords in the college parking lot what seemed like a century ago...and the children he had brutalized... and Merlin...Roberto and the Cobras, and James and his Disciples at the AON building. Then there was the matter of the bounty he had placed upon my head. Stupid bastard was so used to terrorizing people, so enamored with the process of creating fear, he couldn't conceive of the possibility someone would take it personally.

And now there was Sarah. Mutilated. Humiliated. Terrorized. The fact that all of his attempts to subjugate her had seemed only to galvanize her in no way lessened the enormity of the fat man's attempts to break her will. He had trespassed on her humanity.

I gave up my attempts to get Sarah out, persuade everyone to pull back to regroup, heal our wounds. It was a bad idea. We knew where he was. Approximately how many men he had with him. The rest of his soldiers were scattered throughout the mall, disorganized, confused, probably cramming their noses with Bad Boy. It was time to end it.

"Hey, fat man," I yelled. "This world is going to be a much better place without you. You're gonna die today. Tell your soldiers they're going down with you. I saw what you did to the Gaylords, you piece of shit. Your whole fucking war against the Folks is built upon a lie. There's no room for you here anymore."

A few seconds elapsed before he responded. There was a new timbre to his voice, a higher pitch, a reflection of the ambiguity he was beginning to feel at the prospect of being at risk. The clan bully had grown up and for the first time in his life faced an opponent willing to stand his ground.

"You know how many men I got here, McCall?" he barked. He was going to fall back on bravado. "I'm gonna snuff your ass. You been in my business too long."

I asked Roberto if the Messengers were all in one spot. "Far as I can tell. Except for the stragglers. But if they've still got their long talkers, they'll be able to find him."

"If they've still got the balls for the fight," Weasel commented.

"Can we set up a cross fire?" I asked.

"They're in a shoe store for women. Other side of the railing from the three of us up here. About twenty meters. You three set up on their side and we can do it easily."

"What about James' team?" Roberto asked. "Why not bring them up?"

"I don't think it's a good idea to have all of us in one place," Weasel said. "Let's leave them out there. Have our exits covered just in case."

Stevie, Weasel, Sarah and I, accompanied by a limping Duke, who hadn't left Sarah's side since she reappeared, made our way to the top through a series of holes and tunnels and set up in a place called

BLOOD OF THE DOGS

Victoria's Secret. We now had a triangle with twenty meter sides, the Messenger's at the apex.

"On my signal," I said, "we start firing into the shoe store. Three clips. Full auto. Let's see what we can shake out."

We flipped off our glasses and started firing, pouring nearly 600 rounds of the 7.62mm ordnance into the shoe store between our two groups. When the fusillade had ended, we rolled three fragmentation grenades into the store. When the smoke cleared a bit, I flipped my goggles back on and surveyed the results of our barrage through the haze of powder smoke. We had given the store a whole new look, shredding the shelves and counter tops, obliterating the cashier's station, reducing anything still standing into dust and wood splinters.

Nothing moved inside. "Next one's up to them," I said.

I wasn't willing to risk a frontal assault. As it turned out, The Babe was.

Duke gave the warning about ten seconds before it happened. A whine. Ears straight up. "Something's going down," I told everyone. "Make sure you've got fresh clips."

They came out from the rear of the store, en masse, at least forty, moving quickly through the store and out the front. I didn't have time to count. A thundering throng of crazed Messengers, at the peak of a drug high, brave and invincible, firing away with M 16's on full auto. They had a dozen men on their left flank firing at Roberto's position, pinning the three Cobras down, thwarting their attempts to return fire and protect our group.

The Messengers, eschewing the use of their goggles because of the muzzle flashes, mostly outfitted in football or hockey gear, snarling their imagined invincibility, preceded by a wall of 5.56mm M 16 rounds, appeared to be a deranged sports franchise from an alternate universe.

And they were barreling right down our throats. As they ran past Roberto's position, strafing his team mercilessly, none of the Messengers broke away from the main group. They stayed intact, roaring at us with the deafening sound and power of a tornado.

"Get the fuck out of here," I screamed.

Sarah grabbed Duke around his middle and slipped through the back door. Stevie and I each took a different exit, one left, one right, through holes we had carved out of the walls separating the stores. Weasel slipped through a hole in the floor. I ran like hell, letting them have Victoria's Secret. Maybe they'd find the answer to the puzzle while they were in there.

I hadn't heard any of us return a shot during their charge. Roberto's team had scattered at the same time we had. The Messengers' full contingent was intact. Maybe a stubbed toe, couple of drug overdoses. I went down a level and several stores over, before I settled on a position near Lord and Taylor, put my back to a wall and checked on everyone else. No one had been injured, but we were now separate individuals, no longer two teams, and not fully aware of the enemy's movements.

Thinking about our situation, no one injured, no one in imminent danger, I suggested we all scatter and wait them out for a couple of hours. See if any of them crossed our paths.

"Pick a spot with your back protected and two or three exits," I advised. "Sarah," I asked, "where are you?"

"As far as possible from where I was five minutes ago," she answered. "Me and Duke are in the back room of some store."

"Where? What kind?" I asked, planning to retrieve her.

"The store is nothing but empty boxes, garbage and empty shelves and clothes racks," she said. "I have no idea where we are. But wherever it is, it's quiet."

"You got a back door?" Weasel interjected.

"Behind us. It leads to a hallway."

"Are you all right?" I asked, concerned about her wounds.

"The bleeding has stopped. It's wrapped tight. Throbs. Hurts like hell and I'm one handed for now. But it will hold until we finish here."

Merlin came into the circuit then. From the deepest levels of the complex. Weakened from his leg wound, he nonetheless had an important function to perform. His job would be to orchestrate our final surprise for the Messenger troops.

"Why don't we just jump to the end?" he suggested. "My little army is ready to go."

"Too early," I said. "Plus there's too many Messengers left for it to be effective. Probably still close to a hundred out there."

"Main reason," Weasel said, "is we all of us have to be in a safe place first. We're too exposed. Just hang tight, Merlin."

"What are you talking about?" Sarah asked.

I told her.

"Son of a bitch," she said. "Who's idea was that?"

"You need to ask?" I replied.

We settled down to wait them out, open to the possibility that the Messengers would exit in the darkness and head home to lick their wounds. But The Babe was revitalized by his successful break out and temporary victory over our two teams. For the next two hours the Messengers searched the mall, looking for trouble, finding it three times as they encountered James' Disciples, engaging them in fire fights, losing some men, then discovering their adversaries had slipped away through our system of escape hatches.

After the third battle, a particularly fierce encounter far from our positions, we lost touch with Flint's team. It was then that we decided to get proactive—reform the teams and set ambushes while we still had the cover of darkness. The site of our original success, the food serving area, was to be our staging area.

"How am I going to get there," Sarah asked, "when I don't know where I am now?"

"When we get there," I answered, "I'll fire a shot from the Colt 10mm. Move toward the sound. When you see something you could call a landmark, let me know. I'll come get you."

• • • •

"I've got a big problem, Mac," came her soft voice over the headset. The tone of her voice scared me. "I'm sorry. I got lost, Mac. I'm so sorry, honey."

"What is it, Sarah?" I asked. "Just let me know."

"I'm stuck in a hallway, me and Duke." Hesitation. She didn't want to say the rest. "We've got company...The Babe is in front of us, about twenty feet."

"Does he know you're there?"

"Oh yeah. He's got us covered with an AUG. He wants me to bring you here. Duke warned me, Mac. He knew there was trouble. I just turned the wrong way."

"Where are you?" I asked.

"I still don't know," she said.

"Ask him," I said.

"Behind a place called Fannie Mae," she told me.

About two minutes away from my position. A long hall with two entries from the outside and several interior doors leading to offices and bathrooms. He must have caught her in transit from one position to another. I had a choice to come in behind Sarah and Duke or behind The Babe.

"You got any weapons?" I asked.

"He disarmed me. Just a little .22 short in my boot and a couple of knives…and Duke."

None of them would do any good against his bulk and body armor.

"Two minutes," I said. "Listen up, everyone," I said across the band, "keep all the Messengers away from this spot. I'm going to play this out. That means you too, Merlin. Best you can do for us is keep everything ready for when we need the final stake in their hearts."

"You can't keep me away," Merlin said, his intensity burning my ears. "This is mine more than any of yours."

Weasel came on, directing his comments at Merlin. "Stay out of it, Merlin. Let Mac read it first. You could screw the whole thing up sticking your nose in."

Merlin didn't respond.

"Mac," Weasel continued, "I got about twenty Messengers outside my hole here. It's gonna take me ten minutes using the back doors to get there. You're on your own, son. Remember what I've taught you."

"Merlin," I said, "stay in the basement. Get those animals ready. We'll come back to you if we can. This is going to be over real soon— one way or the other. Stevie…How close are you?"

"Very," he said.

"After I'm in, come in behind Sarah and Duke. But no shooting."

• • • •

I stepped into the hall. He was talking to Sarah, snarling and condescending. "...that little party we talked about after its over. You'll forget about him real quick once you had a taste of me."

"You're talking about me?" I asked.

His head whirled at the sound of my voice. He was positioned equidistant between Sarah and Duke's position and mine. At his feet were her weapons, an assault rifle and two pistols. He faced sideways between us, his AUG on Sarah and Duke, an M 16 covering me. We all had the NVG's on. Duke wore a perpetual snarl, his canines showing, throat throbbing with a low growl, Sarah holding him back by the collar. The splint was still on his leg, but I had no doubt that if she loosened her hold, he would charge, leaping to his death from the automatic weapon fire and possibly condemning Sarah to the same fate. We were balancing on a very fine wire.

"Got a problem, McCall," he told me, a smile on his bloated face. "Can't decide if I should kill you and then fuck this bitch or maybe just mess you up a little and make you watch. Think maybe I'll kill you after I finish with the cunt. I'm thinking this bitch ain't your whore, McCall. I think she's your woman. Was your woman. She's mine now."

"What about the truck? The key?" I asked. Each of us still had our rifles leveled at the other. "Without her you won't get them."

He laughed. "I had you figured wrong, McCall. You're just as big a fucking liar as I am. Stick the fucking key up your ass. If there is a key. This is just you and me now. The bitch replaces the truck. I'll be riding her a long time after you're dead, asshole."

I saw Stevie step into the hall behind Sarah and Duke, fifty feet from my position, only thirty from The Babe.

"You're gonna be doing your riding in hell, fat man," Stevie said.

Neither Stevie or I could fire our weapons. The Babe was covered in body armor and the WWII Nazi helmet protected his head. Any stray shots from Stevie would put me at risk, and any shots from me would endanger Stevie, Sarah and Duke. If I tried for a kill shot with the Colt 10mm, chances were the bullet would cut right through his body; and, even though I could surely bring him down, the bullet would keep on flying at high velocity toward Stevie, Sarah and Duke.

The Babe was in an equally awkward position. He wanted Sarah alive, so he couldn't fire in her direction; and now with Stevie opposite me, he couldn't fire at me, because Stevie would return fire and eventually find a soft spot.

The fat man did what I would have done were I in his position. He fired over Sarah's head, making Stevie hit the floor behind her.

"You throw me them guns, boy," he laughed, "or the next time I take out the dog and woman. Pussy ain't worth dyin' for—either for me or you."

I whispered into my mike. "Do it, Stevie. I've got a couple of cards left to play."

The assault rifle and the pistol skittered across the floor, coming to rest at his feet, adding to the pile already started by Sarah's weapons. The Babe turned to me, a victory smile on his fat face.

"What's it gonna be?" I asked. "A shooting or a beating?"

"Ain't got time to fuck with you, McCall. Sure would like to make it nice and slow, but we need to be outta here."

"One thing first. Just one question."

He nodded.

"It's about fat men," I said. "I wonder if its true what the say."

"What's that?" he growled.

"That they got real tiny cocks. Is that true? You got a teeny little cock, Babe?"

"Yeah," said Sarah from the other direction. "That why you like little kids, Babe? Because real grown up women laugh at your unit?"

Right on the button. My goggles couldn't pick up color, but I could see the veins on his forehead pop up like night crawlers. His face had to be crimson. His mouth twisted in a rictus of hate; he tried to decide which of us would go down first.

As he looked between Sarah and me, trying to decide who to fire upon, I reached behind my back and grasped a two foot police model mag light. Four freshly recharged D batteries encased in a titanium tube. 20th cen police used them for clubs in addition to their main function.

"Show me your cock before you kill me," I said. "So I can die laughing." I flipped my NVG's up.

BLOOD OF THE DOGS

The button went all the way in. He stopped thinking and started reacting, turning completely toward me and bringing both assault rifles up so they pointed at my chest. He advanced on me, bellowing his rage.

I brought the mag light up and switched it on, directing the beam straight to the the only thing I could see, the red dot on his night goggles, before he could fire. The light cut a perfect three inch circle in the darkness of the hallway, beginning at my hand and ending at his goggles. His hands flew up to the night glasses and he tore at them, bringing them off his eyes so they hung below his chin. I flicked off the flashlight, brought my NVG's back down, and covered the 15 feet between us and smashed the light on his left wrist, hearing the bone crunch and the rifle in his hand crash to the floor before he roared in pain and brought his right arm and the M 16 crashing down on my left shoulder in a reflexive reaction to the pain.

The force of the blow smashed me into the wall on my left, snapping my head sideways into the hard surface, momentarily stunning me. I fell beneath his feet, and he began stomping furiously on my head and shoulders. Lucky for me he wore Reeboks instead of steel tips.

From behind him, Stevie, Sarah and Duke attacked in unison, crashing against his back and legs, Sarah leaping onto his shoulders and pummeling his neck and shoulders with her fists while Stevie and Duke went after his legs. I crawled back, away from his feet and readjusted my goggles. Above me Sarah was having no effect on The Babe. At nearly four hundred pounds his mass was too much for any of them to be little more than a nuisance. He turned and slammed his back into the wall, pinning Sarah between him and the wall's unforgiving surface. I heard the air whoosh from her lungs. She loosened her hold and crumpled to the floor.

He began pumping his massive legs, running in place, the piston action throwing both Stevie and Duke off him like a horse's shiver shooing away pesky flies. He dropped the M 16 and placed his goggles back over his eyes, focusing on Duke and Stevie, taking one huge stride and then kicking each of them, Stevie in the gut and Duke in the haunches. The blows knocked them each further down the hallway, away from the action. As he went in for more, I screamed his name.

"It's me that's gonna kill you, asshole," I shouted. "They're down, out of the play."

He turned and looked down upon me then, realizing his main objective literally lay at his feet. I pointed the flashlight at his eyes and switched it on. He flinched. But nothing happened. The bulb had been smashed when I had crashed into the wall. The Babe smiled, stepped forward and reached down for me, stripping my pistols away and pulling me up by my Kevlar vest, using only his right hand, and bringing me directly to his face. My feet dangled above the floor as he brought me up to him, face to face, closer than I ever hoped to be to such a putrescence. He was breathing heavily from his exertions. His breath, foul and corrupt, triggered the urge to vomit.

"I'm gonna bust you up and then take you back to my camp," he hissed, spraying my face with gluey spittle. "I got some boys that'd like fucking you in the ass for a few days. When they're done, I'm gonna cut little pieces off you, one a day, until you just roll over and beg to die." He pulled me closer and then flexed his gigantic arm, sending me flying ten feet through the air. I landed on my back and slid another ten.

Slowly and deliberately, exaggerating every motion, he reached over his left shoulder with his right hand and pulled his favorite weapon, the Frank Thomas model Louisville Slugger, from the rig on his back. It looked huge. He caressed it lovingly. Maybe we were right about the cock thing.

I sat up and whispered into my mike, "I think I might need some help here. Stevie, Sarah and Duke are out of commission. This guy's pretty big."

They all answered at once—Weasel, James, Merlin, Roberto. I pulled a few messages from the jumble of their voices.

"On my way."

"Pinned down. Can't get to you."

"Can't find you."

"…his legs or his eyes. That's what you've gotta take away, Mac." That was Weasel. "Watch your footwork. Balance is everything. I'm coming as fast as I can," he continued. Sounded like good advice…for a practice session… I didn't think anything he had ever taught me would help against the monster in front of me, four or five inches taller, two hundred pounds heavier. I couldn't begin to equal his strength.

The Babe began advancing on me then, waving the bat, mouthing obscenities.

"Home run, you little shit. Your head's my fucking ball. Mother fucker, stickin' your goddam nose in my fuckin' business. You know that death dance I talked about, asshole? Split your fucking head like a melon, you really gonna spaz out. You gonna jiggle and dance like a fuckin' retard, McCall."

Scariest thing I had ever seen, this jumbo freak stalking me in the primal darkness of the hallway. Like being stuck in tunnel, far beneath the earth, childhood monsters crawling my way. And I was definitely stuck. If I ran, he might turn back to Sarah, Stevie and Duke. I had to stay.

Nobody's invincible, Weasel had always told us. Find their weakness. It's there somewhere. I back pedaled, scrambling on my palms and heels like a crab seeking a hole, looking for a vulnerable spot on his leviathan frame, one minuscule weakness in a moving wall of flesh.

His left wrist.

I had felt the bones crush under my blow from the mag light. As if reading my mind, he swung the bat with his right arm, showing me his strength and power. Almost too quick to see. But I could hear it cutting the air. You'll never get close, it said.

"Talk to me, Mac." It was Weasel on the headset. "Tell me what's goin' on."

I backed up some more.

"I got an 800 pound gorilla with a baseball bat coming right at me. No guns. No left. No right. I can't get around him. Can't use my speed advantage. I'm fucked, Weasel."

"You got a weapon, Mac. You always got a weapon. Think." His voice was amazingly tranquil and soothing, reassuring. Hard to panic when someone is so calm.

"A fucking clip knife," I answered.

Three inch blade. It would never find a vital organ through the layers of fat. We all carried one. They would cut through anything, even sheet metal. Beautiful all purpose knife. Serrated blade. Sharp as a razor. Strong as a crowbar. No help to me. I needed a samauri sword, not a fucking whittling knife.

Do the unexpected. Use what you got. Weasel's lessons. Always work with the environment.

I had an idea.

"Stay on line," I told Weasel. "I think I've got a chance."

I shook my head and focused. Made it to my feet, still moving backwards. Use my advantages of quickness and speed. Remember Weasel's lessons of footwork. Keep my center of gravity low. If I miscalculated the price would be high. The baseball bat would be an unforgiving force if it found my body.

He rumbled toward me, a big, plodding bear of a man, confident brute force would win the day. After all, hadn't it always succeeded before? When I stopped backing away, he hesitated a fraction of a second, then plunged forward with greater speed, eager to get his bat into my bones and soft flesh. I switched the mag light from my right to left hand and surreptitiously pulled the knife out and thumbed it open, holding it upside down in my right hand so that the blade was hidden by my wrist.

When he was close enough to swing the bat, I feinted to his right, as if I were going to try to engage his arm to keep the bat from smashing into flesh and bone. He bought the feint and swung mightily with his right, grunting with the effort. He was almost too quick for me. As I ducked and rolled to my right, I felt the bat skim across the top of my skull, the breeze of its passing ruffling my hair. It smashed into the wall with a thud, easily blasting through the plaster, showering me with the dust.

As I rolled, I smacked his left wrist with the mag light, refreshing his memory on what a broken bone felt like. He roared in reaction to the pain. I dropped the light and rolled behind him, barely clearing his left side. As I came up, I flipped the handle of the little knife into my palm and reached out with its serrated three inch blade and sliced neatly through his fatigues at the exact point I focused on.

There's these two little tendons behind everyone's knees. They are about as thick as a pencil. Very similar in feel to the Achilles tendon that lies half a meter south. I don't know what they're called. But I do know that without them, none of our legs would work.

It was these tendons on the Babe's monstrous left leg that the little knife sliced through. It went through them so easily that at first I was afraid I had missed, just managed to rip his pants a bit.

He must not have felt any pain. He made no noise before he toppled forward. A cut from a really sharp knife usually takes a few seconds to start hurting.

An avalanche of flesh had come crashing down. He was sprawled out a meter from where I squatted, feet closest to me. He scrambled to his hands and knees, facing me. That part of his legs worked.

"You little piece of shit," he snarled at me. "It's gonna go much harder on you now."

I backed off preparing for another attack, thinking I had missed my target, the little knife hadn't gone deep enough. It was when he tried to stand that he finally understood he was going to die. His left leg wouldn't hold him up. He was a cripple in a world that accepted nothing but perfection.

"What the fuck you do to me?" he asked incredulously. "My leg don't work."

When he put both hands down to his knee, I reached out and yanked his glasses off, stepping back quickly. He was still dangerous, but without sight, his power was diminished further. I continued moving back, keeping my eyes on him. When I felt his discarded weapons, I kicked them further back with my heels. I came to Sarah and helped her stand.

"You OK?"

"Whoozy," she said, inspecting her body. "But I think everything's still in the right place."

She looked down the hallway, where The Babe, without the aid of the NVG's, sat on his double pumpkin ass and tried to find some light in the darkness. "How'd you get him down? Shouldn't we be doing something else? How come he's not charging us?"

I gently put my arm around her shoulder, pulling her close, taking comfort from her safety. "Get me the AUG first. Then check on Stevie and Duke. They got banged up pretty good. Story time later."

Everyone heard our conversation through their headsets and fired questions through the airwaves simultaneously. "We're all fine." I had to say it three or four times before it finally got through to each of them. "He's out of commission. Crippled. We're done. Don't fuck with any of the other Messengers. There's no need to take any more risks. Meet in the basement and we mop up from there. Out."

Sarah handed me the AUG. Down the hall, twenty feet distant, The Babe pulled a Bowie knife from behind his back and cocked his head, trying to ascertain if anyone was near enough to maim. The blade was nearly two feet long, beautifully etched with scroll designs by a 20th cen artisan. My diminutive clip knife was a minnow compared to the razor-toothed, jaw-jutted northern pike power of the Bowie knife.

I sprayed a ten round burst a few feet in front of him, kicking up dust and moldy carpet into his face.

"Slide the knife down to me," I told him.

He complied.

"Listen, McCall," he whined, "I gotta give it to you...all of you. You're tougher than I figured. I was wrong about you. We can deal. I got shit you can use. Anything you want. Bitches, babies, jewelry, guns up the ass—a whole fucking army. Me and you, we can rule this place. Just the two of us. Just fix my leg up. It don't work at all. You can do that. Right?"

"Make your deals in hell," I said. "You're finished here."

Behind The Babe a hallway door slammed open and Merlin limped into the empty space. He surveyed the scene. Our target on his butt; a whimpering bag of flesh; four of us twenty feet away—Sarah, Stevie and Duke alive and moving; me with the AUG trained on The Babe.

"Mother fucker," Merlin said, advancing on the fat man. "You really did get him. Looks like a pile of shit with a head on top."

Merlin came up behind him and pulled a Taurus 9mm, chambering a round. Reacting to the sound, The Babe tried to shrink into the floor.

"I have a gift for you," Merlin told the man who had sodomized him. "It's from the children you defiled. The women you raped. The men you butchered. None of could be here themselves, being dead or sort of fucked up. So they asked me to deliver it."

All of us heard the click of the safety on the nine as he switched it off.

"Please don't."

It was from behind me. Stevie's voice, soft, yet intense. Authority behind the request. He was standing side by side with Sarah. Her good arm was around his waist. His right arm was pressing in on his left ribs. He was in pain.

"You fuckin' nuts?" Merlin snarled at him. "This is the worst piece of filth for five hundred miles. He's a murderer. Torturer. He fucks little girls, Stevie."

"And little boys," Stevie told her. "I know what he is. I lived with him. I was a Messenger for nine years. Remember?"

Merlin stared at him in shock, then understanding. He knew Stevie's life had been tough; had recently been told of Stevie's history with The Babe. Stevie had a claim too.

"Step back from him, Merlin," I said. "He's stronger than anyone I've ever encountered and has nothing to lose."

He took three quick steps back, still keeping the 9mm trained on The Babe's skull.

"I get it," he said. "I don't like it, but I get it. Go ahead." He stepped further back. "Take him yourself, Stevie. He's yours."

Stevie didn't move. "You don't really understand, Merlin," he told him. "I don't want to kill him. And I don't want you to, either."

"Why?" he screamed. It came from way down in his gut. He could give Stevie a run for his money in a pain contest. "Why can't I kill him?"

It ran so much deeper than The Babe. I could hear it in Merlin's voice. All of us could. In the eerie light provided by the goggles, we couldn't clearly see his face. And his eyes were covered. But the volume and tone of his voice spoke of his despair, his hatred. This wasn't only The Babe. This pain was ten or fifteen years old. For Merlin, he was someone else. Maybe several others.

The Babe was Merlin's childhood. The reason he abandoned clan life to live as a recluse. The man cowering at his feet was Merlin's own clan who had driven him out with their blind allegiance to hate, loyalty to system that demanded they forever battle with other foolish men.

He was also the man that had raped him only a few weeks ago. The man responsible for the healing wounds on his face, the bullet hole in his leg and the emptiness in his heart.

"I don't want you to kill him because I like you," said Stevie. "It won't make you happy. You won't feel better about yourself, Merlin."

"Fuck you, Stevie," he bit back at him. "I'm not doing it to feel better about myself. I'm doing it to feel better about him."

Merlin spat in The Babe's direction. The fat man remained silent. He knew the wrong word would result in a bullet in the head.

From behind Merlin, beyond the range of my goggles, a new voice entered the debate. "Listen to him, Merlin."

Merlin whirled, pointing the nine in the direction of the voice, relaxing when he realized it was Weasel. "Scared the shit out of me," he said. "How you do that?"

"It's how I stay alive," Weasel said.

"Tell Stevie to get off my ass," Merlin told Weasel.

"Back off, Stevie," Weasel said.

Stevie didn't answer. We all remained silent.

"Thanks. Now tell him how you'd handle this piece of shit."

"Stevie knows," Weasel told him. "They all know. Was me, fat fuck would be sucking a shotgun barrel."

"Right fucking on target," Merlin replied.

"But it ain't me, Merlin," Weasel continued. "It's you. And Stevie is right. Don't pull the trigger. It doesn't fit you."

Merlin was unnerved, confused by what he was hearing. "You been reading too many fucking books, Weasel. You don't know shit about me. You gonna just let this garbage live? You're fuckin' nuts, you think I'll let that go down."

"He's not going to survive," Weasel said. "And you shouldn't be pulling that trigger."

"How can you say that?" Merlin screamed. "You're a goddam stone killer. You'd ice him without batting an eye."

Weasel stepped closer to Merlin. He smiled and responded.

"Sometimes that's what I am," he said, a hint of sadness in his voice. "And yes, that I would. But we're not talking about me. We're talking about you and Stevie. This isn't right for either one of you. Stevie's got all the guts in the world. He'd give his life for any of us. But he won't be an executioner. And I'd never ask him to. It would change him. Move him in a direction he wouldn't like. One he couldn't come back from. He'd never forget it, Merlin. Neither would you."

Stevie stepped forward, moving away from Sarah, closer to Merlin, The Babe still skulking on the floor between them.

"Look at him, Merlin," Stevie said, pointing down to The Babe. "He's already dead. He's useless and helpless in his world. I know he's garbage. I know it better than anyone here. You heard him tryin to buy his life from Mac. If Mac bit on that, he'd be dead the minute he turned his back on The Babe. I can't do it Merlin. I wouldn't want Weasel too either. But Weasel is the hardest man we have. We need that as much as we need Sarah's conscience. And Mac's courage."

"What do you bring to the table, Stevie?" Merlin asked softly.

"He brings loyalty and love," Weasel told Merlin. "And the ability to see all of us for what we are. And accept us. That's why he doesn't want you to do it, Merlin. Stevie sees some of himself in you."

Merlin's shoulders dropped a little. Some of the venom seemed to drain from him. He recognized Stevie as a fellow victim. Was compelled to listen to a member of the same club.

"Whatta we do with him?" His voice was weak.

He was giving it all over to Stevie. The decision was his.

Stevie grabbed the decision, made it for the group.

"All of us recycle organic garbage," Stevie said. "That's what he is—a sludge heap. We'll give him back to the land. But I won't execute him. Neither should you. I'll defend myself. Help others. Fight someone who can fight back."

The boy, man now, but he was still a boy in our hearts, looked down at the man who had been the dominant male figure for his first nine years—now silent, groveling, mortally wounded, so dangerous that no one approached within reach of his beefy arms—and dismissed him with a wave of his hand.

"Let his own kind do it," Stevie said. "And Merlin pushes the button."

We left then. All of us. Retrieved the weapons, ours and The Babe's. Told Roberto and James we were leaving and picked up the Cobras and Disciples on the way and carefully worked back to the basement, sneaking through our back doors and secret tunnels, avoiding the remaining Messengers.

Roberto and had located the three Cobras who had been silent for so long. They were dead, had succumbed to the Messengers superior numbers. Their bodies were carried back by their clan mates. James, too, has lost soldiers. Our numbers were now seventeen. Sixteen humans, one dog.

The Babe's screams and curses accompanied us part of the way. Filled with anger and fear and panic and disbelief, eventually they subsided as we put enough walls between us and him.

• • • •

In the corner of the basement, behind one of the gargantuan furnaces, there is a large room, combination machine shop and locker area for the workers who tended the complex physical plant in the 21st. It had a good, solid steel door which was rigged by Weasel and Stevie with a two minute delay to blow open when we were safely out of the building complex.

Inside the room were the remnants of three dog packs, over thirty wild dogs, all males, lured into the truck and coaxed into the room by the compelling primal scents of the three bitches in heat that Roberto had given to Weasel.

Behind the door, the dogs inside, having made a tenuous peace in their confinement, were clamoring for their freedom, hungry and enraged by their common enemy.

We packed our equipment, shouldered our weapons and quickly exited via a Byzantine series of newly constructed mouse holes through the lower level service truck entrance of Sears. We returned to the truck, rigged it for defense and all took our positions.

It was then that Merlin returned to the basement, climbed high to the top of an air conditioning unit, and triggered the charges that would blow the door that separated the dogs from the Messengers who remained in the mall. Over the comm sets, it told us all to get clear and we heard and felt a muffled thump. Merlin observed through his night vision goggles the newly formed pack's reaction when the barrier to their freedom was removed.

At first, frightened by the explosion, they cowered in the back of the room, backs down, tails tucked. Then two of them, potential alpha males of the new pack, broke for the opening, barking loudly. The others followed, and the group milled in the furnace room for a few minutes sampling scents left by all of us, looking for danger, searching for a food source. Long time between meals.

It took only a couple of minutes for a few of them to pick up the blood scent from inside the mall. They barked and whirled and communicated their discovery to the others. It took only seconds for the remainder of the pack to grasp the scent. All of them rushed to the open door that led from the basement into the main part of the mall. Nipping at each other's flanks in their frenzy to feed, howling and barking in their furor and rage, they followed the trails of blood, and burst into the mall, chasing out the survivors Messengers, feeding on the dead…

…and eventually working their way to dark hallway where I had cut the tendons in The Babe's fat leg with my little knife.

• • • •

We were never sure just how many of the Messengers made it out of the mall alive. Over a dozen exited from the Lord and Taylor doors, the ones near the truck. In the diminishing darkness of predawn, they moved to the truck, an oasis of safety from the dogs, not realizing the vehicle was already occupied.

After we shot the first few resisters to our demand they disarm, the rest of them surrendered to us. We locked the prisoners in the rear of the truck while we decided what to do with them.

"The place is full of dog shit," complained one of the men, a skin and bones, multiple-tattooed, herpes-sored scum bag whom I recognized from our visit to the Messenger camp. They were all coming down from the drugs and adrenaline rush and were as jumpy as indies at a square dance. I had my own coming down to do and didn't want to mess with him.

"Be glad to leave you here," I said, matter-of-factly. "Of course I can't offer you any weapons. Make a choice. In the truck with the shit or out here with the dogs."

He remained in the truck.

We replenished the crank case oil, fueled the gas tank, ate, and bandaged up and discussed what to do next for about two hours, talking quietly, tired to the bone. When daylight returned, I noticed one of the Messenger prisoners carried a blood stained WWII Nazi helmet. I pulled him from the truck and sat him in front of the seventeen of us who had made it out alive—a jury of fifteen men, one woman and a dog—sitting cross-legged in front of him.

Like us, the man was weary. Stripped of his sports gear and weapons, denied his drugs, he was clearly intimidated by the group before him. His bravado had been leeched from him, like soil from a rain soaked field, by the Messengers' recent defeats. Without the regalia of his decimated clan and the accouterments of war, the Messenger soldier was of normal stature, small hearted—a man few would want to call friend and fewer still would fear.

"How'd you get the helmet?" I asked, pointing to the head gear that sat between us and him like a large soup pot.

The man's eyes kept wandering over to Duke who was laying by Sarah, head in her lap, alert to the prisoner's presence among us despite the fact Sarah was gently stroking his head with her good hand.

Roberto laughed. "Dog's got a bigger rep than any of us," he commented.

I called Duke over to me, closer to the prisoner. He limped over and rested his head on my leg. I felt him relax. He was comforted by the return of Sarah. His eyes bore into the prisoner.

"The helmet," I repeated.

"Souvenir," he replied.

"Bed pan," Merlin countered.

"What happened to the head it usually rested upon?" I asked.

The man shrugged. "I heard the screams and growls from behind a door and went in to see. Figured it coulda been one of my mates. The Babe was in a hallway on his hands and knees. No goggles. No guns. Had a big knife, but it wasn't enough. There was about five dogs in front of him and five in back. They jumped in and out, trying to get a hand or leg. He got a couple, I'll give that to him. But on one swing with the knife, one of the dogs got his other hand and pulled him down on his face. It was over then," he said, looking at all of us. "You know how them dogs are when they get something grounded."

Sarah looked at me, remembering. I knew, all right.

Eleven years ago. Last sensations before I died were the snarls of the pack in my ears and pain of their teeth ripping at my arms, trying to get beneath them to the soft flesh of my throat, guardian of the jugular.

But I didn't die. A perfect stranger helped. I thought Sarah was an angel and I was in heaven when I came out of it.

"You didn't try to save him?" James asked the Messenger.

The man looked at James like, what're you, fucking nuts?

"He was screaming like a stuck pig," the Messenger said. "All girly like. I didn't owe the man shit. He's the one got us into this fucking mess."

All of us stared at the man, silent, nothing to say.

"The helmet rolled free and I took it while the dogs was eating," said the ex-soldier. "They didn't even notice me. It was a big fucking meal for them."

· · · ·

We sent the man back to the stench of the truck bed. He had helped us make our decision. Our prisoners didn't like it. But they did the work. It took them two hours of back breaking labor…after we shooed the dogs away.

CHAPTER FORTY-FOUR

O n the way back to the Wheaton College Messenger compound in the truck, Sarah told me that Billy Graham had been the only big 20th cen preacher that she had known of that hadn't been touched by some kind of financial or moral scandal.

"So what's that make him?" I asked.

"Unique," she replied. "So let's try not to destroy his college any more than the Messengers have already done."

I was driving. Sarah, Merlin and Duke were in the cab with me. Our armor was up. As the truck moved north along 59, it created a gentle breeze that cooled our skins.

The Messengers were in the back with the dog shit and other garbage from the battle at the mall. Stevie, Roberto, James, and our new allies from the Cobras and Disciples were draped across the roof, running boards and the hood. Weasel was in the gun turret, tending to the machine gun. All of them were screaming for me to go faster, even the generally dignified leader of the Insane Cobra Nation. But I kept it slow.

A mile before we entered the Messenger camp, I stopped the truck and we returned the armor to a combat status. Just in case. All of us draped ourselves with weapons. Weasel cocked the HK belt-fed machine gun.

I pulled the black, scarred, malevolent-looking truck to the area where we had met The Babe to negotiate for Sarah's release. Three point turned it so the ass end faced the hill. On the truck's cab and running boards, assault rifles in everyone's hands and another across their chests, all of our survivors except Merlin and I were poised. Sarah had insisted on being up there with the men who had helped in her rescue.

We looked nasty as hell. Planned it that way.

In the midday sun, about fifty or sixty Messengers dotted the hill, sunning themselves, napping off their lunch, reposing in the grass or crooks of the fallen oaks. A bucolic scene. Tough life being a clan soldier.

No guards had picked up our entrance. No soldiers rushed for their weapons. On the hill, the remaining Messengers silently watched our little drama unfold.

Stragglers began to wander up, cautiously observing, willing to wait for us to make the first move. I engaged the mechanism for the truck to dump its contents and climbed on to the roof of the cab, assault rifle draped across my chest. As the bed slowly tipped, the gate opened with a loud clatter, spilling out the truck's contents.

Several pounds of dog shit, a couple dozen living men who smelled bad enough to lose any friends they might have had and two score Messenger corpses slid out, spilling onto the lawn, a gory smorgasbord of blood and bones and canine excrement.

We had made one of the prisoners, the one who complained about the smell, place the WWII Nazi helmet on the skull of The Babe's ravaged remains. The dogs hadn't left much. Nothing to indicate it was their former leader among the raw, bloody flesh and bones.

There were many, many more Messenger bodies back at the mall, dragged out into the parking lot for the scavengers. Also probably a few dozen stragglers roaming indie country—whipped, hungry, low on ammo. We transported enough of their dead back with us to make our point.

The men and women on the lawn began to wander down to get a better look at the entertainment. None of them seemed angered by our offering. Perhaps they were tired of being soldiers during war time. It was a career that could get you killed.

On the truck, we kept our weapons up, non-threatening. We sought no fight.

I jumped down from the roof and banged on the cab door. Merlin handed me the bat.

"Give me a hand," he said. "I want to see this."

Merlin helped Duke out and leaned on the side of the truck, Duke beside him, while I climbed up to the roof of the cab. I stood and surveyed the group of Messengers below us, mostly men, some of their women. No children to be seen. I searched for the toughest looking soldier among the growing audience. He was in the front row, observing impassively, arms across his chest. He carried only a knife and a pistol, but looked mean enough to bite off a rat's head.

I caught his eyes with mine and tossed him the bat. He snapped it out of the air, catching it high up on the barrel and bringing it down to inspect it. Finished, he passed it along. It slowly made its way through the crowd, eventually passing through forty or fifty pairs of hands.

When it reached the back of the crowd, it disappeared for a few minutes and suddenly appeared in the air, transcribing a graceful arc over the crowd, from back to front, spinning slowly end-to-end and landing in the pile of corpses with a wet plop.

The gathering dissipated then, slowly dissolving into groups of two or three, losing its mass and identity like a single drop of blood in crystal clear spring water.

• • • •

Roberto jumped from the hood, signaling Jose' and Flint and all of his remaining Cobras to follow. James and his Disciples disembarked from the sides of the truck. As the two groups of soldiers strode purposefully up the hill behind the remnants of Satan's Messengers, Merlin shot me a questioning look.

"The prisoners," I said. "Especially the children. Both clans are taking the ones that need help back to their camps."

"I'll be damned," Merlin said.

"Sarah talked to Roberto and James about it," I said.

"They didn't need much persuading," Sarah offered.

We stayed with the truck while the Cobras and Disciples climbed the hill. In twenty minutes we saw them crest the hill, begin the trek down with thirty former Messenger prisoners in tow. They were a rag-tag mixture of bewildered, hairless women and big-eyed children. Many of the children were being carried by soldiers.

BLOOD OF THE DOGS

While Merlin manned the gun turret, Stevie, Sarah and I rushed to help. We grouped them around the truck and rushed to find food and water from the Messenger supplies. Duke wandered among the children, accepting a pet from those who weren't afraid, licking every little face that was offered.

For two hours we fed and bathed them in the warm afternoon sun, cleaned the filthy truck bed with clear water from a creek that meandered west of the campus. Soon some of the children began to jabber and the women talked softly among themselves.

• • • •

Before sunset, we loaded them all into the newly cleaned truck bed. Weasel climbed from his turret into the cab, helping Merlin and Duke back inside with him. He started the truck and pointed us in the direction of Roberto's home turf, driving slowly so as not to frighten the children. From there we drove to the James' turf in the city.

Except for the three in the cab and Sarah in the back with the women and children, we all sat quietly on the top of the truck—a warm, cleansing breeze rustling our clothes, pushing the stench of death behind us—satisfied in our minds that Satan's Messengers had ceased to exist.

CHAPTER FORTY-FIVE

"Now that we've been here awhile," Sarah asked, "how do you feel about our new home?"

I put my book aside and straightened her covers, pulling them down so that the top half of her body was exposed to the air...and my eyes. I could handle the distraction.

"You mean living in a place that used to be a pizza restaurant?" I asked.

"Precisely."

"Well, the kitchen isn't bad. And there's plenty of bathroom space. And the neighbors," I said pointing my head in the direction where Stevie and Weasel had carved themselves a cave in the old generator room of the mall, "are certainly nice."

"Yes, I'll give you that," she said.

"And the place is virtually impregnable."

"That's certainly a consideration in these times of strife."

"But," I said in my best husband half of the house hunting team voice, "there are certainly a few drawbacks."

"No garden," she began. "No fresh vegetables, roses, cut flowers for the table."

"No windows," I continued.

"No place for the livestock."

"No livestock at all."

"Perhaps," I suggested after a pause, "we should go house hunting in the spring."

"Oh, sweetie," she squealed, clapping her hands together and doing her best imitation of a 50's sitcom wife, "that would be so wonderful. Do you think the children will want to move?"

"Both Weasel and Stevie are a little tired of trekking through the entire mall to walk Duke," I said. "I think I can talk them into it."

"And a spare room for their little friend?" she asked, referring to Merlin.

"Nothing's too good for the missus," I replied.

"Now that I've gotten my way," she said with a bright smile, "I feel in the mood for a little hanky panky."

"First tell me about the time you saved me," I said.

"No. You first."

"Mine was the first request," I pointed out diplomatically.

"OK." She looked at me, serious now at the recollection of the event that had brought us together. "I had been watching you for two days."

"Why?"

"Because I was alone and you were in my little hunting territory."

"So what did you see?"

"You were so young and strong and handsome, Mac. You made me curious. Sixteen year old girls get curious, you know."

"What did I do that kept you watching?"

"Well for one thing, you didn't hurt anybody or destroy anything. That was certainly unusual. And then when you went to bed, I snuck in and watched. That's when I caught you reading a book by the light of a candle. That was a revelation. At that moment, I thought to myself, there's a man with potential."

"Then what?"

"On the third day you got careless and were surrounded by the dog pack. I knew you were going to die, and the knowledge hurt me."

"Why?"

"Because back then you were this big, stupid, handsome guy, and it seemed like the world might be a little worse off without you."

"And you risked your life for that. Waded into a dog pack guns blasting to save a guy you'd never even met."

"Seemed like the thing to do at the time."

"Shit," I said, disbelieving, "you must have been in love with me."

"Nope," she replied. "Not quite then."

"When?"

She stroked her chin. Pretended to think about it.

"It was the very first instant that I realized that you loved me. That was what pushed me over."

"Which was the first time I opened my eyes and thought you were an angel."

"You got it. You had me hooked from that moment on. End of story. Now tell me about how you saved me."

"Then we fool around."

"Endlessly."

"OK, here goes. Except for a pair of bikini panties, the kind that the women in the music vids wear that are cut up their butts, you were completely naked and helpless. You were surround by fifty blood thirsty clan warriors. I was wounded, bleeding in several places from knife and bullet wounds, but I knew I had to save you."

"Why?"

"Because of your butt. So there I was, naked save for a loin cloth, bleeding all over the place, weaponless save for a Bowie knife clenched in my teeth, facing down fifty clan soldiers…"

"Give me the serious version," she said. "The real one."

I had deliberately gone with a light treatment. The truth still scared me. I became pensive, thinking back. It had been several months since the Messenger attack on the compound and Sarah's capture. Her presence by my side every day and night had helped dilute the power of the fear I felt when I had first awakened from my ordeal in the tunnel and thought she was dead. The terror and panic of that particular moment stayed with me even after her rescue. It remained even now, weaker, but still stubbornly resisting my attempts to vanquish it.

I had been awakened several nights by an insidious nightmare that she was gone, dead and buried, leaving a vast, black hole in my life. In the dream it became a truism that I would be numb, unable to experience happiness, for the rest of my life. She forgave me, in the nightmare, for not being there when she had died. But it didn't help. I would never be complete until I saw her again, and, in the twisted world of the nightmare, I couldn't die.

I drifted into wakefulness each time sobbing uncontrollably, filled with fear and remorse and loneliness, unsure of where or who I was until Sarah pulled me to her and wrapped me in her arms, my head between her breasts, close to her scent. That was when I knew I was awake. When I could smell her.

She held me tightly to her after the nightmares, stroking my head and telling me everything was all right. And it was…immediately. Her soothing voice and familiar smell were more powerful than the desolate dreams of my sleeping mind. She kept saving me.

"I don't think I can talk about it yet," I finally told her. "It was the most frightening thing I've ever experienced."

"You were very brave, Mac," she said smiling sweetly, eyes glistening. "The most courageous hero a girl could ever imagine. I knew you would come for me. Even when that filth pulled me away from the tunnel you were trapped in, I knew you'd come for me. I could feel that you were still alive."

"I fell off my white horse a few times, Sarah," I said. "I had a lot of help."

"And we mustn't ever forget that," she said. "All those brave men, Roberto and his Cobras. James and the Disciples. Stevie. Weasel. Merlin. Our precious Duke. The fact that they helped us, that all of us cooperated, was a passage, Mac. A sign that the basest of human instincts need not reign."

I nodded in assent, thinking of James and the Black Gangster Disciples who had fought with us at the AON Building. Roberto believing me when I told him he had traitors eating at his table. The rules said Cobras and Disciples were natural born enemies, foxes and hounds. Each had joined us to front the Messengers.

"But when we're alone," she continued, "walking in the woods or lying together in the darkness, I fantasize it's just you and me against everyone else. Like when I saved you from the dogs so many years ago. Or that moment in the mall when the lights went on vanquishing the night, and you rose up and conquered my captors. And then we stood clinging to each other in the cleansing light. Sometimes I pretend that the future of the whole world lies with us—just you and me. Is that wrong, Mac?"

"Love is so damn weird," I said. "It makes you do stuff you would never imagine doing before you found it. Or it found you. Like standing outside a collapsed tunnel with scores of clan warriors shooting at you…"

"Or facing down a 400 pound monster in a hallway with a paring knife," Sarah said.

I smiled at her. There was no earthly reason for us to be alive. "Some cultures said that there's a special angel that watches over lovers," I continued. "It's not wrong to dream that we're special. It's part of being in love."

"When The Babe had you trapped in the hallway," Sarah said, "for a few frantic instants I thought his cancer was too powerful for us. We would be consumed. Our love eaten by his disease. My whole body became cold. My insides hollow. When he slammed you into the wall and you crumpled, I saw my future as a black void."

"That's my nightmare," I said, excitedly. "You're gone and there's nothing left for me but emptiness."

"Is it possible we're burning too brightly?"

"You're suggesting we love each other with less intensity?"

"I don't know."

"You go first," I prompted.

She wrinkled her brow and closed her eyes, shutting them tightly, making a caricature of a face in deep concentration. After a minute of effort, she opened her eyes and smiled.

"I can't do it."

"Then I guess we're stuck. I can't either."

"Darling," she said. "Before we start, when are you going to look at the flash drive that you received from your birth family?

THE END

ACKNOWLEDGEMENTS

Patricia, with the book from the first word to the last, is instrumental in its creation. Her ideas, constructive criticism, and support made this a better book. Thank you to my family for their input and patience. Without Jen, Bernie, Amy, and Mike there is no published novel. I am indebted to each of you for your support, suggestions, wisdom, and encouragement. Thanks to Jerry and Social Eye Media for navigating and the ebooklaunch.com team for creating an outstanding cover.

Photography by Myrissa G.

Made in the USA
Lexington, KY
28 August 2018